A KINGDOM SUBMERGED

THE VAZULA CHRONICLES BOOK ONE

DEBORAH GRACE WHITE

LUMINANT PUBLICATIONS

A KINGDOM SUBMERGED

By Deborah Grace White

A Kingdom Submerged
The Vazula Chronicles Book One

First edition (v1.0) published in 2022
by Luminant Publications

ISBN: 978-1-922636-18-8

Luminant Publications
PO Box 305
Greenacres, South Australia 5086

http://www.deborahgracewhite.com

Cover Design by Karri Klawiter
Map illustration by Rebecca E. Paavo

For my Cressy Bell
Because, mermaids

KYONA
GREAT RIVER
LOCH ARINE
VALORIA
BASAL HEADLANDS
WYVERN ISLANDS
BRYFORD
BEXLEY MANOR
VAZULA
TRIPLE KINGDOMS
KELP FARMS
TILSSTED
SKULSSTED
CENTER OF CULTURE
HEMSSTED
OYSTER FARMS
E
S

FAMILY TREE OF KYONAN CROWN   FAMILY TREE OF VALORIAN CROWN

Family Tree of Kyonan Crown

King Catinnae 👑 (dec'd) m. to Queen Elnora (dec'd)

- King Eamon 👑 m. to Queen Luciana
  - Violet m. to Damon
    - Renee
    - Liesl
  - Rory 👑 m. to Kiera
    - Theodore
    - Kiana 👑
    - Steffan
  - Alana m. to Peter
    - Thomas
    - Stella

Family Tree of Valorian Crown

King Malcolm 👑 (dec'd) m. To Queen Marguerite (dec'd)

- King Ormond 👑 (dec'd) m. to Queen Brielle
  - King Matlock 👑 m. to Queen Renata
    - Lachlan 👑 (18)
    - Knox (16)
  - Prince Kincaid m. to Princess Jocelyn
    - Anne m. to Ian
      - Lillian
      - Eugene
    - Norik, Duke of Bexley m. to Elsabeth
      - Laura (22) m. to Edmund
      - Percival (20)
      - Heath (18)
    - Elena m. to Samuel
      - Brody (20)
      - Bianca (20)
    - Leo m. to Maria
      - Jasmine (18)
      - Leonora (16)
      - Lucas (15)
- Princess Lavinia m. to Lord Henrik
  - Imari m. to Anton
    - Magnolia
    - Dustin
  - Ronan m. to Harla
    - Boris
    - Astrid
  - Alora m. to Elias
    - Milton
    - Arthur
    - Marigold
  - Aaron m. to Rosa
    - Max (16)
    - Alex (14)

👑 = in the direct line of succession

<u>Underline</u> = born to power-wielding line

(Brackets) = age at start of *A Kingdom Submerged*

CHAPTER ONE

Merletta's eyes snapped open as she felt the first tentative ray of sunlight touch her face. How had time passed so quickly? She glanced around at the still-dark expanse of water, the surface stretching endlessly in all directions, its undulating motion soothing and familiar.

She righted herself in the water. As much as she usually enjoyed floating on her back until the sun's warmth could touch every inch of her skin, this was no time to get distracted.

This was it. At long last, this was the day.

She glanced upward out of long-held habit. The stars were disappearing as the first streaks of orange reached out from the horizon. Drawing in one final lungful of air, Merletta dove below the surface in a fluid movement.

Instantly, she felt the back of her throat close over. Water passed smoothly in and out of her mouth as she drew it in. The breath she needed filtered through the natural barrier in her throat, but the water itself didn't flow down. It was strange to remember that the sensation of switching between breathing air and breathing water had once felt uncomfortable, even alarming. Now it was as effortless as swimming.

The world below the surface was still dark, but it provided no challenge to Merletta. Her sharp eyes cut through the gloom as she swam the familiar route toward the kelp farms. She hadn't gone far this morning. It was too important a day to get lost in explorations.

She could actually see the start of the uncultivated kelp forest that lay just beyond the farms when that indefinable sense told her she wasn't alone in the water. Twisting quickly, she felt her heart stutter at the sight of the predator stalking her in the gloom.

The shark was big, and the jagged scar across its gills on one side showed it was a survivor. Somewhere in the back of her mind, she noted that although it was far from the largest she'd seen, it was much too large to be this close to the city.

But there was no time for contemplation. The creature realized she'd seen it, and it charged, not giving her time to collect herself. Merletta fought the instinct to swim away, knowing it would catch her. She waited until it was close before dashing toward it, flicking her tail with all her might as she propelled herself underneath the beast. The shark, confused by her bold movement, was too slow to turn in time, and shot past her before twisting in the water to face her again.

Merletta curled her fist, cursing herself for being so unprepared. If only she had her crude stone weapon—but she hadn't brought anything with her on this expedition. She hadn't thought she'd be far enough outside the city to run into trouble of this kind. Knowing her only hope was to incapacitate the creature long enough to get away, she focused her attention between its eyes. The muscles in her arm tensed in determination—whether or not she managed to survive the encounter, this shark wouldn't be the first creature to discover that she was stronger than she looked.

"This is my fifth week on dawn patrol. I think I'm being punished."

Merletta stiffened as the grumbling voice reached her through the gloom of the early morning water.

"Ah, quit your complaining. Someone's got to do dawn patrol."

The murmur of several voices added to the first, and Merletta, her eyes still on the shark, saw the creature hesitate. She knew that sharks had excellent hearing, and it would certainly have heard the patrol. And it probably knew from experience that unlike her, the guards would be armed and in a group.

After a moment's indecision, the creature turned and disappeared into the dim distance, heading away from the kelp forest.

Merletta barely had a moment to breathe a sigh of relief. The voices were drawing closer, and her heart began to race with a different kind of fear. She couldn't get caught by a guard patrol out beyond the kelp farms. Not today.

Propelling herself forward with all her might, she crossed the last stretch of open water in moments and dove into the cover of the kelp forest. She swam several lengths into it before pausing, forcing herself to hold still and listen for the patrol. When they passed by, not far from her hiding place, she tried to keep herself motionless. Her body swayed in the gentle current, in rhythm with the towers of kelp around her.

The plants brushed against her, and it took her a moment to recognize the sensation on her skin of a different type of touch. Jerking in alarm, she barely smothered a shout as the jellyfish trailed along her arm before branching off and disappearing between the fronds of kelp.

Merletta shuddered, her heart once again racing, even as the voices of the patrol became quieter, passing into the distance. She had always been nervous of jellyfish, since being stung during one of her earliest unsanctioned expeditions outside the borders of the triple kingdoms. It had been a difficult—and painful—struggle to conceal the telling injury from everyone at the home.

With the patrol now out of sight and hearing, Merletta turned homeward with a flick of her tail. Passing without incident through the kelp farms, where the workers weren't yet abroad for the day's labors, she entered the city of Tilssted. The sight of a new dwelling under construction, only half carved from a rocky shelf that jutted into the farm itself, made her frown. They couldn't keep encroaching on the kelp farms like this. The triple kingdoms all relied on the farms for food, but none more so than Tilssted, where fancier fare was hard to come by.

The charity home wasn't far inside the boundary. Merletta moved quickly through the outer neighborhood, not sparing a glance for the buildings cut crudely from the rocky mound on which Tilssted was built.

When she reached the charity home, she didn't pause, swimming silently around the side of the building until she reached a narrow opening halfway up the structure. It was good she was leaving. It was getting harder to squeeze through with every passing year. Peering carefully inside, she exhaled in relief when she saw that everyone was still asleep. She was about to slip inside when a quiet voice drew her up.

"Really, Mer? Even today?"

Merletta turned, grinning at the golden-haired mermaid hovering in the shadows near the building, even as she chastised herself for failing to observe that she had an audience. She shouldn't be surprised, she reflected. Letitia had always been the only one to ever notice—or care—what Merletta was up to.

"Especially today," she whispered back. "I'm leaving straight after breakfast, and who knows when I'll get another chance?"

Letitia looked worried, but Merletta brushed off her friend's concern.

"What are you doing here, Tish?" she asked cheerfully. "You've already escaped this place."

"This is your big day," her friend said simply. "I'm going to come with you."

Merletta looked up in surprise. "You remembered," she said warmly. "You're as kind as ever, Tish, but you don't have to come with me."

"I know," said Letitia with a firmness that didn't sit naturally on her gentle face. "But I want to."

Some of the girls in the room were starting to stir, so Merletta didn't argue the point, instead slipping smoothly in through the opening. No one spoke to her as they all made their way down to breakfast. The mutual silence suited her just fine. The only person from the home she had any desire to talk to was lingering outside.

She ate quickly, shoving extra servings into her satchel when no one was looking. After the meal she made straight for the head's office, keen to get the necessary dismissal over as quickly as possible.

The grim-faced mermaid looked her over unemotionally, taking in the small kelp satchel slung over her shoulder. "You're still determined on this course, Merletta?"

"I am," she confirmed, holding her head up and meeting the older woman's gaze. Something flickered over the head's face, and Merletta frowned. She had expected nothing but disinterest, or perhaps amusement at her lofty ambitions. But for a moment she could have sworn she saw quite a different expression in the other mermaid's eyes, one she had felt all too frequently herself in recent days.

But an instant later, it was gone. "You know that if you fail, you can't come back?" The head's tone gave no support to

Merletta's momentary suspicion that the woman was feeling nervous for her.

"Yes, I know," said Merletta, trying to keep her voice level. As if she would want to come back here.

"Well, then," the head said, dismissing Merletta with a flick of her hand. "You are released."

Merletta turned, leaving the office without another word. Tish was waiting for her outside the building. Unlike the head, her nervousness was clear on her face.

As the two mermaids swam away from the building, Merletta glanced back at the large stone structure in spite of herself. As little love as she had for the place, she couldn't help feeling some kind of sentiment at saying goodbye to the only home she'd ever known.

Letitia didn't comment, just swam silently beside Merletta as they made their way into the waking streets of Tilssted. The light of the sun had penetrated even to their depths by the time they made their way into Skulssted. The guards at the border between the two city-kingdoms gave them a suspicious glance, but made no attempt to stop their passage.

Merletta could sense her friend growing more overwhelmed by the moment, but she kept her own eyes ahead, refusing to be intimidated by the extravagance around her. She focused on her goal instead of her surroundings, and before she knew it, they had reached their destination.

Staring up at the elaborate doorway in front of her, she read the words etched into the stone.

Center of Culture.

This was it. She was here.

"Are you sure you want to do this?"

Merletta sighed, trying to restrain her impatience at the question she had heard at least twenty times in the last few days.

"Yes, Letitia, I'm sure."

"It's just..."

Letitia trailed off, and Merletta turned to look at her friend. Letitia was looking around them, her unease clearly written across her face. The other girl didn't need to finish the sentence. The two of them were as out of place in this neighborhood as a couple of tasty herrings in a pod of seals.

"I'm going to be all right, Tish," Merletta said firmly. "I'm going to make it."

Letitia nibbled her lip, an unflattering but kind-hearted skepticism in her eyes. "Why don't you let me speak to my master?" the golden-haired girl offered for perhaps the tenth time. "Maybe there's another shellsmith apprenticeship available." Her pale cheeks colored slightly. "I know it's not glamorous, but it could be much worse, you know. It's better than a lifetime of labor on the outlying kelp farms."

Merletta's expression softened, and she took her friend's hand in hers.

"Tish, I don't think badly of your choice. I'm pleased you've found an apprenticeship, you know I am. It's just...not for me."

Letitia sighed, her expression troubled but resigned as she met Merletta's eyes. "I know," she said softly. "You've always been meant for something more."

Merletta remained silent. For reasons she couldn't explain or justify, she believed the words with all her heart. But while it was sweet of Letitia to say it, it would feel arrogant for Merletta to agree. At least out loud.

"They're not going to be kind to you, you know," Letitia said, her forehead creasing as she glanced toward the ornate double doors outside which they were floating.

Merletta gave a humorless laugh, following her friend's gaze toward the portal into the headquarters of the Center of Culture. "I can handle unkind. It won't exactly be anything new, will it?"

Letitia sighed. "No, I guess not. But you'll have to be careful, Mer. This isn't a home for abandoned kids in the slums of Tilssted. I mean, look around." Letitia did so herself, her unease still clear on her face. "This is Skulssted. And the Center won't be any better. People will be watching. You won't be able to get away with your little..." she glanced around once more for good measure, "...excursions."

Merletta pursed her lips, remaining silent. She had no intention of giving up her outings, but there was no need to tell Letitia that. Her sweet, timid friend would only worry.

Of course, her friend probably knew her well enough to read her silence. That was likely why Letitia looked even more worried than before.

"It's all so secretive," Letitia continued. "I won't even know what you're doing."

"I'm sure I'll be allowed to visit," Merletta reassured her cheerfully. "I'll keep you updated."

She suddenly realized that she was swishing her tail from side to side, and she slowed the movement with an effort. The truth was that she was impatient to be moving, but she didn't want to hurt her friend's feelings by cutting their goodbye short. Tish was almost the only person who'd been kind to Merletta at the home—the last thing she wanted to do was make the other girl think she didn't care about their looming separation.

"It was kind of you to come with me, Tish," she said. She frowned slightly. "Will you be all right getting back to Tilssted on your own, though?"

"I'll swim straight home," Tish assured her. "I won't draw attention to myself."

Merletta nodded. Tish had always been better at that particular skill than she had. If she had only been able—or perhaps willing—to be inconspicuous, her life at the home would probably have been much easier. And yet, she didn't exactly regret the shock waves she'd made. She smiled grimly to herself. At least they'd been as eager to see the back of her fins as she had been to leave. She'd never needed to fear being bullied into staying on as a carer for new arrivals, like some of the more biddable girls ended up doing.

She bid her friend a warm goodbye, watching the other girl propel herself through the water until she was out of sight. As fond as Merletta was of Tish, she didn't need her friend's nerves influencing her at this moment.

As soon as she was alone, she turned back to the doorway in front of her. Early as it was, the gates stood wide. Still, the pearl-encrusted bars didn't exactly spell welcome. They were a reminder of the opulence of the city of Skulssted at large, and of the prestige of the Center of Culture, which Merletta knew lay just through those gates.

She closed her eyes for a moment, steeling herself. It didn't matter that no one else thought she could do this. She knew she could, and she was going to prove it. Sucking in a mouthful of water, she let the familiar salty cool calm her down. The water tasted cleaner in Skulssted, she had to give them that.

Her eyes flickered open. The gates were still there, seeming to beckon and forbid in equal measure. She squared her shoulders determinedly and, with a powerful flick of her tail, surged through the doorway.

CHAPTER TWO

Heath

Heath drew a deep breath, balancing precariously on his miniature island and letting a smile creep across his face as the saltiness of the air assailed his nose. The rock didn't jut far out of the water, meaning that the occasional wave lapped his boots, but it didn't trouble him.

"Better?"

The question made Heath turn. His smile broadened into a grin as he looked at his companion, who was perched on a second rocky protrusion with his tail dangling idly into the water. The dragon, although very small for its kind, wouldn't exactly have fit on the outcrop Heath currently occupied.

"Much better," he acknowledged. "Why is it that my problems always seem to get smaller the closer I get to the ocean, Reka?"

"I don't know," Rekavidur responded, stretching his neck upward and closing his eyes as he extended his snout toward the sun. "But I feel it, too. There's something both calming and exciting about the endlessness of the sea's expanse."

Heath chuckled. "You're very articulate for a dragon, aren't you? Or is the reputation of dragons as being aloof and uncommunicative just wrong?"

Reka's reptilian mouth stretched in a faint smile, and his tone held a hint of condescension as he responded. "Perhaps we just don't waste words where they won't be appreciated. You humans aren't exactly known for any depth of understanding."

Heath laughed aloud. "You're very high and mighty for basically being a child, Reka," he chided.

The dragon sniffed, the sound slightly petulant. "I'm decades older than you, young human. You could show a little more respect."

"My apologies, Mighty Beast," said Heath meekly. But his smile broke out again quickly. He knew perfectly well that his friend wasn't really offended. "But eighteen is considered an adult for a human, you know. You were probably only the size of a pony when you were eighteen, weren't you?"

"Probably," conceded Reka, stretching his wings for balance as he shifted his taloned front feet to avoid them getting wet as a decent-sized wave swept past. He was considerably larger than a pony now. More like the size of two warhorses one on top of the other. Still much smaller than a fully-grown dragon, but Heath knew that he would get there. It would just take another century or so.

"Thank you for coming," Heath said suddenly. "I needed to get away for a minute. A little further away than I could manage by myself."

He glanced back toward the distant shore. He could just make out the rocky cliff where Reka had met him earlier, and the beach to its left. Even his family's manor house was visible, at least to his eyes. It looked like a child's toy house, perched on top of the cliff, some way back from the edge.

"I am glad to help," said Reka placidly, sweeping his tail idly back and forth in the water. "As you know, it is no hardship to me to fly out over the ocean with you. If anything, I wish we were going further."

"Me too," Heath muttered. He sighed, turning his eyes back to the ocean in front of him, although his thoughts remained on the visitor whose arrival had prompted him to make himself scarce.

"Are the dragons worried about all this talk?" he asked curiously. "About magic being dangerous and all that?"

"Worried?" Reka repeated, sounding faintly surprised. "Why would dragons be worried that humans are afraid of magic?"

"I suppose dragons don't have much reason to be worried about anything," said Heath ruefully.

"Not really," Reka agreed, as unconcerned as ever.

Heath sighed again. "It must be nice to be immortal."

"Well," Reka reasoned, still speaking casually, "I don't know if I'm immortal, do I? I haven't yet made my decision."

"You know what I mean," said Heath impatiently. "Just the ability to make that choice is something a lot of humans would kill for."

"Then it is fortunate that there is no way for humans to attain that ability," Reka commented.

Heath had to agree, although he didn't bother to say so. For all his talk of it being nice, he wasn't at all sure that he would choose to be immortal at the cost of being able to one day have children, as dragons could if they wished.

"We are agreed that the dragons have no need for concern, but it seems that you are worried, my friend," Reka said unexpectedly. "Why does the fear of others concern you? Haven't humans always been afraid of magic?"

Heath frowned. "Maybe. But it's one thing for humans to have been afraid of magic when dragons were the only magical creatures around. In case you've forgotten, some humans carry magic now, too. Humans whom I happen to care very much about. Who aren't invincible like dragons."

"Such as yourself," noted Reka.

Heath shrugged. "Well, no one's really sure about that, are they? But my sister, my brother, my father...all of my cousins...I don't like the idea of them being at the center of all this suspicion."

"You have magic too, Heath," said Reka, sounding as close to impatient as the placid dragon ever did. "I have told you many times. I'm just not sure what it is."

Heath remained silent, uninterested in entering into the familiar topic.

"Is he gone yet?" he asked, after a prolonged minute of listening to the sound of the waves lapping against his little island.

Reka glanced back toward the shore. "Well, I see a horse being led to the entrance of your home," he commented.

"Really?" asked Heath, perking up. "Hopefully that means he's leaving."

Reka shook his vast head slowly from side to side. "You really can't see the horse for yourself? Human eyesight is extraordinarily inferior."

Heath smiled. The criticism was a little out of place in this instance, but he felt no need to defend himself. Reka had spent almost no time with any other human. The dragon didn't quite realize how unusual it was for Heath to even be able to see the shore from this distance. Heath's excellent eyesight was the only sign of a potential magical ability that his family had noticed in his eighteen years. It wasn't much to boast about.

"I suppose I should head back soon," Heath said, his eyes resting wistfully on the horizon. "Perce will need someone to vent to."

Before the dragon could respond, Heath glanced down into

the water, and his attention was distracted from his brother's inevitable irritation.

"What's that?" he asked, speaking mainly to himself as he crouched down on his rock. The water, which had momentarily been smooth in the patch just below his feet, was once again choppy. It was difficult to make much out beneath the waves, even for him.

"What?" asked Rekavidur curiously, snaking his long neck down so that his bearded head hovered just above the surface of the water.

"I thought I saw something on the bottom," said Heath, squinting as he attempted to find it again. "It almost looked like a structure of some kind."

"A rock formation?" Reka suggested.

Heath shook his head slowly. "Maybe. But it didn't look like it."

"I'll take a look," offered Reka, a familiar inquisitive light in his eyes. Without waiting for a response, the dragon slid off his rock, disappearing beneath the waves with barely a ripple.

Heath waited above the surface, trying not to let his human limitations frustrate him. He had always been jealous of his friend's ability to explore below the water, but it wasn't Reka's fault that humans needed to take in air much more often than dragons.

It was only a couple of minutes before Reka reappeared, slithering back up onto his rock with surprising grace for a creature his size.

"What did you find?" Heath asked eagerly.

The dragon didn't immediately respond, stretching his neck out over the space between their bastions. Heath suddenly realized why his companion wasn't speaking. He held out a hand to allow Reka to drop his burden into it, freeing up the dragon's mouth for speech.

"I think you're right," Reka said, his tone communicating the faint surprise it always held when his human friend showed any sign of intelligence. "I think there *was* some kind of structure there, once."

Heath's eyes brightened with interest as he looked down at the item in his hand. It looked like...well, like a block from his own stone home might look, if it had been underwater for a very long time. He peered down into the waves again. He would have to come back, on a day when the water was clearer.

"It's strange..." Reka mused, his attention on the depths below them.

"What?" Heath prompted when Reka trailed off. The dragon had a maddening tendency to start a thought out loud, and finish it in his mind.

"I almost thought I could sense something," Reka said. "Some lingering trace."

Heath frowned. "Lingering trace of what?" He raised an eyebrow. "Power, you mean? Magic?"

A ripple passed down Rekavidur's form, from his shoulders to the tip of his tail, in a gesture Heath recognized as a shrug.

"Maybe."

Heath stared down into the ocean, his thoughts swirling like the little eddies of water that formed around his rock. There was definitely something to discover here.

"The visitor has left," Reka said suddenly. "And your brother is definitely angry."

Heath pulled his thoughts away from the water with an effort, frowning slightly at the dragon. "You shouldn't use your farsight to spy on Percival," he chided.

Reka smiled, clearly unrepentant. "It barely counts as farsight from here," he said soothingly. "If it wasn't for the building in the way, I could probably see him with my natural eyes."

Heath sighed, perfectly aware that there was no point arguing with the dragon. "I'd better go back," he said instead. He cast one last longing glance into the water. "This can wait."

"If you like," Reka agreed placidly, pulling his tail from the water and stretching his neck upward one more time. "Ready?"

Reka was already crouching before Heath's nod, and without another word, the dragon launched himself into the air. For a moment Heath's vision was filled with the glint of yellow and purple scales, then he felt the dragon's talons close around his shoulders. The two of them shot upward with dizzying speed, Heath's legs dangling beneath him as they sped toward the shore. He was well used to the sensation, and didn't even spare a thought for the distance between himself and the water below. His eyes were fixed on the shore, and the home that was rapidly growing from a toy house to a full sized manor.

In less than a minute Heath felt his feet touch the grassy surface at the top of the cliff. Reka released his shoulders, landing beside him in a fluid motion.

"Until next time," the dragon said, and Heath nodded absently. In another moment Reka was gone, wheeling north-east over the farmland that formed part of Heath's father's estate.

Heath strode toward his home, reaching the broad stone steps in minutes. He was pleased to see that as Reka had indicated, there was no longer any sign of the unwelcome visitor who had disrupted an otherwise peaceful morning.

"Lord Heath."

Heath smiled vaguely at the servant who greeted him as he passed through the manor's entrance. He had no need to ask the man where the family could be found. Percival's voice was audible even from the entranceway. Heath turned his steps toward the manor's informal dining room. If luncheon was being served he had been gone longer than he realized.

He restrained a grimace as he approached his destination, and the sound of his brother's voice grew in volume. Reka hadn't exaggerated when he'd said Percival was angry. The visiting lord must have been more than usually obnoxious in his criticisms.

"He's just afraid!"

Heath paused outside the door, through which his brother's rant could clearly be heard. He took a breath, trying to put his own emotions to one side and project the calm Percival undoubtedly needed to see right now. If only Laura was there.

"How could King Matlock ever have appointed *him* as Chief Counselor? He's a small, unimpressive man, who's afraid of— there you are, Heath!"

Percival paused mid-stride at the sight of his brother. He had clearly been pacing the room rather than partaking in the elaborate spread on the table before him.

"Hello Percival, Mother, Father," Heath greeted his family, slipping into a seat. "Sorry I'm late."

His parents greeted him with a calm in strong contrast to the storm on their oldest son's face. But to Heath's eye, they both looked troubled, and it surprised him. The strength of Percival's emotions didn't usually throw either the duke or his wife.

"Where did you disappear to?" Percival demanded impatiently, cutting across Heath's surreptitious observation of his parents.

"I was down at the water," said Heath, trying to speak cheerfully. "Just needed to clear my head."

Percival frowned at his brother. "Needed to get away from Lord Niel, you mean."

"Yes," Heath admitted unashamedly as he spread butter liberally on a slice of bread. "That's exactly what I mean."

"Hmph." Percival's voice had dropped to a mutter. "If only we could all be so lucky."

"Well, there have to be perks to not being the heir," Heath

pointed out without rancor. "So what did Lord Niel want this time?"

"He wanted to talk about the tournament," said Percival, throwing himself into a chair at last.

Heath paused, lowering his bread to his plate. "Oh."

Of course. The annual tournament hosted in the capital by the king was due to start in a week. He hadn't even thought of that as the reason for the nobleman's visit, but on reflection, it should have been obvious.

"Lord Niel does have a point, Percival," interjected their father calmly. "As ungraciously as he may have put it."

"Father!" Percival spluttered. "Whose side are you on?"

The Duke of Bexley smiled slightly at his son's outrage, although his voice remained perfectly serious. "It's not a matter of taking sides, Percival. It's a matter of being honest about the truth."

Percival groaned. "Father, I don't even have your gift for exposing truth, and I could still see Lord Niel's simpering excuses for what they were—the insecurity of a weak, small-minded—"

"Precisely," their father interrupted, with a hint of sternness. "Insecurity. And if he feels insecure, you can be certain he's not the only one. I know you're disappointed, but we need to take people's concerns seriously, or the prejudice will only get worse."

"He's right, Percival," their mother added gently. "You said it yourself. Lord Niel is afraid. Missing out on the tournament this year is a small price to pay to reassure him that he has nothing to be afraid of."

"Missing out?" Heath repeated, startled. "He asked you to withdraw altogether? I thought you were already only going to compete in one event, the same as last year."

"I was," said Percival bitterly. "But apparently that's not good enough. And no, he didn't *ask* me to withdraw."

Heath's parents exchanged a brief look, and he sat up straighter in his chair. Whatever Percival was getting at, it was the cause of the tension he could see behind their calm demeanor.

"What do you mean?" he asked cautiously.

"I mean," said Percival, sounding a bit like a sulky child rather than the young man he was, "that our dear Chief Counselor came armed with a royal decree forbidding me from competing."

Heath raised his eyebrows. It was no surprise that Percival was upset—he lived for competition, and the annual tournament had once been the highlight of his year. But the news of a royal decree was a surprise—no wonder his parents were uneasy. Such a restriction was unprecedented.

"What did it say?" he pressed.

Percival shrugged one shoulder as he helped himself to some cold meat. "That it wouldn't be fair, in the spirit of true competition...that the king has no doubt that anyone born with power would be glad, out of loyalty to the crown, to serve the kingdom by undertaking a supervisory role instead of taking an active part in the competition, and so on, and so on." He huffed as he loaded his fork. "It didn't mention any names, of course, but it's basically a specific prohibition against me."

"I'm sure it's not just about you," Heath interjected consolingly.

Percival grunted, giving his brother a look. "It is. This is because of the record."

Heath blinked in confusion. "The record?"

Percival gave an impatient sigh. "The record, remember? If I win this year, it will match Lord Henrik, who won it five times in a row before marrying the princess and withdrawing from the competition." He scowled. "He's our grandparents' age! Is it really so important that his record stands forever?"

"Lord Henrik happens to be my favorite uncle," cut in their father mildly. "And I can guarantee that this restriction doesn't come from him. I can't imagine he would care in the least if you beat his record." He eyed his oldest son. "But you know how popular he and Aunt Lavinia still are. People look up to them, and it would be quite a statement for you, at nineteen years old, to use your power to knock out his record with no sign of stopping."

"You won it at fifteen, Perce," Heath said placatingly. "You still hold the record for the youngest champion, and it's not likely anyone will take it away from you."

Percival didn't look mollified. "If you want proof it's about me specifically, there's more," he grumbled. "Apparently you're still allowed to compete in the archery tournament."

"Of course I'm not competing," said Heath quickly, brushing off this evidence that Lord Niel shared his own skepticism about whether his good eyesight could really be considered a sign of magic. "If you're being excluded, I'm not going to take part without you. I don't care if we don't even go."

Percival's scowl softened at this demonstration of family loyalty, and Heath felt a little guilty at getting too much credit for the generous impulse. The tournament meant nothing to him—it really wasn't a sacrifice.

"You should compete, Heath," Percival said. "You won first place last year, and you're the best archer in the kingdom, fair and square."

Heath shook his head. "Doesn't matter, Perce. I'll stick with you."

"We will certainly all stick together," said the duke, in a voice that brooked no argument. "But there is no question of us not attending the tournament. We will all go, to show our support.

We will not give the impression that the crown is imposing a penalty on us, or that we are unwilling to do our part to contribute to the stability of the kingdom."

"Yes, Father," said Heath quickly.

His gaze passed from his brother's mutinous expression to the worry still lurking in his parents' eyes, before lowering to the plate in front of him. He held back a sigh as he felt the weight of the ocean rock still in his pocket.

He was itching to discover what, if anything, was hidden below the water. But that mystery would have to wait. His feet were back on land now and, as expected, his problems seemed to have grown with the approaching shoreline.

CHAPTER THREE

Merletta tried not to stare at the building that rose up around her. This was no dim stone structure, roughly carved out of the rocky ocean floor, like the charity home she'd grown up in. The receiving hall for the Center of Culture was smooth, pale, and ornate. This structure had been built, not carved. The stone had been quarried from elsewhere, and polished into smoothness. It was inset all over with mollusk shells in pearly white or glinting green, making the very walls shimmer. A small interior coral garden brightened one corner of the space, with skillfully carved stone benches surrounding it.

Merletta swam to the stone desk behind which a mermaid about a decade older than her was seated. The mermaid didn't look up immediately, distracted by something behind the desk that Merletta couldn't see. After a prolonged moment, Merletta cleared her throat, and the other mermaid looked up.

"Can I help—oh," the mermaid said. She ran her eyes over Merletta's entirely unadorned form.

Merletta held her head up, a challenge in her eyes. She knew that the simple shells that formed her only attire, standard for beneficiaries of the home she'd grown up in, were conspicuously different from the decorated and embellished coverings worn by mermaids from Skulssted, or indeed the neighboring city of Hemssted. But she had no intention of showing any embarrassment.

"I'm here to apply," Merletta said boldly.

"For the messenger position?" asked the other mermaid, her voice bored. The disdain in her eyes communicated what she thought of Merletta's chances of achieving even that lowly position.

"No," said Merletta defiantly. "I've just turned sixteen. I want to apply for training as a record holder."

The mermaid looked up, her attention finally caught as her eyebrows shot up. "A record holder?" For a moment she looked too shocked to even be derisive.

"That's right," said Merletta, raising her chin.

The mermaid glanced over her again. "And you're from Tilssted?" she guessed.

"I am," Merletta confirmed.

The mermaid looked around at the room, empty except for the two of them. "Where are your parents?" Her lip curled slightly. "I suppose you don't know how it usually works, but it's traditional for the parents to accompany applicants, to give their blessing to—"

"I know how it works," Merletta interrupted curtly. "I don't have any parents. I was raised in a charity home."

The mermaid just blinked, her expression blank. "You were raised in a charity home?" She paused. "In Tilssted? And you want to apply to be a record holder?"

"I've just said so, haven't I?" Merletta said. She was annoyed to hear the sulky edge to her own voice, but as much as she had prepared herself for derision, it was still hard to take the mermaid's obvious struggle to hold back laughter.

"Well," the other mermaid said at last. "I suppose…I suppose you should take a seat." She gestured toward the coral garden with its stone benches. "I'll call the recruit-master."

"Thank you," said Merletta, as politely as she could.

Swimming over to the nearest bench, she settled herself on its smooth surface and let her tail swish gently back and forth in an attempt to release her nervous tension. She had been dreaming of this day for years—ever since she'd first learned about the Center and its role, when she was a child. She refused to allow anyone else's attitude or behavior to chill the current of her enthusiasm. She was going to make it, like she'd told Tish. She was going to become a record holder, whatever she had to endure these next four years to make that happen.

The employee disappeared through a stone archway, and Merletta tried not to fidget as she waited. It was at least ten minutes before the other mermaid returned, an older merman following behind her. One glance at his face was enough to convince Merletta that whatever else his virtues might be, the recruit-master wasn't known for his patience.

"You're the new applicant?" the merman barked at her. His bristly brows—which had the perpetually puckered look of someone who always had somewhere more important to be— drew even further together. "The one from Tilssted?"

Merletta pushed off the bench, moving to float in front of him with rigidly straight posture.

"I'm Merletta," she said, trying to keep her tone respectful even as she refused to acknowledge the label he had given her. She knew the law, and she let that knowledge buoy her up.

"It's been some years since we've had any applicants from Tilssted," the recruit-master said, a hint of distaste in his voice. "Are you sure you want to put yourself through the application process? It's very rigorous."

"I'm sure, sir," said Merletta evenly.

The merman sighed, looking like he didn't care enough to fight over the point. No doubt he expected her to fail the first round of testing and be out of his hair in no time at all. Merletta set her jaw grimly. He'd soon learn his mistake.

"Come on, then," he said, turning around and gesturing with his head for her to follow. "You'd best come into the Center with me right away. There are some preliminary questions you'll have to answer before we can schedule your test."

"Yes, sir," said Merletta quickly, trying to contain her excitement as she swam after him. After years of being desperately curious to see inside the Center, she could hardly believe the moment had finally come.

In the recruit-master's wake, Merletta passed through the curtain of seaweed that provided a screen for the door out of the receiving hall. The long fronds waved lazily in response to her passage, brushing against her skin with a cold touch that she found faintly unpleasant.

Skulssted sat a little deeper than Tilssted, and Merletta had noticed that it was colder. The Center was the deepest point of the triple kingdoms, so she could only imagine that it would be even worse. She grimaced slightly, secure in the knowledge that the recruit-master had his back to her.

The pair proceeded down a long polished corridor, and Merletta tried not to be distracted by the several doors that opened off both walls. This building might not technically be in the Center, but it was the public face of the revered culture-keepers. There were probably many important things that happened here.

Merletta felt a ripple of excitement go down her tail at the thought that she might soon learn all about those activities. She had taken every opportunity to learn what she could in her sixteen years, and consequently knew considerably more than her peers at the home about the governance and history of their triple kingdoms. But that wasn't saying much. Like most merpeople, Merletta still knew very little about how their way of life came to be. There was so much to discover.

"So did you just turn sixteen?"

Merletta's strokes faltered slightly, startled out of her thoughts by the recruit-master's question.

"Yes, sir," she said. "Yesterday."

The man nodded. "You didn't waste any time."

Merletta didn't need to ask what he meant. Anyone wishing to apply as a record holder had to do so within two weeks of turning sixteen. She'd familiarized herself with the process when she was about six.

"No, sir," she said instead. "Joining the Center of Culture has been my ambition for some years. And," she added conscientiously, "it's customary in charity homes for beneficiaries to seek employment when they reach the age of sixteen. They don't really encourage us to delay once our birthdays have passed."

The recruit-master looked surprised, and Merletta was pretty sure it wasn't the policy of the charity home that he found unexpected. She knew very well that it wasn't exactly common for merchildren to dream of becoming record holders.

But he didn't comment on it. "Is this your first time out of Tilssted?" he asked, still looking forward. She had to work her tail strongly to keep up with him.

"No, sir," she said carefully. "We had outings occasionally, mostly in Hemssted, but once in Skulssted."

A true, if incomplete, answer. Merletta knew better than to reveal her other excursions, but she would very much prefer not to actually lie if she could avoid it. It seemed like a bad way to start out at what she hoped would be her new home. Plus, without family, history, or means, what did she have to hold on to but her integrity?

"Well," said the recruit-master mildly. "I imagine it's a little different from what you're used to."

As he spoke, they emerged out of the building, and it was all Merletta could do to keep her mouth from hanging open like a whale swimming through a krill swarm.

"You could say that," she responded faintly, her eyes scanning the scene before her in amazement.

The building opened onto the edge of a drop off. It wasn't as deep as some others she'd seen, but it was all the more impressive for that very reason. The ocean floor didn't disappear into darkness, but stretched out below her in a breathtaking panorama. The vertical rocky ledge teemed with life, pastel coral sitting smugly between waving fronds of seaweed, and many colorful fish darting in and out of sight. Sea turtles moved lazily across the surface of the coral, occasionally stopping to nibble at a choice patch of algae.

None of this was what captured Merletta's attention, though. It was a beautiful drop off, certainly, but not more so than others she had discovered in her explorations. It was what lay beyond that made her stare like the peasant she was.

There were no other buildings for some distance—nothing but a clear expanse of water, empty except for the varied sea life. But at the lower level of the ocean floor—not so much deeper than where she now floated—rose up an incredible complex that could only be the Center of Culture. If she had thought the receiving hall was impressive, the Center itself put it to shame.

Buildings rose, tall and pointed, their stone sides more smooth and even than any buildings Merletta had ever seen. They had clearly been carefully crafted and meticulously maintained. And it wasn't just a couple of buildings. It looked like a city. Tilssted, Skulssted, and Hemssted had each perhaps looked that way once, but the three cities had expanded so much that they now resembled one sprawling mass of mismatched architecture more than three individual cities.

The Center of Culture, on the other hand, was defined and contained. It was ringed around by a thick reef, giving the impression of a city with a wall, albeit a colorful one. It must have been built on a rocky mound underneath, because it rose in ascending layers, with one pointed spire protruding from the very center, and rising significantly above all the rest. Merletta's heart beat faster in her excitement. Was that where the most valuable records were kept? In the center of the Center? It would be fitting.

She had momentarily paused, but she propelled herself quickly through the water, catching up to the recruit-master as he swam out over the top of the drop off.

Her eyes were fixed on the spire as she followed him. That was where she belonged, right in the heart of where the knowledge was held.

And she would prove it, whatever it took.

CHAPTER FOUR

Heath

"HEEEELP!"

The anguished shout made both Heath and Percival draw up their horses, exchanging looks of alarm.

"It must have come from that group up ahead," said Percival. He moved to nudge his mount forward, but Heath shook his head.

"It wasn't them," he said confidently. "They all look fine to me."

Percival frowned as he followed his brother's gaze along the road before them, stretching toward the capital of Bryford. The only other travelers visible were a great distance ahead, but he didn't dispute Heath's claim. Percival was well used to his brother's unerring eyesight.

"Someone, HELP!"

The shout came again, and both brothers turned their heads to their left, toward a small copse of trees. Heath hadn't even noticed it, but there was a narrow lane branching off the main road not far behind them, heading into the grove.

"Come on," he said, urging his horse off the road. His

supposedly enhanced eyesight didn't give him the ability to see through trees, so he had no idea what they would find. He pushed into the trees to the sound of further cries, Percival close behind him.

It soon became evident that whoever was in distress was on the laneway, not in the grove. Within moments Heath could make out a carriage between the thinning trunks, and a moment later, he emerged from the little copse. He gave an audible gasp, Percival's exclamation coming from behind him.

Before them on the path was an overturned carriage. But it wasn't just on its side. It was a mangled wreck. The lane ran alongside the bottom of a small cliff. By the looks of it, a boulder had detached from the sheer surface, and the vehicle had been unlucky enough to be passing underneath when it fell.

The woman who had shouted for help saw them as they came out of the trees, and she raced toward them, wringing her hands.

"Help!"

Heath hastened to dismount as she approached them, aware that Percival was doing the same. He could barely draw his eyes from the carriage. He had never seen such a wreck, and his first thought was that the woman was lucky to be alive. She must have been thrown from the vehicle when it overturned.

"Please!" she sobbed. "Can you save him?"

Heath had just noticed a man lying not far from the mangled carriage, presumably the driver. Focusing his sharp eyes on the man's form, he noted with relief that his chest was rising and falling, and that his color was healthy. He must simply have been knocked unconscious.

Heath turned to reassure the woman—he was no physician, but he felt confident somehow that the man was fine—but the words died in his throat. The woman's eyes were wild with panic, and an ominous feeling grew inside Heath as she clutched his sleeve. She wasn't talking about the carriage driver.

Before either of the brothers could respond, a faint cry of pain reached them from the direction of the carriage.

"My son," the woman wailed. "He's trapped inside. He's being crushed!"

Heath and Percival exchanged a look of horror before instantly springing into action. They rushed toward the carriage, Percival making for the boulder while Heath crouched down on the level of the ruined vehicle.

"Can you hear me?" he asked, squinting in through the wreckage.

A faint sob was all the response he received, but it was enough to encourage him that the child was alive, and conscious. Pulling a shattered panel of wood out of the way, he caught a glimpse of a limb.

"He's over this side," he called to Percival, gesturing. "Roll it the other way."

The structure shuddered under the weight of the stone, the boulder dropping another inch toward where the boy was huddled. The whole wreck was clearly unstable.

"And hurry!" Heath called.

"But—" The woman's confused exclamation told Heath that she'd approached right behind him.

He didn't turn, keeping his eyes on what little of the child he could see, ready to tell Percival if the boulder's movements were further endangering the boy. He knew why the woman was confused—the boulder was huge, too heavy for three men to shift, let alone one.

But Percival wasn't like other men.

With a grunt, the young man put his shoulders against the mass, his muscles straining as he pushed. The day was warm, and he wore a tunic that exposed his powerful arms. The sight was familiar to Heath, but the woman stared in amazement at Percival's bulging muscles as the boulder began to move. The crushed frame of the wooden vehicle crunched loudly as the rock rolled across it, and the child screamed again. Percival paused, his form straining with the effort of holding the boulder in place as he looked inquiringly at his brother. Heath nodded in encouragement for Percival to continue. The structure around the child hadn't collapsed any further from the movement, and the boy sounded afraid rather than in great pain.

In less than a minute, the boulder was gone, and the wreck underneath it was exposed. The two brothers made short work of pulling the crushed panels of the structure away, to reveal a child of about six or seven, curled in a ball beneath the wreckage. The woman ran forward to scoop her child into her arms. The boy was blinking in the light, his face stained with tears, and he was bleeding from several superficial scratches. But he was moving normally, and his cries had ceased at his sudden freedom. Incredibly, he seemed to have escaped serious injury.

"Thank you," the woman gasped, disregarding Heath and turning to Percival. "You saved him! How—how did you—?"

"We are honored to be of service," said Percival gallantly, sweeping into a bow. "You should get that child to a physician."

"And the poor driver," interjected Heath from where he knelt beside the man. Even as he said it, the man stirred, opening his eyes slowly and letting out a small moan.

Heath released a breath as the man sat up. "It seems you've all been very lucky."

"Thanks to you," gasped the woman, her gaze still on Percival and her eyes bulging. "How did you move that boulder by yourself?"

"We all have our different gifts," said Percival cheerfully. "I'm just glad we were able to help."

"Gifts?" the woman repeated slowly, her eyes widening even further. "Are you one of the power-wielders?"

Heath frowned, a curl of discomfort spreading through him at the awe on the woman's face. And it wasn't because he felt any jealousy. Far from it. The way the stranger was looking at Percival filled him with an undefined alarm.

Percival, however, clearly felt nothing of the kind. "That's right," he said cheerfully, with a little bow. "I'm Lord Percival, son of the Duke of Bexley, and I'm at your service."

The woman responded with a curtsy so low, it could have been to the king himself. Heath's unease grew. It was possible that she was showing such respect because she knew the family tree of Valoria's royals, and was aware from Percival's introduction that their father was cousin to King Matlock.

But Heath doubted it. He was fairly certain that it was Percival's magic that brought the reverence to her eyes. And it struck him that her reaction was exactly what was making nobles like Lord Niel uncomfortable about that outer branch of the royal family that was born with power. Uncomfortable enough to take action.

It also struck Heath, as he observed the glow in his brother's eyes, that the reverence wasn't especially good for Percival, either. He watched his brother, wishing he could put his finger on the alarm he felt at the brightness on the young man's face. Percival had readily used his legendary strength to assist a helpless child, probably saving the boy's life. And he had done it out of a genuine desire to help—he certainly didn't expect anything in return. It was exactly what his powers should be used for.

So why did Heath feel more troubled than ever?

CHAPTER FIVE

"My offices are this way," the recruit-master said gruffly once he had led Merletta across the expanse of the drop off and into the Center itself. Merletta said nothing as she followed him down a broad street. She wanted to take in every detail of her surroundings, but she was too distracted by the feeling swirling around her stomach like a miniature maelstrom. Excitement, or just sick nerves? It was hard to tell. Her eyes bounced rapidly between the gleaming buildings, the elaborate coral gardens, and the merpeople passing all around her. She'd had no idea the Center was so big—it really was like a city of its own.

"Here we are, then," said the recruit-master, as they approached a round and well-decorated doorway. He gestured inside. "In there."

Merletta complied, but the recruit-master didn't follow her. Instead he hovered in the doorway, exchanging words with one of the armed mermen who flanked the entrance.

The guard nodded curtly, turning and swimming away into the open water. Merletta turned to the recruit-master, expecting an explanation. But he just flicked his tail, disappearing down a passageway, presumably back to whatever he'd been doing with his day. Hovering awkwardly in a corner, Merletta waited for so long that she wondered if she'd been forgotten altogether.

But at last, the guard returned, scanning the lobby for her, and gesturing with his head once his eyes latched on to her form. She followed him silently, sensing that he wasn't about to offer any explanations. He led her a significant distance toward the center of the complex, ending in a large square courtyard, flanked by stone pillars but open to the water above. Glancing up, Merletta could see the weak glow of the sunlight far above them.

"Wait here," the guard barked gruffly.

Merletta floated in the center of the square for a few minutes, before a merman who looked to be in his twenties appeared between two of the pillars.

He swam toward her, his eyebrows rising slightly as he took in her appearance. "You're the applicant?"

She nodded, swallowing nervously.

"Well," he said briskly. "I'm to put you through your basic strength and agility tests."

Merletta just blinked. She had to pass physical tests in order to enter the record holder program? She had assumed that all the testing would be focused on her mental capacity.

But the merman didn't offer her the opportunity to ask questions.

"Lift that," he said curtly, pointing to a small boulder to one side of the courtyard. "And place it with those." He pointed to a pile of similar rocks.

Merletta twitched her shoulders, edging her satchel onto her back, before swimming to the boulder indicated. She lifted it with ease, swimming quickly across the space and dropping it on the pile.

"Now that one," said the merman, his tone bored as he

pointed to a larger rock. Merletta hefted it with one arm, and repeated the journey.

"Huh." The merman grunted slightly, his expression unimpressed, and Merletta flushed as she realized he thought she was trying to show off by using only one arm. In fact, it had been an unconscious decision. She had often swum like that when bringing treasures back from her explorations, so as to keep one hand free to wield her crude weapon. Until that moment she hadn't identified it, but she obviously felt sufficiently unsafe and out of place in the Center for her instinctive danger response to be set off.

She would have to work on that.

"Now that one."

She followed the direction of the merman's pointing arm, and squared her shoulders in determination as she saw the size of the final boulder. It was as long as her torso, and significantly wider.

Swimming to it, she wrapped her arms around it to get a good grip. Muscles bulged in her deceptively lean arms as she pulled the boulder from the smooth floor of the training area, holding it at chest height as she swam the mercifully short distance to the pile.

She dropped it with a grunt, turning to the merman for her next task. His eyebrows were once again raised, and it took him a moment to realize that she was waiting for instructions. Merletta suppressed a satisfied grin as he hurried to speak. He clearly hadn't expected her to be able to lift that.

"Come over to these pillars," he said.

Merletta followed obediently, and the merman put her through a series of exercises clearly designed to test her speed and reflexes. They were easy. Unlike most merpeople, Merletta hadn't confined herself to the well-planned passageways and carefully structured gardens of the triple kingdoms. She was well used to darting through reefs, wending her way between sharp coral, and weaving in and out of schools of fish, as nimble as a minnow.

Her tester's eyebrows drew closer and closer together as he watched her, but he made no comment on her performance.

Finally, he took her to another end of the training square, where an obstacle course of sorts was set up, with targets scratched into rocks at various angles. Under his instructions, Merletta picked up some small rocks, darting through the course and flicking them at the targets with a simple sling. As commanded, she stayed constantly in motion, not stopping to take aim. This test was also not especially difficult for her. She just had to imagine that the target was an angry barracuda she had accidentally disturbed. It wasn't like she would normally stop to carefully line up her shot when being chased by a sharp-toothed—and venomous—predator.

When she completed the last stage, flipping around to face the final target with precisely the maneuver she had used on the shark that morning, she turned expectantly to the tester.

"You performed...well," he admitted. He sounded a little begrudging, but Merletta still felt encouraged. It was clear he was impressed. He looked over his shoulder, and she realized the guard who had brought her was still there. He appeared equally surprised by her success.

The guard didn't comment, just beckoning for her to follow before swimming out of the square. She followed him back to the recruit-master's office, where she received an instruction that was beginning to be very familiar.

"Wait here," he said gruffly. "Someone will be along to collect you in a minute."

The guard made his way through one of the many openings coming from the lobby, and Merletta settled back into her same corner, resigning herself to a wait. She had been there for at least half an hour when her attention was caught by a group of several young merpeople swimming across the lobby toward the exit. They were eye-catching because they all wore matching armbands. The two girls in the group even wore uniform shells, not unlike the one Merletta wore from the home, but of much higher quality. Their progress was unhurried, and Merletta looked them over curiously as they approached.

One of the mermen glanced up and saw her watching them, his eyebrow rising slightly at her scrutiny. Merletta met his eye for a defiant second before lowering her gaze, telling herself to think like Tish and be inconspicuous.

"Who was that?" one of the girls said in an audible aside, as the group drifted past her. "Do you know her, Oliver?"

"No," responded the young merman who had looked at her, his tone disinterested. "But she's probably the new *applicant*."

Merletta felt her neck warming at the disdain with which he said the last word, and the derisive noise which came from the girl who had spoken. News had certainly traveled quickly about her improbable application.

"So ridiculous," the girl sniffed, speaking as though Merletta couldn't hear her, although she must realize that she could. "Why would they waste time even giving her the test? It's not like some orphan from Tilssted could actually *pass* it."

The group was almost out of earshot now, but the voice of the other girl carried faintly back to Merletta. "Remember, the law requires the Center to allow any applicant from the triple kingdoms to undertake the test, Ileana."

Merletta slightly relaxed her clenched fists, sucking in a deep mouthful of clear, cold water to calm her emotions. *That's right*, she thought with grim satisfaction. *They can't deny me the chance to earn my place here.*

And she was determined to earn it, no matter what anyone

thought of her background. She would pass that test. She had to.

Unfortunately, she quickly discovered that this mood of powerful determination was difficult to sustain through prolonged waiting. After a while, her stomach began to rumble. She was tempted to slip away and eat the salted cod she had brought from the home, but she was worried someone would come for her while she was gone.

At long last, a middle-aged merman stuck his head into the waiting area and called curtly for her to follow him. He took her into a small office and gestured her onto a stone bench.

For a moment he just regarded her silently, and she tried not to fidget.

"I've been informed that you displayed a sufficient level of physical ability to continue with your testing."

Merletta remained silent, heartened by the information.

"I have therefore been asked to administer the other application tests."

The merman's flat tone made Merletta think that he resented the waste of his time. Most likely he—and others—were hoping she would fail the physical tests without anyone even needing to organize the more complex testing.

The merman proceeded to rattle off a series of questions about her history, barely making eye contact the whole time. Merletta could see his lip curl more with each question she was unable to answer. She pushed down her embarrassment. She was well used to the disadvantages of growing up as an orphan without a family name. There was no reason to let it rattle her now.

Once he had drawn out what little information she could give him, he looked up from the large waxy kelp leaf on which he'd been making short or long slashes according to her answers.

"All right," he said briskly. "The testing."

Merletta straightened her posture as he rattled off what was clearly a rehearsed explanation.

"Any mermaid or merman in the triple kingdoms has the right to apply to the record holder training program within two weeks of their sixteenth birthday. Nevertheless, applicants can only be accepted into the training program if they pass a series of entry tests. The training is rigorous and broad, and requires significant investment from the instructors. That investment cannot be justified unless a trainee at least has the capacity to succeed." He looked her in the eye for once. "I'll be frank—most people don't, even amongst those select few who choose to apply."

Merletta just nodded tightly, feeling like if she opened her mouth she might be sick. So far he had only told her what she already knew.

The merman was already looking down at his leaf again. "The most important quality in a record holder is memory. It's also the most difficult to teach if the aptitude isn't there. Combat and history we can teach, even literacy to an extent. But memory is more difficult to train if there isn't a strong starting point. Therefore we'll start there. If you can't pass that test, there's no point continuing with any others."

"Yes, sir," Merletta managed, again giving a small nod.

She watched with equal parts trepidation and fascination as the merman pulled out a collection of beautifully rounded shells, and an assortment of small rocks in a variety of colors. He explained the format of the test, which required her to remember which color rock sat under which shell as they were covered and uncovered rapidly, and to match rocks to like colors while still covered.

Merletta began to breathe more easily as she followed his instructions, answering correctly every time. The merman was insultingly surprised by her success, his eyebrows going up slightly with each correct answer.

"Well," he said begrudgingly, after several minutes. "You passed the preliminary stage of the memory test." He regarded Merletta silently, his eyes narrowing at her expression. "You look confused. Did you not realize you'd answered correctly?"

"No, sir, it's not that," said Merletta quickly, wondering how to answer.

She wasn't surprised by her accuracy. She knew her visual memory was excellent—it was one of her greatest strengths. In fact, her memory was the reason she was there. Once, when she was a small child, a carer at the home had made a stray comment about her memory being good enough to be a record holder. It was more an expression than an actual suggestion—the carer certainly hadn't intended to create a lifelong ambition with the careless words. But it had stayed with Merletta, and she had gone to great effort to discover who the record holders were, what they did, and what it took to join their ranks. And even from that young age, she had made it a game and a challenge to take every opportunity to test and improve her memory.

"I just..." She hesitated. "I was surprised by the style of the test. It was more...simplistic than I expected." The truth was that it felt like a child's game, the sort she and her fellow beneficiaries had played at the home by gathering together unwanted flotsam and turning it into a competition.

The merman made a disgruntled noise in his throat as he packed the shells and the rocks away. "Yes, well, that's not the normal format of the test. The truth is you're getting an advantage, which hardly seems fair to me, but the law says everyone has the right to apply, so—"

"What do you mean?" Merletta asked sharply. "I'm not looking for a handout. I want to take the same test as everyone else."

The merman looked less than impressed by her interruption. For a moment he just glared at her, then he said, with a slight huff, "Well, that's not really possible, is it? Normally applicants are required to read a complex description, then copy it out word for word ten minutes later, but since you can't read—"

"I can read," Merletta said.

The man stared at her, and this time she didn't think it was her interruption that had thrown him.

"And I can write," she added for good measure. She refrained with difficulty from rolling her eyes as he continued to stare blankly. "Some merpeople in Tilssted can read and write, you know."

"But I thought you said you grew up in a charity home," the merman said. His tone made it an accusation, as if he suspected she had deceived him somehow. "You're telling me they taught literacy there?"

"Not generally," Merletta admitted. "But there was an elderly merman who used to volunteer there. Denton. He was only supposed to teach us symbols, so we could read basic signposts, but he saw that I was more interested than the others." *And more capable*, she added silently. "So he started teaching me to read and write." Her voice took on a reminiscent tone. "He came every week for years."

"Where is he now?" the merman asked, looking slightly suspicious for some reason.

Merletta felt her throat close slightly. It was almost like the feeling of diving below the surface, but she knew it was caused by emotion this time, not by the transition from air to water. "He died," she said shortly. "Years ago."

"Oh," said the merman. He offered no condolences, instead straightening in his seat, his tone turning brisk. "Well, that's good, then. You can take the normal tests."

The memory of her mentor—one of the few genuinely kind-hearted merpeople she had ever met—gave Merletta fresh determination. She focused all her attention on the seemingly endless stream of verbal and written questions put to her. She would like to think that if Denton was still alive, he would have been proud to see her putting his teaching to such good use.

When she performed the first few tests flawlessly, the exercises became increasingly more complex, and it was all she could do to keep up. A few times she knew she had made an error, and she held her breath, expecting to be thrown from the room—and the Center—without ceremony. But apparently some mistakes were allowed, because the testing continued.

It was a struggle to maintain her stoic demeanor when it came time for the written tests. Her fingers gripped the carved coral writing implement firmly, her hands flying over the waxy leaf with incredible speed. Writing had never felt so effortless. Remembering the tortuously slow process of learning to write by scratching in the shifting sand of the ocean floor, she couldn't help but imagine how much easier it would have been to train with such tools.

The testing had been going without pause for almost four hours when the merman finally sat back in his seat. He looked almost as weary as Merletta felt, but his expression was hard to read as he regarded Merletta.

She sat straight, her back stiff and her hand cramped, watching him nervously. *Well?* she wanted to say, but she curbed her tongue.

"You passed," he said at last, and she almost shot out of her seat. "Both the memory and the literacy tests." The merman gave a small one-shouldered shrug. "There were quite a number of errors in there, but within the allowable limit."

Barely, his tone seemed to say, but Merletta didn't care. She'd done it. She'd made it.

She was going to be a record holder.

CHAPTER SIX

Heath

I t was only an hour after their encounter with the unfortunate travelers that Heath and Percival rode through the gates of Bryford.

Once the brothers had assisted the travelers to connect with a larger group heading for the capital—one which had a carriage for the injured travelers to ride in—there had been no reason for them to linger. With promises to take word of the accident to Bryford and send back a physician if possible, they had parted ways with the group.

They had ridden away to profuse thanks from the woman whose son they had saved, and Percival was still whistling cheerfully when the walls of the city towered up above them.

Heath had always liked the city of Bryford, and despite his lingering unease, he felt his heart lift as they entered through the wide wooden gates. The sun was shining brightly, and the pennants fluttering above the thick stone battlements added spots of vibrant color against the already vivid sky.

"Lord Percival!" shouted the guard at the gate cheerfully. "About time for you to show up!"

Percival grinned, acknowledging the greeting with a wave of his hand.

The guard seemed to suddenly notice Percival's companion, adding, "Lord Heath, welcome," in a friendly afterthought.

Heath smiled in a detached way, unable to remember the guard's name. Percival probably knew it, he thought. He smiled to himself as he watched his brother pull up only a couple of streets into the city to talk to a patrol of royal guards.

Heath had reflected before now that Percival would have done well as a guard, or better yet a knight, if he hadn't been the future Duke of Bexley. But as his father's heir, he had quite a different role laid out before him. Heath could have trained as a knight, if he wished. It wasn't uncommon for younger sons of noblemen to do so. But the idea had never interested him in the slightest.

"You're late," one of the royal guards, clearly a friend of Percival's, was saying. "I was starting to think you were going to miss the tournament! You do know it starts tomorrow, don't you?"

"Of course I do," said Percival airily. "Couldn't get away from the estate until now." He jerked his head south east, in the general direction of Bexley Manor. "Our parents won't be here until this evening, but we rode on ahead."

The guard's eyes flicked toward Heath, giving a friendly if vague smile, before his gaze returned to Percival.

"Well, you'd better hurry if you don't want to miss the cut off for signing up. I didn't see your shield on the competitors' board."

Percival shifted uncomfortably on his horse, and his airy tone sounded distinctly forced.

"Oh, I'm not competing this year. Just here to observe."

"Not competing?" The other guard looked at him like he'd lost his mind.

"That's right," said Percival, with an unsuccessful attempt at a chuckle. "Thought I'd better be gracious and give the rest of you lot a fighting chance to win something."

"More like the crown thought they'd better tie your hands," muttered one of the other guards, clearly better informed than his companion.

Heath's discomfort returned in full force, and a cloud descended on Percival's face.

"Oi, Percival!" A shout made them all turn, to see another guard jogging up. "I've just come from the gate," he said, after exchanging friendly greetings. "What's this I hear about you rescuing some child from a crushed carriage?"

Percival shrugged. "It was no big deal," he said, a little too nonchalant. He glanced at Heath. "And Heath helped, of course. We were happy to be of assistance."

"Assistance is an understatement, from what I heard," the guard said, disregarding the mention of Heath completely. "The woman is telling everyone how you saved her boy's life. Says you lifted a boulder the size of a cottage clean off the carriage."

Heath rolled his eyes at this exaggeration. Not that he was surprised, remembering the way the woman had looked at Percival.

"It wasn't quite like that," Percival laughed.

He may as well have saved his breath. A small crowd had gathered, and a couple dozen people were gazing at Percival with an admiration that reminded Heath uncomfortably of hunger. He felt concerned to see his brother at the center of such attention, but in all honesty, he felt even more relieved it wasn't him.

"You're a hero, My Lord," piped up one of the onlookers, and Percival waved a good-natured hand in acknowledgment of the compliment.

"Too bad the crown repays its heroes by shutting them out of the tournament," muttered the guard who had complained before about Percival's hands being tied.

Heath glared at the man. He'd been annoyed enough about the guard riling Percival up, but saying it in front of a crowd was a hundred times worse. Didn't he realize how dangerous such talk was? Judging by his disgruntled expression, Heath suspected he had prematurely placed a wager on some detail of Percival's inevitable victory.

Percival's sunny smile had descended again into a scowl. "Yes, it is too bad," he agreed sourly. Heath shot him a sharp look, and he shrugged. "We should celebrate power," he said lightly. "After all, it's only an accident of fate that prevented power being present in the direct royal line, isn't it?"

A ripple went through the crowd, and Heath's eyes widened.

"Percival!" he hissed. He cast an uneasy glance at their audience, and was unsettled to see a hint of excitement in some of their eyes. Percival had been addressing Heath, but he had a carrying voice.

"Imagine a power-wielder on the throne," Heath heard someone mutter.

"Like Kyona," someone else agreed.

"We'd better go, Perce," Heath cut in, forcing a cheerful tone. "They'll be expecting us up at the castle." He nodded a curt farewell to the royal guards, then wheeled his horse toward the center of the city, glancing back to make sure his brother was following.

But as soon as they were alone, he pulled up his horse. "Percival, what were you thinking?" he demanded. "How could you say that in front of a crowd?"

Percival stared at him. "What are you scolding me for? I was just responding to that guard. All I said was—"

"I know what you said," Heath said grimly. "But what

matters more is what they heard. It sounded like you were saying our family should be on the throne!"

Percival made an impatient noise. "Of course I wasn't saying that! I just meant that if circumstances had been different, King Matlock could have been the one born as the first power-wielder in his generation, instead of Father." He dropped his voice to a mutter. "I'm guessing no one would be complaining about magic then."

"That's not how it sounded," Heath insisted. Percival urged his horse forward again, but Heath leaned over and grabbed the reins, his expression earnest. "Perce, you have to be careful. This is exactly what Father is talking about."

Percival rolled his eyes. "You're quoting Father to me now?" He frowned. "It's easy for you to be so magnanimous in all this, Heath. No one's trying to control you. You're not the one being made a fool of."

Heath sighed. "I know it feels personal, but it's not really about you, Perce." He adopted a bracing tone. "Don't let it get to you. So what if word of the crown's...request has spread around? What does it matter? Better than everyone thinking you weren't entering because you were scared you might lose."

His attempt to encourage his brother didn't meet with much success.

"They wouldn't think that," Percival said simply. "They all know I'd win."

Heath sighed again, unable to think of a response to this unanswerable statement. His brother wasn't being boastful—he was just stating the facts.

It was in a subdued frame of mind that they approached the castle, handing their horses over in the courtyard to a helpful groom. Heath glanced up at the enormous stone basin erected high above the castle's entrance, filled with dancing orange flame. It was impressive, but he had seen it so many times he almost didn't notice it.

He held back yet another sigh. He'd been looking forward to visiting the castle—for reasons of his own—but he was in no mood to appreciate the solid beauty of the stone structure, with its elegant tapestries, and imposing turrets.

They were ushered to a private—but still enormous—receiving room used by the royal family. Food was laid out on a long and beautifully carved wooden table, and the space was filled with members from the extended branches of the royal family. Clearly they were among the last to arrive for the tournament.

The conversation lulled when they entered, and Heath barely held in a grimace at the hesitant way everyone glanced at Percival. His brother evidently hadn't exaggerated when he said that the crown's edict was specifically aimed at him.

But Percival handled himself well, smiling and nodding to everyone as he and Heath made their way toward the king and queen, seated at one end of the long room. Perhaps their father's strict instructions about demonstrating their support for the crown were still ringing in his ears.

The two brothers bowed low to King Matlock and Queen Renata, and exchanged polite greetings with Crown Prince Lachlan—about Heath's age—and his younger brother, Prince Knox. Their duty done, they retreated to the center of the room, where the other young people were laughing and enjoying the food. Heath glanced back at the royals. Crown Prince Lachlan maintained a neutral expression, but Prince Knox was watching the others his age with a hint of longing.

Heath felt a shot of sympathy for the teenage boy, along with gratitude for his own, less visible, status. Lachlan and Knox were his second cousins, but he didn't feel like he'd ever really gotten to know them. By no choice of their own, they were too far removed from him by their station, and the pressure that came with it.

"Look who finally decided to show up."

Heath turned his attention from the two princes, as he felt a genial slap on his shoulder.

"Brody. Good to see you!" He grinned in greeting at the curly-haired young man now whacking Percival's back. No one would accuse Brody of being aloof. Perhaps it was because he was Heath's first cousin—and therefore of equally insignificant status—that he could get away with being as casual as he always was.

"Thought you might be sulking away back at Bexley Manor because you've been barred from the tournament, Perce," Brody added cheerfully.

A spluttering sound drew Heath's attention to the young woman standing just behind Brody. He reached out absent-mindedly to pat her back in an attempt to help clear the wine she had just inhaled.

"Hi Bianca," he said in a friendly way.

"Brody!" coughed Heath's other cousin, glaring at her twin and speaking in a hiss. "You can't say that." She glanced around. "Not here, anyway." Her duty done, she shot a bright smile at Heath. "Hi Heath."

Brody rolled his eyes at his sister, just as Percival, sounding sulky, responded in a mutter.

"Father wouldn't let me. He insisted we all had to come."

Brody chuckled. "I knew you wouldn't be here if you had a choice."

"I'm sure it won't be so bad, Perce," said Bianca soothingly. "It's actually pretty fun to watch the tournament."

"That's right," Brody chipped in. "The rest of us have been doing it for years."

Percival snorted. "I've certainly never seen you compete," he said, raising an eyebrow at his cousin's lithe and un-muscled form. The twins were about Percival's age, and Heath knew that Brody's disinterest in sparring with his cousin had been a source of irritation to Percival since childhood.

Brody grinned. "Oh, I'm not allowed to. Didn't you hear that anyone born with power is requested to take a supervisory role this year?"

Heath couldn't help but laugh, but Percival just grunted, unimpressed.

"Somehow I don't think anyone's worried about you using your abilities with plants to win the tournament."

"Ah well, we can't all be gifted with the strength of five men, cousin," said Brody, elbowing Percival jovially. "I'm just grateful I got something. Just think, I could be like poor old Heath, here."

"Brody," said Bianca, her tone reproachful.

Heath just grinned appreciatively, unfazed by his cousin's humor, but Percival rushed to his brother's defense.

"Heath has power. His eyesight is unbelievable."

"Of course," said Brody, turning to Heath with a sparkle in his eyes that belied his solemn tone. "No archery for you this year, Heath."

"Actually," admitted Percival grudgingly, "they said he can compete if he wants to."

Brody gave a shout of laughter, which he quickly stifled at a long-suffering look from his sister.

"Not considered a threat, hey?" he said to Heath. "That's a bit of a blow, isn't it?"

Heath chuckled. "My pride is deeply wounded, as you can see." He grabbed a drink from a tray being carried past by a servant. "But I'm not going to compete, obviously. I'll be watching with Percival and you lot."

"See that, Bianca?" Brody asked his sister in a wounded

voice. "Heath has his brother's back in his misfortune. Where's that sibling loyalty when I'm out of favor with Mother?"

Bianca rolled her eyes. "There's one small but significant difference—when you're out of favor, you've usually brought it on yourself. Plus," she added reflectively, over Brody's splutters of protest, "as your twin, I have to work a little harder to distance myself from your bad reputation."

Heath was chuckling again, and even the disgruntled Percival was smiling in spite of himself at his cousins' banter. But Brody shook his head sadly.

"No one knows how I suffer."

"Mother probably does," Bianca pointed out. "Being a twin herself. And Grandmother, I suppose." A look of alarm crossed her features, as if she was just figuring something out. "Oh no. I'm going to have twins one day, aren't I?"

"Probably," grinned Brody, elbowing her.

"Where is Grandmother?" Heath asked, looking around. "I was looking forward to speaking with her, but I can't see her."

"She and Grandfather only got back from Kyona yesterday," said Bianca. "They're resting today, but they'll be at the tournament."

Heath nodded, relieved. He had momentarily forgotten about the elderly couple's trip. They had been traveling to the neighboring kingdom of Kyona every summer since their marriage, and they continued in the habit, even in their old age. His grandmother had been a princess of Kyona before her marriage to a Valorian prince, and her brother was Kyona's king.

It was a nice tradition, but Heath was glad they were back. He was very fond of his grandmother, and often found that she had a very helpful perspective on things. He wanted to ask her what she thought about the rising prejudice against those in the court who had been born with magic in their blood. It was presumably a matter of particular interest to her, given that she was the one who had introduced the bloodline—she was the first power-wielding Valorian, really.

"I wonder how their time in Kyona went," he said aloud.

"Yes, I wonder what it's like over there," Percival said, his tone still slightly disgruntled as his eyes flicked to the sovereigns at the end of the room. "With a power-wielder actually on the throne, I'm guessing things run a little differently."

The conversation moved on, but Heath lost track of his cousins' chatter. His eyes remained fixed on his brother, who was still looking toward the royal family. Obviously Heath hadn't been the only one to hear the muttered comments of their onlookers earlier. Whether it was the expression on Percival's face, or the ordeal that the tournament was sure to be, he couldn't say. All Heath knew was that his unease was growing by the minute.

CHAPTER SEVEN

An hour after passing the test, Merletta was still in a state of euphoria. The time immediately after leaving the testing room was a blur. She vaguely remembered being shown to a sleeping area which she was apparently to share with the other female trainees. It had been empty at the time, except for the belongings of its other occupants and the seaweed hammocks strung all over the space, swaying gently with the current.

The mermaid who had showed her the way had raised a disapproving eyebrow when she saw that the small kelp satchel constituted Merletta's only belongings, but Merletta had been far too elated to care about such things.

She was told where to find the dining hall used by the trainees, but given no other instructions. Apparently her orientation would start the following day. Merletta suspected that the mermaid who showed her to the sleeping room expected her to stay there and rest until the evening meal. But no one had expressly forbidden her to wander freely, and she had no intention of floating around all day.

She waited impatiently, barely able to keep her fins still

while the mermaid fussed around, tidying the space. The feeling of restlessness was so familiar to Merletta that she glanced up toward the distant surface in an almost unconscious gesture. The impulse made her smile. She had escaped the home at last, but some things hadn't changed. While she might not have brought many belongings, one thing she had definitely brought with her was the insatiable desire for exploration that had made her the despair of every carer who had ever tried to keep her contained.

Nevertheless, when the other mermaid finally left, and Merletta slipped outside the building, her gaze was no longer directed upward. For once it wasn't undiscovered places beyond the borders of the cities that pulled at her. She had finally reached the one part of the triple kingdoms which she desperately wanted to explore, and she didn't intend to waste the opportunity.

She swam slowly through the passages of the Center, taking in every detail this time. Although the quality of the buildings showed wealth, she was surprised to see that most of them were not covered with the showy decorations she'd observed in the city of Skulssted, while traveling from the home to the Center. And similarly, most of the merpeople passing her were not adorned with excessive jewelry. Even their hair was tied back in a practical manner rather than the elaborate styles adopted by most of the wealthy merpeople she had seen.

Some instinct warned Merletta not to probe too far into the heart of the Center while she was still such an outsider. She skirted the edge of the complex, admiring the beauty of the sea life beyond the edge of the developed area. The creatures were clearly well acclimatized to the presence of the merpeople who lived in the Center. Even the sea turtles showed no reaction to her proximity as she swam alongside their reef. She glanced in fascination back toward the buildings on the other side of the drop off, where the Center ended and Skulssted began. She hadn't realized there was an area of untouched ocean of this size anywhere within the triple kingdoms. It was beautiful.

The light had begun to fade by the time she made her way back toward the trainees' barracks, and its dining hall. She had become distracted by all the new sights, and had lingered longer than intended. The deepening gloom was met by the luminous glow of many lanterns, and Merletta couldn't help but be impressed by how well-lit the streets were. She wondered whether the residents themselves were wealthy enough to all have their own farms of luminescent plankton to replenish the lanterns outside their homes, or whether it was a service provided by the Center.

Some of the street corners even had large conical cages with jellyfish swimming up and down in the confined space, their glow rippling through the water in unceasing motion. Merletta gave these sources of light a wide berth. The shiver that went over her was only in part because of her dislike of the creatures. The Center really was deeper than Skulssted. The chill of the water seemed to reach right into her bones.

Merletta didn't bother going back to the sleeping chamber first, instead making her way straight to the dining hall. She'd forgotten all about her purloined cod in her excitement about passing the test, leaving it in her chamber. But her elation had worn off enough for her to realize just how hungry she was.

She entered the dining hall to general bustle. There were some two dozen merpeople in the room, all presumably holding official roles in the Center.

Merletta made it only a short way into the room when she stopped, blinking quickly at the sight before her. The room was dominated by a long stone platform that seemed to have been carved from the bedrock below. Merpeople were floating around it, chatting and eating, but it wasn't the people or the table that caught Merletta's attention. It was the food.

Never in her life had she seen such a spread. At the home, they had eaten cod and seaweed almost every day, with very little variety in its preparation. Occasionally they would get the treat of rarer fish, and once or twice she had tasted cooked crab, prepared over one of the thermal vents located in the wealthier parts of town.

But even that was nothing to the food being served in the dining hall. The surface of the table was covered with shallow circular indentations, and they were filled with an incredible variety of dishes. There must be thermal vents somewhere within the Center—not that the temperature of the water supported that theory—because there were multiple dishes that appeared to have been seared in the scalding water. There were various types of fish, of course, and the familiar staple of seaweed, but there were also basins of squid, what appeared to be shark meat, and even a large turtle-shell bowl filled with fresh oysters.

Merletta was still hovering in the doorway, staring in stunned silence at the spread, when a mermaid who looked to be in her early thirties paused on her way past.

"Can I help? You look lost."

"Oh," said Merletta, pleasantly surprised by the mermaid's friendly tone. "I was told to come here for the meal, but I'm not sure if there's somewhere particular I'm supposed to sit, or..."

"You're new, then?" the other mermaid asked. "Did you just get a job here?"

"Not a job, no," said Merletta, straightening a little. "I've just been accepted as a trainee."

The mermaid's eyebrows went up. "Oh, good for you! I didn't realize there was a new trainee." She tilted her head toward one end of the stone hall, her long copper braid gliding gently through the water with the motion. "The trainees sit over there. The ones with the armbands."

Merletta followed her gesture and saw five young merpeople. They were sitting in a group around a small stone table set beside the broad platform occupied by the rest of the merpeople.

"Thanks," said Merletta, trying to conceal the sinking feeling in her gut. Even before seeing the faces of the other trainees, she recognized their armbands. They were the ones who had passed through the lobby of the recruit-master's office while she was waiting, the ones who had spoken of her application with such scorn.

Squaring her shoulders, she moved toward them with a flick of her tail. She supposed she knew what type of welcome to expect from her fellow trainees, but it was no more than she'd predicted. Even sweet-natured Tish, who always tried to look for the best in people, had warned her not to expect kindness.

"Is this the trainees' table?" she asked politely, pulling herself up to float alongside the group.

They all turned to look at her, their expressions ranging from disinterest to open hostility. No one looked surprised, however, so she assumed that news of her successful test had already spread.

"It is," said one of the two mermaids in the group, shifting slightly so that there was room for Merletta. Taking a second look, Merletta drew encouragement from the realization that this girl, at least, looked more curious than antagonistic.

Merletta approached the table, occupying the gap the other mermaid had created.

"So," she said, gesturing to the larger table. "What's the occasion?"

"The occasion?" asked one of the young mermen, his forehead creasing in confusion.

"For the banquet," Merletta clarified. "What are we celebrating?"

A couple of the trainees gave poorly stifled snorts of laughter, and the second of the two mermaids shot her a pitying look.

"The occasion is dinner."

"Oh." Merletta felt a flash of embarrassment at her mistake, but she pushed it down. If anyone should feel ashamed, it was the merpeople who ate this way every night while half of Tilssted survived on cod and uncooked seaweed.

"I'm finished, anyway," said the more hostile of the mermaids, pushing herself up from the table with shapely hands.

"Me too," one of the mermen said, following her gesture. The others said nothing, but soon all of them were rising through the water, leaving their mostly empty basins and making for the doorway.

Merletta was left alone at the small round table, painfully aware of the scrutiny of all the other merpeople in the hall.

So much for encouragement.

It was with renewed determination that Merletta followed her fellow trainees from the dining hall after breakfast the next morning. She had decided not to set herself up for further rejection, and had intentionally arrived just as the meal was ending, swiping some octopus tentacles from the table as servers began to clear the food.

"Good morning," she greeted one of the servers cheerfully.

The girl looked up quickly. "Good morning," she responded hesitantly, clearly surprised by the attention.

Merletta caught sight of the other trainees leaving the dining hall, and hurried after them. She hadn't been told where to go for the first lesson of the day—another instance of the wonderfully warm welcome she was receiving—and she figured that tailing the others was her best bet.

Her unconscious guides led her away from the barracks, further into the Center. Merletta's excitement grew as she realized that they were heading for the central structure with the tall spire protruding from its middle. The heart of it all.

They didn't go right into the center of the complex, however. They swam beneath a carved stone archway into a square open space with several doorways coming off it. As they crossed the space, Merletta flicked her tail, catching up to them.

One of the mermen turned slightly, taking in her form without comment. Merletta met his eyes evenly, and he looked away. The six of them made their way through one of the openings on the far side of the central space, and Merletta found herself in a small cave-like room. Layered seats had been carved out of the bedrock on three sides, turning the remaining side of the room into a natural focal point.

The other five trainees settled against the raised seating, and Merletta followed suit.

"Oh. You're here."

Turning, Merletta saw that the voice belonged to the unfriendly mermaid from the evening before.

"Yes," she said shortly. "I was told my training would start today. I'm Merletta," she added as an afterthought.

For a moment there was silence, as five pairs of eyes studied her.

"I'm Sage," said the mermaid who hadn't spoken yet, when the silence threatened to become uncomfortable. "Congratulations for passing the entrance test."

Merletta began to thank her, but a sniff from the first mermaid cut across her words.

"I heard you were given an easier test than the rest of us."

Merletta turned to the speaker, one eyebrow raised. She didn't want to start out by alienating her fellow trainees, but that didn't mean she was going to let them swim all over her, either.

"Yes," she said calmly. "I believe that by some error, I was given an additional test *on top of* all the ones we've all passed."

The other mermaid's expression was more sour than ever, but she was apparently unable to think of a reply.

"You could be a little more polite, Ileana," said one of the mermen, glancing over at the mermaid who had spoken. His tone was mild, but everyone's posture changed slightly, and the hostile mermaid—Ileana apparently—fell silent, looking chastened.

The merman turned to Merletta. "Greetings," he said unemotionally. "My name is Emil."

"I'm glad to meet you, Emil," said Merletta, dipping her head in a traditional greeting.

Emil returned the gesture, his expression disinterested, and turned away. It appeared he had no more to say.

Merletta observed Emil's profile with interest. He looked like the oldest, which might be why he seemed to have the respect of the rest of the group. Like Ileana, he had the classic features considered appealing by most merpeople. Pale skin, fair hair, and faintly purple eyes. He even had the vibrant green tail that many of the girls in the home had often described as the most attractive of scale colors. Ileana's tail was green as well, although not nearly as bright in tone.

Not all of the group matched this ideal. The friendlier of the mermaids—Sage, if she remembered correctly—had skin a shade darker, brown hair, and a tail the pinky-orange color of the coral found in most gardens. And one of the remaining two mermen, although his skin was similar to Sage's, and his tail a deep blue, had even darker hair.

Merletta thought she herself was the darkest in skin tone,

although not by much. She glanced at her tail with some satisfaction, pleased that the vibrancy of the purple-blue scales gave her nothing to be ashamed of. But the momentary surge of pride made her laugh at herself. It wasn't her coloring that made her stand out, of course. She would hazard a guess that none of the other five had grown up in Tilssted.

"Good morning."

The strong voice made everyone sit up straighter in their seats. Merletta followed the others' gaze toward the portal into the room, to see a middle-aged merman enter, his eyes on the large writing leaf in his hand rather than on the group he was addressing.

"Good morning, Instructor Wivell," responded the five trainees as one.

The merman floated across to the empty side of the space. He looked up at last, his eyes scanning the group in an unhurried way before fixing on Merletta.

"We have a new trainee," he said, his face showing neither welcome nor disdain. "Merletta, I believe?"

"Yes, sir," said Merletta, pushing up from her seat.

He nodded. "I am Instructor Wivell. You applied yesterday, correct?"

"That's right," Merletta confirmed.

The instructor nodded again. "And am I correct in understanding that you are not a legacy applicant?"

"Uh..." Merletta hesitated, unfamiliar with the term.

Ileana snickered, exchanging a look with a pale-skinned merman with copper hair and a burgundy tail. But Instructor Wivell didn't seem either displeased or amused by Merletta's ignorance.

"A legacy applicant," he explained, "is an applicant with a parent, or perhaps grandparent, who has trained in the record holder discipline." His eyes lingered on the mermaid who had been friendliest—Sage—and Merletta wondered if she was such an applicant. She tried not to feel jealous. What an advantage that must be.

"Oh," she said, realizing that the instructor was still waiting for a response to his original question. "I'm not one of those."

The instructor nodded. "And you haven't received any formal education, beyond the rudimentary training of a charity home, yes?"

Neither his face nor his voice showed any consciousness that his words might bring Merletta embarrassment, and she tried to appear equally detached as she nodded in confirmation.

"You will have a great deal of water to cover, then," he said, as unemotional as ever. "For now, I will explain the basic structure of our program to you, before we begin our day's training."

A couple of the other trainees sighed, and Ileana grumbled audibly, but Merletta ignored them. She propelled herself back down into a sitting position, leaning forward eagerly. She was more than ready to start learning something.

"The training program is rigorous, and covers multiple aspects of what is required to work with the record holders. You will have three primary instructors. With me, you will study literacy, an area of which you must be a master if you hope to become a record holder. Another instructor will train you in the history of our kind."

Merletta sat up straighter, excited already. The history of how the triple kingdoms developed was one of the areas that intrigued her most.

"Finally, you will receive physical training—including in combat—with a third instructor." He glanced around the group. "If you succeed in becoming a record holder, you will be one of our kingdoms' greatest resources. It is considered important that you are capable of defending yourself from injury or attack."

Merletta raised her eyebrows, wondering who would dare to attack a record holder. But the instructor was barreling on.

"In being accepted into this program, you are joining an elite group. At present, we have only five—now six—trainees undertaking the training." He paused, his eyes fixing on the copper-haired merman who had snickered with Ileana. "You have one fellow trainee in his first year of training—Jacobi."

The young merman nodded tightly when Merletta looked at him, not quite making eye contact. He must be sixteen, then, like her. He did look young.

"If you complete the first year of your training successfully," Instructor Wivell continued, "you will earn the right to take a position as a scribe in the record holder discipline."

Merletta frowned slightly. A scribe? She knew their role was important, but she hadn't gambled everything on this path for the hope of becoming a mere scribe.

"Or," Instructor Wivell went on, "you can choose to continue to a second year of training, as Sage," the mermaid nodded briskly in response to his gesture, "and Oliver have done." Merletta nodded to the merman indicated, the dark-haired one. His eyes were cold as he stared back at her, and she looked away quickly.

"Should they successfully pass second year, they will have the option of serving the Center as a guard, a highly coveted position."

Merletta tilted her head to the side, interested. She had known that the Center guards were different from the general guards of each of the triple kingdoms, who patrolled the borders to make sure nothing dangerous entered the cities. She shuddered slightly as she remembered her encounter with the shark the morning before, then pulled her attention back to the instructor's words. It was news to her that the elite Center guards had once been in the training program for the record holders. Presumably this was why she had been put through a simple physical test before being accepted as an applicant.

"If they continue to a third year, as Ileana has done,"—Merletta could tell that the other mermaid wasn't even looking her way, so she didn't bother nodding—"they train to join the educators."

His eyes rested on the final trainee, the oldest, whom she realized must be nineteen. "And Emil, of course, is in his fourth and final year of training. When he passes, he will become a junior record holder."

Merletta looked at the pale-skinned young merman with increased respect. It hadn't escaped her notice that Instructor Wivell had said *when* Emil passes, not if.

"In each year, you will undertake training in all areas, of course," Instructor Wivell said. "Our intention is for your education to be holistic, regardless of which role you ultimately assume. You will live, eat, and train with your fellow trainees, so you must learn to work together."

Merletta glanced at Ileana in spite of herself. From the twist to the other girl's mouth, working together didn't seem like a very realistic goal.

"Merletta," Instructor Wivell said, calling her attention back to him with a snap. "You will not join normal training today. An educator will be assigned to you for the day, to give you a tour of the Center, and provide the introductory information necessary." He turned away from her, glancing down at his writing leaf. "Oliver, Instructor Agner wishes you to join the same guard squad again today, to continue the training exercise you began yesterday." He looked up again. "The rest of you, we will begin literacy in five minutes."

Without another word, the rest of the trainees rose from their places, tails swishing as they made their way out of the room, clearly all aware of where they needed to go.

"I will show you to the educators' headquarters," said Instructor Wivell, when they were alone. "You will meet here each morning, to kick off the day's training." He paused. "Except for the weekly rest days, of course, such as tomorrow."

Merletta deflated slightly, disappointed to be delayed an extra day in joining the training.

"What do we do on rest days?" she asked curiously.

Instructor Wivell had a slight crease between his eyebrows as he looked at her. "Whatever you wish. It is unallocated time." He thought for a moment. "I suppose most trainees go back to their homes, to visit their families."

Merletta barely held in a snort at the idea of visiting the charity home by choice. Not likely. She could see Tish, she supposed, although she didn't have much to tell her yet, other than the bare fact of her acceptance into the program.

It took only a brief moment of reflection to know what she was going to do with the unexpected free time. A smile tugged at her lips. And it didn't involve visiting anyone or anything within the triple kingdoms.

CHAPTER EIGHT

Heath

"We are down to two contestants!"

The herald's voice rang over the collected audience, his tone slightly pompous.

"Soon, we will have our archery champion!"

The crowd of commoners roared their approval, and Heath clapped politely along with the others in the stand occupied by the royal family and its extended connections.

"You should be out there, Heath," said Percival from beside him, his tone disapproving. "It's foolishness to give up competing just to sit here with me."

"Nonsense," said Heath vaguely, his eyes on the target being set up on the green in front of them. He had told himself he didn't care about the tournament—and it was mostly true—but he had been engrossed in spite of himself by the archery competition.

The tournament was held in a specially constructed arena not far outside the city wall. Their raised stand was located on one side of the large grassy area being used for archery. The hand to hand combat took place in a separate enclosed area nearby, although it was finished for the morning. The solid gray walls of Bryford rose up behind Heath. Further out in the opposite direction he could see a cloud of dust being kicked up from those practicing on the broad dirt oval where the mounted competitions, such as jousting, were held.

But for the moment, everyone's focus was on the archery, which had entered its final round. Heath glanced behind him to the top of the seating stand. King Matlock and Queen Renata were looking on with well practiced smiles. Crown Prince Lachlan looked slightly more interested, leaning forward on his knees, but Prince Knox's smile looked a little forced. Heath remembered that the younger prince was mainly interested in the more physical competitions, like jousting. Archery probably held little appeal for him, but Heath supposed that as it was a final round, the royal family were all expected to attend, to congratulate the champion.

Heath returned his attention to the field. The final two competitors had been called forward to try their hand at the deciding challenge.

"Whew," Percival said with a low whistle, over the gasps and murmurs of the crowd. "That's a long target. Further than last year, surely?" He glanced at his brother. "Do you think you could hit that, Heath?"

"Yes," said Heath simply. "I think so."

He knew so, actually, but there was no need to be boastful. As the first competitor stepped up, Heath's arm flexed involuntarily, his fingers forgetting for a moment that he didn't have his bow in his hand. The competitor raised his bow to eye level, drawing his arm back and taking what seemed an inordinately long time to line the shot up. When he finally released, the arrow whizzed through the air with impressive speed, burying itself in the outer ring of the bullseye.

The crowd let out a collective breath, and many of the watchers began to cheer uproariously. The archer waved to his admirers, a lazy grin on his face, as he stepped back. Heath recognized the man as the one who had come in second to him the year before, and he had no doubt that he would be the victor. The man had probably been delighted to hear that Heath wasn't competing. Even as it occurred, Heath chastised himself for the ungenerous thought.

The final competitor stepped up, taking even longer to line up his shot. The morning was advanced, and the day had become warm. From his seat, Heath could see the beads of sweat rolling slowly down the competitor's forehead as he adjusted his aim slightly. Heath began to fidget with impatience, but finally the archer let his arrow fly. It buried itself in the target, but much further out than the first man's. There were a few groans of disappointment from those who had been cheering for the second man, but they were soon drowned out by applause as the first man raised an arm in victory. Heath could see on people's faces they were impressed that either man could hit the target at all from that distance.

Heath shook his head slightly, his forehead creased. Perhaps Percival was right, and his eyesight was a gift of dragon magic. He wasn't going to say so, but he was pretty sure he could have hit the target more accurately than the second competitor, even if he was shooting from the stands.

He was expecting the victor to be announced, but the herald instead stepped up, waving his arms for silence. The noise of the crowd fell to an expectant hum.

"We have our champion," he began, and the crowd roared again. He held up a hand, waiting impatiently for the noise to drop before continuing. "But there is one final challenge." He turned to the victor. "You have already earned the title, but do you wish to try your hand at the last round?"

The archer looked surprised, but he shrugged, giving a little laugh. "Why not?"

The crowd cheered for him, and he grinned back at them, acknowledging their approval with a wave of his arm. He was led back to the target, which was still placed at its greatest distance from the shooting mark.

The competitor gripped his bow, evidently waiting for the target to be moved again. But instead, a page boy came jogging out from between the stands, carrying a thick length of black material.

"For this challenge," announced the herald importantly, "you will be blindfolded!"

The archer's look of surprise quickly gave way to another laugh, and the crowd laughed with him. It was just the sort of spectacle they loved. Heath watched with interest as the man was given a moment to take note of the location of the target, before the blindfold was attached firmly around his eyes. Then, for good measure, he was spun around several times, until he was staggering a little. The crowd laughed even harder, clapping with delight.

The man spinning the competitor made sure to face him in the right general direction for the target, meaning that his back was once again to Heath. But Heath could still see him wobbling slightly as he raised his bow. He paused for a moment, then let the arrow fly. The range was good, but the aim was way off, the shaft passing considerably to the left of the target.

The man pulled the blindfold off to see the result, shrugging with good-natured defeat as the people cheered for him anyway. Heath clapped along with everyone as the shield of victory was brought out and presented to the man. He had several just like it at home.

"You know what that final challenge was," said Percival from beside Heath, his tone alight with sudden realization. "It was for you."

"What do you mean?" Heath asked with a frown, his eyes still on the ceremony.

"They said you could compete, so they assumed you would. They claim not to think your eyesight is magic, but they set up that final challenge just in case. Because your eyesight couldn't win that shot for you. They must have wanted to prove that you're not perfect—that you *can* miss, just like anyone and everyone would miss that shot."

Heath's frown deepened. "I'm sure it had nothing to do with me. They knew I wasn't competing, and they included it anyway."

Percival shrugged. "I'm not saying it wasn't a good spectacle anyway. Just that I would wager you were in their minds when they introduced it."

Heath shook his head, not convinced. With so many people around them, Percival didn't push the point.

With the archery finished, and the jousting final not taking place until the afternoon, the crowd began to drift away. Heath and Percival stood, but made no immediate move to leave, chatting instead with the others in the stand with them. Percival shared his supposed revelation with the twins, and Brody was quick to agree. Heath rolled his eyes. Whether his cousin actually shared Percival's view was doubtful. He just loved to stir up trouble.

When the stand around them had emptied, Brody turned to Heath with a grin, as if determined to prove Heath's thoughts about him true.

"Well, go on then. Have a go."

"A go at what?" Heath asked blankly.

Percival shot him a disapproving look. "Don't play dumb, Heath. Have a go at the target."

Bianca gave a faint sigh. "Here we go."

Heath looked between his brother and cousins, and the

target still set up on the grass. "Don't be silly," he said, without much conviction. "I'm not competing."

"Of course you're not competing," said Percival tartly. "The competition is well and truly over. But don't try to convince me that you're not itching to try your hand at it."

Heath hesitated. He had been surprised at how difficult he'd found it to sit out and watch. He glanced around at the empty stands. Not a spectator was in sight anymore, everyone clearly having moved on to their luncheon. Where was the harm in just having a try? As Percival said, the competition was well and truly over. And he hadn't even been banned from competing, anyway.

"Oh, all right," he said, grinning in spite of himself as Brody let out a whoop. He saw a troubled crease appear on Bianca's brow, but he didn't stop to ask what she thought.

The four of them hurried down from the stands, and Heath selected one of the practice bows from a nearby weapons stand. He flexed it with a slight frown. It wasn't as good as having his own, familiar bow, but it would do.

"Well then, have a few practice shots," Percival urged, grinning slightly. Heath stepped up to the mark, narrowing his eyes as he took in the target, still set at its final distance. He took one of the arrows Percival was holding out and placed it against the string. His fingers seemed to hum from the tension of the string, and he felt his heart lift a little. It had been too long since he'd engaged in his favorite sport.

Heath drew a deep breath, releasing the air as he released the arrow. It whizzed across the arena, burying itself in the second ring of the target.

"Ehh," said Brody, the grin clear in his voice. "Not quite up to your usual standard, cuz."

"It was a warm up shot," retorted Heath, knowing his cousin

was baiting him, but unable to help giving him exactly what he wanted.

Brody's grin broadened, and Heath shook his head as he took another arrow from Percival. He forced himself not to be goaded by Brody's chuckle, taking his time to line up the shot. This one hit the bullseye dead center, and Percival cheered.

"Show us it wasn't a fluke," he said, holding out another arrow.

Heath rolled his eyes at his brother's exuberance, but he couldn't help grinning himself. He hadn't seen Percival in this good a mood since before the tournament began. Once he had sent three more arrows into the center of the target, Percival declared him ready for the final round. Brody, always full of restless energy, ran the distance to remove the final arrow from the target, leaving it clear.

"Come on, Bianca," said Percival imperiously. "Hand me your kerchief."

Bianca sighed, but didn't actually protest as she handed it over. For all her disapproving clucks, Heath got the sense that she was as curious as the boys as to how he would perform when blindfolded. So was he, if he was honest.

Percival tied the kerchief firmly around his brother's eyes, then spun Heath around forcefully. He spun him more times than the competitor had been spun—so many that Heath's head was reeling when Percival finally let go.

He staggered slightly before finding his footing, his arms a little shaky as he raised his bow. He blinked pointlessly behind the blindfold, unable to see anything. With a slight shake of his head, he acknowledged himself impressed that the victor had been as close to the target as he had.

Heath drew a deep breath, determined to at least make a creditable shot for his audience of three. After all, being a good archer wasn't just about eyesight. He'd trained in the sport since childhood, honing a natural aptitude with extensive time and persistence.

He could hear the chuckles and murmurings of Percival and the twins behind him, so at least he knew he wasn't about to shoot anyone by accident. As he pictured the target, trying to assess where exactly it was, he gave a gasp.

"What is it?" Percival asked from behind him.

"Nothing," said Heath quickly, lowering his bow. He raised his hand, surreptitiously confirming that the blindfold was still in place. So why could he see the target? He turned his head slightly to the side, but he couldn't see the stands, the bright summer sky, his brother. Everything was blank, the blindfold doing its job. But when he turned forward again, he could see the target, alone in the blackness. What was happening?

"Well, come on, Heath!" goaded Brody. "If you're going to admit defeat, say so at once, so we can go get some luncheon."

Heath didn't respond, just raising his bow again. He couldn't see his bow, or his hand in front of him. He could only see the target. Perhaps it was a trick of the mind, a very effective picturing of what was in his thoughts. Most likely the target wasn't anywhere near where he was picturing it to be. Nevertheless, he lined the shot up carefully before letting the arrow fly.

Although he couldn't see, he could hear the deadly hum of it slicing through the air, followed by the unmistakable thud of the metal hitting the target.

Heath ripped off his blindfold, staring at the arrow, which was buried in the dead center of the bullseye. The hit was met by total silence, and he turned to see all three of his companions looking at the target in astonishment. His eyes were on Percival as his brother's gaze flicked to him. Heath only had time to take in Percival's startled expression before Brody distracted him with his cheers.

Heath turned toward his cousin, not missing the fact that

Bianca looked more alarmed than impressed. A moment later Heath's own alarm grew, as shouts and cheers from further away reached his ears.

"He did it! The Duke of Bexley's son hit the bullseye with the blindfold on!"

Heath wrenched himself around, gasping as he took in the several spectators who had regathered, unnoticed by him. He had been sure the arena was empty except for his little group, and he was dismayed to realize his mistake.

Their eyes were wide, their expressions similar to that of the woman whose son Percival had saved from the crushed carriage. Heath had rarely had anyone look at him like that, and if he was honest, it was a little intoxicating. His alarm grew at the realization that he was enjoying the sensation, and he dropped the bow as if it was burning metal.

"We were just messing around," he called, trying to sound cheerful rather than terrified. He pulled Bianca's kerchief from around his neck, where it had slipped, and waved it in the air. "It wasn't a proper blindfold—I could see the whole time."

The watchers deflated slightly, most of them nodding in disappointed acceptance of this explanation for Heath's impossible feat.

"Still impressive," one of them called, and Heath saw that one or two were watching him skeptically, not looking entirely convinced.

He swallowed nervously, hastening to return the bow to its stand. "That was a mistake," he muttered to Percival, his hands shaking slightly as he took the remaining arrows from his brother, placing them in their holder alongside the bow.

"Why did you do that?" Percival demanded, and Heath looked up in surprise at the anger in his brother's voice. "Why did you tell them you could see?"

Heath was silent, not sure how to explain to his brother that it had been true, in a sense.

"If people are afraid of your capabilities, that's their problem, not yours!" Percival insisted.

Heath shrugged. "You heard what Father said. We're not supposed to be drawing attention to our...talents right now." His voice turned wry. "And you've already made enough of a spectacle with your little speech the other day."

Percival opened his mouth, clearly ready to argue further, but Heath glanced over his shoulder and stiffened. The discomfort in his stomach blossomed rapidly into full scale alarm at the sight of his father, standing several feet away with a very sober look on his face.

The Duke of Bexley had his mother on one arm, and the elderly princess was watching Heath with great interest.

"Father," Heath stammered. "Grandmother."

Percival spun around at his brother's words, even as their grandmother spoke.

"That was very impressive, Heath!" Her tone was warm, and Heath managed a small smile. She was possibly his favorite person in the world, but her approval couldn't quite make up for the look of grave concern on the face of her son beside her.

"I thought you chose not to compete, Heath," said the duke mildly.

"I did, Father," said Heath quickly. "I didn't even want to compete..." His words trailed off as his father raised one eyebrow. The duke's gift was an ability to identify deception, so he would surely realize, as Heath had done himself, that those words weren't entirely true. Heath exchanged a look with his brother, who gave him a sympathetic grimace. They had often bemoaned how unjust life was, to give them a father with such an ability.

"I was just fooling around, Father," Heath tried again. "I

didn't mean for anyone but Percival, and Brody and Bianca, to see." That much at least was entirely true, and it was clear that the duke knew it.

His look of disapproval disappeared, but the concern in his eyes lingered as he glanced at the few spectators still in the stands. They wouldn't be able to hear what was being said, but they were watching the exchange with great interest, and the buzz of their conversation could be heard even from where Heath stood.

"Well," said the duke, in a voice clearly intended to close the topic, at least for now. "Your grandmother heard that you particularly wanted to speak with her, Heath, so we came looking for you."

"Grandmother," Heath greeted the princess again. "How was your time in Kyona?"

"Lovely, thank you, Heath," she said, her eyes thoughtful as they rested on him. "Why don't you come and have a cup of tea with me, so I can tell you all about it?"

Heath nodded, swallowing nervously as he offered his arm.

"Thank you, Norik," she said to the duke, dismissing him with a wave of her hand. "And I'll see you three at the jousting final," she added to Percival, Brody, and Bianca with a smile.

They all murmured their agreement to their grandmother, taking their dismissal in good part. Heath and the older woman walked silently together. Their progress was slow, due to frequent interruptions as the princess—still very popular with the people—responded to the many greetings of courtier and commoner alike. They didn't attempt conversation until they were settled in her receiving room, and the servant who brought their tea tray had bowed herself out.

"Well," said the elderly princess, leaning back in her chair. "That was quite a shot, Heath."

Heath smiled wanly. "A good shot, but a bad decision."

"Hm." His grandmother didn't speak for a moment, just assessing him with her steady scrutiny. "Don't try to tell me you're not troubled," she said at last. "I can see that you are."

Heath sighed, and she nodded decisively, as if he had confirmed her words aloud.

"I thought so." She leaned forward, pouring him some tea. "Tell me everything."

CHAPTER NINE

Merletta

Merletta flicked her fins as she made her way through the passages of the Center. She was up early, but not so early that the complex was deserted. Every now and then she passed another mermaid or merman. Most gave her a brief nod once they took in her uniform shells and the armband now affixed to her upper arm. She couldn't help but straighten her back a little with pride. The difference was noticeable in the reaction of strangers to her appearance.

She swam quickly across the drop off, passing through the receiving hall and out into Skulssted, heading north. She had no particular desire to visit Tilssted, and she certainly wasn't planning to go to the home. But that direction seemed the safest, as anyone watching her would assume she was visiting her old accommodations. Plus she was well practiced in exiting the city from that general location.

It was surreal, swimming through her old neighborhood. It had only been a couple of days since she lived there, but it felt like a lifetime. So much had changed.

She gave the district where the charity home was located a

wide berth, not eager to bump into anyone she knew. She was just entering the kelp farm when the sound of arguing voices drew her attention. Hanging back, she tried to avoid detection as she observed a scene that had become all too familiar in recent years.

A broad-shouldered merman—presumably the owner of this stretch of farm—was locked in a hot dispute with some builders. The cause of their argument was clear from the stones stacked nearby and the chiseled bedrock that indicated the beginning of a new construction. Merletta shook her head. If the regent of Tilssted kept trying to push the settlements into the farms like this, these shouting matches were going to turn into armed clashes. She'd heard that the regents of the other two cities put great pressure on Tilssted to take more than its share of the growing population. But Tilssted had to start sticking up for itself. Their resources were already stretched much too thin.

She slipped past the mermen, disappearing between the towers of kelp. The sun had risen now, way up above the surface, and the farm laborers were already at work. But she didn't need to worry about them. Long experience told her they weren't interested in reporting her wanderings to the guards.

She decided to ascend closer to the surface before leaving the kelp farms, as the workers tended to start low and go higher throughout the morning, meaning they were less likely to see her actually leave the outer boundary of the city. She nodded as she passed a pair of middle-aged mermaids who had begun their methodical journey up one of the tall kelp towers, and they barely glanced her way as they nodded back.

"Probably escaping one of those homes," one of them said quietly to the other, stifling a yawn. Clearly they couldn't see her armband through the fronds of kelp.

"As long as she doesn't get too high, and start to dry out."

Merletta smiled to herself as the other mermaid's anxious reply reached her through the water. The woman obviously had a kind heart, but she didn't need to worry about Merletta.

It was evident that the two workers thought she was exploring the kelp farms. It probably didn't occur to them that she would want to go beyond. She wouldn't be the first merchild to choose to live as a castaway on the streets, seeking refuge in the kelp farms at night, instead of enduring the restrictions of a charity home. She had considered it, before the elderly merman had begun teaching her to read. After that point she realized that however insufficient it might be, the education she could attain at the home was worth putting up with all the rest.

She traveled up the kelp tower until the water began to lighten considerably from the morning sun. Turning, she put on speed as she darted through the leafy tops of the structures, passing out of the farm and into the less cultivated kelp forests within minutes. Her instinct about the workers' patterns was right—she didn't pass another soul within the kelp farms.

Now she just had to worry about avoiding any patrols, and she would be fine. Well, that and the dangerous sea creatures that populated the area outside the triple kingdoms. The presence of these animals was the reason there were guards constantly patrolling the borders. As much as no one was supposed to leave the triple kingdoms without a valid reason, like the hunting parties, it wasn't actually the job of the guards to keep merpeople in. But they wouldn't hesitate to give her a hard time if they saw her wandering where she shouldn't be. Experience had proven that.

Shortly after leaving the farms for the forest, she felt the slight release of tension that told her she was crossing the barrier at the boundary of the triple kingdoms. The sensation was so familiar that she barely noticed it, continuing without a check.

Merletta reached the edge of the forest, floating between the wild kelp for a moment as she checked that the water was clear. Open water beckoned, still gloomy in the dim light of the early morning, even though the surface was only a few fathoms above her. She closed her eyes for a moment, drawing a swirl of cool salty water into her mouth. Then she propelled herself out of the fronds, plunging into the ocean's expanse. This was one of her favorite moments—the feeling of freedom that came from leaving the city behind. The elation she felt as her strokes took her out into open water, with nothing visible on any side, was indescribable.

She struck out without a clear direction in mind, almost giddy with the freedom of it. Usually, her explorations had been limited to the very early hours of the morning, before she'd be missed at the home. But if she had understood Instructor Wivell correctly, she had an entire day free, with no one particularly caring what she did with it. Such a liberty was completely unprecedented in her life.

She soared above the jagged edges of a familiar canyon, its points and twists partially hidden by the gloom, given how high she was. Feeling as unfettered as the great seabirds she'd seen wheeling overhead, she swam quickly, flicking her tail rapidly until she was out beyond the normal patrol ring of the guards. There might be all manner of unpredictable sea beasts out here, but she'd take them over the depressing predictability of an armed merguard any day. She patted the satchel slung tightly across her chest to reassure herself. She had brought her weapon today.

The water was getting warmer up so high, and she dove a little deeper, giving herself time to acclimatize before she reached the surface. Spotting a fever of rays up ahead, she pushed herself through the water with a smile, eager to join them. She slowed her pace when she reached them, weaving in and out between their sleek, flat bodies, running her fingers along their backs and watching as they gently flapped their wings in response. It was a large fever, the mass of golden-brown bodies stretching almost as far as she could see. They were beautiful, moving in tandem, their path through the water effortless and unhurried. If only merpeople could coexist as peacefully, Merletta thought ruefully.

Increasing her pace, she progressed through the fever, her eyes passing disinterestedly over the stingers stretching out behind each creature. This was one of the many delights merpeople like those two farm workers missed out on by embracing the fear of the open ocean they were taught from birth. Merletta had been told of the dangers of these creatures, of the deadly power of their stingers, as though they were monsters in the night. What she'd never been told, and had needed to discover for herself, was that they were gentle by nature, not aggressive, and not to be feared unless provoked. Most merpeople never gave themselves the opportunity to learn that information.

A sudden shaft of sunlight, cutting through the layers of water with random precision, turned the brown of a nearby ray into gold. Merletta looked up, her attention drawn from the creatures beside her to the world above. She darted forward, pushing upward as well as outward, ready to feel the sun on her face again.

She broke the surface with a splash of delight, her throat opening involuntarily, and the fresh, beautiful air passing down it. There was something truly liberating about the sensation.

She had once cut a sea turtle free, after it had gotten caught in a fisher's net set up to catch cod. She often thought of that moment when she emerged at the surface and felt the blockage in her throat open—it was surely the same feeling. She remembered also her punishment when the fisher complained to the head of the charity home about his ruined net. But she had never regretted her intervention. Sometimes at night, she dreamed she was tangled in a net and woke thrashing and breathless. In her dreams no one came to help her, but there was no need for the turtle to be trapped in the same fear.

Merletta shook off such dark thoughts. She was at the surface now, the most free place she'd ever found. The sun was strong, hardly a cloud to be seen. Merletta stretched out on her back, closing her eyes and letting the warmth soak into her skin and scales. The incredible feeling of genuine heat she experienced at the surface was worth the increased awareness she now had of how cold it really was in the depths. The Center was even colder than Tilssted.

Her eyes still closed, she allowed herself to drift, gentle swells carrying her up and down. Most merpeople would be in great danger of getting lost if they did such a thing, but Merletta wasn't worried. She knew the area well—most likely she was currently drifting over the large reef shaped like a mermaid's tail.

She smiled to herself as she imagined the reaction of the kind-hearted farm laborer if she could see what Merletta was up to. Half of Merletta's body was out of the water as she floated on her back, the sun touching her from the crown of her head to the tip of her tail. The other mermaid would probably expect Merletta to dry out at any moment. Merletta chuckled at the thought. She had once been so ignorant, too.

The head at the charity home had actually told them directly that allowing a substantial part of their bodies to be outside water for too long would cause them to dry out. Merletta was fairly sure the head had done it in order to discourage illicit expeditions like her own. But after testing the theory more than once with no ill effect, she'd been foolish enough to confront the head with her lie. She'd been young then, and not wise enough to foresee the inevitable consequence of her confession.

But perhaps it had been worth it—she'd been punished severely for her trips outside the boundary, and had been watched closely for months. But the head had also grudgingly admitted that mermaids couldn't actually suffer the fatal malady of drying out simply from sticking their heads out of the water for too long. It made sense to Merletta that it was safe for her to look above the surface—why else would her throat have the ability to open and close as needed, allowing the transition from breathing water to breathing air? Clearly the charity home taught its beneficiaries a warped version of the truth to discourage exploration.

But she was no longer stuck in the charity home. She was a trainee of the Center now, and she would soon be learning the more complete truth on a range of topics. The thought warmed her almost as much as the sunlight on her skin.

Eventually she flipped over, diving back below the surface to cool off from the intensity of the sun. She found she'd drifted further east than she'd guessed, the reef some distance behind her. She turned, heading north with relaxed strokes. She glanced at the skin of her arms as she swam, reflecting, as she had many times before, that her increased exposure to sunlight may be part of what made her darker than other mermaids with similar coloring.

Most of the merpeople went to the surface very rarely, and even then only in organized groups which traveled straight upward from the cities. Merletta had never come across anyone else willing to brave the dangers of the open ocean alone as she did. And in fact, she thought, glancing around her, it wasn't as dangerous as she'd been led to believe. Perhaps another instance of exaggeration by the trainers at the home.

As if to contradict her thoughts, a glimpse of white to her

left drew her attention. She shuddered as she caught sight of a bloom of jellyfish, grateful that it was moving away from her. There were some hazards, certainly.

But Merletta wasn't for a moment tempted to turn back. Not when she had a whole day for exploration. She'd been this far out a couple times, but never in this direction, and she was eager to see what she might discover. Passing another reef, she dove down to duck inquisitively around the coral. She was well and truly outside the triple kingdoms now, and the creatures weren't used to the presence of merpeople like those in the reef surrounding the Center. Fish darted away from her, even a small reef shark weaving away at her passage.

The reef wasn't far under the surface, and sunlight slanted through in thick shafts. Merletta glanced up as something obscured the light for an instant. She laughed with delight at the underside of a dolphin, leaping in and out of the water. She was closer to the surface than she'd realized. Brow furrowed in confusion, Merletta glanced around. She'd assumed the reef had grown up on a large rocky shelf which reached toward the surface. But in fact, the area was quite sandy, the ocean floor itself seeming to slant upward indefinitely. How could that be?

Merletta propelled herself upward, following the dolphin's lead. Within moments, she reached the surface, pushing her unrestrained hair out of her eyes as she scanned the open sea. She turned, looking for the dolphin, and her eyes grew round at a sight she had never seen before.

"Land," she breathed.

It had to be. The dry ground before her was no rocky shaft sticking out of the water as she had seen a few times in other places. It was a huge expanse, rising to such a height that the sea would never cover it, no matter what the tide. Merletta blinked furiously, but the vision didn't disappear.

She swam slowly toward it, as if in a trance, hardly able to keep her eyes open against the brightness.

Because it was so very bright.

It put the colorful coral gardens to shame. The land was bordered by sand like that of the ocean floor. But this sand looked like it had never been touched by water, and was much lighter and brighter than it should be in the sparkling sunshine. The land rose beyond the sand in a green mound, covered in plants that were nothing like the kelp forests Merletta knew. They were much too green, much too bright, and only rustled ever so slightly in the light breeze, instead of swaying constantly in the current.

It was land, no doubt about it. But how was it possible? The triple kingdoms had been established far from the land for the merpeople's protection, everyone knew that. Their ancestors had discovered that merpeople weren't safe close to land—it was one of the few things that even the common people were taught about their history. The children at the home had often repeated the bedtime stories late at night, speaking of the fierce and bloodthirsty beasts that populated the land, and would kill any mermaid on sight. Dragons, they were called.

Some of the carers used to threaten disobedient merchildren —such as Merletta—with banishment to the surface to dry out or be hunted and eaten by the fearsome monsters. The stories had frightened her as a small child, but she had long ago learned to roll her eyes at such nonsense.

Merletta started as her tail thumped against something hard. She looked down, realizing with a jolt of fear that the water had become so shallow that she wouldn't be able to swim for much longer. She glanced up toward the land, a familiar frustration rising in her. She was beyond the borders of the cities—she was supposed to be free of the endless restrictions on her desire to discover. But here she had found the most exciting place she'd ever encountered, only to have a new barrier appear to prevent her from exploring it.

But for all her boldness, she had no desire to dry out. She sighed, pushing back toward deeper water, and beginning to swim alongside the land, deep enough that her tail encountered no obstacles. She scanned the shoreline in fascination, desperately curious to know what, if anything, was hidden inside those green mounds.

After several minutes, her sharp eyes picked something out on the surface of the ground. She paused, treading water as she observed it. What in the ocean could it be? It didn't look like a plant. It looked like...but her thoughts were impossible, so she risked going shallower, her eyes straining for a better look.

She shook her head in disbelief. It couldn't be...how could it have gotten there? But, though the stone looked eroded—even though there was no water surging around it to explain such a phenomenon—it certainly had the structure of a building. Looking further along the shore, Merletta's eyes widened as she saw more of the same thing. It almost looked like a mertown, except that it was deserted. And fully dry. How could anyone live in such a place? Impossible to survive.

Merletta felt a strange sensation passing over her, shuddering across her skin, and rippling down her scales. It was half fear, half excitement.

She didn't know what she'd discovered here, but she knew down to her fins that she'd discovered something.

Something big.

CHAPTER TEN

Ordinarily, Heath would always feel better after a cozy chat with his grandmother. But he sat through the jousting final in a mood of considerable anxiety. He had hoped that the snow-haired princess would reassure him. But it turned out she was also feeling greatly concerned by the tensions arising over the power-wielding branch of the royal family.

At no point in their conversation had she chastised him for his display, but Heath still felt guilty as he saw the many eyes darting in his direction throughout the jousting. Clearly news of his feat had spread, and not everyone believed the excuse he had fabricated.

He barely took in the actual competition. He had never been interested in jousting at the best of times, and he was far too distracted by the attention he was attracting. Even Percival seemed to be less attentive to the fight than usual, his eyes flicking from the crowds to his brother. Unlike their father, he didn't look concerned. If anything, he still looked frustrated by Heath's attitude.

Heath didn't bother arguing with him about it. His brother

might not like it, but he was starting to see the duke's point. Without even competing in the tournament, he'd managed to create exactly the kind of spectacle the crown was clearly trying to avoid. And it only highlighted the divisions forming over the issue of power. He wasn't sure what made him more uncomfortable—the looks of awed admiration, or the disapproving glares of the fastidious. He even saw the archery champion watching him sullenly, and he wished he could sink into the stands below him. He had never intended to take the focus off the man's victory.

As they made their way down from the stands—having clapped vaguely for whichever helmeted knight had claimed the victory—a disgruntled muttering caught Heath's ears.

"...typical of these power-wielders. Couldn't stand not being the center of attention. Always having to strut their supposed abilities."

Heath felt his ears warming. He would have kept walking, but unfortunately Percival had heard the comment as well. He turned around, a mulish expression on his face.

"Do you have something to say?" he challenged the speaker, a young nobleman, not too much older than him.

The man looked from Percival to Heath, his expression unrepentant, before sweeping off with his companion.

"Bunch of puffed-up, judgmental—"

"Just drop it, Percival," Heath cut him off, with unusual sharpness. His brother looked at him, his face showing that he was surprised, and a little hurt.

"I'm sorry, Perce," said Heath, softening. "I know you're just trying to defend me. But I can't blame people for their reactions. I'm the one who did something stupid, and I'm not sure I can criticize other people for being afraid."

"Afraid?" Percival repeated, frowning in confusion. "You mean resentful."

Heath's frown mirrored his brother's. The other man's fear had been as clear as day to him. Had Percival really missed it?

He entertained a momentary daydream of slinking off alone, to avoid being a spectacle at the luncheon, but he knew he couldn't do it. It would be seen as confirmation that he had done something wrong, and wouldn't help with the crown's attempts to convince everyone that all was well with the power-wielders. But as soon as he was released from the meal, he made his way to the castle's enormous records room.

He had been hoping to visit the place since arriving, but had been too caught up in all the social functions surrounding the tournament to make good his escape. As he entered the quiet sanctuary of the records room, he pulled the block Reka had retrieved from the ocean out of his pocket.

He ran a hand over its edges as he walked, his footsteps echoing in the large space. He had examined it in some detail since Reka gave it to him, and he was becoming increasingly convinced that it had been worked by some kind of tool.

"Lord Heath. It's wonderful to see you back in Bryford again."

Heath looked up, smiling at the record keeper who was hurrying toward him. The man had always had a liking for him, appreciating his genuine interest in learning, a rarity among the young people of the court.

"I'm pleased to be back," he said simply. "And," he added, his smile turning rueful, "pleased to have a moment's escape from the chaos of the tournament."

The older man chuckled. "Well, here you'll find a haven. I doubt you'll encounter another soul. Not much interest in the records room when there's a tournament happening. So what can I help you with?" He chuckled. "Here to look at maps of far off places again?"

Heath smiled absently. "Something a little closer to home,

actually." He held up the rock. "I found this in the ocean near Bexley Manor. I'm interested in the history of that area. Were there any settlements there that I don't know about?"

"Hmm." The record keeper took the rock, examining it with interest. "None of any significant size, at least not that I know of. It does look as though it was part of a building though, doesn't it? Although greatly damaged by a long time under water, of course."

"The thing is..."

Heath hesitated, not wanting to sound foolish. But the record keeper was watching him encouragingly. The man had always taken him seriously in the past, never implying that he would grow out of his childish desire to explore and discover, as others had done.

"The thing is," he tried again, "it was out pretty deep." He gave a brief description of what he had seen, and where he had found the rock. "And it didn't look like a loose piece of rubble that had been washed into the ocean. It looked like the remains of an actual structure, right there on the ocean bed."

The record keeper frowned thoughtfully. "That doesn't seem possible, does it?" he mused. "How could a whole building end up that far out to sea, with any of its structure intact?"

"Is there..." Heath turned the rock over in his hand. "Is there any possibility that something could have been built underwater?"

The record keeper looked surprised. "I've never heard of such a thing. How would the builders manage it, if it was as deep as you say? And why would anyone bother?"

"I don't know," said Heath absently, his eyes still on the rock. "Could the water level have risen, maybe?"

"Not by that much," said the record keeper, shaking his head. "I think the most likely explanation is still that the remains of a building near the shoreline washed into the sea a long time ago." He gestured to the back of the room. "I can show you where to find records of the settlement of that area."

Heath nodded, trying not to feel disappointed as he followed the record keeper. It wasn't as though he'd really expected the man to know anything concrete. He browsed through the records indicated, but after skimming several census documents regarding villages in the area, and a dozen reports of harvest returns, he had well and truly lost interest. He turned away, confident he wouldn't find anything of use there.

He knew he should probably return to the tournament—the next round of the hand to hand combat was due to start that afternoon—but instead he found himself wandering toward a more familiar section. He had spent many happy hours in his childhood reading accounts of early Valorian travelers. He'd never been to the South Lands—he'd never even been to the neighboring kingdom of Kyona—but he knew all about their customs and their climates.

He still hoped that one day he might get to see them. When he was younger, any time he'd wanted to escape his problems, he'd daydreamed about persuading Reka to just pick him up and fly him there. He knew that while the voyage would take humans three weeks by ship, it would take the dragon a matter of hours by air.

He smiled to himself, but there was an edge of sadness to the expression. He was old enough now to realize that outrunning his problems was no solution. And the growing problem facing his family was suddenly feeling much more personal than it had the day before.

He ran his hands over a fairly recent tome about Balenol, the South Lands kingdom that had once made slaves of the Kyonans, but which now had an uneasy peace with the North Lands kingdoms. The borders were shut for many generations, but by the time this record was written—in the time of his grandparents—travel between the kingdoms had been growing more common. Heath didn't pull the record from the shelf. He had read its accounts of hot, sticky air and prowling jungle cats many times.

He wandered toward the door, without much purpose, reluctant to leave his sanctuary. He paused at a polished wooden table, his eyes running curiously over the parchment spread out there. The title at the top read "Foreign Lands".

"What's this?" he asked the record keeper, who was sorting rolled parchments nearby.

"Hm?" the man asked, glancing up briefly. "Oh, that's an index I'm working on. It's past time I cataloged that collection, but I've tended to focus more on our Valorian records. They're usually in greatest demand." He grinned. "Except when you're in town, of course, My Lord."

Heath smiled absently, his eyes scanning the parchment. He saw now that it was an alphabetical list of place names. There were markings next to them, obviously indicating the relevant records according to some system of the record keeper's. He saw many names that were familiar from his reading, like Nohl, the capital of Balenol, and Thirl, the capital of neighboring Thorania.

His eyes caught on the entry at the bottom of the parchment, the name entirely unfamiliar.

"Vazula," he read aloud. "Where's that? And why is there a question mark next to it?"

The record keeper wandered over. "Ah, that. I'm not entirely sure if I should include it, that's all. It's mentioned in one of the records, but I can't be sure of its accuracy. The source is unknown, and I suspect that it's actually an account of a legend, accidentally categorized with the travel records by my predecessor."

"Can I see it?" Heath asked, his interest piqued.

"Of course." After a moment's search, the record keeper retrieved a tightly rolled scroll from a top shelf. "Be my guest."

"Thanks," said Heath, unfurling the scroll on the smooth surface of the table, while the record keeper wandered up beside him. He scanned the words quickly, aware that he shouldn't really be lingering so long. It seemed to be a record of a voyage, made by the ship's captain, although Heath could understand why the record keeper had been unsure whether it was fact or legend. The captain appeared to have had a fondness for dramatics, his descriptions overly poetic, and his style reading like that of an epic tale rather than a practical ship's log.

"It seems old," Heath commented, noting the formality of the language.

"It is," the record keeper confirmed. "There's no date, but I would guess that it's hundreds of years old. This is almost certainly a copy, but it's still one of the oldest records in here. Certainly worth preserving, regardless of its factual basis." He chuckled. "Just perhaps not in the section regarding the customs of known lands."

"On our voyage back from the lands of the east," Heath read aloud, "we once again stopped at the island kingdom of Vazula. Our stay was brief, for we sensed that our presence was an unhelpful distraction from the conflict at hand."

He glanced up. "What conflict? And what 'lands of the east' is he talking about? I thought there was nothing further east from Valoria, other than Wyvern Islands."

The record keeper shrugged. "No idea. It's clear from the wording that this isn't his first record of such voyages, but this is the only one we have." He began sorting again. "And it would be more accurate to say that there's nothing accessible further east from Valoria. We have no records of lands out that way, but we can't be certain. The waters are simply impassable."

"Really?" Heath asked, surprised. "I didn't know that. I was always told that there isn't anything there."

The record keeper chuckled. "It is an explanation commonly given to those who might be tempted to try their hand at passing the 'impassable' waters." His expression grew grave. "It took many many shipwrecks for our ancestors to accept that we cannot sail east more than a few days' journey."

Heath looked back at the record, his mind reeling from the new information. He scanned the page, his eyes widening at the sight of a familiar word further down the record.

"We left them with our good wishes," he muttered, again reading aloud. "They are truly a noble people. I am sure they will learn to live in harmony with their magical brothers. But I shall say no more here. I am bound to secrecy."

Heath stared at the page, a sense of excitement mounting. The record keeper glanced up and read his expression.

"Reached the part about being 'bound to secrecy', have you?" He chuckled. "That captain certainly loved to be dramatic."

"He talks about their magical brothers," said Heath slowly. "What does that mean?"

"Poetic language, I imagine," said the record keeper vaguely. "It's in his style, isn't it?"

Heath didn't respond. The record keeper was right about the captain's style, but Heath was convinced there was something real behind the flowery words.

"I wonder if they did find a way to coexist," he muttered, mainly to himself.

The record keeper looked up quickly, his voice a little sharper. "What was that?"

"Nothing," said Heath quickly, stepping back from the record. "I'd better be going. Thank you for your help."

The record keeper was watching him, a shrewd look in his

eyes. "It's just a legend, My Lord, I'm almost certain of it. Did you see the fantastical descriptions he gave of maelstroms and sea monsters?"

"Yes, I saw," said Heath quickly. "Probably just a legend, as you say."

He could feel the older man's eyes on him as he hurried from the records room, but his thoughts were elsewhere. He didn't even feel self-conscious at the strange looks he got from passing servants as he muttered aloud to himself, caught up in his musings.

"Vazula."

Heath had been dreading the final round of the hand to hand combat, knowing that Percival would be as cross as a bear through the whole thing. But as it happened, he spent most of the morning mulling over the intriguing revelations of his visit to the records room the day before.

Percival, of course, had no such distraction, and it was his grunts and mutterings that eventually pulled Heath's attention back to the fight. The final two contestants were locked in a well-matched struggle, the clang of their swords and the clinking of their chain mail regularly swallowed by the crowd's enthusiastic encouragement. Heath glanced at his brother, taking in the frustration written plainly across his face. He didn't need his brother to speak to know that Percival was thinking he could easily have bested either one of the competitors.

The same thing had clearly occurred to others, as well. Many eyes were flicking in their direction, and this time it wasn't just Heath who was the focus of their attention. Percival, with his ability of unnatural strength—a magic gift that was simple to understand, and impressive to witness—had always been popular among the common people.

One of the knights finally defeated the other, and the crowd erupted in cheers. Heath smiled briefly as the victor made his way to the royal stand to pay homage to King Matlock and Queen Renata, and to receive his token of victory.

The king and queen had only sons, no princesses. The king's sister had a daughter, who carried the honorary title of princess, but she was recently married, and not present at the tournament that year. The role of giving the victor the customary kiss therefore fell to one of Heath's many second cousins.

Lady Magnolia's mother was a cousin to the king, just as Heath's father was. But while the Duke of Bexley was the son of the former king's brother, Magnolia's mother was the daughter of the former king's sister. She had inherited the older princess's fiery hair, and—if rumors were to be believed—her irrepressible personality, as well.

She gave the kiss with flourish, her face dimpling mischievously as she bestowed on the winning knight a congratulatory—and undeniably flirtatious—smile.

Heath chuckled indulgently at the display, exchanging grins with his other cousins. Glancing along the line of the royals, he saw Magnolia's grandmother, Princess Lavinia, sitting beside his own grandmother. The princess's hair was no longer fiery in color, but her eyes still sparkled with mischief.

The sight of her husband sitting beside her made Heath's smile slip away, however. It wasn't that he had any dislike for the elderly lord who held the tournament's record. On the contrary. Their story was a bit of a popular romance, Lord Henrik only being the youngest son of a viscount, and managing to win the princess's hand by a feat of valor. But the carefree good humor clear on the couple's face was a strong contrast to the pleasant but careful smiles worn by Heath's own grandparents, sitting next to them. It was a reminder that, unlike Magnolia's grandmother, Heath's grandfather, brother to the former king, hadn't married a Valorian. He had married a Kyonan with magic in her blood, introducing the mixed blessing of power to Valoria's royal family.

Heath glanced back at Magnolia, smiling and waving to the admiring crowd. There was a reason Heath's sister Laura, equal to Magnolia in rank, had never been asked to undertake this role. Just as there was a reason that Magnolia could afford to be cheerful and cheeky and the center of attention, without raising comment. She didn't carry magic, and no one was afraid of her, or suspicious of her intentions.

Heath drew a deep breath, his thoughts once again returning to the mysterious reference to Vazula and its supposedly magic inhabitants. The thought that had been growing in his mind hardened into determination. He would leave the capital the next day, and call on Reka as soon as he reached home. If there was any chance that a kingdom existed somewhere where magic and non-magic people had been successfully coexisting for centuries, he wanted to find it.

He smiled slightly to himself. Yes, generations of Valorians had deemed the East Seas impassable.

But they had never tried traveling by dragon.

CHAPTER ELEVEN

"Good morning trainees."

Merletta pulled her attention to the merman in front of her with an effort. She'd been so distracted by her thoughts about the land and its impossible structures, she hadn't even noticed him enter the small room. She straightened in her seat. This was her first day of real lessons, a day she'd been preparing for and dreaming about for a decade. It was no time to get lost in daydreams.

The merman glanced at the small group as they chorused a greeting.

"Oliver is still with Instructor Agner, preparing for his testing, is he?"

The mermaid with the coral-colored tail—Sage—spoke up. "Yes, sir."

The merman nodded, his eyes gliding over to Merletta. "And we have a new trainee," he said.

Merletta swallowed as she rose from her seat. "Yes, sir," she said. "I'm Merletta."

"It wasn't a question," he said shortly. "I know your name, and I know where you come from. I'm not sure what game you're playing, but I won't allow this program to be made into a mockery, understand?"

"Y-yes sir," said Merletta, too stunned by the open hostility to feel angry.

"Then resume your seat, and do not interrupt my class," said the merman.

Merletta sank back down to the stone bench, a flush creeping up her face. Ileana and Jacobi snickered at the other end of the bench, and the anger made its belated appearance. What right did this merman have to humiliate her in front of her peers, for no reason but which city she came from?

"I am Instructor Ibsen," the merman said, his eyes still lingering on her with an expression colder than the deepest point of the Center. "I will teach you all you need to know of our history to be accepted into the ranks of the educators, and more."

Merletta glanced at Ileana, remembering that as a third year, she was preparing to take her educator exam. Merletta was as determined as ever to pass all four years and join the elite record holders, but she thought that the educator role was the next most appealing. It would be a wonderful service to go throughout the triple kingdoms, educating the regular merpeople on those basic aspects of their history which were common knowledge. She only wished the home had been considered important enough to warrant a little more attention from the educators.

Ileana glanced over and saw her looking, the other mermaid's eyes narrowing. Merletta met her gaze challengingly for a moment before looking away. Being an educator wasn't appealing enough to pursue if it meant working with Ileana.

"Our new trainee will require the most basic of introductory lessons," said Instructor Ibsen. "We will use it as an opportunity for you all to demonstrate how you would explain our history to a child."

Merletta felt another flush rising, but she kept her expression unyielding. She had earned her place here, like any of them, and she would not allow herself to be intimidated out of claiming it.

"Jacobi," Instructor Ibsen said, and Merletta's fellow first year straightened. "How did the triple kingdoms come to be?"

"Three brothers traveled here from the deepest ocean," responded Jacobi instantly, the words clearly copied directly from a lesson. "They founded the three cities of Skulssted, Hemssted, and Tilssted. They, with their wives, were the first monarchs of our kingdoms."

"Good," said Ibsen, turning to the next youngest trainee present. "Sage. Tell us about the establishment of the triple kingdoms."

Sage shifted, her voice clear and confident as she answered. "The brothers ruled side by side in harmony, establishing the three cities, which at that time were spread apart. They had an ancient magic, and combining their power, they created a barrier around their cities. These wards are still in place, keeping dangerous creatures out, and protecting the merpeople from detection by any unwanted visitors, such as dragons."

Sage paused, and Merletta fidgeted in her seat. She'd heard all this before, of course. Every merchild knew this much. But Sage wasn't finished.

"Over time, the population grew such that the cities merged together, forming the triple kingdoms. The lines between the cities became less distinct."

Merletta barely held in a snort. *Tell that to every single merperson who's sneered at me for daring to apply to the Center when I come from Tilssted.*

"Now," Sage continued, "the triple kingdoms operate largely as one people."

Merletta could hold in her questions no longer. These simple explanations had never satisfied her, and here at last was her chance to find out more.

"But where did the brothers come from?" she asked. Everyone's eyes turned to her, their expressions ranging from intense disapproval to mild surprise.

"I already said," Jacobi answered, looking irritated. "From the deepest ocean."

"Yes, I know," said Merletta impatiently. "But where in 'the deepest ocean'? Did they come from another merkingdom? And if so, is it still there? Do we have brethren out there somewhere?"

Instructor Ibsen cleared his throat, and she turned her attention to him, hoping for an answer to a question that had long made her curious.

She was disappointed.

"I thought I told you not to interrupt my class," he said, his brow stormy. "I didn't invite you to ask questions. I invited Jacobi and Sage to give you information."

"But if they were educators, giving this information to regular merpeople, wouldn't their audience be likely to ask questions?" argued Merletta. "Shouldn't they prepare for how to answer them?"

One of the instructor's eyebrows twitched as he stared her down. Then he turned abruptly to Jacobi. "How would you answer such a question, Jacobi? Try to imagine your fellow trainee is a common merchild." His lip curled. "It shouldn't be too difficult in this instance."

Jacobi turned to Merletta, a slight smirk on his face. "Thank you for your interest," he said, again sounding as though he was repeating a set line. "But I have no more information to give regarding that topic. Accept the history you have been told as a gift."

Merletta frowned slightly. She might not be getting the answers she wanted, but she was certainly learning a great deal.

It was discouraging. She was very familiar with this approach to questions—it had been standard practice at the charity home. But she had thought it was merely the repressive atmosphere of the home itself. Surely here in the Center she would get better answers than that. That was certainly not the type of educator she would be, if she ever ended up in that role. She opened her mouth to say as much, but stopped herself, trying to think a bit more strategically.

She turned to Instructor Ibsen, her tone careful. "I understand that Jacobi has completed his task, but he's speaking to trainees, not actually to common merpeople. You said you would teach me everything I need to know to be an educator, and more. Surely the educators have more information than that?"

Ibsen's eyes had been gradually narrowing the whole time she spoke, and they were now the smallest slits. But after a moment's silence, he begrudgingly answered.

"The brothers came from another settlement of merpeople, but they—and their wives—were the last survivors of that people. The rest were wiped out by the dangerous creatures that live in the deep ocean. The brothers survived the destruction, which is why they created the wards that protect us. So it couldn't happen again."

Merletta opened her mouth, then closed it. There were some holes with that story, but it was clear from Ibsen's demeanor that she wasn't getting any more answers on that topic, at least not today. She had to remind herself that she had a lot to lose now that she was a trainee, with a genuine chance at a better future.

This was no place to mouth off like she so often had at the home.

"Jacobi," said the instructor, turning away from Merletta, "you answered satisfactorily. Sage," his expression was still a little dark as his gaze settled on the second year mermaid, "do you know where you went wrong?"

Sage didn't immediately answer, and Ibsen opened up the question. "Can anyone else tell Sage her mistake?"

"Yes, sir," said Emil, the fourth year student, calmly. "She answered more than the question asked. You asked her about the establishment of the triple kingdoms, and she blurred her answer from that into a discussion of our kingdoms' current politics. The extra information muddied the water, and confused her listener."

"Precisely," said the instructor, clearly pleased. "Well explained, Emil." He turned to Sage, his eyes flickering darkly to Merletta. "Our new trainee has demonstrated exactly why it is unhelpful to provide information that has not been sought. She became caught up on details that were not important, instead of focusing on what you were actually saying."

Sage nodded thoughtfully, clearly accepting the chastisement.

Merletta's first instinct was to contradict Ibsen and point out that her question about Jacobi's insufficient explanation bore no connection to Sage's answer. But at the last moment she changed her mind. She wasn't here to argue, she was here to learn. And she had many questions.

"Since we're discussing the topic of the merging of the triple kingdoms," she said, trying her very hardest to make her tone respectful, "why is it that we can't expand beyond our current borders?"

Ileana made an impatient noise in the back of her throat. "Haven't you been listening to a word? The cities are surrounded by a magic barrier, and it's not safe to live outside it. We've already expanded to the edge of the barrier, so any more expansion must happen inward. That's how the cities have merged into the triple kingdoms."

Merletta flicked her tail, frustrated. "Yes, I know that. But what if some amongst the population wanted to take their chances? Perhaps they could live in settlements just beyond the barrier if they built more natural defenses. They could be close enough to have support from the triple kingdoms as needed. There are plenty in Tilssted who I'm sure would be brave enough to at least try."

"It is not a matter of bravery, but of stupidity," said Ibsen harshly. "You are again providing a helpful demonstration for the class, this time of the ignorance that has made Tilssted so much less prosperous than its neighboring cities. It is simply too dangerous to live outside the barrier."

"But—" Merletta paused. She had again been about to contradict, picturing the stretch of ocean she had traversed the day before. It wasn't so wildly dangerous from all she'd seen. But she stopped herself just in time. She couldn't make that argument without revealing her excursions outside the barrier. "But I've been told that most of the creatures in the ocean aren't aggressive," she said carefully. "Surely they're not so much to be feared." She gave a small shudder. "Except for jellyfish, of course."

A snicker drew her attention to Jacobi. "She's afraid of jellyfish?" he mocked, in a carrying whisper. Ileana wore a look of open disdain, and even Instructor Ibsen had a sneer on his face.

"In any event," Merletta pushed on, forcing herself to ignore their derision, "we've already expanded so far inward that we've merged. There's no more room to increase. More and more of the inhabitants of Tilssted are being pushed into the kelp farms.

What will happen in another generation or so? We simply won't fit."

"We'll be fine," said Ibsen dismissively.

"But how?" Merletta insisted.

"Enough questions," growled Ibsen. "You're here to learn, not take over the lesson."

"But how can I learn if I don't ask questions?" Merletta asked, her frustration bursting from her.

"That's enough!" Ibsen's calm gave way for a moment, revealing an anger beneath that was more alarming than his icy hostility.

He took a moment to breathe, calming himself before continuing, and Merletta reined in her own frustration, her heart rate spiking slightly. She'd been trying to be careful, but she'd still pushed too far, as usual. She had to remember that this wasn't the home. If she wasn't careful she would get herself thrown out before she'd begun.

"I wouldn't expect you to understand," Ibsen said at last, speaking in a more measured tone. "And allowances must be made for your ignorance, being only at the very commencement of your study. But these are matters for far wiser and more experienced minds than yours to worry about. These things move in cycles, and problems right themselves in a natural course."

Merletta lowered her head respectfully. She was far from convinced, but "ignorant" or not, she knew well enough that further defiance would achieve nothing useful in this instance.

"This is what happens when they let Tilssted trash into the program," muttered Ileana to Jacobi.

Instructor Ibsen must have heard her, but his face remained impassive, and he made no move to chastise the third year mermaid. Merletta shook her head slightly, not sure whether to be angry or simply to laugh. If they thought they could deter her by rudeness or coldness, they had no idea of either her determination or the life she had led in the charity home. It would take a lot more than snide remarks to send her swimming.

"Ileana." Ibsen broke the uncomfortable silence at last, and for a moment Merletta thought he would call Ileana into line after all. But he merely continued with his lesson. "We have discussed how the triple kingdoms came to be, and discussed the dangers of the open ocean."

Not really, Merletta thought mutinously, but she kept her mouth shut.

"Explain the other key dangers we must warn our population about."

"There are three great dangers to a merperson," Ileana responded promptly. "The dangers of the open ocean we've covered, as you said, Instructor."

She nodded to him, her tone obsequious, and Merletta barely refrained from rolling her eyes.

"Another," Ileana continued, "is the danger of drying out. As this can only happen if every part of a merperson is out of the water, right down to the very tips of their fins, we are safe from that death if we simply stay under the surface."

Merletta nodded along absently. She had long ago discovered that this information wasn't really a secret. Everyone else knew how drying out worked—it was only the beneficiaries of the charity home who were taught a more restrictive definition.

"The third," Ileana said importantly, "is land."

Merletta stilled, her attention fully caught.

"Our ancestors were wise in establishing our triple kingdoms in the deep ocean. It is dangerous for merpeople to be settled near land, and not just because of the risk of drying out. It is also because of the presence of dragons on the land. They are barbaric creatures, and particularly enjoy the taste of merpeople. They will hunt us down if they see us—another reason for us to stay below the surface and inside the barrier unless we have essential business that takes us outside it, like the patrol guards, or the hunters."

"Correct," said Ibsen, his tone bored.

Merletta sat back, considering Ileana's words. She was surprised. She had thought that the tales of the dragons' aggression were an exaggeration, added to make bedtime stories more frightening.

"Are dragons really particularly aggressive toward mermaids?" she asked, forgetting for a moment that she wasn't supposed to be asking questions.

Ibsen drew a long breath in through his nose, his irritation clear, but apparently her question wasn't offensive enough to earn a chastisement.

"Yes," he said shortly. "They are."

"Are they also aggressive toward other creatures?" Merletta asked. "Or just mermaids?"

"They do not hunt other sea creatures," said Ibsen. "They need land to settle on, so they don't usually stray too far from it. Since they mostly stay on land or in the air, they do not generally dive below water looking for food. That is why we are only at risk if we go too close to land, and too close to the surface."

"No, I meant are they aggressive toward creatures on land," Merletta clarified. "Do land creatures live in fear of them like we do, growing up on tales of their violence?"

Ibsen frowned slightly at her. "Growing up on tales?" he repeated. "Of course not. I suppose, in as much as the fish fear the merhunter or the shark, land creatures might fear the dragons." He observed Merletta for a moment. His scrutiny was sharp, and he seemed to realize that she wasn't satisfied. His eyes narrowed. "But such animals can hardly tell tales. There are no intelligent creatures on land other than dragons. Only simple beasts, similar to the fish, or the turtle. As merpeople rule the sea in dominion over the simpler creatures, dragons rule the land and the air. And it is to the mutual benefit of us and them that our territories are separated by such impassable natural barriers."

Ileana shifted slightly in her seat, but Merletta ignored her. She didn't care whether the older girl was yet again glaring at her. There was too much to think about. She opened her mouth to contradict the instructor, but closed it again, remembering both her need to protect her secrets, and the fact that she had pushed him too far already today.

He narrowed his eyes again as he looked at her. She lowered her gaze under his scrutiny, and he turned away, apparently satisfied. But inside, Merletta's mind was a maelstrom of confused questions. She didn't know exactly what she'd seen the day before, on the land, but one thing was certain. It was built by something, and that something wasn't dragons. And it was fully out of the water, so it couldn't have been carved by mermaids, either.

But if neither dragons nor mermaids left it there, what did? And where were they now?

There was only one conclusion. She needed to get back there, and soon. There were a lot of questions to be answered.

CHAPTER TWELVE

"**A**re you ready?"

Heath turned quickly, marveling for the hundredth time at how silently dragons could move, given their size. He hadn't even heard Reka approach. And his eyes had been focused eastward, out over the seemingly endless expanse of ocean, so he hadn't seen the dragon either, as he presumably wheeled in from the direction of Wyvern Islands more toward the north.

"Yes," he replied, stepping up to meet his friend.

Reka was perched right on the edge of the cliff, his tail dangling over the lip. He shifted slightly, causing several bits of rock to dislodge and fall toward the water far below. His eyes passed over Heath's tall form, taking in the rucksack slung securely over his shoulder.

"Interesting," the dragon said, his voice bright and curious. "When I detected your call with my farsight, I assumed you wanted to explore the structure we found under the water at our last meeting. But you appear to have come prepared for a more significant journey."

"That's right," said Heath. "You've often said you wish to explore further across the sea. I'm finally on board."

Rekavidur tilted his head to one side, regarding Heath closely. "I thought you felt you must put your explorations aside for the present, because of your family's troubles."

"Well," said Heath, shrugging one shoulder. "I'm actually hoping that this time my explorations might help with my family's troubles." He swung his gaze back out to sea, squinting toward the horizon, despite knowing perfectly well that if there was anything out there, it was far beyond even his sight.

He looked back to find himself under the intense scrutiny of the dragon.

"What?"

"You haven't forgotten, have you, that dragons can tell when humans aren't being honest?"

"Of course I haven't," said Heath, nonplussed. "What I said was true."

"Hm." Reka snaked his long neck forward until his reptilian head was inches from Heath's face. He sniffed, not unlike a dog scenting its food. "Then why did you have a flavor of deception about you?"

Heath thought back, evaluating his words, and gave a self-conscious chuckle. "Oh, I see. Well, it *is* true that I'm hoping this might help with what's going on in my extended family." He gave a sheepish grin. "But I also can't deny that I'm glad of the excuse to explore beyond where we've been before. I suppose you could say my motivations are mixed."

He sighed. "It might be a fool's errand, but I really do want to help find a resolution for what's happening. When I was in Bryford I read a record about a land to the east where magical and non-magical people have been coexisting for a long time. Maybe even centuries."

Reka exhaled in surprise, sitting back on his haunches. The

cliff beneath him shifted slightly, another chunk falling into the ocean below, but it didn't seem to bother him.

"Magical people in a different land? That seems unlikely. Before the birth of your grandmother, and her twin, dragons were convinced that no other creatures could safely carry magic. If there were magical people in a nearby land, we would have known long ago that humans can in fact wield power."

Heath shook his head. "I don't think it's nearby, at least not in human terms. And would you really expect to know about it? I thought you told me that most dragons aren't interested in exploring beyond their lands. Isn't it true that the colony your father came from in Kyona didn't even know about the colony on Wyvern Islands until your father went questing with my grandmother to find more dragons?"

"It is," Reka confirmed.

"And those colonies are only a couple of hours' flight from each other, at dragon speed!"

"What you say is true," Rekavidur said, with that faint tone of surprise Heath had long ago learned to ignore. "I suppose, based on that reasoning, it is possible that there could be lands to the east that no dragon from my colony has ever explored, and that our farsight does not reach." He flicked his tail slightly. "But surely humans, who are more prone to expansion, would have explored it."

Heath shook his head again. "The water is impassable, apparently. No one can sail more than a few days eastward." He grinned slightly. "How long would it take you to fly the distance of a three day voyage?"

"Carrying you?" Reka tilted his head to one side. "An hour, maybe two."

"Excellent," said Heath briskly. "Then we can be back before the evening meal."

Reka looked Heath over again, a shrewd expression on his reptilian face.

"Where does your family think you're going?"

Heath shrugged. "Just to explore along the coast."

The dragon shook his head slightly from side to side. "Remarkable how easily humans deceive one another."

Heath fidgeted uncomfortably. "I didn't exactly lie. I just wasn't very specific." His voice turned stern. "So there's no need for any sanctimonious comments about how dragons don't lie to each other."

"It is good that we do not," said Reka placidly, "since humans do so enough for both species."

Heath cast his eyes heavenward, but the dragon continued unperturbed. "So. Where is this supposed land?"

"Vazula," corrected Heath. "The record called it the island kingdom of Vazula. And all I know is that it's east of here."

"Very well," said Reka amicably, and Heath smiled.

It was one of the great things about having a dragon for his closest friend. They didn't tend to be daunted by requests that humans would have found unreasonable, or even impossible. There wasn't a whole lot that was impossible for dragons.

Reka crouched, preparing to take to the air, but he paused at Heath's sigh, angling his head inquiringly.

"Sorry," said Heath. "It's just that it'll be hours of flying, probably several hours without pause, by the time we have to turn around and head straight back. It's quite a long shot that we find any land out there. My shoulders are going to be in agony."

A rippling shrug passed down Rekavidur's body. "That is the cost of your exploration," he said, no trace of sympathy in his voice. "If you're trying to ask me to let you ride on my back, then don't."

Heath rolled his eyes at his friend's flat tone. "I wasn't going to ask that, so there's no need to get high and mighty with me. I know dragons don't let people ride them."

"I should think not," said Reka indignantly. "We are not horses."

"All right, all right," sighed Heath. "Let's do this."

He barely had time to brace himself before he felt Reka's talons on his shoulders, the dragon moving with the lightning speed of his kind. In seconds, they were ascending with such rapidity that moisture streamed from Heath's eyes. As always, Reka somehow managed to avoid piercing Heath's shoulders with his razor-sharp talons, but Heath nevertheless resigned himself to an uncomfortable journey.

Reka streamed due east, toward the morning sun, and the coast of Valoria soon fell away. By the time Heath glanced behind him, Bexley Manor was once again a toy cottage, barely visible even to his eyes. He looked forward, much more interested in what might lie ahead.

Rekavidur rose incredibly high before leveling out. Heath tried to keep his eyes on the horizon rather than on the water far, far below him. He knew that Reka would never drop him, but it was still incredibly unnerving to look down and see the distance between his dangling legs and the choppy surface of the ocean. There was no circumstance in which a human could survive that fall.

The sun continued to rise in the sky as they flew toward it, the sea sparkling incessantly in the light. Although summer was over, the day was warm, and Heath was soon wishing that the sun was high enough for him to be in Reka's shadow.

They covered the distance quickly. Absurdly quickly. Heath knew that if they were traveling over land, the scenery would be nothing but a blur at the impossible speed Reka was moving. But with endless ocean beneath them, there wasn't much to see. The water looked the same in every direction, and Heath had no difficulty scanning the expanse for any signs of land. He saw the occasional rocky outcrop, and even more rarely a sandy spot of land barely big enough to be called an island.

Time moved slowly, and as predicted, Heath's shoulders began to ache. After about an hour of flight, he noticed that some of the miniature islands appearing from time to time had palm trees on them. He'd seen trees like those a number of times, further along the coast of Valoria. Apparently they grew everywhere in distant Thorania, where the air was supposedly thick and heavy. In fact, now that he thought about it, he realized the air he was currently flying through was becoming increasingly heavier.

He was just pondering this change when he caught sight of something away in the distance on his right that made him startle so strongly that Reka dipped his giant head to look.

"Are you all right, Heath?" The dragon spoke effortlessly, his voice somehow clear and loud in Heath's ears despite the wind rushing past in an endless torrent.

"Look at that!" Heath shouted, pointing south. "Is that...is that a maelstrom?"

Reka glanced at the spot in the distance, where the waters surged with sudden violence, and a hole could be seen in the ocean. "Looks like it," he said, his voice unconcerned. "Perhaps that's what makes the area impassable for human ships."

"I guess they're real, then," said Heath, dazed. "Not just sailors' tales."

After another half an hour, Heath was feeling extremely tired and sore, his eyes stinging from the wind, and his limbs starting to go numb. He was thinking with dread of the reality that whenever they did finally turn around, they would only be halfway through their journey. It was probably time to call this venture the wild goose chase it was. But he couldn't quite bring himself to ask Reka to change course. They'd come so far already. Further than any Valorian had in living memory, he was sure of it. What if it was just a little bit further? It would be a shame to lose the ground—or water—they'd covered.

He kept his mouth shut, reasoning that they could rest on one of the tiny islands on the way home.

And then, suddenly, he felt a ripple pass over him from head to toe, sending something powerful jolting through his body.

"What was that?" he shouted, but before Reka could answer, Heath's attention was captured by the sight before him, and he forgot all about his question.

At the speed they were traveling, his gasp was of course lost, flung violently away the moment it left his mouth. But there was no need to call out—Reka had clearly seen the island as well, judging by the sudden slowing of his flight.

Because island it was. The land before Heath was no barren outcrop of rock, or random circle of sand. It was a proper island, a hundred times the size of anything he'd seen so far. It was half ringed by a semicircle of white sand, but the ground rose up from the beach into jungle covered slopes, with cliffs on one side. The sun was as fierce as ever, and the island was an explosion of bright color against the sparkling turquoise of the shallower water around it. Most of the land was covered in green foliage, and viewed from above, it looked like an unevenly cut emerald. From his aerial view, he could see the reef just below the surface of the water, creating a natural ring around the island.

It was beautiful.

"Vazula," Heath whispered, the word once again stolen by the wind.

He had no proof of course, but he was certain he had found the island kingdom. His excitement mounted, along with a shot of nerves. What if the people of Vazula weren't friendly?

Perhaps they would resent his intrusion into their hidden paradise.

Reka didn't need any instructions from Heath to realize they had reached their destination. He had already slowed his pace significantly, and he began to descend toward the island. Within moments, he had set Heath down gently on the white sand at the water's edge, alighting beside him.

"Well," said the dragon, shaking out his wings before folding them against his sides. "It seems that there is land out here after all." He glanced back toward the west. "And not far from Valoria's shores at all. Apparently you were right."

Heath nodded absently, not bothering to point out that in human terms, they had traveled a substantial distance. "Do you hear any sign of inhabitants?" he asked instead. "I couldn't see anyone from the air."

The dragon closed his eyes for a moment, breathing deeply and listening in silence. "No," he said, but he kept his eyes closed, his head cocked slightly to one side as he inhaled. A deep rumble vibrated through his chest. "Hm."

"What is it?" Heath asked.

The dragon shook his head slowly from side to side. "I'm not sure yet."

Heath narrowed his eyes. "You're feeling magic, aren't you?" he said, excitement building within him. "There really are magical people living here!"

Rekavidur did his rippling shrug. "Perhaps."

Heath waited, aware there was more behind the dragon's words, but Reka didn't elaborate.

"Well, let's have a look around," Heath said at last, accepting that his friend would share his thoughts when he was ready, and not before.

He adjusted his rucksack more comfortably across his back, and started toward the jungle. He crossed the sand quickly, beginning to climb the rocky section of land beyond it. The air was thick and hot, and sweat was already beading on his forehead. The dragon loped beside him, taking the rocks in easy strides, but keeping to a slow pace so as to remain in line with his companion.

"Heath, look."

Heath pulled his eyes back from his contemplation of the beach behind him, and their lonely tracks on the otherwise untouched sand.

"What is—" He cut himself off, seeing at a glance what had captured Reka's attention.

Rising up from the jungle was a stone wall, clearly constructed by human hands. Heath's heart leaped at this sign of human habitation, and he surged forward. But his elation was short-lived. The structure wasn't far from the beach, and he reached it within a minute. But it was evident even before then that the stone wasn't part of a building so much as a ruin. He slowed his pace, passing under a crumbling archway into what had surely once been a wide courtyard.

It was hard to get a sense of its original size, given the creepers tangling across the space, and the trees forcing their way up between the paving stones. But it was certainly no natural structure. The stones had clearly been cut, and the remains of a stone wall of impressive height rose up on the far side of the courtyard. That building, too, had been reclaimed by the jungle, overgrown with vines, much of its stone surface covered with moss.

The abandoned ruins were beautiful and eerie in equal measure, and Heath felt a chill pass over him despite the hot stickiness of the air.

"No one's lived here for a long time," observed Reka unnecessarily, dislodging a loose stone as he squeezed his reptilian form through the archway behind Heath.

Heath nodded absently, his eyes scanning the structure before him for any clue as to what had happened here.

"Perhaps, like your people, those with magic had conflict with those without magic, and they eventually annihilated one another completely."

Heath turned to the dragon, a snippy retort on his lips, but his words died at Reka's familiar inquisitive expression. The dragon wasn't making fun of Heath's fears. He was perfectly serious. A shudder passed over Heath's form as he turned back to the ruins.

"Let's not assume the worst," he said firmly. "Maybe they just moved to a different part of the island." He turned back toward the archway, hefting his rucksack with determination. "Come on. Let's go deeper."

CHAPTER THIRTEEN

"As most of you know," Instructor Wivell's eyes lingered on Merletta for a moment, "this is the hall of the scribes."

Merletta ignored the veiled reference to her ignorance, as she was fast becoming used to doing. Ileana's snide comments were harder to take, but she did her best to tune them out as she scanned the vast space before her.

"That's right, take a good look," Ileana taunted in a quiet but audible aside, as their literacy instructor drifted over to speak to one of the scribes. "This is where you'll be working, if you're *very* lucky and somehow manage to fluke your first year tests."

Merletta bit back the retort that rose to her lips. The day had barely begun—it was far too early to let Ileana bait her.

"That's no way to speak, Ileana," chided Sage unexpectedly. She gave Merletta a small nod, her lips curving up at the edges in what was almost a smile. "The scribes have a very important job, and to join their ranks is an honor."

Merletta turned away quickly, not quite able to return the smile. Her face, which had remained stony at Ileana's snide remark, was heating in a flush. Sage clearly meant to be encouraging, but her attempted kindness was even worse that Ileana's sneers. She may have phrased it more politely, but she clearly thought Merletta had little chance of succeeding beyond the first year of study.

"All right."

Merletta turned gratefully to Instructor Wivell, who began to rattle out directions.

"Emil," he turned to the fourth year student, "the head scribe is expecting you. I believe he intends to continue your lessons on etymology. Once he is finished, return to my classroom. Instructor Ibsen has filled me in on your most recent topic with him. I will test you—I hope you've been upgrading your mind palace since last time. If there is time afterward, we will run through some simple spaced repetitions."

Emil nodded, swimming briskly away.

Merletta blinked at the unfamiliar word, but didn't bother to ask for an explanation. She had been in classes for less than a week, but she had already learned to be sparing with her questions. It wasn't that she was unwilling to face the inevitable battle—she just wanted to choose the right ones, to make it worth it. At least Wivell seemed to actually want her to learn something, unlike Ibsen, the history instructor.

"Second and third years," Instructor Wivell turned to Ileana, Oliver, and Sage, "records maintenance."

The three young merpeople nodded, flicking their tails with purpose as they crossed the room. Clearly they knew where they were supposed to go.

"First years." Instructor Wivell turned to Merletta and Jacobi. "With me."

Jacobi shot a disgruntled look at Merletta, but she ignored him. She had well and truly learned to disregard the other trainees' regular complaints at having to cover the same water they'd already studied, given the arrival of a new trainee. It was hard for her to sympathize—having been denied the opportunity to learn anything of substance all her life, she couldn't imagine being so resentful just because she had to hear this crucial information more than once.

Wivell was swimming across the room, his posture stiff and upright. As Merletta hurried to follow him, something brushed across her arm.

"Jellyfish!" Jacobi hissed in warning, and Merletta spun in alarm, running a hand across her arm in a panicked gesture.

But all she saw was Jacobi's fins as he pulled them back under him. His snicker brought heat rushing to her cheeks. She narrowed her eyes, hoping he couldn't tell how much his prank had made her heart race. The slimy sea snake.

If Wivell had noticed the interaction, he gave no sign of it. "The scribes are the lifeblood of the Center," he was saying, with his usual unconcern.

Merletta shook off her irritation and swam after him, looking around the large space with interest. The scribes were set up in rows, seated at long stone benches. These surfaces didn't have indents like the table in the dining hall. Instead they were totally smooth. And spread across the surface, in front of the scribes, were bundles of large waxy leaves. The scribes were scratching on the surface of the leaves with sharpened prongs of coral, much like the one Merletta had been given to use for her test.

"The development of our language into a written form is one of the greatest achievements of merkind," the instructor continued. "The ability to preserve information for others to read later is invaluable. But it is of course a resource that requires constant maintenance, as no written records can survive more than a few years."

"So long?" Merletta asked, startled. She thought of how quickly all of her own scratchings had always disintegrated.

"With the right treatment," Instructor Wivell said, nodding. "We prepare the writing leaves with a special compound, and sometimes seal them after they've been written on. That process is one of the things your fellow trainees are studying as they learn about records maintenance."

Merletta was silent for a moment, impressed. She looked around again, taking in all the leaves stretched tightly across the stone surface.

"The scribes are all using coral," she pointed out. "Why don't they use sharpened rocks?"

"They do sometimes," said Instructor Wivell, his tone neither encouraging nor impatient. "But in most cases, it damages the writing leaf too much, and the records don't last as long."

Merletta nodded absently, a slight frown on her face as she pictured the inscription over the doorway to the Center's receiving hall.

"Records would last much longer if carved into stone, wouldn't they?" she asked. "Why don't they do that?"

Jacobi sighed audibly, but Merletta ignored him. It was surely a reasonable question.

"As you would know," Wivell answered calmly, "we carve into stone for signposts and other such purposes. And we do engrave some records in that way. But it's not practical for the majority of records. For the records to actually last a significantly longer period, it must be chiseled deep into a stone of decent size, and that process is very time-consuming. But also, stone is not an efficient medium to store." He gestured at the leaves. "These take up much less space."

He folded his hands behind his back again as he continued. "The scribes you see are only one of many teams of merpeople whose sole job it is to copy the contents of perishing records onto fresh ones. The process is constant. There are also others who inscribe stone as necessary."

Merletta scanned the room again, amazed that this was only a fraction of the scribes. There were dozens of merpeople in the room.

"Are these scribes all former trainees, then? Who passed the first year, and chose not to continue, or who failed to pass second year?"

"No, of course not," said Wivell. "There aren't that many applicants to the training program. An individual can apply specifically to be a scribe, and undertake less complex training for that particular purpose. A high level of skill in literacy is necessary, even for a junior scribe, but many of the other qualities required to undertake our program are not as crucial in this role. For example, the superior memory."

He glanced at Merletta. "The role of a scribe is not a role of such trust and honor as that of the record holders." He gestured across the room. "These employees are copying out records to do with governance, finance, and other such important but uncomplicated matters. The most important records, such as those relating to our history and our culture, are the province of the record holders. That knowledge is primarily preserved not in a physical form, but in the record holders' memory."

Merletta's forehead creased slightly. There was something strange in that explanation, but she couldn't quite put her finger on it. She filed the thought away for later, her mind still caught on the issue of the written records.

"It would save so much time and work if the records could be preserved for longer," she mused. "All these scribes, copying records day in and day out, and I can only assume that the longer our kingdoms are around, the more the volume of records to preserve increases." She glanced upward, almost unconsciously. "I bet air is less destructive than water. Perhaps we could find a way for the records to be stored above the surface line."

"That," cut in Wivell with unusual sharpness, "is a foolish suggestion."

Merletta pulled her gaze downward, meeting his eyes in surprise. She had been speaking her thoughts aloud, not really expecting the suggestion to be taken seriously, and she was surprised by the strength of his response. He seemed to realize he had overreacted, because he took a moment to collect himself, pulling in a swirl of water through his mouth before continuing.

"Look at these scribes." He gestured again to the room. "They are valuable and hardworking citizens of our kingdoms. Would you expose them unnecessarily to the risks of the surface? Imagine how much time they would need to spend going back and forth if such a system as you propose was pursued. Any potential—and likely minimal—benefit we gained from our records being dry above water would be far outweighed by the risk of our citizens drying out."

"I wasn't really making a proposal," said Merletta carefully, still trying to read the normally unemotional merman. "I was just thinking aloud."

"Yes, well. Your desire to improve the system is admirable," Wivell said, unconvincingly. "But you can rest assured that on all such matters, wiser and more experienced heads than yours have considered every angle and selected the best option."

A small cough drew Merletta's attention to Jacobi beside her, and he sent her a smirk. She just stared blankly back at him, wondering how he could really think that she had been the one to come out of that encounter looking foolish. She subsided, but inside she felt a sinking disappointment. Instructor Wivell's chastisement had been almost identical to that of Instructor

Ibsen. *Smarter merpeople than you have reached this decision, and it's not for you to question it.*

She had hoped the Center would be different, that as a trainee she would be encouraged to ask questions, to think differently, to seek answers that might improve the way things were done.

But she was quickly discovering that for all its luxury and opportunity, the Center was more like the grimy charity home than she would ever have imagined.

Merletta swished her tail absentmindedly as she chewed her way through a modest serve of squid. Her thoughts were once again on the land she had discovered. Only two more days until the next rest day, when she had every intention of going straight back there. Ibsen's incongruous claim that dragons were the only intelligent land creatures had only increased her determination to explore the structures further, and to figure out exactly what it was she had discovered.

She pulled her thoughts back to the present, glancing at the food in her hand. She had to admit to herself that she enjoyed being able to eat what had previously been the rarest of treats for breakfast every day. She eyed a bowl of oysters nearby, but drew her gaze away quickly. Thinking of Tish, who was almost certainly eating kelp and cod for every meal, she couldn't bring herself to partake of such extravagant luxuries.

Still, perhaps she should try the unusual looking fish in the table's central basin. She was sure she hadn't tried that type before, and since it seemed to be fish, it didn't feel as decadent as oysters.

She piled some onto her plate, glancing around the dining hall. Her forehead creased slightly as she looked from the bustle of the long table to the empty seats around her. She had stopped avoiding the main meal times, figuring that if they all needed to work together, the other trainees would just have to get used to her. So she was here at the normal breakfast time, and had no idea why the round table was empty except for her.

"Good morning."

She looked up, surprised to see Sage greeting her. The coral-tailed mermaid wasn't overtly rude like some of the others, but she didn't usually go out of her way to speak to Merletta.

"Good morning," she replied, glancing around and seeing that Sage was alone. She gestured to the basin before her. "Fish?"

"No, thanks," said Sage quickly. "The rest of us ate early, so we could be at training on time." She glanced at Merletta's food, and started visibly. "You're not eating that, are you?"

Merletta stared at her. "I was going to. Am I not allowed?"

"That's pufferfish!" Sage said, eyes wide with alarm.

Merletta pulled her hand away from the basin with a gasp. She would never have guessed that the innocuous looking dish was one of the most poisonous foods in the ocean.

"How in the sea did it get served in the dining hall?" Sage said, her face pale. "It's used as pest control, but I can't imagine how it got confused as merperson food. Anyone preparing food should know it on sight." The mermaid scrutinized the other tables carefully. "It looks like it's only on this table, so hopefully no one's eaten any." She waved a servant down and explained the situation. He hastened to remove the dish, eyes wide with horror.

"Thank goodness I came looking for you," Sage said, still looking shaken. "I can't imagine how such a mistake was made. I'm sure the kitchen staff will have a fit when that servant reports it."

Merletta's eyes were narrow as she gazed around the room.

Sage seemed genuine, but Merletta didn't have any difficulty imagining how a poisonous dish had ended up at just the trainees' table, when she was the only one still to attend the meal. The truth had dawned on her the moment Sage used the term "pest control".

"Well," she said mildly, "thank you for warning me." She wasn't fooled into thinking it was some accident, but she had no intention of showing her hand. She knew very well how these things worked. Anyone at the charity home who went crying to the carers when another beneficiary pulled a stunt like this learned very quickly that they had just put a target on their back.

"Did you say you came looking for me?" she prompted.

"Oh, yes," said Sage, shaking herself out of her stupor. "I saw you weren't there, and wondered if you knew we start early on training days..."

Her words trailed off as Merletta surged quickly from her seat, all thoughts of the prank forgotten. "I'm late?" she asked anxiously.

"Not if we hurry," said Sage, her brown braid swirling around her as she turned toward the door. Merletta hurried after her.

"What do you mean training days?" Merletta asked as they swam out of the dining hall. "Are we doing something different from normal today?"

"So no one did tell you," said Sage, half to herself.

Merletta couldn't resist a small snort. "Are you surprised?"

Sage remained silent, and Merletta let it drop, not wanting to push when Sage was showing the first sign of concern Merletta had received from anyone in the Center.

"Usually on the last two days of the week, we all train with Instructor Agner," said Sage, her forehead still creased. "We didn't last week because he was putting Oliver through some practice tests."

"But not you?" Merletta asked, looking sideways at the other mermaid as she kept pace with her. They had left the building and were making their way in the general direction of the tall spire at the center of the Center. "Aren't you both second years?"

"We are," confirmed Sage, leading Merletta down a side street in an apparent shortcut. "We're both seventeen. But Oliver is older than I am. His birthday is only a couple of months away, so he's preparing for his second year test."

"The one that will qualify him to become a guard," mused Merletta. "If he decides to stop there."

"That's right," nodded Sage. "But he won't stop there. He wants to continue, like Emil."

"And Ileana," prompted Merletta.

Sage was silent for the briefest moment before answering, her face more than usually expressionless. "Yes, and Ileana."

Merletta hid a smile. It was heartening to know she wasn't the only one who didn't really like the abrasive older girl.

But the smile quickly dropped away as she flicked her tail, eager to get there as quickly as possible. She had no clue what Instructor Agner was like, and she didn't want to start off by being late. The home had been brutally harsh on tardiness, and she had no idea what rules there were in the Center about such things. Could Instructor Agner throw her out of the program for that? Instructor Ibsen, at least, would surely be glad of the excuse if she gave him half a chance to use it.

"Thank you, by the way," she said quietly.

"What?" Sage flicked a glance her way.

"Thank you," Merletta repeated. "For coming to get me."

Again Sage hesitated slightly before answering. "It didn't seem fair," she said, shrugging one shoulder uncomfortably. "For everyone else to know, and you not to."

Merletta chuckled. "Well, fair isn't really the way it works, not when you're from Tilssted," she said without rancor. She shot another look at the older mermaid. "So I really do appreciate it."

Sage nodded, passing through a square entranceway.

Glancing up, Merletta realized they were in the same courtyard where she had taken her physical test. Stone pillars marched along all four sides of the square, and today, a number of sparring matches were taking place in the middle of the space. Merletta watched with interest as she followed Sage around the edge of the courtyard toward the other trainees, who were floating in a group on one side of the square.

Ileana greeted Merletta with her usual scowl. Her head was angled to the side, in Jacobi's direction, and the scowl turned to a snort of derisive laughter as Jacobi ran a hand across his arm in a convulsive gesture. Merletta stiffened at the memory of Jacobi's jellyfish prank, but she refused to show any embarrassment. How had she been such a fool, revealing an area of vulnerability in front of the whole class like that? Of course someone had instantly exploited it.

They had reached the group now, and Jacobi sighed audibly.

"You just couldn't help yourself, could you, Sage?" he drawled.

Merletta narrowed her eyes at him, her gaze encompassing Ileana as well. Even without the jellyfish prank to precede it, she doubted she would have had difficulty guessing who was behind the pufferfish incident.

"That's enough, Jacobi," said Emil, his tone as cold and unemotional as ever. Jacobi fell silent, exchanging a resentful glance with Ileana.

Merletta smiled at Emil in thanks, but the fourth year student had already lost interest in the petty exchange. His attention was back on the older guards who were training in the courtyard. Merletta sighed internally as she also watched the guards, who were fighting with long-handled spears. She had a feeling she would miss Emil next year, when Ileana would be the most senior of the trainees.

"Ah, you're all here, excellent!"

Merletta turned quickly, straightening her posture as a middle-aged merman approached them. Unlike most other mermen, his hair was cut short in a practical style, and he wore no adornment of any kind. He carried a staff in his hand, of a knobbly length of treated driftwood.

"And I am at last meeting the new trainee," the merman continued brightly.

Merletta blinked, taken aback by his cheerful tone and his friendly smile. Did he not realize she was from Tilssted?

"Merletta, isn't it?" the merman prompted, when she continued to just float there in stunned silence.

"Yes, sir," she said, finding her voice at last. "I'm Merletta. I started the program last week."

"Oh, I know all about that," he responded, with a slight chuckle. "In fact, I know all about you. I'm Instructor Agner, although you can just call me Agner, and I'm glad to have you in my training."

"You are?" Merletta asked, unable to help herself.

Agner chuckled again. "Of course I am. I heard about your impressive performance in your physical entry test. I also heard that you passed the literacy and memory tests with the highest score we've seen in some years. Very well done, very well done."

Merletta blinked more rapidly than ever. She had? She remembered the second tester's condescending tone as he'd told her that she'd made lots of errors, as though she had only just scraped through. For a moment she felt annoyed, but she shook it off, allowing herself an internal smirk. They might not want her here, but they weren't going to find it easy to get rid of her.

"And from Tilssted, too!" Agner was continuing. "All the more impressive, as I assume you've had no formal education?"

Merletta acknowledged it numbly. It seemed he did know her origins, then. She glanced at the other trainees, to see how they were taking Agner's comments. Emil looked as unresponsive as ever, his face giving no indication that he'd even heard the instructor. Ileana, of course, looked furious. The two second years—Oliver and Sage—were looking at Merletta thoughtfully, although Oliver looked far from happy, while Jacobi simply looked stunned. It must have occurred to them, as it had to Merletta, that if she'd had the highest score "in some years", she had probably outperformed all five of them.

"Well then," said Agner. He rubbed his hands together jovially, apparently unaware of the reaction he had created among his trainees. "Let's begin with some warm ups, shall we?" He scanned the group, his eyes resting for a moment on each face. "Sage. How about you pair up with Merletta, show her how we do things?"

It seemed he wasn't totally oblivious to everyone's frame of mind, Merletta thought dryly, as she moved to join Sage. They did a series of warm up exercises, which Merletta found unfamiliar but quite enjoyable. It was good to get the blood pumping, especially in the chill of early morning in the depths of the Center.

"Well, you seem to be in good shape, Merletta."

The instructor's voice from close behind her made Merletta start. She hadn't realized he was watching.

"I'm surprised you found the opportunity to keep so active while living in a charity home," he added. "From all that I've heard, I thought it was quite a restrictive life."

"Yes," Merletta responded carefully, studying his face. Did he somehow know about her trips outside the barrier? Was he trying to trap her? But if he was suspicious of her, he hid it well.

His expression remained genial. "It is a restrictive life in many ways," she said. "But they certainly didn't encourage us to be idle."

True, if not entirely forthright.

"Well, then," said Agner, still speaking brightly. "Let's try you out in combat." He scanned the group. "Ileana. Would you care to start Merletta off?"

Merletta kept her face as neutral as she could, but inside she groaned. Ileana was the last person in the group she wanted to be matched with on her first attempt at combat. The older mermaid moved forward, her slight smirk confirming all Merletta's fears. She was certainly not going to take it easy.

Not that I want her to, Merletta thought defiantly, as she propelled herself into the area indicated by Agner. She took the staff he handed her, noting that Ileana took particular care in selecting her own.

Merletta passed her fingers along the surface with interest, never having felt such an instrument before. Driftwood was rare —these were expensive weapons. At least they were blunt, unlike the spears being used by the real guards further across the courtyard. Their weapons seemed to be similar staffs topped with stone spearheads. They looked like more expertly sharpened versions of the weapon Merletta had long ago fashioned for herself.

It's just like fighting that shark, she thought firmly, gripping the unfamiliar tool as she and Ileana began to circle. *Go in with confidence, and you'll frighten the predator away.*

She surged forward, raising the weapon. She barely even saw Ileana move, but she certainly felt the other girl's staff connect with her midriff. She fell back through the water, grunting with pain. She righted herself quickly, her eyes narrowing at the barely contained glee in Ileana's eyes.

I can do this, she chanted to herself. Ileana was hanging back, and Merletta was once again the first to move. Gathering her energy, she flicked her tail in a sudden and powerful motion, cutting through the water toward her opponent.

She didn't have even a moment's warning before her tail exploded in pain. She could hardly make sense of the other girl's movements—all she was aware of was a stinging pain in her tail, followed rapidly by a whack to the head so hard it made her vision spin. She blinked, confused for a moment at how she was now facing the opposite direction, but before she could spin back around, Ileana dealt her a solid blow to her back, making her drop her weapon and clutch it.

She scrambled to retrieve the staff, but Agner's chuckle broke into her anger, as the instructor signaled that the fight was over.

"Well, well, whatever they taught you at the charity home, I guess they didn't train you in combat."

Merletta ground her teeth, fighting the feeling of humiliation. She refused to even look at Ileana—she could feel the smugness radiating off her.

"Don't be discouraged," said Agner cheerfully, swimming toward her. "We'll get there. You're already a fighter here." He touched the end of his own blunt weapon to her forehead with a grin. "And that's the bit that's hard to teach. We can train you to be a skilled fighter. That part's easy." He turned to the rest of the group. "Emil. You and Ileana can demonstrate for Merletta what a bout between skilled fighters looks like."

The older trainee swam forward calmly, a staff gripped between his hands, and Merletta sank back to join the others. She was only too glad to be out of the action for a moment.

It might be easy from where Agner was floating, she thought ruefully, her head still throbbing as she rubbed her stinging back. But she had a feeling she had a lot more of those blows coming before she would be called a skilled fighter.

By the end of the second day of training with Agner, Merletta's whole body ached. Each of the other trainees had taken their turn at defeating her with embarrassing ease, but mercifully they had returned to their normal training regimes after that. Merletta had been assigned to join the exercises being undertaken by new recruits to the training program for the standard guards. It seemed their training also took place in the Center. Even they already had enough training in combat to make short work of Merletta, of course.

But she was still in a cheerful mood as she once again made her way out of the Center early in the morning on her second rest day. Bruises aside, there was something satisfying about training. And unlike her other instructors, Agner was not only friendly, but seemed dedicated to actually teaching her something. It was a welcome change.

As she passed through the kelp farms, nodding in a friendly way toward a lone laborer, she turned her thoughts from the Center to the world outside the triple kingdoms. She didn't meander this time, passing through the barrier and heading straight toward the north east. She crossed the familiar canyon, and wove through the tail-shaped reef. She hung back in the coral, floating silently on the current as a small hammerhead shark passed not far away. It was past their common feeding time now, but better to play it safe.

Her excitement began to mount as she noticed the slope of the ocean floor, slanting gradually upward. She flipped her tail, moving more quickly through the water. When she caught sight of the reef, she directed herself straight upward, breaking the surface and breathing in the fresh air.

She blinked the water away quickly, her eyes eagerly scanning the horizon. There it was.

The land.

It was still there. She swam alongside the reef, looking for a good place to pass through it. The tides were different from last time, and the reef was closer to the surface. She caught sight of the structures on the land, and renewed her efforts to pass through the reef. She had to get a closer look.

She found a spot where the natural barrier was only sparse, and darted through it, sending dozens of tiny fish fleeing from her approach. The water quickly became too shallow for her to swim fully upright, and she was soon horizontal, her belly almost touching the sand. She floated in the shallows, observing the stone structures from a distance. They were definitely buildings, albeit not very well maintained ones.

But how had they gotten there?

She moved slowly along the shoreline, floating on her belly with her back out of the water. Her hands gripped the sandy floor of the ocean as she used them to pull herself along. It was a strange and pleasant sensation, feeling the coolness of the sand between her fingers at the same time as the warmth of the sun beating on her back. And the water itself was luxuriously warm here, warmer than she'd ever felt before.

Something floated toward her on the surface of the water, and she eyed it warily. She hung back as she studied it, but it didn't appear to be alive. Hesitantly, she reached out and picked it up. It was round, like a pearl, but much larger, and brown. And although it was hard, it had a rough, almost hairy texture to its surface. She rapped on it with her knuckles, and it made a knocking sound. Taking another look at the land, she noticed a profusion of similar items growing on some of the tall plants that protruded from the sand. This one seemed to have fallen and ended up in the water. She gave it a sniff, her interest piqued. It smelled good...perhaps even edible. She stashed it in her satchel for further examination later, then continued to wander in line with the shore.

Her restriction chafed her the further she went. If only she wasn't confined to the water. She was sure she'd be able to pull herself along the dry ground in the same way she was pulling herself through the shallows. If only that wouldn't cause her to dry out, that was.

Looking up, her heart leaped at the sight of a passage of water that jutted into the land up ahead. She hurried toward it, still pulling herself by her hands. The tall green plants hung over it, coming all the way out into the water. The water was slightly deeper at the entrance to this passage, and Merletta dove below again for a moment. The plants continued underwater, and she approached one with interest. It wasn't green under the surface, but brown. And it was hard and solid, unlike a kelp tower. It was so solid, in fact, that it didn't even sway with the water.

Merletta frowned as she ran a hand along its rough surface. It was familiar, but it couldn't be...

She snapped a piece off with an effort, staring at the short section in her hand. It was driftwood. An untreated version of the driftwood staff she'd been using as a weapon in her training for the last two days. But how was that possible? Driftwood was a product of the sea, coming from the deep ocean and floating up to the surface, everyone knew that. It didn't come from land.

Just like there are no intelligent creatures on land bar dragons, a voice in Merletta's head said grimly. *Just like floating too long on the surface will dry you out.*

The thought swirled uncomfortably inside her. She had long ago gotten past her outrage over the lies she'd been told at the charity home. But the Center was a different matter. That was where she was supposed to get answers. And the suspicion growing inside her now—that the inconsistencies between what she'd seen and what she was being taught were not errors but intentional untruths—was much more unsettling. It made her feel adrift in the open sea, like she had no point of foundation.

She opened her kelp satchel, stowing the short length of driftwood—or just wood, she thought dryly, since it hadn't been adrift at all. Then she once again let her head break the surface, dodging between the wood-plants, which above the waterline were covered with green leaves, as she made her way down the passage. It was taking her away from the structures, but her excitement still grew as the water allowed her to travel further into the land.

The passage soon opened up into a large circular mass of water, lined halfway around with the strange, solid plants. The part that wasn't overhung with them was lined with rocks below the water, but above the water gave her a clear view into the green heart of the land. To her excitement, she could even see a glimpse of one of the stone structures through the leaves. She swam toward it, her hands pulling her over the rocky surface once the water was too shallow to properly swim through.

"Look at this, Reka. I think there's a lagoon through here."

Merletta froze at the sound of the unfamiliar voice, her head whipping back toward the deeper water. Had someone followed her? Her first instinct was to pull herself out of the water, so they couldn't see her, but she mastered it quickly. She had no desire to dry out.

"There is a lagoon! It's beautiful."

Merletta turned her head back toward the rocks, confused at the direction the voice was coming from. It sounded like it was on the land, but of course it couldn't be. Did the water continue further than she'd realized? She hovered, still frozen on the surface, not sure which direction to flee.

"Do you think it connects to the ocean, or is it just—"

The words came again just as a figure emerged from the

green. Merletta's heart stopped beating at the sight before her, and her eyes grew wide. For a moment she was incapable of moving, her gaze riveted to the creature before her. Her eyes traveled from the ground upward, her heart beginning to beat again, except at double time.

A shudder of half fear half fascination passed over her as she realized that the creature's strange hide was a covering, and the skin underneath was just like a merman's, pale like Emil's, or Jacobi's. The coverings were rolled up at the arms, and she suspected that if they were removed altogether, his top half would look exactly like a merman's. That is, if a merman could float upright with no tail and out of the water.

When she reached his face—for the creature was a he, judging by his voice—Merletta started involuntarily. She'd been so lost in her examination of the strange arrival that she hadn't even realized he'd stopped speaking abruptly. It was evident now that he'd done so because he'd seen her just as she'd seen him. His eyes were latched on to her head and shoulders, which protruded from the water, and he looked almost as startled as she felt.

"Hello," he said, breaking the silent standoff with a voice that was unexpectedly gentle. "Do you live here?"

Merletta just stared at him, her mind totally incapable of forming any coherent thought. What was she seeing? Was she dreaming, still fast asleep in her hammock at the barracks after all?

"I don't mean any harm," the creature said quickly. "My name is Heath. I'm so glad you're here. I was hoping to meet the people who live on this island."

Merletta blinked. Island? Is that what this land was called? And he thought she lived here? A strange and unexpected longing rose up in her. It would be a beautiful place to live. She wished she could be like him, free to wander the surface of the land, instead of bound to the water by her scales.

"Heath?" A gravelly voice, altogether different from that of the creature before her, emerged from the green.

Merletta's eyes darted toward the sound, and she suddenly regained control of her limbs. She had no desire to be seen by yet another strange creature. She started to shuffle quickly backward across the underwater rocks.

"No, wait, please don't go!" Heath said, extending a hand as he took a few steps toward the water.

Merletta paused for a moment, her eyes finding his. For one long heartbeat she was held in thrall by his eyes. They were so much like hers, as if he was one of her kind, instead of an impossible, mythical creature. But she heard his unseen companion approaching through the trees, and with a last glance at the first creature's impossible form, she dove below the water, swimming as swiftly as a marlin toward the familiar safety of home.

CHAPTER FOURTEEN

Heath

"Wait!" Heath called, splashing into the shallows. But the girl was gone, with barely a ripple. He scanned the surface of the lagoon, but he could see no sign of her head, with its wild, dark hair, breaking the surface anywhere. She must be an excellent swimmer.

"Heath?" Reka emerged from the trees, his reptilian head snaking from side to side as he sniffed the air. "Did I hear you speaking to someone?"

Heath turned away from the water, swallowing his annoyance. He was fairly certain it was the dragon's approach that had frightened the girl away, but his friend couldn't really be blamed for that.

"There was a girl!" he said, pointing toward the water. "Swimming in the lagoon."

"Really?" Reka tilted his head to the side, his eyes bright with interest. "Are you sure?"

"Of course I'm sure!" spluttered Heath. "She was right there, where the rocks are. She dove between the mangroves."

"And you spoke with her?"

"Well, I spoke *to* her," Heath amended. "She didn't respond.

She sort of just...stared at me. Then she dove under the surface, and disappeared." He frowned toward the lagoon, his eyes once again scanning the smooth water. "She hasn't come up for air. Do you think she's all right?"

"I know nothing about her or her situation, so I have no idea," said Reka simply.

Heath rolled his eyes, but he was in no mood to be distracted by his friend's usual literal interpretation of human speech.

"I hope she is," he murmured, mainly speaking to himself. He wanted to find her, to ask her for answers to all his burning questions about this lost kingdom. But it was more than that. He didn't like the idea that he'd scared her off. Just like Reka said, he knew nothing about her, or her situation. But when their eyes had locked, for that moment, he'd seen something familiar in them. Some reflection of his own restlessness, perhaps.

He shook off the fanciful thought. "We should find her," he said firmly.

Reka's eyes were narrowed in focus as his gaze swept the area. "I don't think you'll find her," he said placidly. "I can neither see nor hear any sign of anyone but us."

"But..." Heath frowned at the water. "Where did she go? She must have gotten out of the water somewhere. Maybe we can find her tracks."

"You can look," said Reka, with maddening unconcern. "But I don't think you'll find anything." He sniffed the air. "Anyway, it seems you were right, so that should be some consolation."

"Right about what?" Heath asked absently, splashing over the rocks in the shallow water, disregarding his wet boots.

"About magic carriers living here."

"What?" Heath's head whipped back around, his attention fully caught. "Why do you say that?"

"Because that girl, whoever she was, had magic," Reka said, rippling his scales comfortably. "You really can't feel it? I can still sense it quite strongly, even though I'm confident she's no longer here."

"No, I didn't feel a thing," Heath said, his forehead creasing.

"Hmm," mused Reka. He was silent for a long moment, deep in thought, while Heath splashed through the shallows, looking for any sign of the girl.

"I'm not altogether surprised, on reflection," the dragon said at last. "It's very strong, but it's different from your family's magic. Not flagrant like your brother's—rather, subtle, pervasive."

Heath turned back to the lagoon, shrugging one shoulder. He didn't know what the dragon meant, but he still couldn't sense lingering magic. He closed his eyes for a moment, trying to focus. Or could he? There was some taste to the air...it was familiar, niggling at his memory in a way he couldn't put his finger on.

"What was she like?" Reka asked, interrupting his thoughts.

Heath opened his eyes. "She was...beautiful," he said, almost involuntarily. He thought about her dark hair, and expressive eyes. Her features had been quite delicate, but she had certainly not projected an air of refinement. "And...wild, somehow."

He frowned slightly. It was difficult to put his impressions into words. He had once seen a jaguar, one of the large cats that prowled the jungles of Balenol. It had been brought across the ocean to be shown as a curiosity in the North Lands, and it had created quite a sensation. But Heath had hated the spectacle. The creature was majestic, and seeing it locked in a cage, restless and aggressive from its confinement, and from the discomfort and fear of the sea voyage, had been distressingly wrong.

Something about the girl reminded him of that moment.

He shook his head slightly, trying to find a more concrete answer to the dragon's question. "She had dark hair," he said at last. "And skin a bit like a South Lander's. And she was dressed..." he felt a slight flush rise up his neck, "...unusually."

"What do you mean by unusually?" Reka pressed curiously.

"She, uh..." The flush rose further as Heath thought of her attire. With his superior eyesight, he had been able to see the droplets of water running down the warm skin of her bare shoulders as she moved. Just as he had been able to see the drops clinging to the thick mass of her long dark eyelashes.

He cleared his throat. "She wasn't wearing much at all, actually. I could only see her torso, but all she had on were a pair of these large sort of shells, connected together somehow. Oh, and a length of some kind of seaweed or something wrapped around one upper arm."

"That is unusual," said Reka, sounding fascinated. "I've never come across a person dressed in such a manner before."

Heath flushed all over again as a thought occurred to him. "Maybe she was bathing, and we interrupted her. It might explain why she left in such a hurry."

"Maybe," said Reka, clearly unconcerned. "Or maybe the people here dress that way, because of the heat."

"Could be," Heath agreed, his eyes drawn back to the water. "I wonder where she went. I must have been distracted, and missed her getting out of the lagoon." He frowned toward an opening in the mangroves. "Unless she swam out to the ocean before leaving the water."

"Maybe her magic allows her to breathe underwater," suggested Reka.

Heath looked over at him, startled. "Is that possible?"

Reka did his strange rippling shrug. "Who knows?" The dragon looked up at the sky. "We should depart soon, if you still wish to return home in time for dinner."

"Who cares about dinner?" protested Heath. "We need to find that girl! Or at least, find the settlement she comes from."

"I don't think you'll find her," Reka repeated. "But I have no objection to looking."

"You're sure you didn't see anything from above?" Heath asked.

"I told you," Reka said patiently. "I couldn't see any signs of human habitation, but the jungle is too thick on most of the island for me to be able to say with any certainty."

Heath hefted his rucksack onto his shoulder determinedly. "Well, we know now that there *must* be human habitation somewhere. We just need to look harder."

But after several more hours of exploration, Heath had to acknowledge that even if there was anything to find, he wouldn't be finding it that day. They discovered extensive ruins, including ones quite close to the lagoon where he had seen the girl, but no sign of current habitation. He didn't explore the ruins at all, his focus entirely on the search for the girl and her people. But the island paradise was, to all appearances, deserted.

The sun was hanging low in the sky when he finally, reluctantly, asked Reka to take him home. They took to the air with a whoosh that momentarily flattened all nearby vegetation, but Heath barely noticed the familiar sensation of his stomach dropping to his knees. His thoughts were on the mystery of the girl's identity, and he twisted precariously in Reka's talons, watching Vazula as it shrank from an island to a glittering emerald in the middle of the ocean, then disappeared altogether.

He sighed, turning his gaze to the endless water before him and resigning himself to the discomfort of the journey. It would take the dragon an hour and a half to carry him back to Bexley Manor. He would miss dinner for certain, and he started to wonder what he was going to tell his family. Not so much about this excursion—one day of unexplained absence he could probably get away with. But it wasn't going to be just one day. He was going to come back the next day, and the next. As long as it took to find answers.

Three days later, Heath was almost boiling over with frustration. His plans to return immediately to Vazula had been thwarted the instant of his arrival home, and he was still fuming over the whole incident.

Reka had set him down outside Bexley Manor at twilight. As usual, the dragon hadn't lingered, pausing just long enough to assure Heath that he would return at first light the next day. But apparently even that had been too long.

Heath soon discovered that he had chosen the timing of his excursion poorly. Not that he could have predicted that would be the day the sanctimonious Chief Counselor decided to once again descend on the Duke of Bexley's family, full of carefully-worded accusations, and veiled threats of further restrictions.

It seemed that Heath's performance at the tournament had rattled the nobleman even more than Percival's feats of strength. He had apparently waited all day for the opportunity to admonish the young man, and the arrival of the truant so late in the day, and by dragon no less, had certainly done nothing to improve his temper.

Heath narrowed his eyes, although he wasn't seeing the target on the other side of his father's training yard. His vision was clouded by his anger. Usually practicing his archery was a guaranteed way to relieve stress, but truth be told, he couldn't remember ever being this riled up.

His hand reached mechanically for an arrow but didn't immediately pull it from the quiver, his fingers running compulsively up and down the fletching as he remembered the scene he had walked in on a few days before.

"Here you are at last, Lord Heath," Lord Niel had said in an accusing tone, before his family had even had the opportunity to greet him. "You've certainly kept me waiting a long time."

Heath blinked, pulling his thoughts from the island with difficulty. "Lord Niel," he said blankly. He looked in confusion to his parents, both seated in the receiving room where Lord Niel was pacing, but their stony expressions gave him no clue as to what was going on. "My apologies for the inconvenience. Had I known I was expecting you, I would have—"

"You certainly seem to be allowed a great deal of license," Lord Niel had interrupted. "Gone from morning until night, with no one able to give me a clear answer about your whereabouts."

Heath raised an eyebrow, his polite tone taking on a frosty edge. "I wasn't aware that my whereabouts were any concern of yours."

His father gave him a warning look, but Lord Niel disregarded his interjection anyway.

"And I see that rumors of your closeness to your pet dragon haven't been exaggerated," Lord Niel barreled on, gesturing to the window. Clearly he had seen the manner of Heath's arrival.

Heath forgot his rising anger for a moment in the absurdity of it all. His lips twitched, a hint of humor creeping into his voice. "You'd better not let Rekavidur hear you calling him my pet, My Lord."

"Is that a threat?" Lord Niel pounced on the comment, turning swiftly to face Heath with a martial light in his eye.

"Of course not," said Heath quickly, all desire to laugh gone.

The poorly disguised satisfaction in the nobleman's eyes alarmed him more than all of Lord Niel's grumbling. The older man was looking for an excuse to make trouble. Heath was smart enough to realize that he needed to be careful not to give him any reason to complain to the king that Heath's friendship with Reka was a threat to Valoria's non-magical citizens.

Lord Niel drew a deep breath, his eyes narrowing as he looked Heath up and down. "I have been discussing with your father the importance of demonstrating to all of King Matlock's subjects that there is unity within our royal family, among those who wield power as well as those who do not."

"And I have already reminded you, My Lord, that my family and I are well aware of that fact." The duke stood to his feet, looking down at Lord Niel from his superior height. His tone was uncompromising, and the lift of his eyebrow, although subtle, somehow pointed out more clearly than words that in spite of Lord Niel's role as Chief Counselor, as a duke, and a cousin to the king, the Duke of Bexley held considerably higher rank.

"I understand your concerns," Heath's father went on, "but I will not tolerate any insinuations against either of my sons. My family remains—as we have always been—unswervingly loyal to the crown, as we have demonstrated in every way. Have you forgotten that through my long service as His Majesty's chief advisor on both foreign relations and matters of justice, the gift with which I was born has benefited Valoria more times than can be counted?"

"Of course not, My Lord Duke," blundered Lord Niel, but Heath's father wasn't finished.

"Or that only recently, Lord Percival was able to save the life of one of His Majesty's subjects by intervening in a near-fatal accident?"

For a long moment, Lord Niel was silent, his eyes narrowing as they rested on Percival. Heath's stomach dropped as he realized with an inexplicable flash that the Chief Counselor had somehow heard of Percival's careless comment the day before the tournament began. Was he about to accuse Percival of treasonous talk? Not that Percival would have to worry about any consequences from the crown. Their father would murder him first if he found out about it.

But it seemed that Lord Niel had no intention of airing that information in front of the duke, at least not at the moment.

"You misunderstand me, Your Grace," he said, his words polite but his expression still hard. "I was not speaking of your actions, or those of Lord Percival. I was speaking of Lord Heath's display at the tournament." He turned to Heath. "I have been told that although you appeared to hit the target while blindfolded, you were not in fact wearing a proper blindfold, and could see the target when you took aim. Is that true?"

Heath met the nobleman's gaze for a measuring moment. "It is," he said at last. His conscience only pricked him slightly. Considered in a certain light, everything Lord Niel had just said was true.

Lord Niel relaxed slightly, his gaze assessing Heath. "I see. So I was correct in my understanding that you have not been gifted with..." He trailed off, then cleared his throat. "It is unfortunate, then, that a different impression was received by a number of those who observed you."

"Indeed," said Heath, his voice cold and his face expressionless.

Lord Niel just watched him for a moment, his fingers drumming absently against the hilt of the dress sword he wore. "You should know," he said abruptly, "that there are those who are not comfortable with your close association with the dragons. Some consider it unwise—even irresponsible—for humans to make themselves vulnerable to such unpredictable creatures."

"Indeed?" Heath said again, tilting his head in a polite gesture, even while his gaze remained unyielding.

Lord Niel hesitated. "And I suppose you don't intend to tell me where you were all day, either?"

Heath raised his eyebrows, doing his best to copy the haughty manner his father adopted when someone overstepped their boundaries. It was the kind of skill a duke needed, but Heath rarely had to use.

"You suppose correctly, My Lord."

Lord Niel waited, looking to the duke and duchess in apparent expectation that they would chastise their son. But no one said anything more, and eventually he took his leave in a less than gracious manner.

That whole encounter had been bad enough, but the conversation with his parents that followed it was even worse. As much as Heath felt a little guilty for the tension his little exhibition at the tournament had created, he still couldn't believe that his parents were clipping his wings.

How was he to blame for Lord Niel's paranoia, or the fear some Valorians still felt toward dragons? Three days it had been, and they still weren't allowing him to leave the manor. What did they think he was going to do if not directly supervised? It wasn't like he was inciting Reka to set fire to anything. The two of them just wanted to explore together, and not even within the boundaries of the kingdom.

Not that his parents were aware of that detail. He was glad they hadn't asked him to tell Lord Niel where he'd been—he would have been astonished if they had given way to the pompous nobleman's presumption. But when they were alone, such restraint disappeared immediately. Heath had told them he and Reka had been exploring together, and had declined to give details even when pressed.

His refusal to elaborate was at first mainly a mulish response to the accusations made against him. But even on sober reflection, he thought it best not to reveal the full extent of his explorations to his parents. It was partly because he was fairly certain they would tell him not to undertake such a long—and potentially hazardous—journey again. But it was also partly because he first wanted to somehow prove that Reka was wrong in his guess that the coexistence of magical and non-magical people on Vazula had led to everyone wiping each other out.

He didn't think that information would encourage anyone in their current situation.

"A bit more annoying when the prejudice is directed against you, isn't it?"

Heath turned, lowering his hand from the quiver as he watched his brother approach across the training yard, sword in hand.

"It is," he acknowledged. He gave his brother a dry look. "No need to look so happy about it."

"Sorry," said Percival, his grin contradicting his words. He clapped his brother on the back. "Just glad to have company in my disgrace, that's all." His expression turned serious as he studied Heath's mutinous face. "Don't let anyone wear you down, all right? You've done nothing wrong."

Heath sighed, drawing an arrow from the quiver at last. "I know."

He lined up the shot, inhaling deeply, then released it. Both brothers watched impassively as the arrow hit the bullseye dead center.

"Mother and Father know it too," Heath added. "They're not really angry with me. They just don't want to give anyone extra reasons to be suspicious of us."

He drew out another arrow. "The truth is, I don't even care about the prejudice. Not really. I'm just annoyed about being kept kicking my heels here because..."

He trailed off, and Percival looked at him, his forehead creased. "Because what?"

"Nothing," said Heath. He wasn't entirely sure why he hadn't told his brother about his discovery of the abandoned island kingdom, but every time he went to say it, he found himself reluctant to share the secret.

"Lord Niel just wants to take his insecurity out on anyone he can," he said instead. "Even he doesn't really think I have magic."

"Well that's his mistake, then," said Percival staunchly. "No one without magic could have hit that shot."

"I told you," said Heath impatiently. "I could see the target."

Percival's frown deepened. "I tied the kerchief myself, Heath."

Heath poked his brother in the stomach with the tip of his bow. "I guess kerchief-tying isn't part of your magical abilities."

Percival rolled his eyes, but let the matter drop. Heath returned his attention to the target, his conscience niggling at him. Again, he wasn't sure why he didn't want to confide the full truth in his brother. He hadn't hesitated to tell both his grandmother and Reka the details, and both of them had received the information placidly enough. But then, they had both always insisted that they could sense magic in Heath, without knowing its form. Telling his brother—the ever-confident Lord Percival, known throughout the kingdom for his legendary strength—seemed like more of a risk, somehow.

Heath went to bed that night in a sour frame of mind, having just tried without success to convince his parents to let him out of the cage. He was starting to contemplate directly disobeying their instructions, something he hadn't done since childhood.

"Reka," he called to his empty bedchamber as he prepared for sleep. "Still no point coming tomorrow. I'm still a prisoner. Apparently I have to lie low for a few more days."

He threw his tunic petulantly across the room onto a carved wooden chair. He knew that his friend would hear the message. Reka's farsight was tuned in to Heath, and calling the dragon by name was always enough to get his attention. Of course there was no way for Heath to hear any response.

As the thought occurred to him, an image flickered before his mind's eye, of Reka. Heath blinked, thrown by how real the picture seemed. Reka was sitting on his haunches, his head tilted to one side as he listened to Heath's complaint. The dragon's form and mannerisms were familiar enough that it was no surprise that Heath's imagination could conjure up a convincing image, but the surroundings were somewhere he'd never been before. Heath shook his head to clear it, wondering how much resemblance his imagination bore to the reality of what the dragon colony on Wyvern Islands looked like.

He slept fitfully, his mind as always on the island, and his strange encounter with the only inhabitant he'd been able to find. Who was she? Was she the sole survivor of some terrible tragedy? Her eyes, filled with a restlessness that spoke to his soul, haunted his dreams as they had the last three nights.

But just before dawn, he fell into a dream that for once had nothing to do with Vazula.

"Mama, Mama, who's he?" A five year old Heath tugged on his mother's skirts as they wandered through Valoria's summer markets.

"Hush, Heath, where are your manners?" his mother chided. "It's not polite to point."

"But he's not normal."

"Heath!" his mother said, her tone shocked. She shot an apologetic look at the stranger in the market. "My apologies, sir."

The man inclined his head in acknowledgment of her words, but his expression remained cold. Heath stared at him, unable to pull his eyes away. There was something chilling about the older man's face, something alien.

"But Mama, why's he different?"

"That's enough, Heath," his mother said firmly, tugging him away. "No more excursions to the markets until you can learn to behave with the manners fitting your station."

"But he's different," Heath insisted, his shrill little voice rising. "He's different!"

He continued to protest, even after his mother had handed him over to one of their personal guards, and the man had dragged him gently but inexorably out of the public eye.

"He wouldn't stop saying it," his mother reported to his father later that evening, her tone still disapproving. "I was mortified. The poor man was simply walking through the market, minding his own business."

She all but rolled her eyes when her husband responded with eagerness rather than seconding her rebuke.

"Maybe it's a sign of his magic coming out! Maybe he could see something you couldn't." He got down to his young son's level, his expression encouraging. "What was different about him, Heath? Can you remember?"

Heath shrugged his little shoulders. "Dunno. He felt different, that's all."

"You felt something, did you?" The duke still sounded pleased. "That's good, Heath." A pointedly cleared throat from behind him made his expression turn more serious. "But your mother is right, you know, little one. You mustn't be rude. We get to enjoy lots of good things because of our position, but it also means we need to take more care to be kind and polite to people. Understand?"

"Yes, Father," Heath said obediently, although he was still confused as to what exactly he'd done wrong.

"Good," said his father with his gentle smile. His eyes turned eager again. "But about this feeling you had. Can you feel it now? When you look at me?"

Heath shook his head.

"Have you felt it before?"

He shook his head again.

"Hm." The duke rocked back on his heels, exchanging a look with his wife. "I thought he might have been sensing magic—it's often the first sign of ability, you know—but it doesn't seem like it."

"I don't think so," the duchess said. "I've never seen the man before. I don't think he was part of the extended family, and he didn't look Kyonan. So he couldn't be a power-wielder."

"What did he look like?"

She shrugged. "Just normal. Nothing remarkable."

"No, Mama," Heath corrected, frustrated. "He was different."

"I know, little one," his father said absently, tousling his hair. He shrugged his shoulders, speaking again to his wife. "No matter, there's plenty of time for his magic to show itself."

Heath woke with a start, lying still in his bed as his eyes adjusted to the dim light of the early dawn. Why had he been dreaming about that old incident?

He sat up, rubbing his face blearily. It had felt much more real than a dream should, much more accurate in every detail. It was like his dreaming mind had fully relived a memory that had long been buried. He'd all but forgotten about that encounter in the marketplace. Now that he thought about it, that was the first time he'd begun to understand that he and his family had to be careful of how people saw them. It had become something he lived by, like the rest of the power-wielding nobles, and it was the reason for his current frustration.

But he didn't think that was why his mind had chosen to pull that memory up from the depths of his awareness. There was something else, something pulling at his mind, some threads trying to connect. He groaned. It was going to niggle at him until he figured it out, just like the many mysteries of

Vazula were niggling at him while he was being prevented from continuing his exploration of the island.

Drawn like water down a whirlpool, his thoughts flowed without resistance back to the island. For a moment he was distracted from his dream, reliving the encounter by the lagoon.

He gasped. The lagoon!

That was the connection he was missing. He had told Reka he couldn't sense any magic lingering there after his encounter with the girl, but when he'd tried again, he had felt something. It was different from the magic he felt from his family, but it had seemed familiar somehow. He remembered being unable to put his finger on it at the time.

He realized now that the memory it had triggered was that of the incident in the marketplace when he was a young child. His unconscious mind had connected for him the threads that his waking thoughts couldn't quite bring together.

He frowned, his thoughts swirling wildly at the introduction of yet another mystery.

What did it mean? How was he ever going to find answers to any of the questions that kept appearing with every layer he peeled back?

He had to get back to that island.

CHAPTER FIFTEEN

Merletta raced through the kelp forest with less than her usual caution, her thoughts still in a whirl. She had barely stopped for breath since leaving the lagoon, and her heart was beating wildly.

What had she just seen? Who was he? *What* was he?

She swam into the heart of Tilssted without thinking, forgetting in her distraction that she lived in the Center now. By the time she came to herself, she realized she had made her way to a corner of the city where she often used to hide when she wanted to escape the home for a while, but didn't think she'd be able to get past the barrier.

She settled against the wall of the natural cavern, closing her eyes and letting her breathing slow. She needed to think through what had just happened, without any prying eyes watching her.

What she'd seen was impossible. She shook her head, trying to clear it. As impossible as finding land so close to the triple kingdoms.

What kind of creature had she just discovered? Two things were certain: he wasn't a dragon, and he wasn't a simple beast, like a fish or a squid. He had spoken to her! And even if he hadn't...She remembered his eyes, the very depth of them, the way they'd locked on hers, speaking as intelligently as his words...

She shook the thought off, unnerved by her own reaction. Surely it was his kind who had built the structures she'd seen on the...what had he called it? The island. But he'd said he was hoping to meet the people who lived there, so presumably he didn't actually live there himself. So where had he come from?

She strained her memory, searching for the details of the stories the merchildren had told each other at the home. The most popular had been the scary tales of careless merpeople being eaten in one bite by the fierce dragons who apparently lurked on the surface, waiting to snatch up unwary wanderers. But there had been other stories, too. Myths like sea witches who dwelt in the deep ocean, ready to grant wishes.

Casting her mind back, Merletta pulled up a vague memory of another myth, about land-dwellers who were restricted to the land by their form. Creatures similar to mermaids, but without tails, or mermaid intelligence. The legends were that they so envied the merpeople's ability to roam the water freely that they used to gather enough driftwood to make structures, and ride across the surface of the water on them, trying not to fall in, because if they were fully submerged they would die, just as mermaids would die if they dried out.

Merletta couldn't remember much detail of these tales. She had heard them only once or twice, many years ago. She had always been less interested in the make believe, and more interested in the secrets of their own history. But she had an excellent memory, she reminded herself. She screwed her eyes shut more tightly in her effort to remember what these land-dwellers had been called.

Humans!

Her eyes sprang open, satisfied that she had found the word. The land-dwellers from the myths were called humans.

She shook her head again, slowly this time, still too stunned to fully believe what she'd seen. It seemed humans weren't a myth after all. They were real, and they were *close*. And they were more like mermaids in both form and intelligence than the stories had claimed.

It was almost too much to take in. She had thought that in finding the land, she'd made a big discovery. But it was nothing to what she'd seen today. Her initial shock and panic began to ebb, excitement taking their place.

There were creatures of intelligence living on the surface of the land! Creatures capable of speech, and of building houses. They might be restricted from entering the water, but they could roam the land at will. If merpeople could cooperate with these humans, both groups would have twice the reach they'd had before. Who knew what they could discover, what new and better ways of doing things could be found with this extra source of information?

She pulled the round, brown object from her satchel. This item alone had a myriad of possible uses. She ran a hand over the rough, sturdy surface. Perhaps it could be cut in half, and used as a covering, instead of shells. Or fashioned into a bowl. And it might even be a new source of food. With the triple kingdoms expanding too rapidly for their infrastructure, there was always more demand than there were resources to meet it. No one knew that better than an orphan from Tilssted.

She sat in the cavern for a long time, wrestling with her thoughts. A lifetime of sneaking around, of disproportionate punishments and undeserved snubs, had created an instinct of secrecy in her. The first thought in her mind was definitely that she shouldn't tell anyone what she'd seen. Who knew what the repercussions would be for her if those at the Center found out about her frequent unsanctioned trips to the surface?

But there were greater factors to be considered. She struggled with herself, pushing her own fear of consequences down in favor of what the triple kingdoms could gain from this discovery. She would have to face whatever punishment she might be given. It would be worth it for the merpeople of all three kingdoms to have such an opportunity. Perhaps in time her misdemeanor would be forgiven when everyone saw the full possibilities of this discovery. Besides, if the legends were true, and humans couldn't fully dive below the water, then it wasn't as though they were any threat to merpeople.

For a moment Merletta was distracted from her resolution, lost in the memory of the human she'd seen on the island. His eyes hadn't been dark like hers, but a dusky blue, like the sky after a spring storm. And they had seemed gentle. She had fled from him in her shock, but considering the matter now, in the safety of the triple kingdoms, she didn't actually believe he was dangerous. There had been nothing threatening about him.

She was suddenly overwhelmed by an illogical desire to return to the island then and there, to see him again, and find out who he was and what he knew. But she shook it off. She had more pressing things to consider. Like how she could communicate her discovery in a way that it was most likely to be believed and least likely to get her thrown from the training program.

She had decided on an approach by the time she arrived at class the following morning with her fellow trainees. She had barely been able to sleep the night before, too nervous and excited to let the gentle rocking motion of her hammock lull her into calm. The other trainees seemed to be in good spirits, chatting about what they'd done on their day off. It seemed that most of them had visited their families, as Instructor Wivell had predicted.

"How about you, Merletta? What did you do on your rest day?"

Merletta turned, instantly wary. But it was Sage who had spoken, and the other mermaid's face showed neither suspicion nor hostility. She was even giving Merletta a tentative smile.

"I, uh..." She searched her mind for something she could say that was true, but not dangerous. "I went back to Tilssted for a little while."

Sage nodded, her expression still friendly, if a little awkward. "Nice that you got a chance to visit your fa—friends."

Merletta held back a smile at Sage's slight flush, certain that the other mermaid was chastising herself for starting to say the word "family". There was no need for her discomfort. Merletta wasn't sensitive about being an orphan. She'd had her whole life to get used to the idea.

She glanced around the group, noticing with surprise that the rest of the trainees had been listening to the exchange, a couple of them even doing so without hostility on their faces.

When her eyes passed to Emil, he nodded gravely. "Good morning, Merletta."

"Good morning, Emil," she responded, a little stunned.

It took her a moment to identify why his greeting seemed so significant. She suddenly realized she wasn't sure she'd ever heard the young merman—or any of the trainees—actually address her by name before. But Sage and Emil had both just done so, and even Oliver wasn't glaring at her. Ileana still was, of course, and Jacobi was ignoring her altogether, but it was still a huge improvement.

She searched her thoughts, trying to identify the cause of this change, and she decided it must have been Agner's revelations. Apparently the information of her excellent test results had earned her some measure of respect. She sat a little straighter in her seat, a flash of pride passing over her. Unlike the rest of the group, she had earned her place here without the advantage of help from anyone.

Instructor Ibsen drifted into the room soon after, and Merletta's momentary satisfaction slid away. She swallowed nervously. It was unfortunate that the history instructor was the least friendly, because his class was the most obvious opportunity to lead into her revelations. She ran a hand over her satchel, reassuring herself that she'd remembered to bring the hard round plant for demonstration.

She had decided not to interrupt, but to wait until he offered the chance for questions. Being Ibsen, it was some way into the class before the opportunity arose. Ibsen invited questions, and Jacobi, her fellow first year, raised a hand.

"Yes, Jacobi?" the instructor said, nodding invitingly to the trainee.

"You said that the instructors fall within the training department of the Center rather than the record holder department. Are they the same thing as the educators?"

"Good question," nodded Ibsen. "They are not exactly the same. The educators also fall within the training department, but their role is to work with the public. The instructors are a separate discipline who conduct training and education within the Center. They are drawn from all disciplines, and generally serve only a term as instructors. For example, when Emil is a junior record holder," he nodded to the nineteen-year-old, "he will also answer to Instructor Wivell—the chief instructor. That is because part of his role as a junior record holder will be to help with training others."

Jacobi nodded, his question answered, and Ibsen glanced at the rest of the group. "Any other questions?"

Merletta cleared her throat. "I have a question."

Instructor Ibsen turned to her, his eyebrows already drawing together in disapproval, and his tone anything but encouraging. "Oh?"

Merletta sighed internally. He hadn't even heard her question, and he was already angry with her. Out of the corner of her eye she saw Sage looking between Jacobi and Merletta, but she didn't allow herself to become distracted.

"You said last week that it's too dangerous for merpeople to live anywhere near land, because of the dragons."

"I meant," said Ibsen, in a long-suffering voice, "questions about the establishment of the Center, which we were discussing." He turned away, as if dismissing the topic, but Merletta had nerved herself up for this, and she wasn't going to give up easily.

"I know, sir, but I was wondering whether it's possible that there could be benefits of living near land that might outweigh the risks. For example, surely there are resources that appear on land that we don't find in the ocean, that we could use for materials, for tools, maybe even for food!"

"I can assure you that any potential benefits *do not* outweigh the risks," Ibsen said, his tone bored.

"But what if the risks have been exaggerated?" Merletta pushed, shifting forward in her seat. Her hand strayed toward her satchel. "Wouldn't it be worth at least considering what we might find? Perhaps we could discover a way to—"

"Enough." Ibsen cut her off, his voice dismissive. "Others more qualified than you have weighed the risks and the benefits, and we are only safe if we stay within our own borders."

"But are we safe if we're running out of space, running out of food, always struggling for enough resources?" Merletta argued, her frustration rising at the familiar non-answer.

"I said, enough." Ibsen's voice had taken on a deadly calm that did little to hide his growing anger.

Merletta held back a grunt of frustration. She was only

trying to help the triple kingdoms—that was her only reason for raising the matter. Was his prejudice against her background really so strong that he wasn't even willing to consider something that might benefit everyone?

She drew in a deep swirl of water, collecting herself. She had braced herself for personal consequences—she still had to try.

"What if there are land-dwellers—other than dragons," she hastened to add, "who could talk to us, tell us things we don't know, help us expand our capabilities? How will we know if we don't—"

"What part of 'enough' didn't you understand?" Ibsen growled, and Merletta fell silent, alarmed by the sudden fury in his eyes.

"Land-dwellers?" muttered Jacobi in an audible aside to Ileana. He gave a slight snicker, apparently oblivious to the deadly edge to Ibsen's demeanor. "Is she talking about humans and those types of myths?"

Merletta's eyes flicked to the duo, her expression resentful, but she was surprised by what she saw. Jacobi looked smug and condescending as he made fun of the slum-dweller who believed in bedtime stories. But for once Ileana wasn't joining in with his mocking. She was avoiding his gaze, looking at Ibsen with a carefully blank expression. Her eyes darted to Merletta, then quickly away when she saw that Merletta was watching her. Her face was devoid of its usual glare, her expression remaining unnaturally empty.

Merletta's forehead creased, confused by the other mermaid's manner as she followed her gaze back to the instructor.

"As I said," Ibsen emphasized, "I was inviting questions on the content of today's lesson. We were not discussing the dangers of the land. That is subject matter far more advanced than your level of study."

Merletta opened her mouth to protest, but a sudden thought made her pause. She closed it, watching the instructor thoughtfully. He seemed to take her silence as acceptance, and continued the lesson, speaking briskly.

Merletta stole a glance at the other trainees. Emil was as unexpressive as ever, and Oliver looked no different from usual. Sage, however, looked a little confused, and while Jacobi still wore a smirk, Ileana showed no sign of her usual enjoyment of Merletta being chastised. She was still unnaturally expressionless.

Merletta looked from them to Ibsen—who was speaking casually but still looked angry to her eye—and her suspicion hardened to certainty.

They know.

Her head whirled at the realization. *All that talk of it being more advanced than my level...the instructors know about humans.* Her gaze passed from the confusion of Sage—a second year—to the uncharacteristic demeanor of Ileana—a third year. *And so do the older students. They've been taught about them.*

As if the discovery that humans were real wasn't enough of a shock, now she had to come to terms with the fact that their existence was being actively concealed from the population by those whose job it was to educate them. But why? Why were they keeping it a secret? They must have their reasons—perhaps they genuinely believed it was too dangerous for everyone to know. Perhaps humans were a threat in ways Merletta didn't understand.

But thinking of the man she'd seen on the island, it was hard to believe it.

Besides, she thought angrily, not even pretending to listen to the lesson anymore, even if they were hiding it from the public, why were they hiding it from the younger trainees? She thought back to what Ibsen had said, and she scowled as she realized the reason. In her case at least, the instructor was surely hoping she'd fail her next test, and never advance to the level where she would be taught such things. They obviously didn't want drop outs to have that information.

The thought was sobering enough to pull her from her anger. This was more than a petty vendetta against someone from Tilssted. This was organized deception, and it made her question everything. It also made her extremely glad that she'd exercised some caution at least, and hadn't blurted out to the class that she'd seen a human herself. Who knew what that would have led to? She was glad not to find out.

One thing was certain. She would have to be more careful than ever.

Merletta tried to pay attention to the rest of the class, realizing that the history and hierarchy of the Center was probably valuable information for her survival within it. But her thoughts were too chaotic to focus for long on anything. And knowing that the instructor, with the knowledge of at least two of the other trainees, was intentionally providing false information to the group, made it hard to take anything he said seriously.

When the class ended, and the trainees began to drift out of the room and toward lunch, Merletta was still so distracted that she reached the open street before she realized she wasn't alone. She turned to Sage, surprised to see the other mermaid keeping pace with her. The rest had all gone on some distance ahead.

Merletta waited, watching the coral-tailed girl with wary eyes. Who could tell what Sage might know that Merletta didn't? Perhaps Merletta's questions to Ibsen had revealed things to the older student that she hadn't intended to reveal.

"Merletta, I, uh..." Sage cleared her throat, obviously struggling to find the words. "I just wanted to say that I thought that was...you know, harsh."

Merletta came to a stop, staring at the other girl in surprise.

"I just wanted you to know," Sage glanced around to make sure they were alone before rushing on, "it's not always like that. I mean, it wasn't like that for the rest of us, as first years. Instructor Ibsen is never exactly friendly, but we're usually allowed to...to ask questions."

Sage fell silent, and Merletta continued to stare at her.

"Why are you telling me this?"

Sage shrugged uncomfortably. "I just...I just didn't think it was fair," she said. "The difference. I don't really understand it."

Really? Merletta wanted to retort. *You weren't exactly falling all over yourself to welcome the new trainee from Tilssted.* She refrained, though, interested to hear what else Sage might have to say. She remembered the way the other mermaid had looked between Merletta and her fellow first year during the class. It was heartening to discover that Sage had not only noticed the vast difference in Ibsen's treatment of Jacobi and Merletta, but had been made uncomfortable by it.

Sage's next words made her glad she hadn't made a snippy reply. The older girl clearly knew what Merletta must be thinking.

"I also wanted to say I'm sorry that none of us have been very welcoming."

Merletta observed her for a moment, noting the flush on the other mermaid's cheeks. It wouldn't be the first time someone had tried to use kindness as a trap, but Sage certainly seemed sincere.

"Thank you," Merletta said at last. "I appreciate it."

Sage nodded awkwardly, and the two of them began swimming again, heading toward the dining hall.

"Do you really think there could be resources on land that we could use?" Sage asked, her tone more natural again. "That there could be intelligent creatures?"

Merletta shrugged, keeping her voice casual. "Who knows? Anything is worth considering, isn't it?"

Sage had never been hostile, and had just shown her more kindness than anyone else at the Center, but she was still far from what Merletta would consider a friend. She had no intention of trusting the other trainee with her secrets.

Still, she thought, as Sage voluntarily sat next to her at lunch, friend or not, it was certainly nice not to be surrounded by enemies.

The other mermaid was still chatting with Merletta in a friendly way when they reached their sleeping quarters. The room was empty but for them, and Merletta found herself speaking more freely than she had since arriving at the Center. She was entertaining Sage with a description of her first carer—an eccentric mermaid who had liked to adorn her hair with live sea snails—as she sank into her hammock. She was just nestling her tail between the hammock's folds when she felt a horrifyingly familiar touch on her scales.

She surged out of the hammock with a scream that brought Sage tumbling out of her own sleeping area. Merletta backed away, her eyes wide with fear as the jellyfish emerged into sight, its diaphanous white body glowing faintly in the darkness.

"What's wrong?" Sage asked urgently, her eyes passing from Merletta's terrified expression to the intruder now drifting away across the room. The other mermaid's expression softened. "Oh, I forgot. You're afraid of jellyfish, aren't you?"

"So should you be!" protested Merletta. "That's a box jellyfish! Its venom is excruciatingly painful, and more often than not, fatal!"

Sage put a hand to her mouth. "Are you sure?"

"Of course I'm sure," said Merletta shakily. "How did it get in here? No type of venomous jellyfish should even be inside the triple kingdoms, let alone in someone's hammock!"

Sage raised one shoulder helplessly. "I just assumed it had gotten loose from one of the lanterns. It does happen sometimes."

Merletta gave her head a vehement shake. "They don't use box jellyfish in the lanterns," she said. A shudder ran over her frame. "Trust me, I've been paying attention."

"Oh my." The lazy voice from the doorway made both girls turn. "How did a jellyfish get into our sleeping quarters?"

Merletta glared at Ileana, her suspicions instantly raised. One hand balled into a fist as she started forward. "Is this your idea of a funny prank?" she hissed. "That could have killed me."

Ileana's expression was cold as she stared Merletta down. "And what a tragedy that would be."

"Ileana," said Sage sharply, her forehead creasing. "Do you know anything about this?"

Ileana raised an eyebrow. "Of course not," she said haughtily. "What are you suggesting? It's hardly the first time a jellyfish has gotten loose from one of the lanterns."

Sage glanced at Merletta, her expression uncertain. "That's what I thought, too."

Merletta didn't bother reiterating what she knew to be true. Even if she could convince Sage, there was nothing the other girl could do about Merletta's suspicions. She considered reporting the incident to one of the instructors, but quickly dismissed the idea. She had no proof of foul play, and they weren't exactly eager to assist her.

She remained silent, letting Sage take the lead in calling the appropriate person to remove the dangerous visitor. Her face remained impassive, for Ileana's benefit, but inside she felt afraid and alone. She'd put up with this type of pettiness all her life, but these pranks went beyond anything she'd experienced at the home.

She had been wary of every bite she took since the pufferfish incident. Now she couldn't even sleep without fear.

The rest of the week passed painfully slowly, her nerves on high alert. Her lessons with both Ibsen and Wivell were more draining than interesting, since Merletta couldn't help receiving everything they said with suspicion. The cheerful energy of Agner, even with his brutal disregard for how bruised she always became during training, made for a nice change of pace during the last two days.

But it was all just filling in time, counting down until she was free.

Bruised or not, she was up before the sun on the next rest day. After several uneventful days, she was no longer quite so much on edge. But she was still eager to get out of the Center for a while. Plus, now that she knew she couldn't rely on what her instructors were telling her—much as she'd never had confidence in anything the charity home head had told her after exposing the older mermaid's lie about drying out—she was more determined than ever to find her own answers.

She covered the distance to the island even more quickly this time. In spite of her recent scare, she was focused enough on her goal to swim within a couple fathoms of a bloom of jellyfish rather than go a longer way around. When the land finally appeared before her, she was overcome by a jittery feeling of anticipation. Would the human be there again? A small cowardly part of her was hoping he wouldn't be, and she would be off the hook. But mostly, she was sure of her course.

Because she'd decided that it was time to be bold in finding answers. This time, if he approached her, she wasn't going to flee.

CHAPTER SIXTEEN

Heath's spirits lifted as he saw the island appear. It was worth every minute of the uncomfortable flight to be approaching Vazula again.

He had left before dawn and fully intended to be gone all day. It probably wouldn't go far toward convincing his father that he'd been right to allow Heath to once again roam free with his dragon friend. But in that moment, Heath didn't care. Valoria seemed distant and unimportant. It was the island that occupied his every thought.

Would the girl be there?

Heath started when he felt the ripple of strange power pass over his body just as they began to descend. He'd forgotten to ask Reka about it last time, distracted by his first glimpse of Vazula.

"Did you feel that power?" he asked, as soon as the dragon set him down on the sand. "I felt it last time, too."

"Of course," said Reka simply. "It is curious, is it not? Most telling."

"Telling how?" Heath asked impatiently. "Do you know what it is, then?"

"Don't you?" Reka asked, clearly surprised. He considered his human companion. "But then, I suppose you've never entered a dragon realm before, have you?"

"Dragon realm?" Heath repeated, startled. Whatever he'd expected, it hadn't been that. "What do you mean?"

"I mean that the power we just felt indicates a magical barrier, such as that which surrounds Wyvern Islands, where my colony lives. I understand there is a similar one around Vasilisa, the home of the colony within Kyona's borders. It is generally not possible for humans to cross it." Reka paused. "Not on their own, in any event. Any human could enter if I were carrying them, I imagine. But the fact that you can sense the barrier is evidence of the magic in your blood."

"In my bloodline, at least," Heath amended.

Reka shook his head in silent disagreement, but didn't enter on the disputed topic of Heath's power, or lack of it. Heath was glad. He had other things to think about.

"That's probably why the sea is impassable to ships," he mused.

"Most likely," Reka agreed placidly.

Heath considered the matter for a moment, his eyes straying to the jungle that started where the beach ended. "So what does that mean?" he asked. "The fact that Vazula has a magical barrier around it?"

Reka blinked at him. "Have I not just answered that question? It means that humans cannot cross it, not without a dragon, or magic of their own."

"Yes, I got that," said Heath. "I mean, why is it there? How did it get there?"

"If that is what you meant, then why was it not what you asked?" Reka complained. "I begin to understand why my father always told me that humans are poor communicators themselves, yet absurdly quick to be frustrated with the communication of dragons."

"Never mind that," said Heath quickly. He had no desire to hear another long-winded recital of all the lessons Reka's father had imparted to his son about humans, gleaned primarily from his interactions with Heath's grandparents. "It doesn't matter how the barrier got here. Let's see if we can find the gi—the people who live here."

"It might not matter to you," Reka retorted, "but it is a matter of great interest to me to know what became of the dragons who lived here."

"The dragons who...what?" Heath paused in the act of stepping over a large rock. "Okay, I'm totally lost."

"What do you mean?" Reka asked, his head tilted to the side as his gaze passed from Heath to the jungle ahead of him. "How can you be lost? We haven't even left the beach yet."

"No, Reka, I meant—" Heath cut himself off, drawing a deep breath and willing himself to be patient. He had waited a week to look for the girl and her people again. Another few minutes wouldn't make a difference.

"You think the magic barrier means that dragons once lived here?" he tried again.

"I don't think anything of the kind," said Reka, sounding slightly offended. "I know that dragons lived here, and I didn't need the barrier to tell me that. The evidence of their presence was obvious to my senses when we were here last time, just as it was indisputably clear that they are no longer here. The question raised by the barrier is why they didn't remove it when they left, and by extension, what caused them to leave."

Heath stared at his friend. "You could tell last time that dragons once lived here?"

"Certainly," said Reka calmly, his expression a trifle smug. "You couldn't?"

Heath closed his eyes, shaking his head slightly. Reka's father might think himself an expert on humans, but Heath had heard the tales, too. And he was starting to understand what his grandmother had meant when she told him once that there was little logic to be found in what information dragons did and didn't consider necessary to share.

"No," he said aloud. "I couldn't." He frowned slightly. "Are you sure what you felt wasn't just the same magic that hung around the girl I saw?"

"Positive," said Reka.

"I wonder what did happen to the dragons," said Heath, looking at the ruins visible from where he stood. "I wonder if it was the same thing that happened to the humans."

"Unlikely," said Reka with maddening superiority. "Humans are easily displaced or disposed of. It would take considerably more to dislodge a colony of dragons. I conclude that the dragons must have left by their own choice."

Heath rolled his eyes. "Of course you do." He hoisted his rucksack up on his shoulder. "Enough chitchat. Let's go."

He led the way up the beach, the dragon loping unhurriedly behind him. For lack of a better place to start, Heath headed for the lagoon again. Reka lingered behind to sniff curiously at a ruined archway, so Heath was once again alone when he pushed his way through the trees and emerged at the edge of the inlet. His eyes scanned the area eagerly, and he froze where he stood.

She was actually there.

Heath blinked a few times to make sure he wasn't hallucinating. As much as he had come here looking for her, the idea that she would just be floating there waiting for him was too absurd for him to actually believe it.

And yet, there she was.

It was undoubtedly the same girl. Her wild, tangled hair and the restlessness in her dark eyes were unmistakable. He'd never seen anyone quite like her.

Their eyes locked once again, and he had to fight his first impulse. Running toward her and shouting for her not to disappear again would probably have the opposite effect. Instead he stepped forward tentatively, extending a hand, palm open, in a gesture of peace.

"Please, don't leave," he said carefully. "I'm not going to hurt you."

"Yes, I did lose my head a little last time, didn't I?" she responded frankly.

Heath blinked, his hand dropping to his side.

"I don't usually startle so easily," she continued, her words clear despite an unfamiliar accent. "I've just never seen a creature like you before, and it rattled me more than I care to admit." She swam closer to the shore, her strokes sure and confident. "The truth is," she said matter-of-factly, "I didn't actually think you existed until I saw you."

"I, uh...what?" Heath said stupidly. This encounter was not going the way he had expected.

"But I'm very glad you came back. I wanted another chance, and I have so many questions. My name is Merletta, by the way."

"I'm...Heath," Heath said. He would have liked to have thought of something wittier to say, but his mind was still blank.

"Greetings, Heath," she said. Her tone was stilted with the awkwardness of someone who was unused to formality, but felt the need to attempt it. As a result of his noble rank, Heath had often come across such demeanor in those of the poorer classes.

For a moment they just regarded each other in silence, then she shook her head slightly, her posture relaxing into something much more natural.

"Sorry," she said, with a slight chuckle. "It's a bit awkward, isn't it? Trying to have a conversation with you up there and me in here."

"Uh, a little," said Heath, a small smile breaking through his stupefaction. He had wondered why she was still in the water, but hadn't liked to mention it. His eyes flicked down to her torso, then quickly back to her face. She was only wearing the large shells again.

The girl—Merletta—seemed to take in his slight flush, because she tilted her head to the side curiously. It only made his face grow hotter. He had worried that he'd again interrupted her in an attempt to wash, but he was a little reassured by her obvious confusion as to his reaction. Most likely her attire was normal according to the customs of her people, and she had no idea why it seemed so strange to him.

Mercifully, Merletta chose not to comment on the silent interaction. "I don't mind if you don't," she said instead, and it took Heath a moment to realize she was talking about her earlier comment regarding being in the water. "I suppose we'll have to just work with it, because it's not like I'll be coming out there, is it? And I'm guessing you're not coming in here anytime soon."

"You...you want me to go into the water?" Heath asked, distracted from his embarrassment.

"What?" Merletta seemed bizarrely startled by the question. "No, of course not! I don't mean you any harm."

Heath opened his mouth, then closed it again, more confused than ever. They might both be speaking the language of men, but she may as well be using dragon speech for all the sense her comments made.

"Um...thank you?" he said, his tone making it into a question.

She clearly realized he was confused, and her brows drew together as her eyes found his. For a long moment their eyes were locked, foreheads furrowed as each tried to read the other.

Even as his heart beat more quickly, Heath found his mind relaxing. Merletta was throwing him like no one he'd ever met before, but at the same time, there was something about her that set him at ease. He took an unconscious step forward across the rocks, bringing him closer to the water's edge. That something in her eyes was still there, that restless energy that made him think they would understand each other, if given the chance.

"How did you get here?" she asked abruptly. "Where did you come from? You don't live on this land, do you?"

"No, I don't live here," Heath said, shaking his head slightly and coming out of the trance he'd been in. "And actually..." he hesitated, "I flew here."

Merletta's eyes were suddenly as round as coins. "You can fly?" she breathed. She'd been leaning toward him, her hands on the rocks, and she pulled herself up so she was fully supported on her arms, the movement seeming unconscious.

"Well, not me personally, obviously," Heath chuckled, unable to help his eyes straying down her form as more of her emerged from the water. "My friend Reka agreed to—DRAGON'S FLAME!"

The exclamation broke from him involuntarily as he leaped backward, his eyes riveted on the area where Merletta's hips should be. His gaze passed from the unnerving sight of her warm brown skin melding into shiny purple scales over to the enormous gold-tipped fins protruding from the water off to one side.

For several stunned seconds he just stared, feeling his eyes growing wider with each heartbeat. Then his gaze passed to her face. She looked confused, and wary. She was still up on her arms, but was leaning slightly back toward the water, as though ready to flee.

"You have a tail," Heath said stupidly. "You have...an actual tail."

"Yes," she said slowly. "Naturally."

"It's just...I don't..." Heath tried to pull himself together, moving back toward her with an effort. His thoughts were swirling wildly, but underneath it all, he still knew that he didn't want her to run away. Especially not now he had a whole host of new questions. "I don't have one of those," he said, with a weak attempt at a smile.

"Of course not," said Merletta, half-laughing. "You're a human." She paused, her face growing uncertain again. "Aren't you?"

"Yes," said Heath, a hysterical laugh threatening to bubble up out of him. He passed a hand quickly over his face, drawing a deep breath when the vision didn't disappear. "Sorry," he said. "I've just never had to clarify that to anyone before. But yes, I am a human. And are you...are you a mermaid?"

"That's right," said Merletta, nodding. Her eyes passed over his face, their expression fascinated. "You didn't know that? What did you think I was?"

"I thought you were like me," said Heath frankly, and something in Merletta's eyes warmed. He gave a small smile, crouching down by the water's edge. How was it possible for her to seem so...human?

"You see," he explained, "I didn't know mermaids were real. They're just a myth where I come from. An ancient legend that no one has ever actually believed. Or so I thought."

Merletta nodded eagerly, pulling herself even further toward him in response to his movement. She was propped on her elbows now, just the lower half of her tail dangling in the water. Heath's fascinated eyes followed the movement of her tail, as it gently swished back and forth. It was probably rude to stare at it, but he couldn't help himself. It was less terrifying and more beautiful by the second, strangely. The scales seemed to change as the tail moved, from purple to blue to green and back again. And all of it sparkled in the sunshine in a way he was certain no fish tail ever had.

"That's exactly what I thought about humans," Merletta was saying, her tone expressing the fascination he felt. "That you were just a myth, something from a bedtime story. My people don't even know about this land, let alone its inhabitants. But when I saw the structures on the shore, I knew *something* must have built it." She lifted one hand, brushing her long, dark hair back over her shoulder in a tangled mess. "But even in the craziest myths, I never heard anything about humans being able to fly!"

"Oh, no," Heath hastened to clarify, laughing apologetically. "Humans can't fly. When I said I flew here, I meant—"

But he cut himself off at the sound of her sharp gasp. He had clearly lost the mermaid's attention, her eyes now fixed on something over his shoulder, and an expression of pure terror on her face.

CHAPTER SEVENTEEN

For an instant, Merletta remained frozen, her arms locked in place as her blood thundered in her ears.

A dragon.

Was this it? Was she about to die? Merletta's paralysis suddenly lifted, her arms jerking uncontrollably as she scrambled to move. But she forgot how far she'd inched up the rocks in her eagerness to connect with the human—Heath—and discover all the answers he could provide. She wasn't used to being so far out of the water, and her fear made her clumsy. Instead of pushing back into the water, she somehow managed to flip her tail up onto the rocks with the rest of her.

A horrible pain seized her, and she felt her whole body spasm. Her agonized gaze passed from the dragon to her own form, and she realized with a jolt of horror that only the very tip of one fin was still in the water. Panic seized her, and her hands scrabbled frantically at the rocks in a frenzied attempt to pull herself back into the ocean. She was breathing too fast, unable to properly take in air, as a hot, dry sensation rushed over her body, starting from her fins and moving up her tail.

She reached the water at last, throwing herself in with a splash that was anything but graceful. She could hear Heath shouting to her from above the surface, but she kept her head under for a long moment, taking in deep steadying mouthfuls of water as the painful prickling feeling subsided. She twisted in the water, running a hand down her tail to reassure herself that she was in one piece.

So that was what drying out felt like.

It was just as painful as she'd imagined. Merletta shuddered. That had been far too close. She'd had some narrow escapes in her adventures outside the barrier, but she'd never been that close to death before. And it was self-inflicted, the result of a mere moment of distraction. She'd had a good reason, perhaps, but even the fear of the dragon paled in comparison to the terror that had just passed through her entire being.

The dragon.

Merletta's eyes darted upward. She could see the beast—it was now close behind Heath, its huge form skulking over him. Her instincts told her to flee deeper into the water, but from all she'd been told, that would be useless. Dragons were much too fast, below water as well as above it, for her to be able to outswim an attack.

Of course, it was possible that what she'd been told wasn't true. But then, she'd thought that the tales of land always being infested by dragons must be an exaggeration. Apparently some of the warnings were real.

And yet...the beast had made no move to attack her, even when she was so distracted that she would have been embarrassingly easy to pick off.

Merletta waited until her heart rate had slowed slightly, then re-emerged above the surface. Heath was at the lagoon's edge now, on his hands and knees as he watched her below the water. Merletta had assumed that the plants surrounding this body of water would make it hard to see in from above, but his gaze was latched on her as she rose, in a way that told her he'd been watching her the whole time.

"Are you all right?" he asked the moment her head cleared the surface. His concern was evident in every line of his face. "What happened? You looked like you were having a seizure or something."

Merletta tore her eyes from the dragon with difficulty, meeting Heath's gaze. "I almost dried out," she said, a shudder passing over her. "I can't believe I was so incredibly careless."

Her eyes darted back to the dragon, who was watching them silently, his head cocked to one side as he listened to their conversation. The whole situation was beyond bizarre. Was she really chatting casually with a human, ignoring the fact that a deadly dragon hovered nearby? Perhaps it was all an unusually vivid dream.

"Dried out?" Heath repeated, his brows drawing together in confusion. "What do you mean?"

"Oh, I forgot you don't know anything about mermaids," Merletta said distractedly. "We can't get all the way out of the water." Heath still looked confused, so she clarified. "Or we die."

His eyes grew wide, the concern turning to open alarm. "Are you safe now?" His gaze passed over her, bobbing in the water with her chest above the surface. "Do you need to go deeper?" He stood up, splashing into the shallows. "Don't come closer—I can come to you instead."

"It's all right," Merletta said, her face stretching in a smile that wasn't quite natural, thanks to the adrenaline still coursing through her body. "This is safe. Besides, you need to be careful. Don't you have the same risk, but you know, opposite?"

Heath shook his head. "I can fully submerge myself without dying. I just have to come up for air very frequently."

"Huh." Merletta couldn't help but feel a little disgruntled. "Seems unfair."

She caught a spark of humor in Heath's eyes, but her attention passed to the beast behind him.

"Ah, yes," said Heath, following her gaze. "Is that what frightened you in the first place? Sorry about that. Reka, this is Merletta. She's a...a mermaid." He stumbled slightly over the word. "And this is Rekavidur. He's a dragon."

"I know what it is," said Merletta warily. The dragon so far had remained silent. "And I'm not interested in its name so much as I'm interested in knowing whether it's going to eat me."

"Eat you?" repeated Heath, startled. "Of course not!"

"Dragons don't eat humans," said the dragon placidly. His voice was gravelly but deep, like the muffled scrape of stone grinding on stone at the bottom of the ocean.

"Well, I'm not human," Merletta reasoned, trying to keep her gaze on the dragon's face. Her eyes kept being drawn back to its enormous talons, resting on a rock just at the water's edge.

"Aren't you?" the dragon asked, its tone thoughtful. "You seem like a human to me."

"Seems like a—? Reka," cut in Heath, exasperated. "She has a *tail*."

"Yes, except for that part, of course," conceded the dragon, as calmly as ever.

Heath rolled his eyes. "Small detail," he muttered.

"So dragons don't hunt mermaids?" Merletta asked cautiously.

"Hunt them?" the dragon replied, his tone surprised. "Speaking for myself, I'd never even heard of such a creature before now." He considered the matter for a moment. "But I wouldn't have thought so, in any event. I've never heard of a dragon eating a creature intelligent enough to be capable of speech. Killing, yes," he clarified. "Eating, no."

"Reka is definitely not going to eat you," Heath said firmly. "Or kill you," he hastened to add.

"Is that how you flew here?" Merletta asked, putting the pieces together. "With the dragon?"

"My name is Rekavidur," the dragon said, his tone reproachful. "Your manners are lacking, to refer to me as 'the dragon' after we have been formally introduced."

"My apologies," said Merletta, taken aback by the reproof. "I didn't think a creature such as yourself would have any interest in a proper introduction with me."

"That is understandable," said Rekavidur, inclining his head regally.

Merletta examined the dragon for a moment. He was nothing like she'd expected. Which was in keeping with everything else that had happened that day, really. She looked from him to Heath. "Are you his pet, then?" she asked curiously.

The spark of humor leaped back into Heath's eyes, but it was extinguished a moment later, as the dragon answered for him.

"Yes, in a manner of speaking."

"In a manner of speaking?" Heath repeated, his tone outraged. He glared at Rekavidur, who just gave him a strange kind of rippling shrug. Heath turned to Merletta. "No, I am *not* his pet. We're friends." He shot a glare at the dragon. "And equals."

Rekavidur gave a snort of laughter so pronounced that a tiny spurt of flame actually shot from his mouth, extinguishing immediately in a miniature puff of smoke. Merletta edged backward in the water, her eyes widening slightly.

"Equals," the dragon repeated quietly, chortling to himself.

"You know, I defended you when someone called you my pet recently," Heath told him, clearly disgruntled.

"What?" The dragon's mirth disappeared instantly, and he

puffed himself up to an impressive height. "Who dared to refer to me in such a manner?"

Merletta edged even further back. The creature was majestic, no doubt about it, and he looked incredibly dangerous in his anger.

But Heath just rolled his eyes, evidently not impressed. "Never you mind." He returned his attention to Merletta, pointedly turning his shoulder on Rekavidur. "To return to your original question, yes. Reka agreed to carry me here, which is what I meant when I said I flew. I come from Valoria, a kingdom far to the west of here." His eyes grew curious. "Where do you come from?"

Merletta hesitated for a moment. She was aware that any of her fellow merpeople would see it as an enormous betrayal for her to give any information about their kind to a human, let alone a dragon. Even this conversation would probably be enough to have her expelled from the Center forever.

But she pushed the thought aside recklessly. Why, she couldn't say, but she felt a connection to this Heath that she had rarely felt with other merpeople. She couldn't be sure of course, but she suspected that everything he'd so far told her was the truth, which was more than could be said for anyone in the Center.

"My kingdom is in the depths of the ocean, not far from here," she said. "We call ourselves the triple kingdoms, because we're made up of three small kingdoms, which have merged into one, in a manner of speaking."

"Incredible," Heath murmured. He frowned suddenly. "But you say that no one in your kingdom even knows about this island?" She nodded, and his eyes searched hers. "So you have no idea if anyone still lives here? Or what happened to them if they don't?"

"None whatsoever," said Merletta. "I don't even know what this place is called."

"It's called Vazula," said Heath absently. "This is—was—the island kingdom of Vazula, I'm almost certain."

"Vazula," repeated Merletta. She studied the human's face. "You look disappointed."

"What?" Heath shook himself out of his abstraction. "No, no, I just thought you might know...I was hoping to find out more about the history of this place, to find out if it was possible to co-exist..." He trailed off, smiling at her in a way that set off a strange feeling in her stomach, like she'd eaten old squid. "But that doesn't matter now. Believe me, I'm not disappointed to have met you instead of finding my answers."

She gave him a smile of her own, uncharacteristically shy all of a sudden. "Well, I was hoping to learn something of the inhabitants of this place, too, but I'm certainly not sorry to have encountered you." She looked past him, letting out a huff of frustration. "I wish I could explore properly, but as always I'm blocked."

"Maybe I can help," said Heath brightly. "I can be your eyes up here. What do you want to know?"

Merletta tilted her head to the side as she regarded him. She couldn't help but smile at his enthusiasm. "I want to know who built those structures, for one thing. Do you think it was humans?"

"Oh yes, definitely," Heath nodded. "But I haven't been able to find any sign of them still being here. I searched for hours last time, after I saw you. I assumed you were from a settlement on the island somewhere."

Merletta laughed. "I still can't believe you thought I was a human." She shook her head, her eyes passing slowly over Heath's form. "I certainly didn't mistake you for a merman, not even for an instant." She reached forward, tugging lightly on the strange fabric wrapped around his legs. "What are these coverings? Why do you wear so much over your whole body?"

"Uh..." Heath looked faintly pink, and she observed the changes in his face in fascination.

"I'm sorry," she said. "Should I not have asked that? Is it normal for humans to cover themselves?" She glanced at the dragon. "Rekavidur doesn't seem to be wearing coverings."

"Of course not," said Reka calmly. "Like you, I have scales. Humans do not, and they try to overcompensate for it with their excessive use of clothes."

"That's not quite how I would put it," said Heath dryly. His flush had subsided, and there was a smile in his eyes as he looked back at Merletta. "Yes, it is normal for humans to wear clothes, even in this blasted heat. Mine are simple compared to many people's. And of course you can ask that. You can ask me anything. I'm sure you're as curious about my people as I am about yours." He glanced around, his eyes latching on to a large flat rock nearby. "Come on."

He made his way over to it, sitting on its surface with his legs fully dangling into the water. He didn't seem to mind being wet. Merletta wondered if all humans were like that, or if he was unusual, like her with her love of being on the surface.

"Is that..." Heath gestured to Merletta's shells, trying to sound casual and not quite succeeding. "Is what you're wearing normal for mermaids?"

Merletta followed him over. He had chosen the spot well, as the water was deep enough for her to properly float, even while leaning her elbows on the rock. She looked up into his face, fascinated by the familiarity of his features. If she kept her eyes off the disconcerting legs, he could absolutely have been a merman.

"Yes," she answered belatedly. "Mermen don't have them, of course, but all mermaids wear shells like these." She grimaced.

"Well, not like these, exactly. Mine are also simple. Mermaids like to adorn themselves, and those who can afford it wear very elaborate coverings, among other things." She chuckled to herself. "I saw a mermaid from Skulssted once who had such an enormous rope of pearls in her hair that you could hardly see the hair at all." She shook her head. "But that's Skulssted for you. Pretentious with their wealth a lot of the time." Her tone turned dry. "You can be sure that us beneficiaries weren't exactly strutting around with ropes of pearls."

"Beneficiaries?" Heath repeated curiously.

Merletta looked up, thrown all over again by the sight of his legs—clad in black—still dangling in the water. She'd almost forgotten. He was so easy to talk to, it was hard to believe he was an impossible, mythical creature.

"Oh, that's what we're called," she responded absently. "In the charity home where I grew up. I'm an orphan." She added the explanation matter-of-factly, no particular emotion attached to it, but Heath's eyes instantly softened.

"I'm so sorry," he said. "It must be devastating to lose both of your parents. I would be heartbroken to lose mine."

Merletta blinked, for a moment unsure how to answer. It occurred to her that she couldn't remember anyone ever saying such a thing to her. People from outside the home tended to look down on the orphans, as though their misfortune said something about them and their worthiness. Even Tish, the sweetest mermaid in the kingdoms, had never actually told Merletta that she was sorry her parents had died.

With shame, Merletta realized she'd never said that to Tish, either. She'd never thought of it. Being orphans was just part of who they were, not something they could change, and not something there was any point bemoaning. Those at the home didn't encourage the beneficiaries to seek sympathy over it.

And yet Heath, not only a stranger, but an unfamiliar

species, had gone even further than sympathy. He'd actually put himself in her place, imagining how he would feel to live her experiences. It was an unheard of reaction to her misfortunes, and she found it strangely empowering.

"Thank you," she said at last, her voice quiet. "You have a very kind heart, I think." She shook her head slightly, her voice growing more cheerful. "But it's all I've ever known, so it's not so devastating, really. My parents died when I was an infant. I have no memory of them. The home didn't even know who they were —I have no last name." She looked curiously at Heath. "How about you? You have a family, then?"

He nodded, his expression still subdued, apparently on her behalf. "Yes, my parents are both living, and I have an older sister, Laura, the sweetest person you'll meet. She's twenty-two, and was married about a year ago, so she doesn't live with us any longer. Then there's my brother, Percival, who's twenty." He chuckled to himself. "Perce is a force to be reckoned with." His eyes returned to hers, a humorous light in them. "Then there's me."

Merletta nodded, but before she could answer, the dragon broke in. "I find your magic fascinating."

Merletta started, not having realized how close the huge scaled creature had approached. He was perched on the rocks to one side of her, but he had snaked his long neck toward her, and he was sniffing the air faintly.

"My magic?" she repeated warily. "What do you mean?"

"You're a creature of magic," Rekavidur said simply. "You weren't aware of it?"

"I...I don't think so," Merletta responded hesitantly. She glanced at Heath, whose brow was furrowed in thought. "I mean, I know that our ancestors had an ancient magic that allowed them to create the barrier, but that's long in the past now. None of us have magic that I've ever heard of."

"Curious," said Rekavidur, apparently to himself. He sat back on his haunches, regarding her. "You are telling the truth, or at least, as best you know it."

"Of course she's telling the truth," said Heath defensively, and Merletta raised an eyebrow. She hadn't been offended by the dragon's comment. Dishonesty was so universal in her experience that she couldn't blame Rekavidur for questioning her truthfulness. She was completely unknown to him, after all.

"What was that about a barrier, Merletta?" Heath asked. "Are you talking about the ring of magic that's around this island?"

Merletta shook her head. "No, I'm talking about the barrier around the triple kingdoms. It's not a physical barrier—it's a ward of sorts that keeps dangerous creatures out, and prevents us from detection by..." she glanced at the dragon, "by outsiders." She looked back at Heath. "We're well outside it now. The island's not within it." She grimaced slightly. "The island is most definitely not within it. The truth is, I'm not strictly supposed to be outside the barrier. Only the guards and the hunters usually leave. I have to sneak out." She gestured to the water behind her. "But there's so much to discover—a whole ocean! How could I want to stay confined in one small bubble of it?"

"I know exactly what you mean," said Heath, a familiar light in his eyes. "I feel the same way." He glanced at the dragon. "So does Reka, although he won't admit to being restless. It's what drew us together. His colony encourages exploration even less than my people do."

The dragon didn't respond, still scrutinizing Merletta in silence, apparently trying to identify her supposed magic.

"Is that some kind of satchel?" Heath asked, pointing to the strap over Merletta's shoulder. "It looks like kelp."

"It is kelp," said Merletta, patting it. "It's where I store my treasures." She pulled out the round brown object she'd picked up last time, holding it up to show him. She'd brought it with her, not wanting to leave it at the barracks as potential evidence of her wanderings. "Like this. I'm not sure what it is, but I'm thinking it could have a lot of uses! It smells like it might be edible, and I wonder if it could even be used as a more practical covering than shells."

"It's a coconut," said Heath, taking it from her with a smile.

His fingers brushed hers as he did so, leaving behind a tingling sensation. His skin was as warm as the sun on the sand, nothing like the cold smoothness of merpeople's skin.

"It's the fruit of a tree," Heath continued, and she pulled her attention back to his words. He looked behind him, gesturing. "That tree, see? There are lots up there. They don't grow where I live, but there are other parts of the coast where you can find them." He turned the round object in his hand. "Coconuts have a kind of milk inside them that you can drink, and a part you can eat, as well. And the husk can be useful, too, like you said. But first you have to get into it."

He grinned. "Normally it's a real pain. You have to get a sharp rock, and it can take ages to get it right. But we can cheat." He turned to the dragon, who'd wandered off a little way, sniffing the area of rocks where Merletta had almost dried herself out. "Oi, Reka! Could you help us out, please?"

The dragon reached out absently, slicing the coconut cleanly in half with one talon before returning to his explorations. Heath turned back to Merletta with a grin. He broke off some of the white substance inside, taking a bite out of it before offering the same piece to Merletta.

"Try some."

She reached out a tentative hand to take it. She could still see where his teeth had marked it, and she nibbled a corner from the same place. It was like no flavor she'd ever tasted before. Everything she'd ever eaten was salty and heavy, but this was light, fresh, pleasant. It was delicious. She looked up at Heath, a lightness she'd never felt before sweeping over her, buoying her up in the water.

"What's a tree?" she asked abruptly. "And what's milk?"

Heath smiled, his eyes as warm as his skin as he leaned forward on his rock.

"Where should I begin?"

CHAPTER EIGHTEEN

Heath

The sun was again hanging low in the sky before Heath finally admitted that he needed to head home. If he'd been reluctant to leave last time, after only catching a glimpse of Merletta, it was nothing to how he felt now, after actually speaking with her.

She was a mermaid! An actual mermaid. He'd been talking with her for hours, and yet it still didn't quite feel real. She'd stepped—or rather swum—right out of myth and into his reality, and it was going to take some getting used to.

She'd spent most of the day asking him questions about life on the land, and he'd been only too happy to answer, keen to keep her there and talking for as long as she was willing to stay. But he had so many questions of his own, and it would be maddening not to get the chance to ask them.

"Yes," she said, when he finally admitted that he had to leave. "So do I." She glanced at the position of the sun. "I didn't realize it had gotten so late. I shouldn't really be beyond the barrier after dark." Her forehead creased slightly. "The sharks will be hunting soon."

"Will you be all right?" Heath asked in alarm. "Is it safe for you to travel home alone?"

He cast his eyes out in the direction of the ocean, anxiety rising in him as he pictured Merletta being stalked by a shark. She was still almost a stranger, but somehow the thought of harm coming to her was distressing. Perhaps it was because of what had happened earlier, when she had almost dried herself out, or whatever it was called. Her blind panic had been hard to witness, like an animal thrashing in a snare, knowing the hunter was approaching.

But Merletta just smiled. "Thank you, but I'll be fine. I've been doing this for a long time. I know how to look after myself."

Heath nodded, still uneasy, but sensing it would be a slight on her capability for him to protest further.

"Will I see you again?" he asked instead.

"If you want to," Merletta said simply.

He gave her a friendly smile. "Of course I do. There are about a thousand questions I want to ask you."

Merletta laughed. "I suppose I should give you a turn," she acknowledged. She glanced over her shoulder toward the ocean. "They keep us pretty busy in my training program," she swelled slightly with pride as she said it, and Heath made a mental note to ask her about the program next time, "but I get a rest day once a week. I can come back then."

"I'll be here," Heath promised.

He hid his disappointment. A week felt like a long time to wait. But it might help with his family if his mysterious absences were spaced apart a little.

He twisted around, pulling one leg from the water and resting his elbow on his knee. "I wonder where Reka has gotten to." The dragon had lost interest in their conversation hours before, wandering back toward the ruins.

Heath turned back to Merletta, noting how her eyes followed the change in his posture with fascination. He smiled to himself. It was easy to forget that she was as amazed by his legs as he was by her tail. He'd feel self-conscious about not being more muscled, like Percival, except that he knew Merletta had absolutely no one to compare him to. In her view, he was the epitome of humanity. The thought made him chuckle.

"Will you tell your people about me?" Merletta asked suddenly, a guarded expression in her eyes.

"Do you want me to?" Heath asked.

Merletta shook her head without hesitation. "No, I don't."

"Then I won't," said Heath simply.

"Thank you," said Merletta, still speaking carefully. "I suppose it seems strange, it's just that—"

"You don't have to give me an explanation," Heath cut her off. "I won't expose you if you're not ready to be exposed."

A strange look passed over the mermaid's face. Heath waited curiously, hoping she would share the thought in her mind.

"I think you're telling the truth," she murmured at last, seeming to speak mostly to herself.

"Of course I am," said Heath calmly. He leaned into the elbow that was still resting on his propped up knee. "Merletta, I will never lie to you."

Her expression was impossible to read. "But you'll lie to your own family for my sake, if they ask you where you've been?"

Heath shrugged. "I won't lie. I'll just decline to answer."

Merletta raised an eyebrow. "And they'll accept that?"

"Probably not," Heath acknowledged, with a rueful smile. "But that's my problem to worry about." He glanced back over his shoulder again. "Reka!" he called.

The dragon ambled into sight, and Heath pushed himself to his feet. "Until next week, then, Merletta."

The mermaid was already sliding back into the water, her

expression enigmatic enough to make her look the part of a mythical creature.

"Until next week, Heath."

"Heath? Did you hear me?"

"What?" Heath turned to his brother, emerging from his distraction. "Sorry, Percival, what did you say?"

"I said we're leaving now. Are you sure you're not coming?"

"I'm sure," said Heath impatiently. He glanced at the sky. "If you want to get to Bryford before noon, you'd better leave."

Percival frowned. Heath could see through the open window that a groom had brought his brother's horse around to the front of the manor, but Percival made no move to leave.

"What's up with you, Heath?"

"What do you mean?" Heath asked defensively.

"I mean what's got you so distracted? I'm surprised you don't want to come."

"To an official meeting of the king's nobles?" Heath raised an eyebrow. "I'm surprised you *do* want to go."

"It's not just some meeting," Percival reminded him disapprovingly. "It's an audience to discuss the question of whether restrictions should be placed on power-wielders. You really don't have an opinion on that?"

"Of course I do, but I doubt I'd even be welcome," Heath hedged. "Neither one of us has a real position in court. You're just scraping by because of being the heir. I don't have any such excuse."

Percival gave him a look. "You're not that oblivious, Heath. Don't try to pretend you don't know that plenty of the real persuading will happen outside of the official meetings. I'll be surprised if any of the other power-wielders fail to attend."

"Yes, well, I'm not really one of those, am I?" Heath said vaguely.

"You're part of this family, aren't you?"

The new voice made both brothers turn, and Heath squirmed a little under his father's steady gaze.

"Of course I am, Father," he said.

"Then this affects you as well," the duke said calmly. "Whatever your level of magic."

"I know it does," Heath acknowledged. "I didn't mean that I don't care. But I don't see why I need to be there. It's not like I have any influence with the court."

The duke regarded his youngest son for a long moment, his expression steady. "I have often found," he said at last, "that it is difficult to assess our own influence. We do not have the perspective from within our own skin."

Heath said nothing, not in the mood for platitudes.

"Come on Heath!" Percival said with a scowl. "What if your absence is taken to mean you have no objection to the proposed restrictions?"

"More likely it will be taken to mean that I don't have magic, and I'm therefore not directly involved," Heath said dryly.

"For the record," his father said, cutting off Percival's reply, "I also think it would be wise for you to be present for this event." There was a moment of silence, then the duke sighed. "But I am not going to force you to attend."

Heath lowered his gaze, unable to meet his father's eye. The whole situation was unfortunate, to say the least. If it was any other time, he would have been more than willing to attend this hearing in support of his family. He would have insisted on it, whether it affected him directly or not.

But of course the king had to schedule the discussion for tomorrow. Heath simply couldn't bring himself to miss his rendezvous with Merletta, not for anything. Quite apart from not being sure he could stand to wait another entire week, he wasn't at all confident she would come a second time if he failed to show up as promised. And it wasn't as though he could go looking for her under the ocean, to tell her why he'd been delayed. His family would simply have to manage without him.

And they would manage just fine. He was telling the truth when he said he had no influence. If he went, it would just be for moral support, and the absence of that wouldn't make any real difference. Or so he told himself as he saw them off shortly afterward, trying to push down the guilty feeling threatening to rise within him.

"See you in a few days!" he called to his brother, waving half-heartedly.

Percival didn't respond, just sent him a dark look as he pulled his horse ahead of the carriage carrying their parents. The sight of the carriage made Heath's conscience twinge again. Even his mother was attending, although she certainly had no magic in her blood.

But he refused to dwell on it. He had other things to think about.

"Reka?" he called to the empty air, as soon as he was alone in the courtyard. "How soon can you come? If you're up for it, I'm ready whenever you are."

He turned back toward the house, hurrying to grab his things. He knew that if Reka was so inclined, he could be there within minutes. Merletta wouldn't be returning until the following day, but that didn't mean there was nothing to discover on Vazula.

He had at least three days without his family looking over his shoulder, and he intended to spend every possible minute of it on the island.

∽

"You were here most of yesterday?" Merletta's expression was hard to read.

"That's right," said Heath, watching her face with fascination. She had such expressive eyes. It made him feel inexplicably connected with her emotions, even when he was completely unable to guess her thoughts, as was the case now. "What is it?"

"I don't know..." She swished her tail slightly from one side to the other, in a gesture he was already coming to recognize as her thinking stance. "It's just strange to think of you being so close by, and me not knowing it."

Heath smiled. "I found it strange, too."

"You took long enough to mention it," Merletta said, sounding a little disgruntled.

Heath smirked slightly. "Well, I thought if I showed you what I found, you might be too distracted to answer my questions about mermaids."

"You found something?" Merletta had been floating on her back, her arms behind her head, and the droplets on her skin long since dried by the afternoon sun. But at his words, she instantly straightened, so she was bobbing upright in the water.

"I did." Heath said, still grinning.

He leaned back, reaching across the rocks toward his rucksack. He had taken his boots off this time, and rolled his leggings up, so that he could dangle his legs in the water without getting his clothes saturated. He'd noticed how Merletta kept scrutinizing his feet when she thought he wasn't looking, clearly fascinated by the unfamiliar appendages.

"Well, I found it, if we want to be precise," interjected Reka, lifting his head lazily from where it was lying across the rocky shallows, along with the rest of him. The jagged surface didn't seem to bother him in the slightest, the sharp edges clearly not able to penetrate his hide. He looked absurdly relaxed, taking up an enormous proportion of the lagoon's edge as he stretched out like a cat in the sun. His tail dangled into the water, swishing peacefully from side to side in a gesture similar to Merletta's.

Heath just rolled his eyes at the majestic image. "You did not. You directed me to the building, but I found the record."

"Record?" Merletta repeated eagerly. "You found a written record?" She swam right up to Heath's rocks, her eyes alight. "But how is it possible if this place has been abandoned for so long? Surely writing leaves don't last that long, even above the surface."

"Writing leaves?" Heath asked, pausing in the act of retrieving the half-disintegrated parchment from his rucksack. "You mean paper?"

Merletta's eyes grew round as she caught sight of the parchment in his hand. "What's that?" she breathed, resting her elbows on the rocks in her eagerness.

"It's called paper," Heath explained. "It's made from trees, and it can last generations if taken care of." He grimaced slightly as he glanced down at his treasure. "Which this one hasn't been, of course." He looked back up at Merletta, realization washing over him. "I hadn't even thought about it, but of course you couldn't exactly have paper underwater. No trees, but also, it wouldn't last, would it?"

"I should think not," Merletta said, her eyes still riveted to the ancient letter. "This changes everything," she muttered. "Half the function of the Center would be unnecessary."

"What do you mean?" Heath asked, curious. She had already explained about her trainee position in the merkingdoms' Center of Culture, but he wasn't sure what paper had to do with it.

"Never mind that now," said Merletta impatiently. "What does it say?"

"See for yourself," Heath offered, holding it out to her.

She hoisted herself partially up onto the rock, taking the parchment in her hand.

"It seems to be a letter," said Merletta, fascinated.

Heath just nodded, watching her as she read the paper. It was incredible to see a mermaid reading the language of men with as much ease as he had. But that was only part of what held him in thrall. The delight of discovery that lit her whole face was like watching his own emotions from the outside. It was a novel experience, and it warmed him to her considerably.

"'I was grieved to read in your last missive of the troubles plaguing Vazula since I left,'" Merletta read aloud. She ran her fingers down the page. "Most of the rest is illegible." She screwed up her face in her effort to read the faded words. "'You should join me in Albury,' unreadable, unreadable, 'wealth of this land not exaggerated,' blah blah, 'I await your reply.'"

She stared at the page for a moment after she'd finished. "Where's Albury?"

"No idea," said Heath, lazily wiggling his toes in the cool water. "Never heard of it."

Merletta looked up at him, a smile growing on her face despite her difficulty in deciphering the message. "It's incredible," she breathed. "If this place has really been abandoned for as long as we think, this message has survived for centuries!" She shook her head. "I can hardly believe it. Imagine being able to record your thoughts and experiences like this, knowing they would last beyond your lifetime."

Heath returned her smile. "It's fascinating to read the words of someone long gone, I agree," he said. "It doesn't have quite the same effect on me, I suppose, because I'm used to the existence of ancient records. In fact, it was just such a manuscript which sent me looking for Vazula."

"Well," said Merletta, her eyes still riveted on the paper. "It might be commonplace in your world, but this would change my world completely."

"I am curious, though," Heath said, stowing the paper safely away again when Merletta handed it to him. "What's a writing leaf?"

"I'll bring one to show you," Merletta said absently, her eyes on Reka, who had just slipped off the rocks and into the lagoon, and was twisting through the water with an agility to match the mermaid's. "Next time."

"Yes," Heath agreed, his lips curving up into another smile. "Next time."

CHAPTER NINETEEN

Merletta spun herself around in a body roll as she swam to class, just for the sheer joy of it. It wasn't her upcoming history lesson that had her in a good mood, either. She'd become familiar with Instructor Ibsen's teaching style, and she had little expectation of today's class providing any genuinely useful information, any more than the previous dozen had.

And yet, she'd been learning a great deal over the last several weeks, nevertheless.

Her mind went back to the most recent rest day, a couple of days before. Heath was teaching her to whittle wood, and it was the most fascinating challenge she'd ever undertaken.

She could still hardly believe the effectiveness of the knife he'd produced. Metal, he'd called it. It cut with so much more precision than stone, or coral, and was a hundred times stronger and more durable than fish bone. Heath had been impressed by her demonstration with the writing leaf and coral implement she'd swiped, but it was nothing to his revelations. She patted the satchel at her side, elated at the thought of all the ways her treasure could be useful.

Her cheeks warmed as she remembered the smile in Heath's blue eyes when he'd insisted she keep the knife. He'd said they were common back home, that he had plenty more, but still... receiving gifts had never really been a part of her life, and the gesture meant more than he could possibly know. She shook her head slightly. She had no idea why the human seemed to have taken such an instant liking to her, but she wasn't about to discourage him.

Merletta was just hurrying through a simple breakfast—even after all these weeks, she still couldn't quite bring herself to gorge on the delicacies routinely provided—when a voice hailed her.

"Good morning, Merletta."

She turned, smiling a friendly greeting as she swallowed her mouthful of squid. "Good morning, Sage."

"You're up early this morning. You were gone before I even woke."

"I went for a morning swim around the reef," Merletta explained cheerfully. "Sometimes on lesson days, I feel the need to stretch my fins before we start. It's a long time of sitting still."

Sage smiled. "You don't do well with sitting still, do you?"

Merletta grimaced at the reference to Ibsen's criticisms the day before, when he'd reached the limit of his patience and chastised Merletta for her fidgeting. She'd tried to keep still, but her thoughts had been on Vazula, as usual, and she was itching to reach the next rest day. Heath had promised to bring a map of his kingdom, and she couldn't wait to examine it. The only maps she'd ever seen were crude ones carved into rocks as signposts. The possibilities of a map on paper were incredible.

"I never have," she sighed to Sage. "It was constantly getting me in trouble at the home."

"What was the home like?" Sage asked curiously.

Merletta looked at her in surprise. It was the first real sign of interest anyone in the Center had shown about her past. Well, about her actual experiences, anyway. Snide comments about her background were still common from both Ileana and Jacobi, although the other trainees had started to lose interest in such petty barbs.

"It was dreary," she said frankly. "And depressing. Life was predictable, with no variation, no excitement, and a lot of hard work. Beneficiaries often have to compete for the same apprenticeships, so there's more rivalry than friendship, and the carers were mostly not very warm. They wanted us to know our place, and didn't encourage us to have big ambitions."

Her tone turned dry. "When I announced, years and years ago, that I was determined to apply here, it didn't make me very popular." She gave a sad smile. "Tish was the only one who didn't sneer at me, but I don't think even she believed I could do it."

"Tish?" Sage asked.

"Letitia. My only true friend in that place. She turned sixteen a few months before I did, and started a shellsmith apprenticeship." Merletta's eyes became unfocused for a moment as she thought how she'd neglected her friend in her excitement over her new discoveries. "I should really visit her, see how she's doing."

"Sounds like a challenging environment for learning." Both Merletta and Sage turned in surprise at the new voice. "I'm impressed you were able to learn enough to perform so well in the entry tests."

"Good morning, Emil," said Merletta carefully, as the fourth year trainee settled next to Sage and began to scoop oysters out of a basin.

He'd never been insulting, and had shown her a basic level of respect since Instructor Agner's revelations about her results, but this was the first time he'd ever joined her and Sage at a meal like this.

"It took a great deal of effort and application to get any kind of education, if I'm honest."

Emil nodded. "Admirable." He nodded to the other trainee as well. "Sage."

Sage nodded back to him, but her eyes returned quickly to Merletta. "I think you're skilled at working within a difficult environment to learn in."

Merletta grinned at the carefully worded comment. She'd take any support she could get, however veiled. "Are you referring to Instructor Wivell's disinterest over whether I learn anything, or Instructor Ibsen's open determination that I don't?"

Sage hesitated for a moment, her gaze passing around the room to make sure no one could hear them, and her face turning slightly pink as she glanced at Emil. But her expression was determined as she responded. "Both. I think the prejudice against you due to your origins is not only unfair, but entirely impractical."

"Ah well, life isn't fair, is it?" Merletta said cheerfully. "Like you said, I don't need an easy ride in order to learn. The resources available in the Center are like nothing I've seen before. I spend most of my spare time in the records rooms, you know, reading the public records. I'm learning an incredible amount, even if most of it isn't in class. Did you know that because of their sheer size, the kelp farms actually bring in more income than the oyster farms? Even counting both oysters and pearls."

"I agree with Sage," Emil said calmly, cutting off whatever reply Sage had been about to make. Both mermaids turned to him in open astonishment.

"The reluctance of our instructors to properly teach you is

detrimental to all our learning, and seems to me a strange use of the resources of this place."

There was a stunned silence. Merletta could hardly believe her ears. Was Emil actually criticizing the program? She had never suspected that any such thoughts were hidden behind his impassive expression. Outwardly, he had always seemed to keep the line of the instructors' approach.

"It is to your credit that you're managing to learn as much as you are," Emil continued, nodding to her again.

"It certainly is," Sage added, with another small smile of encouragement. "To be honest, I think Ibsen is getting increasingly frustrated by how well you're keeping up."

Merletta chuckled, shaking off her stupefaction over Emil's interjection. "Well, he might not like me, but he can hardly have all the public records, and all the trainees' resources, locked away just to spite me, can he? It's no secret he's hoping I'll just fail first year and disappear back to Tilssted," she added cheerfully, "but he won't find it so easy. I'm as difficult to dislodge as a barnacle, or so the carers used to tell me. I'm going to do everything I can to pass."

"I hope you succeed," said Emil unemotionally. With a final grave nod, he rose up in the water, drifting toward the door of the room, his food barely touched.

"Well, that was unexpected," said Merletta, the moment he was out of hearing.

"It certainly was," Sage agreed, staring after him. "I think that's the most real conversation I've ever had with him, and I've been here almost two years. Not to mention before."

"Before?"

"I grew up a few streets away from Emil," Sage explained.

Merletta raised her eyebrows in surprise. "Really? I didn't know that."

"Yes, we're both from Skulssted. Same as Jacobi, although

his family lives on the other side of the city. Jacobi and I had met a few times, but only because both of our mothers are record holders."

"So you're both legacy applicants," Merletta mused, glancing at her fellow first year, his copper hair standing out across the dining hall. "That must be nice."

Sage shrugged. "In some ways. It also comes with a lot of pressure. I think Jacobi feels it more than I do. My mother was thrilled that I wanted to apply, but she wouldn't have pushed me to do it if I didn't want to. I don't think Jacobi ever had much choice." She lowered her voice. "Don't tell him I said this, but sometimes I get the sense that he's afraid of not being good enough to pass the program, and letting his family down."

Merletta studied the young merman thoughtfully, noticing for the first time the slight tension in the way he swished his burgundy tail back and forth, even while resting. She felt chastened. She'd been so reactive to Jacobi's hostility that she'd never spared a thought for the struggles the other trainee might be facing himself. Sage's willingness to reach out to Merletta wasn't an anomaly—Merletta wasn't the only trainee she'd watched with sympathy. She had taken a little while to show it, but underneath all her caution, Sage had a heart as kind as Tish's.

Merletta looked back at the other mermaid, to find Sage watching her seriously.

"Emil's not wrong though, that it's a waste not to properly teach you. I'm glad I'm not the only one to notice how differently the instructors are treating you from the rest of us. I've never seen them be so obstructive with anyone else."

Merletta just shrugged. Being singled out, in a negative way, was something she was very well used to from the home. She had always stood out, and her unwillingness to fall into line had ensured that she was constantly under scrutiny. She liked to think it had made her tough.

"Not all the instructors," she reminded Sage with a grin. "Agner has taken to me well enough."

"That's an understatement," said Sage dryly. "But it doesn't make me feel better for you. He works you twice as hard as the rest of us. I don't know how you can still swim by the end of some of his sessions."

"It's because he sees my potential," Merletta said thickly, speaking around a mouthful. "Or at least, that's what he claims." She chuckled at Sage's pained expression. "Believe me, I don't mind. I like it. I can actually beat Jacobi now, but I still have a long way to go to match you older students."

"I'm pretty sure you could match me," Sage admitted. "I've never excelled in combat the way Ileana has."

Merletta frowned. "Now why go and ruin a perfectly nice breakfast together by talking about her?"

Sage stifled a giggle, glancing around to make sure the other trainee wasn't in earshot. Her gaze shifted to a large bruise on Merletta's side, down where her skin met her scales, and her smile dropped away. "That bout with her last week was hard to watch, to be honest."

"Nothing I can't recover from," said Merletta unconcernedly. "I'll best her eventually, you'll see."

"I believe it," said Sage, with conviction. She considered Merletta curiously. "Is it true that Agner has said he'll start training you with the sharpened spears next week?"

Merletta nodded. "If I can satisfy him with my staff fighting this week."

Sage looked impressed. "That's early to start with spears. I didn't until the start of second year." She lowered her voice again. "Jacobi is as prickly as an urchin over it. He still hasn't started with spears, and he's been here months longer than you."

Merletta shrugged again. "Is it true that when you train with a spear, you get to keep it? Take it with you everywhere?"

Sage nodded. "You become responsible for your own weapon. Mine's stored in the barracks."

"Why don't you keep it with you?" Merletta asked, glancing at Sage's empty hands.

"Why would I need to carry a spear around in the Center?" Sage asked blankly. "And it's not like anyone's going to steal it from our barracks." She hesitated. "People don't really steal in the Center. Is that...is that why you carry your satchel with you to meals?"

Merletta wasn't surprised by the question. She'd noticed that while the other trainees all carried satchels to class, they often left them in their sleeping quarters during meals.

She gave a dry laugh. "You mean, because I'm from Tilssted, and therefore think there are thieves everywhere? No. I just like to be prepared, that's all." *Plus, I don't want anyone to find the evidence of my adventures while I'm out of the room.*

"Have you thought about tying back your hair?" Sage asked suddenly, and Merletta blinked at the abrupt change of topic.

"Why?"

Sage shrugged uncomfortably. "I just think it would help, that's all. The rest of us wear ours in braids, and it's more practical, plus it looks a little less...wild."

A defiant spark flared up in Merletta, and she was tempted to respond defensively. They had always been required to wear their hair in tightly confined—and unflattering—styles at the home, and Merletta had been relishing the freedom to let the dark waves float freely around her since becoming a trainee.

But the look in Sage's eyes made her pause. She realized that the other mermaid wasn't trying to criticize her, she was trying to help her. It was the memory of Emil's expressionless face as he unexpectedly voiced his support for her that made up her mind. She had always operated with stubborn defiance, and it had gotten her incredibly far. But perhaps it was time for a more strategic approach.

She had assumed that Emil, and even Sage to an extent, was fully in line with the views of those in power. But it was becoming increasingly clear to her that she couldn't judge people's true opinions and concerns by the reactions they publicly showed. Those who knew the Center—and the program—much better than she did seemed to think it was important to give at least the appearance of compliance.

Perhaps it was time she learned something from them.

"Thanks for the tip," she said mildly. "I'll braid it from now on."

She had to admit, in a particularly grueling training session a few weeks later, that it was more practical to have her hair out of her eyes.

Not that it was preventing her from being pummeled by Ileana.

"Good, Ileana, well done," said Agner brightly, when Ileana scored a solid hit to Merletta's tail. "I do wish you'd decided to stop at the end of your second year. We would be glad to welcome you into the guards."

Merletta grimaced as the other mermaid withdrew, a smirk on her face.

"Thank you, Instructor, but I plan to be a record holder."

"Yes, yes, you all do," sighed Agner. "But the life of a guard is much more active, you know, much more invigorating."

Merletta winced as she touched a tender spot on her chest. "Invigorating, you call it?"

Agner chuckled. "I didn't say it was easy. You did well, Merletta. Your reflexes are good, but you're still not fighting strategically enough."

He swam forward, tapping his staff to her arms in a clinical way, a slight frown on his face. "More upper body strength would definitely help. You're still a little too scrawny to really fight at the level of the older students. One bout with Emil, then he and Ileana can join the guard squad for patrol, and I'll run you through some weights exercises."

Merletta nodded, gripping her spear tightly as the fourth year merman swam forward to meet her. His face was as unexpressive as ever as the two of them circled one another. She had learned to be a little smarter since her first fight with Ileana, and she waited for him to make a move.

His arm flashed out, as quick as an eel, and she was only just in time to parry the move. Emil drew back, then struck again, still using the blunt end of his spear. She was ready for him this time. She deflected the wooden handle, thrusting hers toward him in an attempt to break through his guard.

He blocked her easily, then came back at her with such force that she knew she wouldn't be strong enough to deflect it. She twisted nimbly, propelling herself through the water and dodging his attack.

Emil spun as well, keeping her in his line of sight. Merletta made a bold thrust while he was still in motion, hoping to catch him off guard.

But he was too quick, and the next thing she knew, the end of his spear was connecting forcefully with her chest, pushing water from her mouth with an oomph.

"And you're speared through the heart," Agner said cheerfully, calling the hit.

Emil withdrew the moment Agner spoke, looking neither triumphant nor apologetic. Just his usual impassive self.

"You're improving, Merletta," Agner said, as Emil swam away to join Ileana where she was preparing to leave with the guard squad. Merletta followed him with her eyes, a little jealous. She couldn't wait until she was advanced enough to get to join patrols. It would be an interesting change to go outside the barrier on official business instead of sneaking out.

"I think you're ready to start with the sharp end next week."

That got her attention.

"What? But you just said I was speared through the heart."

Agner chuckled. "Obviously we'll start simple." He observed her shrewdly. "I believe in pushing my trainees hard, Merletta. Provided the potential is there, I think it's the best way to get results. You're excellent proof, in fact. Look how far you've come in a few short months."

Merletta nodded. "I'm just grateful you're willing to push me at all, Instructor."

Agner raised an eyebrow. "The other instructors still giving you a hard time for being from Tilssted, are they?" He shook his head. "They'll come around. Just show them you have what it takes. They're worried about seeing their fusty program overrun by the lower classes, but they know how to appreciate intelligence." He grinned at her. "Tilssted was my favorite part of the triple kingdoms to patrol, you know, back when I did such things. There's a rawness about the merfolk there which I like."

"We are pretty raw," Merletta agreed, grinning back. "Sometimes I miss it. At least you know where you float with Tilssted dwellers. Here, it's a bit harder to know what's under the surface." She was probably being too honest, but she couldn't help liking the casual cheerfulness of the combat instructor.

"Well, like I said, they'll come around when you show you're capable of keeping up," said Agner. He flashed her a wink. "And if you're not capable, and you flunk out of their classes, you can always apply directly to be a guard. I'll whip you into shape in no time."

Merletta chuckled, appreciating the encouragement, but not at all interested in taking the offered out. She wanted to learn to fight well, to be able to defend herself from both merpeople and other sea creatures. But being a guard didn't interest her. She wanted answers, and she was becoming increasingly convinced that she wasn't going to get them in first year. She had to progress, whatever it took.

CHAPTER TWENTY

"How's this?" Heath asked, squinting as he tried not to look directly at the noonday sun.

Merletta laughed openly. "You look like a baby sea turtle, still learning how to swim."

"Hey," Heath protested. "I've been able to swim since I was a child."

"Maybe, but floating on your back is all about balance," said Merletta. "If you keep kicking your legs like that, you're going to overturn."

"Easy for you to say," grumbled Heath. "You don't have legs. I can't help kicking them a little. It's involuntary."

"Well, you asked me to teach you," said Merletta, splashing water over his bare chest with a grin. She poked his side. "At least you're not all wrapped up today. All those coverings must hamper your movement. You look much more natural now, almost like a merman."

Heath righted himself, trying to be as nonchalant as she was about her touch. They were floating above the reef today, past the breakers, rather than in the lagoon. Back home autumn had already turned into winter, but on Vazula, it seemed to always be hot. The sun was particularly fierce today, and he had discarded his tunic before going in the water. Merletta still didn't really understand the concept of clothing, and she was much more casual about touching him than anyone he'd ever met before. It was exhilarating and terrifying in equal measures.

"You show me how it's done, then," he said, sidestepping the topic of clothing.

"All right," Merletta agreed, stretching onto her back compliantly. She closed her eyes, looking utterly relaxed as she floated, her body perfectly still, moving only with the gentle swell of the waves.

His eyes darted to the warm skin of her shoulders, mesmerized by the way they rose and fell with her breathing, as if mimicking the rolling waves. Sometimes, like in this moment, she seemed almost to be a part of the ocean. And yet, at the same time, there was something so human about her. After months, he still wasn't quite sure what to make of her.

She opened her eyes suddenly, and he wasn't quick enough to avoid being caught staring. For a moment the silence stretched between them, uncomfortably charged, as Heath cast around for something suitable to say.

"You're wearing your hair differently," he said at last, his eyes latching on to her thick dark braid. She was still watching him closely, the tension hanging between them, so he tried to adopt a teasing tone. "It makes you look less like a wild creature of ocean legend."

He expected her to laugh, but she didn't. Her face didn't change, but he got the strong impression that she was trying to decide whether his comment was a compliment or the reverse.

"I like it," he added quickly. "I just wondered about the change."

She sighed, leaning her head back against the water much as he might rest his head on a cushion. "I'm trying to blend in a little more at the Center," she said. "Not put everyone's backs up so much. Or at least," she amended, "choose which things are worth putting their backs up over."

"That's wise," said Heath, nodding.

"Do you think so?" There was an element of anxiety in her voice as she turned to him. "I don't want to let them change me into a conforming trainee, who doesn't question what she's taught."

Heath smiled, daringly reaching out to tweak her braid. "I think it would take a lot more than a change in hairstyle to do that." His expression grew more serious. "I've always believed in the importance of choosing your battles. Or, if I'm honest," he added ruefully, "avoiding battle altogether wherever possible."

He sighed, his eyes drifting overhead to where Reka was hovering, far above them, riding the current of the wind as he sniffed out the traces of dragon magic still lingering around Vazula. He had lost interest in Heath and Merletta's endless lessons, teaching each other about their respective peoples. His main interest in coming to Vazula now was in attempting to unravel the mystery of its missing dragon inhabitants.

The thought made Heath feel guilty. His whole excuse for coming to Vazula in the first place was that it wasn't just exploration for the sake of satisfying his curiosity. It was a genuine attempt to find answers about how Valoria's growing magical population could successfully integrate. But the truth was, since meeting Merletta, he had all but forgotten about that quest. He hadn't even explored the ruins in weeks now. Instead he spent all his time in the shallows, pretending that his new companion, and the endless depth of discovery she represented, didn't belong to a completely different world, one with no possibility of crossover with his.

"What battle are you fighting now, Heath?" Merletta asked, her voice searching, and unusually gentle.

He looked up quickly, and this time she was the one watching him. But she didn't look in the least embarrassed. Her forehead was creased in concern, and she was clearly expecting a serious answer to her question.

Heath released a long breath. "It's more the battle I'm not fighting," he admitted. "And I'm struggling to decide whether I should be."

Merletta regarded him in silence for another moment, her eyes flicking to his arms, which were working harder to keep him afloat the longer he was treading water.

"Come on," she said, gesturing with her head toward the shore. She turned, flipping from her back and slipping below the surface in one fluid motion.

Heath followed much more clumsily, and soon they were both resting their hands on the sand of the shallows. Merletta turned over, sitting on the sand, with her tail in the water, and the waves lapping over her.

"Be careful," Heath said anxiously, as a receding wave left more than half of her tail out of the water.

Merletta just smiled, not bothering to respond to the warning. She closed her eyes for a moment, leaning back on her hands and turning her face up toward the sun. As much as he didn't want to be caught staring a second time in one afternoon, he couldn't stop his eyes from being once again drawn to her form. She looked unusually peaceful as she soaked in the sun, reinforcing his impression that she was relaxed above the surface in a way that was probably rare in her underwater life.

He remembered thinking she was beautiful the first time he'd seen her, back when he thought she was human. If anything, she seemed even more beautiful now. Her eagerness for life drew him magnetically, but his own admiration unnerved him. When they were floating in the water, it was alarmingly easy to forget for a moment. But here, in the shallows, it was impossible to miss the way her slim, graceful form merged into an enormous—and very not-human—tail.

The whole thing was discomfiting, to say the least.

"It's so warm in the sun," Merletta said, her words startling him out of his scrutiny. His eyes darted to her face, but she still had her eyes closed, her face turned up toward the sky. "Sometimes I wish I could stay up here forever. I can't help but be jealous of you. The depths of the ocean are freezing."

Heath smiled. "Don't be too jealous. It's warm on Vazula, but back in Valoria it's winter now. There's snow on the ground, and the king will be holding his Winter Solstice Festival soon."

Merletta opened her eyes at last, her gaze bright with curiosity. "What's snow? And what's the Winter Solstice Festival?"

Heath held in a smile as he explained snow to her. As always, she was an eager listener. She would surely be an excellent student, if her idiotic instructors would only give her a chance to actually learn.

"And the Winter Solstice Festival is our biggest celebration," he added, once her questions about snow came to an end. "It happens in the middle of winter, on the shortest day of the year. The other one is the Summer Solstice Festival, but that's not quite such a big event. Probably because there are already lots of galas and such in summer. But there's nothing else happening anytime around the Winter Solstice. People brave the weather to come from all over the kingdom to be part of it, my family included. It's an impressive festival, especially since the dragons became involved. It's a little different every year—I'll describe it for you after it happens. It's only a few weeks away."

"Is it?" Merletta asked, interested. "It's at a similar time to our celebration, then. We only have one—Founders' Day. It's when we celebrate the establishment of the triple kingdoms, many generations ago. We always had simple games and a special meal even at the home. I'm interested to see what it will be like in the Center." She looked out over the ocean thoughtfully, presumably in the direction of her underwater home. "Curious that it's so close in timing to your major festival."

"I guess so," Heath shrugged. His eyes slid past his companion, to the spear buried point down in the sand, less than a foot into the water.

"That's quite a weapon, by the way," he said. "I guess you passed the first round of spear training, then."

"I did," Merletta confirmed. Her voice was full of a grim pride. "It's the most brutal training yet, but it's worth it to get to keep the spear."

"Is that what this is from?" Heath asked, letting his disapproval show as he gestured to a long thin slice on her arm.

"What's that?" Merletta asked, following his gaze. "Oh, yes, that was Ileana," she said matter-of-factly. "We're not supposed to use the sharp part of the spear in training, obviously, but that's Ileana for you. She'd skewer me if she thought she could get away with it." The mermaid tilted her head to one side. "And she probably could if it was Ibsen, or even Wivell, who taught combat."

Heath frowned, his mind full of dark thoughts about the hostile mermaid he'd never met, and the negligent instructors who allowed the other trainees to mistreat Merletta. He didn't like the nonchalant way in which Merletta spoke of her injuries, either, but he realized he had no legitimate reason to comment on either issue.

"Was that Ileana, too?" he asked instead, pointing to a bruise just below one of Merletta's collarbones.

"No," she said, looking disgruntled. "That was Oliver. I'm still annoyed about it—I can beat him now, more often than not, but I let my guard down." She sighed. "If only I could beat Ileana. She clearly struggles to keep up in the other classes, but I can't deny that she's excellent in training."

She suddenly sat up straighter. "All this talk of training reminds me! Did you bring your bow?"

"I did." Heath got up to retrieve the weapon, lying on the sand some distance away. He grabbed his quiver of arrows as well, bringing them to the water for Merletta's examination.

"I can't wait to see how it works!" Merletta said enthusiastically, running her fingers along the taut string. "Do you think I could learn to use it from the water?"

"I'm not sure," Heath said, considering it. "I think it would be hard to hold yourself steady enough without being able to anchor yourself to the ground."

"It sounds like an amazing weapon," said Merletta wistfully. "We can only throw things a very short distance underwater, or a little further if we use a sling. It would be a huge advantage to be able to hit something as far away as you claim a bow can do." She turned eager eyes to him. "Can you demonstrate for me?"

"Of course," said Heath. He glanced around. "See that coconut?"

Merletta nodded, and Heath stood, taking aim carefully. He released his breath, and the arrow whizzed through the air, hitting the coconut dead on, and knocking it from its tree. It fell into the water, and Merletta dove forward at once, swimming to it and bringing it back with her.

"Amazing," she breathed, turning the coconut over in her hands. The arrow still protruded from it, and she touched the feather fletching with curious fingers. "This is from a bird," she exclaimed.

"That's right," said Heath easily. "What's my next target?" he asked, wanting to show off a little. He glanced up at the dragon still visible some distance above them. "Should I shoot Reka?"

Merletta gave a snort of laughter. "I'm guessing it wouldn't hurt him?"

Heath grinned. "I doubt he'd even feel it. But it would probably make him angry enough to refuse to carry me home." He sighed, and his voice dropped to a mutter. "Which wouldn't necessarily be so bad."

Merletta didn't respond, and when Heath glanced over, she was once again watching him with that searching expression.

"Tell me," she said, and it wasn't a request.

Heath squirmed uncomfortably, not at all sure where to begin. For reasons he couldn't fully explain, even to himself, he had neglected to mention before now about the magic that ran in his family's blood. He was silent for an uncomfortably long time, but Merletta didn't push him. She just waited, watching him expectantly, and suddenly he let go of something inside himself.

"The problem is power—you know, magic," he said in a rush. "Or maybe that's the solution, I don't know."

Merletta looked confused, but she didn't speak, letting him continue. It all came out in a rush, about his Kyonan grandmother whose parents had imbued dragon magic from their exposure to the colony in Kyona's mountains. How she and her brother had consequently been born with an innate magical ability, unprecedented in the history of humans. How she had married a Valorian prince, introducing magic into the royal family, although not into the direct line of the throne. He told Merletta about the rising tensions, and his concerns over Percival, who seemed to have somehow ended up at the heart of it all.

"As the only one without an obvious magical ability, I have the choice to sort of stay out of it, in a way the rest of them don't," he explained. "The truth is that I've muddled along well without power all these years by learning to keep my head down." He thought about it, smiling slightly as he amended, "And to not take myself too seriously." He sighed. "But Percival sees it as a lack of loyalty whenever I don't weigh in. He thinks that everyone else will assume I agree that the power-wielders should be restricted, and sometimes I worry that he might be right."

He raised his hands helplessly. "But what am I supposed to do? Argue on their behalf when I'm not even one of them?"

Merletta looked out toward the ocean, considering his words in silence. "So you're part of the royal family," she said, the direction of her thoughts taking him by surprise.

"Not really," he said quickly. His status was another thing he'd avoided mentioning. He hadn't wanted to admit it, after hearing just how disadvantaged she was. "We're too far removed from the king to really be considered royal."

"But your grandparents are a prince and princess, and your father is a duke." She didn't wait for Heath's nod of acknowledgment, turning to look at him. "Should I be calling you Lord, or something?"

"Of course not!" said Heath, squirming uncomfortably. "I would hate it if you did."

Merletta was silent for another long moment, then her gaze returned to the horizon again. "It doesn't seem likely that you would be the only one not to inherit power," she said at last. "I suspect that Reka is right, that you have some kind of magic, but haven't yet fully identified what it is."

Heath waited, but she fell silent, apparently having nothing more to add.

"That's it?" he protested, eyebrows raised. "You looked so pensive, I thought for sure you were going to give me some helpful advice!"

"Advice?" Merletta repeated, giving a humorless laugh. "How can I give you advice? I can barely navigate my own world, let alone yours, which I know absolutely nothing about."

She frowned. "But I will say that I find it strange you think your ability to advocate for the power-wielders is *lessened* by you

—supposedly—not being one of them. I've often thought those of us in Tilssted would be taken more seriously in our struggles if someone from outside were to speak up on our behalf. No one listens when we do it." She sighed. "It's one of the reasons I wanted to join the program at the Center. But it quickly became clear that my position as a trainee makes little difference on that matter. I'll always be from Tilssted, as far as they're concerned."

Heath mulled it over for a moment. "So you think I should speak up? Get involved?"

Merletta shrugged. "I'm not going to tell you what I think you should do. That's up to you." She considered him thoughtfully. "If you did decide to get involved, what would you do?"

It was Heath's turn to shrug. "No idea. There was a meeting a few months ago, where the king invited input from his court on the issue. All the power-wielders went. I didn't go because..." he glanced sideways at her, "well, I didn't go. And Percival's been in a bit of a huff with me ever since, to be honest."

"What did the king decide?" Merletta asked curiously.

"He hasn't yet," said Heath. "He's obviously conflicted about it, and both camps are annoyed that he's not instantly siding with them."

"And you feel caught in the middle," Merletta guessed.

"I side with my family, of course," he said quickly.

Merletta gave him a look. "That's not an answer. Don't get me wrong, I understand your loyalty. If I had a family, I'd do anything to protect them. But I was asking what you actually think."

Heath sighed. "I don't want to see anyone put under restrictions," he said. "But—even though I don't think I could ever admit it to Percival—I can kind of see the other side. I mean, it's not exactly fair to have someone with the strength of five men competing in a tournament against normal competitors, is it? And although I would never be afraid of anything my family might do, because I trust them, people who don't know them so well…"

Merletta nodded. "It is a problem." She stared off into the distance for another prolonged moment, then turned back to him, a cheeky grin crossing her features and breaking the moment. "Don't take this the wrong way, but it's kind of a relief to hear that your mythical human society is beset by problems just as complicated as ours."

"Thanks for the support," laughed Heath, sending a generous splash of water in her direction.

For all the joking, the conversation stayed with Heath. Merletta's words—*if I had a family, I'd do anything to protect them*—circled throughout his mind as Reka flew homeward. She had spoken them without judgment, but they shamed him nevertheless.

Merletta had grown up an orphan, with almost no one to even care what became of her. And yet she had applied for her position partly with the hope of helping the plight of others from her city. He had been taking his family, and their support, for granted. He was giving them less loyalty than they deserved by trying to stay on the sidelines in a fight that affected their very selves. It was time for him to stop avoiding involvement.

He said goodbye to Reka on the clifftop, steeling himself as he walked toward the manor. Like he had told Merletta, he had no idea what he was going to do. But he was determined to do something.

He was shivering by the time he entered the gates, his clothes still not fully dry from a day spent mostly in the water. It had been fine in the temperate air surrounding Vazula, but in the bite of a Valorian winter, it was brutal. He'd have to start taking a change of clothes. Although, he thought with a dry chuckle, he might have to be creative in finding an opportunity to change. Merletta probably wouldn't realize that she should give him privacy, and would instead be fascinated by the opportunity to watch a human replace his "coverings".

"Decided to return, did you?"

Heath turned quickly, the laugh dying in his eyes as he took in his brother's sulky expression. He sighed. Percival was becoming difficult to live with.

"Yes, Reka just dropped me off."

"I saw." His brother regarded him for a moment, eyebrows raised. "Have you been swimming? In winter?"

"It wasn't so cold," Heath answered evasively.

Percival's eyes narrowed. "Where do you two go? Every week, like clockwork."

"You know how Reka and I get," Heath hedged. "We love to explore."

"That's not an answer." Percival sounded less than impressed.

"What do you care?" Heath challenged. "I thought you were focused on this edict that's supposed to be coming from King Matlock."

"I was," said Percival shortly. "And it would have been nice to think I had the support of my own brother."

Heath frowned. "Would have been?"

"Edict's out, it's done," said Percival.

Heath straightened, an ominous feeling growing within him. "And? What did he decide?"

"He sided with *them*," said Percival, the venom in his voice causing alarm to swirl around Heath's stomach. "We've been summoned to attend Bryford within the next month. We dangerous power-wielders are to be registered. Like cattle."

Heath raised an eyebrow. "You're being very dramatic."

"Actually," Percival pushed himself off the wall he'd been

leaning against, "I haven't gotten to the dramatic part yet. No one's announced it, but the rumor is that once we're registered, and our powers are assessed, we're going to be restricted in using them."

"Restricted?" Heath repeated slowly. "Restricted how?"

Not that he really even needed to hear the answer. The angry sneer on Percival's face told him what a disaster these restrictions would be, whether reasonable or not.

"We can only use them at the request of His High and Mighty Majesty."

CHAPTER TWENTY-ONE

"You seem low lately."

"Hm?" Merletta looked up absently. "Sorry, Sage, what were you saying? I was distracted."

"Yes, I know." Sage smiled. "That's what I was saying."

"Oh." Merletta laughed unconvincingly, and Sage's forehead creased in concern.

"Seriously, what's going on? I thought everyone liked Founders' Day. You missed all the festival games, and you've barely even glanced at the banquet. In case you haven't noticed, there's enough food here to feed the whole triple kingdoms."

"It's certainly a lot of food," Merletta conceded, glancing around the large open space. Or at least, it seemed large when empty. She knew that from all the times she'd swum past it in her explorations of the Center. But at the moment, it was so packed with merpeople that the space seemed cramped.

Everyone was dressed for the occasion, mermaids wearing their most finely-wrought shells, their wrists adorned with delicately carved rings of coral, and their hair braided with pearls. Even many of the mermen wore their hair in elaborate braids.

Emil, across the room, had his fair hair pulled partially back into a braid. It flowed down over the rest of his hair, which was floating freely around him. It wasn't dissimilar to the way Sage's brown hair was styled, but the effect was entirely different. Emil looked like a warrior, whereas Sage looked dressed for a dance. Perhaps it was the blossoms poking out from her tresses, or the periwinkles circling her neck on a delicate strand.

And Sage wasn't wrong about the elaborate feast. It was a hundred times more impressive than anything the charity home had ever put on. Merletta could only imagine the work involved in preparing that much food over the thermal vents and transporting it all to the Center. The food was spread over many tables, and they were all lined with diaphanous green plants. Their crenelated edges undulated gently in the constant currents created by the feasters moving about the space. Darkness had begun to fall, and plankton lanterns were glowing in every corner of the banquet area.

It was a spectacular sight, but somehow Merletta didn't feel very festive. And it wasn't because she had nothing to wear except her usual standard issue shells. And her satchel, of course. A few of the attendees had thrown confused looks at the kelp bag. They were probably trying to figure out where Merletta fit. Her armband declared her as a trainee, but the only others wearing satchels were servers, or guards, who were on duty and therefore needed access to supplies. She didn't care if she looked odd. She wasn't going to leave her treasures unguarded for a whole evening.

The fact that she'd missed the games, while a little disappointing, also wasn't the cause of her low mood. She would have liked to at least watch them, but Founders' Day fell on a rest day, and she hadn't even considered staying in the Center for it.

Much good that determination had done her.

"I'm sorry," she sighed, turning to the other trainee. "I'll try to be better company."

"Never mind about that," said Sage, still frowning. "Are the instructors getting you down?" She glanced around and lowered her voice, a sure sign she was about to say something not completely supportive about either the program or the instructors. Her private defiance was growing, but her public facade hadn't changed at all. "Ibsen was out of line the other day, with that slur about not having a name."

"I don't care about Ibsen," said Merletta impatiently.

It was mostly true. Normally she brushed off the abrasive instructor's insults, but it had stung a little to see Ileana's sneer. It had taken Merletta a while to identify the change, but she finally had to admit to herself that she had been more sensitive about her orphaned status since discovering that Heath was some kind of noble.

That had been nearly two months ago, and it was almost the last conversation they'd had. He'd come only briefly the following week, and had said that he'd be unable to come for a while.

She'd assumed he meant one week, maybe two. But it had been five weeks of absence now, five times she'd made the swim all the way to the island, only to wait in growing depression for the entire day, with no sign of a dragon growing steadily larger in the westward sky.

Five weeks.

Even the heavy downpour of rain the week before—one of her favorite things to experience at the surface—had done nothing to improve her mood. She'd never been a big worrier, but she couldn't help being afraid that something had happened to Heath.

Or that he'd lost interest in her.

The thought flashed through her mind that such an idea was almost worse. But she immediately chastised herself for the selfish thought, and for her continued abstraction, pulling herself back to the mermaid beside her. She needed to stop daydreaming about humans and focus on where she was.

"I'm glad you're not letting him get under your scales," Sage was saying, flicking her decorated brown tresses over one shoulder.

Merletta stared for a moment in growing panic, wondering how Sage could read her mind, before the other mermaid's next words reminded her they were supposed to be speaking of Instructor Ibsen.

"He's just cross that you performed so well in that practice test."

"I should hope I performed well," Merletta said dryly. "I barely slept the week before with how much time I spent in the public records chamber." She sighed. "It would certainly be nice if I actually had help from my instructors in studying, instead of having to do most of it out of class time."

Sage grimaced sympathetically, and for a moment they floated in silence. Merletta glanced toward the opening to the banquet hall, and the open water beyond. The days were at their shortest, and soon it would be truly dark. She could see the glow of a jellyfish cage at the entrance. She shivered slightly.

"But why are we talking about my practice test?" she asked, turning suddenly back to her companion. "Your real test is only a couple of weeks away!"

"Yes, and I'm sick of talking about it," Sage said firmly. She gave a slight shudder. "And thinking about it."

"Are you nervous?"

Sage gave her a look. "Am I nervous? Have you forgotten that combat is my weakest area? And that if I fail second year, my only fallback is to be a scribe, spending my entire life copying and re-copying harvest records for posterity? Yes, I'm nervous."

Merletta opened her mouth, then closed it again. It was times like this that it was hardest to keep it in. It was so absurd to think that generations of scribes were copying records onto writing leaves day after day after day, when the human world had the means to make records that could last for centuries. But she had no idea what would happen if she told Sage about the island, and Heath, and everything.

She shook her head slightly. She was trying not to think about Heath.

"You can do it," she said instead, in a bolstering tone. "You're better in combat than you think you are. You beat me easily last time we fought, remember?"

"It wasn't easily," Sage said dryly. "And I'm pretty sure I got lucky." She sighed. "But thanks. It's just so unfair that I have to pass guard training to progress. I don't want to be a guard—why can't I skip straight to the educator assessment? That I can at least study for."

"You'll get the chance to take that test," said Merletta firmly. "And you'll be all the tougher and stronger for having passed your guard test first. Oliver passed. I'm sure you can."

If possible, Sage looked even more nervous. "Talking about Oliver's test is not going to make me feel better. Did you see how nervous he was before he went in?"

Merletta nodded. "He looked almost as green as Emil's tail."

The joke failed to get a smile out of her companion. "And when he came out, he looked even worse. I get the sense he only just scraped by, which is terrifying. He's definitely a better fighter than I am."

"Surely it can't all be about combat," Merletta said. "He really won't tell you a thing about the assessment?"

Sage shook her head. "Of course not, and I haven't pressed

him. We're not allowed to talk about the tests to younger trainees, especially the guard test. It's supposed to test your ability to respond to the unexpected."

"I know," said Merletta matter-of-factly, "but I wondered if you insiders really kept to those rules, when no one's looking."

"You're an insider, too, Merletta," Sage said firmly. "You've earned your place as a trainee, like anyone."

Merletta just gave her a look, and Sage sighed.

"Besides, Oliver wouldn't feel any loyalty to me. He's from Hemssted, remember? They look down on those of us from Skulssted."

"They do?" Merletta blinked. "I thought Skulssted was the wealthiest of the cities."

"Oh, it is," Sage confirmed. "But Hemssted has more influence for all that." She rolled her eyes. "At least, they like to think so. You know what they're like."

"Not really," said Merletta, fascinated. "I thought Skulssted and Hemssted were united in looking down on Tilssted."

"Well, we are, generally," Sage admitted apologetically. "But that doesn't mean we don't bicker amongst ourselves as well."

"Huh." Merletta locked the thought away for later. It was new information to her, but Sage still looked unusually anxious, and she thought it best to change the subject. "What about after the test, though? Surely you're looking forward to a break?

Sage smiled. "Yes, I am. It will be nice to go home for a whole month."

"And if your test is in a couple of weeks, your birthday must be only a month after that, right? What will you do for that?"

"My family will host a party, I imagine," said Sage, looking slightly awkward as she always did whenever talking about her family. Nothing Merletta said seemed to convince her that she wasn't sensitive about being an orphan. "Turning eighteen is kind of a big deal."

"It certainly is," Merletta agreed, with an encouraging smile.

She turned her attention back to the room, her eyes skating over the various attendees. She saw Ileana, looking irritatingly polished and glamorous. She was wearing some of the fanciest shells Merletta had ever seen.

At least she wasn't glaring at Merletta for once. Her gaze was directed elsewhere, and following it, Merletta noticed a silver-haired merman on the far side of the space, surrounded by a knot of important-looking officials. Glancing around, she realized that more merpeople than just Ileana were watching him out of the corners of their eyes.

"Who's that?" she asked, nodding in his direction.

Sage followed the gesture, her forehead creasing. "You don't know who that is?"

Merletta shook her head.

"That's the Record Master," said Sage. "The most senior merman in the record holding program. In the whole Center of Culture." She paused. "So in all the triple kingdoms, really."

Merletta raised an eyebrow. "Surely the regents of the three cities would disagree with that."

Sage shrugged one shoulder. "They might not admit it, but they must all know that the Center is the real seat of power in the triple kingdoms."

Merletta was silent, surprised by this plain speaking. She had begun to get the impression that most of those who worked and lived in the Center shared that view. But she hadn't heard it said before now. Perhaps it was Sage's status as a legacy applicant that made her take that stance so confidently.

"I've heard of the Record Master, of course," Merletta said eventually. "He doesn't look like I expected." He looked, in fact, quite ordinary. "What's he like?"

Sage gave an incredulous laugh. "I have no idea. He's basically the ruler of the triple kingdoms, Merletta. It's not like I've spoken to him."

She'd barely said the words when the Record Master's eyes suddenly flicked to them. Both trainees froze, and Merletta wondered if Sage was also filled with the same unnerving feeling that he knew what they'd been saying. It was impossible, of course, with how far across the room he was. But his gaze remained fixed on them nevertheless.

With the most casual of movements, he began to float through the throng, exchanging a word here and there with those he passed. The officials surrounding him stayed where they were, but two expressionless guards drifted across the room with the Record Master, flanking him. Merletta turned away, not wanting to be caught staring. A suggestion that they find food was on the tip of her tongue when Sage gave a strangled hiss.

"Merletta!"

She turned, and her eyes widened as she saw what had made Sage speak. The Record Master's eyes were on them, and he was undoubtedly coming their way.

The two mermaids had time to do no more than exchange a glance before he was upon them.

"Happy Founders' Day, Record Master," Sage said breathlessly, inclining her head in a respectful gesture. Merletta did her best to copy.

"Happy Founders' Day to you as well, trainees," the man replied, with a glance at their armbands. His voice was deep and calm, and his expression was relaxed as he looked them over. His eyes settled on Sage. "I think I have met your mother. You are a legacy applicant, are you not?"

"I am, sir," said Sage, sounding dazed. "It is my honor to continue my family's tradition."

The Record Master bobbed his head in acknowledgment,

before turning eyes the color of a storm cloud to Merletta. He examined her in silence for a nerve-wracking moment.

"And you are our Tilssted applicant, I believe."

He didn't phrase it as a question, but Merletta answered anyway. "I am, sir," she said, holding her head up. She refused to be ashamed of her background, even in front of the Record Master.

He nodded slowly. "Admirable, to have achieved so much with so little advantage."

"Thank you, sir," said Merletta carefully.

His piercing gaze was still fixed on her face, his expression impossible to read. "What is your name?"

"Merletta, sir."

There was another long moment of silence as he seemed to measure her with his eyes. "Well, Merletta, even just gaining entry to the program is an achievement of which you may be proud."

Merletta wanted to raise her eyebrows at the way he spoke, as if he was literally giving her permission to feel proud. But she controlled her features, knowing better than to do or say anything that might offend.

"Thank you, sir, I am. And I'm just getting started."

He regarded her for another second before turning away. "Enjoy your evening."

And with that, he was gone, off to speak with the next lucky attendee. Sage sucked in a mouthful of water, letting it out in a shaky stream.

"I can't believe we just spoke with the Record Master!" she gushed. "And *he* approached *us*! Wait until I tell Mother!"

Merletta gave her a tight smile. She hadn't been especially impressed by the encounter herself, but it had clearly been an exciting event for Sage, and she didn't want to ruin it for her friend. She thought she felt someone's eyes on her, and she turned to see Ileana glaring at her with an expression of absolute loathing. Clearly she also placed a high value on the Record Master's attention, and from what Merletta had seen, she had gotten none of it. Merletta met the other mermaid's glare boldly. She couldn't care less what Ileana thought.

"You were right that you're just getting started, you know," Sage said unexpectedly. "The entry test is the easiest of them all to pass. We've been talking about my test, but you should be thinking about yours. It might feel like ages away, but it'll come around quickly."

"It can't come soon enough, as far as I'm concerned," said Merletta frankly. "I'm determined to do well enough to prove to Ibsen and Wivell that they're not getting rid of me anytime soon. And then I get to move to second year. I don't want to be a guard any more than you do, but I'm actually looking forward to a year with more focus on physical training. At least it's easier to measure my progress."

"Or lack of it, in my case," Sage sighed.

"Enough," said Merletta firmly. "You're getting yourself down for no reason. You're going to pass this test." She rose into the water. "Let's go."

"Go where?" Sage looked up at her, bewildered.

"We've both eaten more than enough, and floating around at a banquet isn't going to help you pass your test. We're going to go train. You need to stress less, and prepare more."

"But...it's Founders' Day." Sage looked out through the doorway. "And it's dark."

Merletta rolled her eyes. "We're at the bottom of the ocean. It's always dark."

Sage looked at her strangely, and Merletta realized it had been an odd thing to say for a normal mermaid, one who didn't spend every available moment at the surface.

"You know what I mean," she said briskly, trying to cover her blunder. "The lanterns will be on, so no excuses. We're going to whip you into shape for your test."

Sage glanced around the space, a small smile spreading across her face. "You know, I think you're right. All these important people are just making me nervous." She rose from her seat as well, following Merletta toward the exit.

They had almost made it from the room when she surprised Merletta by speaking again.

"Thanks, Merletta. You're a good friend."

Merletta turned away quickly to hide the flush of pleasure rising up her neck.

Friend. It was a nice word.

Most of the trainees seemed to feel a bit flat in the aftermath of Founders' Day. But Merletta's mood lifted a little as the week dawdled by. She knew it was foolish—chances were that Heath would again fail to show up. But she couldn't help looking forward to the end of the week. It had become habit.

And it wasn't just the rest day. She also found the two days before it to be the least frustrating of the week. Of course, they were the most difficult in another way, since Agner continued to push her mercilessly. But she always came out of training feeling like she was getting somewhere, which was more than she could say for her other classes.

Agner told her exactly what to do to improve, in stark contrast to Ibsen. Even Wivell had been visibly reluctant in teaching her how to construct a mind palace, and she was developing it only with Sage's occasional coaching rather than any assistance from the instructors. She was struggling to get the hang of it, and reluctant to spend much time trying. It was a fascinating concept, of course—the idea of storing information in imagined rooms within her mind, to be retrieved at will like belongings from a shelf. But didn't help that Wivell had insisted she must base her mental building on her childhood home, with which she was most familiar. She didn't like spending large chunks of time mentally wandering the hated halls of the charity home. Although if she could overcome her distaste, it would probably be a benefit that there were so very many rooms there, in which to store the information she was to learn in her courses.

But all that was a problem for another day. On training days, she didn't have to swim through her mapped out mind palace. Nor did she have to drill herself on previous lessons in an attempt at solidifying information through interval repetition.

Better yet, today she had no need to reflect on the fact that Safe Mermaids Don't Break Surface in order to remember the stages of the triple kingdoms' establishment: search, magical barrier, designing, building, and stabilizing. Today she could focus on building her physical strength—a much more quantifiable goal.

As was her custom, she got up early on the first day of training, intending to reach the courtyard before class began. She liked to get in some extra warm up exercises. She crept around quietly as she got ready, knowing that Sage wasn't fond of early mornings. She wouldn't have cared if she woke Ileana up, but the third year mermaid seemed to have woken even earlier, because her hammock was swinging empty.

Merletta swam into the training courtyard in a determined frame of mind, her thoughts on the defensive technique Agner had drilled her in the week before.

She was so focused on her training, she didn't even hear anyone approach. The first thing she knew was an excruciating pain in her tail, as something hit her, hard, from behind. She spun in the water, trying to see what had come at her, but before she could get a good look, she was whacked across the face so hard it made her head snap back and her vision spin.

She recognized the weapon this time—there was no mistaking the brutal crack of a training pole. And equally familiar were the snide voices.

"Whoops, didn't see us coming, did you, Tilssted?"

"Didn't they teach you how to watch your back in that slum of yours?"

Merletta pulled herself upright in the water, infuriated by this overt attack. But her vision was still blurry from the hit to the face, and before she could do more than bring her own spear up, Jacobi had butted the end of his pole into her stomach.

Water was expelled from her mouth with a choking rush, and she doubled over as pain blossomed from her center. Her vision had cleared enough to see Ileana's next move coming, however, and she managed to parry the thrust with the length of her spear.

"What are you doing?" she hissed, eyes narrowed in anger.

"Teaching you your place," Ileana spat, her own features contorted as she pursued her attack.

Merletta was hard pressed just to hold her off. She couldn't maintain her position—Ileana was forcing her back across the courtyard, Jacobi taking advantage of every opening to land painful blows to her arms and tail.

"You think you're one of us?" Ileana grunted. "Rubbing shoulders with the Record Master? You will *never* be one of us."

Merletta stared at her. "That's what this is about?"

Her distraction cost her, as Ileana finally managed to break through her guard. The older mermaid shoved Merletta right in the chest with the end of her weapon, and Merletta was thrust backward, giving an involuntary gasp of pain.

Ileana's eyes narrowed in triumph, and a spark of defiance leaped up within Merletta. She surged forward, taking the other trainee by surprise, and landing a solid blow to the side of her head. She used the butt of her spear—however dishonorable this attack might be, she didn't even consider using the blade, not when Ileana and Jacobi had come against her with only training poles. But Ileana clearly didn't appreciate the forbearance. She hissed in pain and anger, pure hatred leaping into her eyes.

She fell on Merletta with renewed vigor, raining blows on her head that Merletta could barely defend against. Merletta darted backward, only to find her back against a wall. Before she could blink, the shaft of Ileana's pole was laid across her throat, and the older mermaid was pressing all her weight on it.

Stars danced before Merletta's eyes, and she could barely pull in water. She struggled against Ileana's grip, but the pole only pressed in harder. She began to thrash more and more wildly, panic setting in. Her spear fell from her nerveless hands, and she scrabbled uselessly at Ileana's arms.

"Ileana," muttered Jacobi, sounding nervous.

"Quiet," Ileana hissed. "I know what I'm doing."

Merletta's eyes were bulging, blackness creeping in at the corners of her vision. She locked eyes with Ileana, and for a terrified moment, read the intention of the older girl's eyes. This wasn't some cruel prank. Ileana was genuinely trying to kill her.

An instinct deep within Merletta awoke, and she knew that she had to fight now, or die. Calling on an extra reserve of strength she didn't know she had, she brought her tail up with a furious surge. It caught Ileana solidly in the chest, and the other trainee's grip slackened enough for Merletta to throw her off. She dove down to retrieve her spear. She had just brought it up in front of her, serious now, when a cheerful voice called across the courtyard.

"Now that's what I like to see! Trainees enthusiastic enough about the art to be here at the crack of dawn!"

All three of them turned, lowering their weapons at the sight of Agner, swimming calmly across the courtyard. A quick glance at her attackers showed that Jacobi looked afraid, and Ileana mutinous.

"Who's winning the bout?" Agner asked brightly, his eyes passing between the three of them. He raised an eyebrow at Merletta's weapon. "A spear against a training pole, Merletta? That's not your usual style."

Merletta was silent. Her whole body had begun to shake as shock set in, and for a moment she couldn't master any words.

"Merletta?" Agner pressed, looking mildly concerned.

"Ileana just tried to kill me," Merletta gasped, drawing in a mouthful of water in a shuddering motion.

"Stop being so dramatic, Merletta," said Ileana, schooling her features into an impressively convincing look of disdain. "If you can't handle a decent fight, don't accept my challenge."

"Accept your challenge?" Merletta echoed. "You attacked me, two to one! I didn't even know you were here!" She glared at the other girl, her hands tightening convulsively on her spear. "I let the jellyfish go, and I was willing to dismiss the pufferfish as a stupid prank. But this is too far, Ileana. You just tried to murder me!"

"Whoa, whoa, whoa," said Agner, and Merletta was infuriated to hear a laugh in his voice. "Let's not get carried away. I know emotions can run high in a bout between such..." he glanced between the two mermaids, "passionate rivals. But it's best to leave those frustrations in the practice yard. No need for accusations." He turned to Ileana. "What's this about pufferfish and jellyfish?"

Ileana shrugged a careless shoulder. "I have absolutely no idea what she's talking about, Instructor."

Merletta narrowed her eyes. Enough. She should have reported the other incidents. It was foolish to think those pranks were like the ones she'd experienced at the charity home. Any one of them could have killed her. She had thought before now that it might have been ignorance that led Ileana, and most likely Jacobi, to choose such dangerous jokes. But this went beyond any prank.

"I want to see Instructor Wivell," she said abruptly. "He's the chief instructor, right?"

Jacobi looked more nervous than ever, but if Ileana felt any fear of being exposed, she showed no sign of it. Her expression was a perfect blend of disdain and boredom.

Agner sighed. "Merletta, I would encourage you not to make more of this than necessary. The other instructors don't appreciate being appealed to about injuries sustained during training."

"I want to see Instructor Wivell," Merletta repeated stubbornly.

An hour later, her blaze of determined anger had abated, and she felt close to tears as the aftermath of the incident began to wear her down. The fact that she'd been kept waiting so long didn't bode well for Wivell's reception of her complaint.

When she was finally waved into his office, she was disheartened but not surprised to see the stony look on his face. When she stated the details of the three potentially fatal attacks, his expression didn't change in the slightest.

"Do you have any proof that these weren't just accidents, or that any trainees were involved?"

"Not for the first two," Merletta admitted angrily. "But believe me, Ileana was very much involved when she had her staff pressed to my throat an hour ago!"

Wivell waved a dismissive hand. "I don't count that incident," he said, sounding irritated. "Injuries sustained during training are inevitable and necessary if trainees are to reach the requisite level of combat skill."

"Injuries like this?" Merletta gestured furiously to the bruises now blooming all over her body. Her voice was still raspy from the pressure on her throat. "And it wasn't in training! They were waiting for me before class started, and attacked without warning!"

Wivell was unimpressed. "I am aware that Instructor Agner encourages his trainees to initiate their own bouts, and to test their skills in a variety of settings."

"I'm telling you, she was trying to kill me," Merletta insisted.

Wivell raised an eyebrow. "That's quite an accusation. From what I understand, *you* were the one fighting with a sharpened spear, not your classmates."

Merletta opened her mouth in frustration, but closed it again. Angry tears sprang to her eyes as she realized she should have listened to Agner. It was clear that she wasn't going to get anywhere with this complaint. It was also clear now why Ileana and Jacobi had come at her with training poles instead of spears. A chill passed over her at the realization of how easily they could have gotten away with making her death look like an accident.

"The other two incidents, then," she said. "What was my crime there?"

"If these incidents happened," said Wivell calmly, "why didn't you report them at the time?"

"Because I didn't think I'd be taken seriously," Merletta snapped. "I can't imagine what would have given me that impression."

Wivell sighed. "I don't appreciate my time being wasted, Merletta. I'm sure that at the charity home, such outbursts as this weren't uncommon. But in more civilized society, we try to control our emotions."

Merletta propelled herself toward the door without another word. There was no point in saying more. She didn't know if

Wivell supported the attacks against her, or if he simply didn't believe they'd happened. Either option was equally possible.

But it didn't matter which it was, because the message was clear. As long as it could be explained away as an accident, the instructors weren't going to step in to protect her. Not even if her life was on the line. She was on her own.

CHAPTER TWENTY-TWO

Heath

Heath shifted his feet impatiently on the flagstones, earning him a reproving look from his mother. He stilled, but a moment later found himself drumming his fingers against the hilt of the dress sword he was required to wear for the occasion.

"What's up with you, Heath?" Percival muttered from beside him. "I'm usually the one who can't stand still for the lighting of the flame."

Heath grunted. "Turns out you were right all along. This ceremony takes forever, and it's freezing out here."

"Boys," their mother reprimanded, her mouth somehow not moving, and her placid for-public-occasions expression remaining firmly in place.

The brothers fell silent, although Heath could still sense the slight smirk on Percival's face. He rolled his eyes at no one in particular, reminding himself that he was supposed to be the reliable one as he cast his eyes over the crowd lining the edges of the large courtyard. He turned his attention back to the king's customary speech.

"And we are honored to mark the passing of another year of peace with our allies."

"Ah," muttered Percival, straightening slightly. "Now it gets interesting."

"Maybe to you," Heath whispered back. "But some of us have actually seen a dragon before."

"No need to get high and mighty, Dragonfriend," Percival started, but at another glare from the duchess he fell silent. He would likely have done so without his mother's intervention, because a moment later a furious wind swept the courtyard where they stood, setting the pennants above the castle flapping frantically.

As if to mimic the wind, a hushed muttering spread over the gathered crowd. And for all his talk, even Heath couldn't help but be impressed—and a little intimidated—by the sight of half a dozen dragons descending on the courtyard, right on cue.

The winged reptiles were enormous, filling the entire square. The sound of their talons touching down on the flagstones below was like metal on glass. Despite his repeated exposure to Reka, Heath felt an involuntary shiver of fear pass over him. Reka was so large compared to a human, it was easy to forget that, as an adolescent dragon, he was much smaller than most of his kin.

The dragon in front of the group was five times larger than Reka. His size showed his age, as did his deep burgundy color, so much darker than Reka's bright scales.

"Greetings, King of Men," the dragon said, inclining his head ever so slightly toward King Matlock, where he stood on a raised platform at one end of the castle courtyard. "We come to celebrate our peace."

Heath's eyes passed over the dragons, and he gave a start of surprise. He hadn't noticed the smallest member of the group at first, but there was no mistaking the familiar form. Reka was looking at Heath, and when their eyes met, the dragon flicked his head slightly to one side in a gesture of greeting. Heath smiled back, intrigued. Reka had never joined the ceremony before, and Heath wondered whether it might be a sort of rite of passage for the young dragon.

The burgundy dragon was inclining his head toward another one of the group as he spoke.

"I speak for the colony on Wyvern Islands, and my brethren represents the colony at Vasilisa."

At his words, a medium sized dragon moved forward, his scales still fairly bright in hues of purple, green, and blue. He dipped his head in recognition of King Matlock, but his eyes quickly searched the royals arranged around the king for another face.

"Jocelyn," the dragon said, extending his enormous head toward Heath's grandmother. "Greetings."

The elderly Kyonan princess smiled, moving forward to lay a hand briefly on the dragon's outstretched snout.

"Hello, old friend," she said softly. "I am glad to see you."

"And I you," the dragon said solemnly. He turned his attention back to the king.

There was no sign of emotion on King Matlock's face, but Heath noticed a few of the nobles wearing slightly sour expressions. It seemed they did not appreciate the display of loyalty shown by the dragon toward the power-wielding, Kyonan princess rather than her nephew, the king.

"King of Men, my name is Elddreki, and although I dwell now on Wyvern Islands, I bring greetings from Vasilisa, in Kyona's mountains. We are glad to be at peace with our human neighbors from both kingdoms."

The king bowed, and the dragon dipped his head again. At

the talk of peace, Heath felt a new sense of appreciation for the familiar ceremony. It was merely symbolic—it wasn't as though Valoria had ever actually had war with the dragons, and if they ever did, the mighty beasts would wipe the human kingdom out with ease. But there was value in remembering the relationship between them.

And as much as some might resent the deference shown to Heath's grandmother, they should be grateful to her. She was the first true dragonfriend Valoria had ever had, and it was only since her arrival in their kingdom that the Flame of Friendship had existed. After all, it wasn't as though the dragons really had anything to gain from declaring peace with the kingdom of men whose land they shared, or anything to lose from being at enmity with them.

If what Heath's grandmother had told him was true, it was entirely due to Elddreki's influence that the dragons had decided to formally mark their pre-existing peace with Valoria. And that influence had been exerted purely on the basis of the unusual friendship between Elddreki and Heath's grandmother. His thoughts grew somber as he remembered the other part of his grandmother's explanation—or more accurately, warning. By renewing the ceremony annually, the dragons had a very simple way of withdrawing from the declaration of peace without going back on their words. They needed only to let it lapse.

Heath had assumed that Elddreki, probably the best known dragon in Valoria, would undertake the rest of the ceremony, as he had done every year within Heath's memory. But instead, he stepped slightly to the side, revealing a yellow female dragon of a similar size to himself, and Reka beside her.

"My offspring, Rekavidur, would be honored to speak."

The king turned to Reka. If he felt any surprise at the change, he masked it in his usual expert way.

"Greetings, King of Men," said Reka, in the formal cadence of the dragons. "I am Rekavidur, and I am honored to have been chosen by my colony to renew our symbol of peace." King Matlock assented with equal formality, but Rekavidur wasn't done. To Heath's astonishment, the young dragon turned to him. "Greetings, Dragonfriend," he said, and another murmur passed through the crowd.

Heath felt Percival shift beside him at this serious—and extremely public—use of the title he had flippantly thrown at his brother minutes before.

"Greetings, Rekavidur," said Heath, after a moment's stunned silence.

He had no idea what, if anything, he was supposed to add, but apparently Reka was satisfied. The dragon turned away from Heath, to the castle's entrance. He pushed from the ground, a rushing wind sweeping around the courtyard as he took to the air. Within moments, he was hovering above the stone basin, in which the flame was flickering. The fire was as faint as Heath had ever seen it, given that it had been a year since its last replenishment. The magic was designed to keep the Flame of Friendship going for only a year at a time, so the dragons and humans could renew the symbol of their peace annually.

"May our warmth sustain you in the dark of winter," Reka said formally.

Heath hid a smile at the young dragon's lofty tone. He hadn't needed his grandmother to explain this other reason for the dragons' involvement in the festival. Thanks to his friendship with Reka, he was well aware that dragons, for all their elusive majesty, were extremely fond of formalities and ceremonies.

Reka opened his jaws wide, and Heath's full focus returned to the present. Even from the ground, Heath could feel the heat spreading from the dragon's mouth as fire built within him.

Icicles melted all around the basin, causing miniature waterfalls to flow down the castle's stone walls.

Then Reka let out a gush of flame—orange with the slightest purple tinge—which engulfed the stone basin. The fire within roared back to full strength, and the crowd cheered. As if on demand, snow began to fall, gentle white flakes drifting onto Heath's hair, and sizzling as they landed on Reka's scales, still warm from the magic of his flames.

"All right," Heath admitted to his brother, smiling in spite of himself. "The ceremony isn't so bad."

Percival chuckled, a slight edge to the sound. Glancing at him, Heath realized his brother's admiration was mixed with a measure of fear. It was easy to forget that most people weren't as used to dragons as Heath was. The magical beasts still unnerved most humans. And not without reason, he reflected, glancing up at the sheer size of them. It wasn't just their physical strength, either. There was a presence about even the smallest of dragons. Only a fool would cross the creatures.

The dragons didn't stay long beyond the lighting of the flame, but Heath found the opportunity to approach Reka while the king was exchanging formalities with the burgundy dragon.

"Why did you greet me like that?" he asked, when he had checked that no one was listening.

Reka did his rippling shrug. "It was my father's idea, actually. He has noticed the increase in the time we spend together, and he suggested that the change should be marked."

Heath frowned slightly, his gaze passing to the larger dragon, who was in speech with Heath's grandparents. "What did he say about our trips to Vazula?"

"He does not know about Vazula," said Reka calmly.

Heath raised an eyebrow. "I thought dragons don't lie to each other."

Reka gave a huff of irritation, and Heath tried not to smile at his friend's lofty tone. "I did not lie. I never even considered such a thing. My father did not ask where we had been, just confirmed that I have been with you."

"If you say so," Heath said lightly.

His eyes traveled to his own father, standing respectfully behind his elderly parents as they conversed with the dragon Elddreki. Reka could act as grand as he liked, but the dragon's omissions sounded suspiciously like Heath's carefully crafted explanations to his own parents.

Heath drummed his fingers on the table impatiently, the good humor that had enlivened the Solstice ceremony, and the gala that followed, long gone. "What's taking so long?"

Brody raised an eyebrow. "Probably the king doesn't realize he needs to hurry up to suit your schedule."

"You know I didn't mean that," Heath grumbled.

"Relax, Heath," said Percival, stifling a yawn. "This process has been going for days, what's another half an hour?"

"Days?" Heath shot his brother a look. "You mean weeks. It's over three weeks we've been kicking our heels here."

"What's up with you, Heath?" Brody stared at him. "You're usually the one keeping everyone else calm. What's your hurry?"

Heath rolled out his shoulders. "I just didn't realize that by coming to this registration discussion, I was signing up to move to Bryford. When I agreed to come, I thought we'd be here a week beyond the Solstice at most."

"Agreed to come?" Bianca repeated, leaning around her brother from her seat at the long table. "It was a summons. Didn't you have to come?"

"Gray area," said Percival, helping himself to the refreshments set out in the middle of the table.

"Ah, of course," said Brody, nodding wisely. "Because of the weak power thing."

"Thanks for that, Brody," said Heath dryly.

Both of Brody's eyebrows went up this time. "Now I know something's up. You never react to my jabs. Why are you so annoyed about being here?"

"It's because he's missing his weekly dates with Rekavidur," Percival supplied helpfully, his words coming out thickly around a mouthful of pastry.

"Oho, who's that?" Brody asked, grinning broadly at his cousin. "Is there a girl, is there?"

Heath could feel a flush rising, and was relieved when Percival unwittingly rescued him.

"No, no, I'm talking about his dragon friend."

"Oh, that's right. I forgot his name." Brody deflated slightly, then gave Heath a strange look. "You and your dragon friend have weekly dates?"

Heath rolled his eyes. "Reka has nothing to do with it. He won't care that I'm gone for weeks. He probably won't even notice. I just don't like being kept here like a prisoner."

"Well, you can complain all you like, but I'm glad it's taking this long," said Percival frankly. "I think King Matlock must be rethinking the whole thing, or it would be over by now."

Brody frowned. "Don't get me wrong, I'm glad Grandmother intervened. But I don't understand what took her so long. She barely said a word when it was first discussed, a few months back."

"She had to be careful, didn't she?" Bianca pointed out. "If she changed the king's mind, it wouldn't exactly help our cause, would it?"

"Why not?" Percival asked, looking confused, but Heath instantly saw what his cousin meant.

"Because her power is change," he answered for Bianca. "And it's very strong. Of course. If she'd spoken a word about it, everyone would think she'd used her magic to change his mind."

Bianca nodded. "It's delicate. From what I've heard, it's Grandfather who's done all the persuading."

"Any idea why it's just us here, though?" asked Jasmine, another cousin. She had so far remained silent, and she sounded nervous. She was Heath's age, but her timidity had always made her seem younger to him.

Before anyone could hazard a guess, the door to the long dining hall opened, causing them all to look up.

They all pushed themselves hastily to their feet as King Matlock entered the room, flanked as usual by his guards. Crown Prince Lachlan was at his side, and a court scribe followed them in, parchment and quill in hand.

They settled across the table from the five cousins, and they all sat as well. After exchanging respectful greetings, Heath surreptitiously examined the parchment before the scribe. Most likely none of the others would be able to read it upside down and from that distance. But from what his sharp eyes could make out, it looked like the king had just come from a meeting with their non-magic counterparts in their generation of the extended royal family. Heath glimpsed Magnolia's name—the second cousin who had bestowed the victory kiss in the tournament—among others.

The realization filled Heath with foreboding. Dividing them into two camps seemed like the opposite of what the king should be doing.

"Thank you for your attendance, Lord Percival, Lord Brody, Lady Bianca, Lord Heath, and Lady Jasmine," said the king formally, naming them in age order as though he was reading from a mental census list. "I wish to speak with the five of you specifically, because you represent those adults in the power-wielding branch of the family who have not yet reached the age of twenty-one."

Heath exchanged a curious look with his brother. What was the significance of the age of twenty-one? That must be why Laura, at twenty-two, hadn't been included in this meeting. At least the fact that the king wished to speak with those who had reached adulthood explained the exclusion of Jasmine's two siblings, and their two other cousins.

"The decision I have reached will affect you all soonest, although in time it will also impact those of your cousins yet to reach their majority."

Heath felt Percival fidget in his seat. He showed no outward sign himself, but he also wished the king would get to the point.

"The matter of registration is to be put to one side for the time being," the king continued, and Percival went unnaturally still. "At this stage, all the crown seeks is the loyalty of those of its subjects who have power."

"Your Majesty," cut in Brody, inclining his head in the closest thing to a bow he could manage while seated. "I think I speak for us all when I say that you have our absolute loyalty."

"Thank you, Lord Brody," said King Matlock gravely. "I value your words. However, it is not in your power to speak for everyone."

Was it Heath's imagination that the king's eyes lingered for a moment longer on Percival than on anyone else as he scanned the group? If Lord Niel had heard about Percival's ill-advised comments about power on the throne, then the king must have as well. Did he suspect Percival of treasonous thoughts?

"The suggestion has been made that those subjects born with power can do a great service to our kingdom by swearing their loyalty to the crown, and thereby reassuring the rest of the population—and indeed demonstrating to other kingdoms—that Valoria is united and strong. After careful consideration, I have approved this suggestion. I know you will all be happy to provide this service for your kingdom. The ceremony will take place on the occasion of the relevant individual's twenty-first birthday."

There was a moment of silence as everyone processed his words.

"Just to be clear, Your Majesty," said Heath carefully. "Am I correct in understanding that this ceremony will only be conducted for those born with power?"

"That is correct," said the king briskly. His eyes passed over the group again, but Heath couldn't help but notice that Prince Lachlan, beside him, had his gaze fixed steadily on Percival. His expression was impassive, but something about his demeanor made Heath incredibly uneasy.

"Do any of you wish to comment on this matter?" the king continued. "Or ask any further questions?"

His tone didn't encourage discussion, and after a moment of silence, King Matlock nodded curtly. "Thank you for your attendance," he said again. "I am sure you are eager to return to your homes, but I would be grateful for your continued patience as we work out the details of this arrangement. I'm sure you will wish to have input into the form of the ceremony, which will be an event worth celebrating as each of you take your full place in society. I look forward to working more with you all in the future, and seeing how your unique talents can best flourish."

The king stood, and they all stood as well. But after his retinue had left the room, the five cousins sank back down into their chairs. Unsurprisingly, it was Percival whose face looked the stormiest.

"If Father was here, he'd be able to confirm what we already know—that last comment was an absolute falsehood."

"Lower your voice, Percival," said Bianca, her tone unusually sharp.

Percival looked mutinous, but Heath agreed with Bianca. He was becoming more and more convinced that this whole process had arisen from Percival's words that day, before the tournament. This was no time for him to be overheard calling the king a liar.

"Well, this is taking things in a bit of a new direction, isn't it?" Brody said thoughtfully.

"It's good, isn't it?" Jasmine interjected hesitantly. "I didn't much like the idea of being registered, so surely it's a good thing the king isn't doing that after all?"

"He didn't say he wasn't doing it," Percival corrected her. "He said it's being 'put to one side for the time being'. There's no way the others are going to stop pushing for it, having come so close to success. It might take another decade, but it will happen eventually."

"Unless we can find a way to bring everyone together," said Heath absently, deep in thought. Percival just shrugged one shoulder, still moody.

"It's interesting that he called just those of us between eighteen and twenty-one," mused Brody.

"And interesting that they waited until well after the dragons' attendance at the ceremony," muttered Percival. "I suppose they didn't want to risk them being offended."

Brody ignored the comment, continuing on his train of thought. "It didn't seem that he really wanted our opinion on the matter, did it?" Percival snorted, but again Brody ignored him, pushing on. "Clearly he'd already made up his mind."

Heath remained silent. Brody was undoubtedly right. It had been clear from what he could read of the scribe's notes that the other group—their non-magic peers—had been given substantially more opportunity to have input into the matter. But he didn't think it would be helpful to share that information. Not with the storm still hovering over Percival's brow.

For a moment Heath was distracted, the thought of storms reminding him of the island, and the day when he and Merletta had been caught in a tropical downpour. She'd taught him to float under the surface, face up so as to watch the incredible sight of rain hitting the water from below. What was she thinking about his continued absence? He hadn't intended to be gone this long, and he hated the thought of her arriving each week in the expectation of seeing him, only to be disappointed.

He shook the thought off. He had more immediate problems to worry about.

"Clearly it's our generation the crown is worried about," Brody was continuing. He cast a surreptitious glance at Percival. "I didn't hear any talk of our parents having to swear loyalty."

"Perhaps he feels they've already demonstrated their loyalty, through their service," Jasmine interjected timidly. Her eyes were also on Percival, and when he noticed it, he sent her a glower which made her instantly look away, her face turning pink.

Heath gave his brother a reproving look before smiling encouragingly at Jasmine. "I'm sure you're right," he said. "And with a little time, everyone will see that our generation is equally loyal."

"It's an insult," Percival said forcefully. "We're all loyal, and we've never given anyone any reason to think otherwise. Making us declare it in some public ceremony is not only humiliating, but it suggests we weren't loyal before. Or at the very least, that we can't be trusted to be loyal without being forced into it."

Heath was silent, exchanging a thoughtful look with Brody. It was predictable that Percival would be angriest about it, but he wasn't entirely wrong. The fact that as the oldest of their generation—other than their married sister, Laura—Percival would be the first to go through this ceremony, wasn't going to help.

Heath sighed, banishing all thoughts of Vazula and Merletta even further from his mind. His brother was going to need all the help Heath could give him to get through this. Hopefully, without being accused of—or actually committing—treason.

CHAPTER TWENTY-THREE

Merletta sighed, tossing the leaf up with a flourish, and watching it drift back down to the stone bench in front of her. It was impossible to focus on her own study when she knew that Sage was taking her test right now. She glanced up through one of the many long openings in the ceiling of the records hall. The light in the distant sky was waning. Sage had been at it for most of the day. It was certainly a grueling assessment.

Merletta had been projecting confidence for the sake of the other mermaid, but the truth was she was nervous for her friend. Oliver really had looked ill when he'd emerged from his test.

At least Ileana had stopped trying to scare poor Sage. Apparently the third year mermaid had passed her guard test with a brilliant result, and she'd been making smug remarks for weeks about what an ordeal the test could be for more timid trainees. It had made Merletta want to punch her in the face—she knew perfectly well that Ileana's increasingly disdainful attitude toward Sage was a direct result of the growing friendship between her and Merletta.

The thought of Ileana made Merletta's hands ball into fists. She had plenty of reasons to want to punch the older trainee in the face. It was almost impossible to believe that such a short time ago, Ileana had tried to kill her, and now things were just back to normal.

That is, if she really had tried to kill her. Merletta had been so sure when she surged into Instructor Wivell's office. But the very normality of Ileana's behavior toward her since then had made her doubt herself. Could the other mermaid really have tried to kill her one minute, then gone back to cold silences and petty insults the next? Agner had refrained from mentioning the incident again, and Merletta had the impression he was trying to be gracious and not embarrass her for her disproportionate display of anger.

Just an instance of emotions running wild after a brutal bout between two bitter rivals.

Easy for him to think that way, when he wasn't the one who had to sleep in the same room as Ileana every night. But the other mermaid had shown no sign of aggression toward Merletta since then, and over time, things had almost begun to feel the same as before. After all, short of dropping out and swimming away back to Tilssted, Merletta didn't see what more she could do about her suspicions.

Except watch her back, of course.

Merletta winced as she shifted in her seat. Most of her injuries had healed now, but a couple of places were still stiff, and sometimes she felt a phantom pressure on her throat.

She hadn't even told Sage the full details of how she acquired the particularly vicious bruises. Sage hadn't taken either of the previous pranks seriously, and Merletta couldn't bear to hear her friend tentatively offering the same explanations that Wivell had. She also didn't want to put Sage in the position of choosing sides between Merletta and the instructors. She was afraid of what the other trainee's choice might be.

Plus Sage had needed to focus on her upcoming test. And now Ileana's test was less than a month away, so she had her own problems to worry about. And one way or another, Sage would be past the ordeal soon. Merletta knew there were no second chances to take any of the tests. You passed, or you failed, that was it.

She really hoped Sage passed.

She glanced around the records hall, unsurprised to see Jacobi sitting at the other end of the space. It was becoming more common to see him studying outside classes as well. His first year test was scheduled to happen not long after Ileana's third year test. His birthday must be close to Emil's, because Merletta had heard that the fourth year's test was set for the day after Jacobi's.

Then, in only a few months, it would be her turn.

She picked the writing leaf back up again, trying to convince herself that she was interested in the history of how the oyster farms were established. The minutes swirled by at a glacial pace, and Merletta read the same words over and over again without them making any impression on her mind.

"Wasting your time over here, aren't you?"

Merletta sighed, looking up at the unwelcome interruption.

"What do you want, Jacobi?" She couldn't be bothered sparring verbally with him. She was too stressed about Sage's test, and too tired from the long swim to the island on her rest day—long and unnecessary, since Heath had failed to appear for the seventh week in a row.

"I want you to learn your place, Tilssted," the copper-haired trainee sneered. "A little clue—it's not in the Center."

Merletta just rolled her eyes. He had barely spoken to her

since the incident in the training courtyard, and she'd been delighted at their mutual avoidance of one another. Even before that, she'd been trying to be more forbearing with him since hearing Sage's comments about his family. He was still a slimy little sea snail, of course, and he'd still helped Ileana attack her. But he hadn't shown the murderous hate the other trainee had, and to her own irritation, Merletta still felt the occasional—and very uncomfortable—twinge of sympathy when she noticed him glaring at her.

"It's not like you're going to pass the test to go on to second year," Jacobi continued, apparently unable to stop until he got a reaction.

Merletta flicked her tail in irritation. She didn't want to deal with Jacobi right now. "Let's just let our results talk for us, Jacobi."

Jacobi's eyes narrowed in anger, and Merletta belatedly realized what the source of his persistent insults must be. She had outperformed him in the recent practice test by quite a lot. She could only imagine that if she passed the final test, without any advantage of blood or upbringing, and he didn't, he would be utterly humiliated.

"If they even let you take the test," Jacobi sniffed. "It's not like any of the instructors want you here."

Merletta didn't respond, frowning. His words were petty, and she was fairly confident he didn't know anything she didn't, but the comment still touched a nerve. The thought had occurred to her before now that someone—Ibsen, probably—might try to prevent her from progressing by rigging the test, or some other type of foul play. It was one of the reasons she was trying to keep the line a little more, at least outwardly, and had refrained from pressing her accusations against Ileana further.

And since she had taken that approach—keeping her questions to herself, studying in her own time rather than pushing the instructors for assistance, even braiding her hair—things had become a little easier. Ibsen was still unpleasant, but Wivell at least seemed content to ignore her rather than pursue any vendetta against her. He hadn't even made mention of her unsuccessful complaint.

The thought that someone might interfere in her testing was all the more unsettling because she knew there was nothing she could do about it.

"At least you'll be able to go back home to your beloved slums soon," added Jacobi spitefully, clearly taking her silence as a sign of the success of his taunts. "You should really be reading up about your people over there, instead of taking up perfectly good study space here."

Merletta ignored the jibe, but she did follow his gesture with a bemused frown. "You do realize that's not the section on Tilssted, right?" She pointed to a different part of the records hall. "Tilssted's records are over there."

Jacobi rolled his eyes. "You think I don't know that? I wasn't talking about Tilssted's records. I was talking about the orphan records."

"Orphan records?" Merletta asked, her forehead creasing in confusion.

"You really don't know anything, do you?" Jacobi scoffed. "I would have thought that *being* a nameless orphan, you would at least know that you lot are all—"

"Merletta!"

Both trainees turned as the clear voice cut across the usually silent records hall, interrupting Jacobi's insults.

"Sage!" Merletta abandoned her fellow first year without hesitation, uninterested in any further conversation with him. Her heart lifted as she took in her friend's demeanor. She didn't need Sage's next words to know the outcome.

"I did it! I passed! I don't think it was by much, but I did it!"

"I'm so glad!" Merletta cried, grabbing Sage's hands and spinning them around in the water. "And not at all surprised. I knew you could do it!"

"Sshhh!!" The angry hiss made both mermaids look up, to see the record holder currently in charge of the hall swimming toward them. "This is a haven, not a carnival!"

"Sorry, sir," said Sage apologetically. "I got carried away."

"I wasn't speaking to you, trainee," the record holder sniffed. His eyes narrowed as they rested on Merletta. "You may not have value for knowledge in *Tilssted*," he growled, "but here our records are considered sacred. You should treat this hall with more respect."

"But, sir," protested Sage. "I was the one who—"

"Our apologies, sir." Merletta cut her off with a slight shake of her head, pulling her friend along by the arm until they were out of the building.

"That was so unfair," Sage started, frowning back toward the records hall.

"Never mind that," said Merletta. "You did it! You're a third year!"

Sage's face brightened instantly. "I know! I can hardly believe it."

Merletta smiled as they began to swim back toward their barracks. "I want to say tell me all about it, but I guess you can't."

A slight shudder passed over Sage's tall figure. "I'm glad I'm not allowed to talk about it. I don't want to at all."

"Well, you can forget all about it now," said Merletta. "You never have to do second year again."

"Hooray for that," agreed Sage emphatically. "Now let's cele-brate with dinner. I'm starving."

Merletta readily agreed, and the two of them made their way to the dining hall, chatting brightly.

It wasn't until the meal was almost over that Merletta suddenly realized what had been niggling in her mind ever since she'd left the records hall with Sage.

"What is it?" Sage asked, in response to Merletta's sudden gasp. "What's wrong?"

She glanced nervously over her shoulder, and some part of Merletta's mind noted how much the test had shaken the normally placid mermaid. But she had no space to think about that now.

"My satchel!" Merletta shot up out of her seat. "I don't have it. I think I left it in the records hall."

"Oh," said Sage vaguely, looking confused at Merletta's reaction. "Well, we can go back and get it after the meal. The hall is open at any hour to trainees, remember."

Merletta shook her head. "I need to go now."

"But...what's the hurry?" Sage looked utterly bewildered. "No one's going to steal it, not in the Center."

But Merletta was already halfway to the door. She didn't want to explain it to Sage, but the thought of someone finding her satchel, with its illicit treasures, was one of her greatest fears.

She swam rapidly through the dark streets of the Center, reaching the records hall within minutes that felt like hours. She swam straight in, ignoring a disapproving look from the record holder who had scolded her earlier. A quick search was enough to confirm that her satchel was no longer there. Her heartbeat sped up.

"Excuse me, sir?" She approached the record holder, refusing to be put off by his glares. "I think I left a satchel here. Have you seen it?"

"I know nothing of any satchel," sniffed the merman haughtily. "I am a record holder, young lady. It is not my role to pick up your things when you are so careless as to leave them behind!"

Merletta didn't respond, a sick feeling rising in her stomach. She did another lap of the hall, now deserted except for the record holder, but there was still no sign of the satchel.

There was nothing for her to do but give up, returning to the dining hall with reluctant strokes. She cursed her own carelessness in leaving it behind. She usually carried it with her everywhere, but she'd been so distracted by Sage's arrival that it had slipped her mind.

Quite apart from the danger of discovery, she was devastated at the thought of losing all her little treasures. The length of wood, the coconut...a lump rose in her throat...Heath's knife. With two months of his absence, it had started to feel like her only link to the warm-hearted human.

"Did you find it?" Sage asked, as soon as she rejoined her friend at the round table.

Merletta shook her head, not trusting herself to speak with the lump still in her throat.

"Oh, that's frustrating," said Sage sympathetically. "Probably someone picked it up as lost, and it'll find its way back to you soon enough."

Merletta still didn't respond. Sage, with her legacy status, and absence of anything to hide, clearly had no concept of why Merletta would be anxious about someone else having access to her belongings.

Their meal finished, they made their way to the barracks. Sage was still buzzing from her successful test, and Merletta didn't want to bring her down. But she was so dismayed over the loss of her satchel that she felt ill.

"Oh, Merletta, there you are."

Merletta looked up warily at the lazy greeting that met her as she passed into the female trainees' sleeping quarters. It was never a good sign when Ileana was speaking to her by choice.

"Ileana," she acknowledged, her eyes narrowed venomously, but her tone cautious.

"I have something for you."

The words made Merletta's head snap up, her eyes fixing on the small kelp satchel dangling from Ileana's hands.

"Where did you get that?" she snapped, reaching out to snatch it, then thinking better of it and dropping her hand.

"Jacobi found it," said Ileana, an unnatural smile still on her face. "Apparently you left it behind in the records hall. He gave it to me to pass on, since he obviously can't come into our part of the barracks."

"Oh good," said Sage cheerfully. "See, Merletta? I said it would turn up."

Ileana's smile turned into a smirk, and Merletta's feeling of unease tripled.

"Aren't you going to thank me for returning your belongings?" the older mermaid asked, her tone as smooth as a polished pearl. She raised a challenging eyebrow. "It is yours, isn't it?"

Merletta hesitated, the desire to have it back warring with an instinct that told her Ileana was trying to trap her. But she could hardly deny ownership after Sage's comment. She snatched it off Ileana, saying nothing either in thanks or acknowledgment. But Ileana's look was even more smug than before as she relinquished the satchel, before drifting toward her hammock.

Sage chatted happily on, oblivious to Merletta's tension. At the first opportunity, Merletta surreptitiously surveyed the contents of the satchel. She was both relieved and alarmed to see that everything was still there, not a piece missing.

She glanced at Ileana, who was swinging gently in her hammock, her eyes closed and an expression of satisfaction on her face. Merletta was genuinely surprised that the older girl hadn't taken anything. But what did it mean?

She wasn't sure what Ileana was up to this time, and possibly Jacobi with her. But one thing was for certain—it was nothing good.

CHAPTER TWENTY-FOUR

"Three weeks!"

Heath closed his eyes, drawing a deep breath as he attempted to calm his frustration. He released the breath and the arrow, but the thud of the arrowhead hitting the center of the target did nothing to improve his mood.

"Three weeks since the king made his decision, and they still haven't finalized this ceremony business. Who cares about the stupid details?"

He turned to his brother, who was supposedly practicing archery as well, but in reality was moodily throwing arrows point down into the ground at his feet, picking them up, and repeating the process. Percival had never had the patience for archery. He preferred a fight where he could be up close and personal with his target.

"I don't think anyone cares this much about the details," he said darkly. "They just want to keep us all here to see how we're taking it, so that we're under the crown's eye and unable to do anything drastic for long enough for our reactions to settle."

Heath lowered his bow, surprised by the unusually

insightful comment from his brother. "You're probably right, actually."

"No need to sound so astonished," Percival muttered. He threw his bow down, abandoning all pretense at archery. "I don't blame you for being annoyed. It's a couple years before your 'ceremony'"—he spoke the word with a sneer—"and no one's worried about you, anyway. There's no reason you should be forced to sit around in Bryford all these weeks." He sighed. "I've never fancied being carried through the air, my legs dangling precariously, but it's starting to sound appealing even to me. Maybe Reka can come rescue us both, and I'll join you on your adventures instead of enduring this stuffy court."

Heath snorted. "You're not invited on our 'adventures' thank you. You'd be very much in the way."

Percival just rolled his eyes. Heath tried to imagine his brother on the abandoned island, but it was hard to picture. He would get bored there very quickly.

It was obviously a moot point. He had told Merletta he wouldn't expose her, and telling his brother would certainly be doing that. Not to mention Heath quite liked being the only human she knew. He'd been compared to his brother—and not favorably—all his life. It had never bothered him much, since he didn't care about the achievements Percival most valued. But in this instance, he had a feeling it might.

"Come on," he said, returning his bow to the stand. "We both need to get out of our own heads."

"Yes," Percival agreed, straightening. "I could do with a good gallop. A race to the falls, perhaps?"

Heath shook his head. "No, I was thinking I'd see if I could find Grandmother. Taking tea with her usually clears my head."

"Tea with Grandmother?" Percival repeated incredulously. "That's your idea of a good distraction?"

Heath just laughed. "It'll help, trust me."

Percival continued to grumble all the way through the castle, but Heath ignored him. The servant they approached was able to locate the elderly princess quickly, and to Heath's relief, she was delighted to make time for them. The last thing he wanted was to get roped in to racing Percival. Once his brother's competitive instincts were set off, the afternoon would descend into an endless series of challenges, from which Heath would find it difficult to extricate himself.

"It's nice to see you here, Percival," the former Kyonan said, once they were all settled in her private receiving room. There was a humorous sparkle in her eyes as they rested on her oldest grandson, who was turning the delicate teacup over in his hand with as much fascination as one might view a two-headed dog. "I don't often get the pleasure of a visit from you."

"Yes, Heath dragged me," said Percival unashamedly.

"You're very gallant." Their grandmother said the words with a chuckle, and Percival grinned responsively.

"It's not your company that's the problem, of course, Grandmother. It's sitting still and drinking tea." He raised an eyebrow hopefully. "I don't suppose you want to race me to the falls, do you?"

Percival sounded like he was only half joking, and Heath cast his eyes toward the ceiling.

"I'm a bit past that, I'm afraid," said their grandmother, still chuckling. "Your grandfather would probably take you on. He forgets how old he is."

Her eyes passed to Heath. "I'm sorry you're stuck here so long. I've been trying to convince the king that it's time to release you all. Matlock is like his father, very meticulous and methodical about everything he does. Which is very admirable," she hastened to add. "But his own sons are so well behaved, it's easy for him to forget that most young people don't deal well with boredom."

"You mean your sons weren't well behaved?" Heath asked mischievously.

She laughed aloud. "If only. The things your father got up to..." She smiled at him, and the laugh in her eyes faded to something more serious. "How are you faring, Heath?"

"I'm fine," Heath shrugged. "I'd like to go home, of course."

"Home?" Percival snorted. "It's not home he's missing."

"Oh?" The elderly princess raised an inquiring eyebrow at Heath, and he fidgeted uncomfortably in his seat.

"It's nothing," he said quickly. "Reka and I had been exploring together, and it's true that I'm missing the freedom."

"Every week," interjected Percival, now examining the pitcher of cream. "Like clockwork. They'd disappear for the entire day, but Heath refuses to say where they've been."

His grandmother pinned Heath with a searching look, and he squirmed even more.

"Hm," she said at last, turning her attention to her cup of tea.

Heath let out a long breath. She wasn't going to interrogate him in front of Percival. He should have known he could count on her not to put him in a corner.

"Rekavidur?" she said instead. "Elddreki and Raqisa's dragonling? The one who attended the ceremony this year? I knew you had a connection of sorts, even before he singled you out at the Winter Solstice. But I didn't realize you spent so much time together."

"Just recently," Heath shrugged. "And he's not really a dragonling anymore. I was as surprised as anyone that he greeted me at the ceremony." He grimaced. "He didn't give me much of a reason for it when I asked him, but I've given it a lot of thought. I think he was trying to give me the status of dragonfriend to help counteract my lack of power."

His grandmother gave him a skeptical look. "Somehow I don't think that's it, Heath."

"What do you think about this whole ceremony require-ment?" Percival cut in abruptly. "It's an insult, surely?"

Their grandmother hesitated, her eyes measuring the irate young man before her. "If you can find a way to *not* view it as an insult, I think that would be wise."

"That's not really an answer, Grandmother," said Percival, unimpressed. "I was asking your opinion."

She smiled, but there was a sadness to it. "Royalty has to be careful with the luxury of opinions," she said.

Her shrewd gaze made Heath wonder uncomfortably if she, too, had heard about Percival's slip of the tongue. He grimaced. If only he could wind back time and stop his brother from ever opening his mouth on the subject.

Percival didn't seem to share Heath's discomfort. He prob-ably had no thought of that long-ago conversation in his mind at all, and he looked mutinous at their grandmother's refusal to weigh in.

The elderly princess sighed as she took in his expression. "Don't think too harshly of the king, Percival. He's inherited a complicated situation, that was none of his making, and he's trying his best to find a way through it."

"It wasn't of your making either, Grandmother," said Heath, frowning at the guilt he saw lurking behind her gentle words. "You didn't choose to be born with power, and you've benefited the kingdom so many times by using your gifts."

She patted his hand fondly. "Thank you, Heath. You have a kind heart." She smiled. "And an observant eye. I can't deny that I have been troubled by all this. The possibility of passing my power to my descendants was one of my greatest fears when I was your age. But that was before I learned to see it as a force for good, not evil. I keep reminding myself that it's not a bad thing to have magic growing in our community."

"Of course it's not a bad thing!" said Percival, looking

shocked and a little offended at this sign of uncertainty from the family's original power-wielder. "Like Heath said, you've done so much good with your gift." His tone turned hopeful. "Are you sure you couldn't do it now?"

The elderly princess shook her head firmly. "I'm sorry, Percival, but I'm very sure. This isn't some crisis, brought on by evil interference, which requires the help of my power to break its hold. This is a real and complex problem, and we need to find a resolution in the natural way. If I used my power to change King Matlock's mind for the benefit of our family, it would not only exacerbate everyone's fears, it would prove them to be justified."

Percival looked sulky, but Heath knew in his bones that his grandmother was right.

"Is it really so bad, Grandmother?" he said. "I don't mean the ceremony, I mean the registration idea. I feel foolish to ask, but is there any great harm in keeping a record of who is and isn't born with power?"

"Heath!" protested Percival. "I know you're obsessed with knowledge and records, but come on! Whose side are you on? You want us to be restricted, so we can only use our powers if specifically requested to by the king?" He raised his muscled arms helplessly, and his voice turned sarcastic. "How would that even work? Would I be prevented from lifting things anytime I'm not in His Royal Majesty's presence?"

"That talk of restrictions was just a rumor," Heath said quickly.

"Actually," cut in their grandmother, "it was exactly what was intended."

Heath stilled, aware that Percival was looking at him smugly, although his eyes remained locked on the princess.

"It wouldn't be workable at all," she said, glancing at Percival. "I tried to explain how impossible it would be to simply not use some types of power. But it's hard for those outside of the situation to understand that." A frown creased her forehead. "But it's not about taking sides, and Heath's question isn't foolish." She met Heath's eye seriously. "I believe that the king meant well with the idea of registration, but I won't deny that it made me very uneasy. Have you ever heard of humans being registered and cataloged like that?"

Heath shook his head slowly. "Percival did say it made us like cattle," he acknowledged. "It is a little unusual to force people to be registered in such a way."

She nodded. "It is unusual, but not unheard of. I *have* seen it, or something not unlike it. When I was young, there was talk in Kyona of registering those whose parents and grandparents had once been slaves in Balenol, classifying them differently from the rest of the population." She shook her head. "It was a very dangerous suggestion, planted by an enemy of Kyona whose intention was to see the kingdom rip itself apart. And it would certainly have worked if the plan had gone ahead." Her expression was more serious than Heath had ever seen it. "They were even talking of branding the freedmen, as they were called." She nodded to Percival. "Like cattle."

"But that's surely a different matter," Heath protested. "No one's talking about branding the power-wielders!"

"Not yet," said the princess gravely. "But these things are delicate, and taking one step in a bad direction can be more dangerous than you might think."

"You see?" Percival said, gesturing to their grandmother. "Like I said."

Heath didn't respond, mulling over his grandmother's words. "So you think whoever came up with this idea is an enemy of Valoria?" he asked. "That the intention is to make us all turn on each other?"

"What?" His grandmother looked startled. "No, I didn't mean that. I was just reflecting on what happened in Kyona."

Heath nodded absently. She seemed genuinely surprised by his question, but he wasn't entirely satisfied. He'd certainly been given a lot to think about.

Another week crawled by, and the formal events Heath was required to attend all seemed pointless, like their sole purpose was to justify the continued presence of the power-wielders. Heath was convinced now that Percival had been right, and that they were being kept close so they could all be monitored for any sign of defiance.

From the way some of the nobles watched Percival in particular, Heath had come to two conclusions. The first was that a great many people were aware not only of Percival's careless words about the throne, but of the sympathetic reaction of some of the population. The second was that in keeping them all in Bryford, the king was trying to prove to his court that the situation could be managed without registering or restricting anyone. And certain members of the court—Lord Niel included—were almost certainly hoping to see behavior that would convince the king of the opposite. Lord Niel even watched Heath with an eagle eye whenever they were in his vicinity. Perhaps he was still simmering over the incident with the archery competition, or perhaps it was just the inevitable result of the unexpected visibility Heath had achieved when Reka had greeted him at the Solstice.

Heath therefore tried to behave with circumspection, hiding his impatience as best he could. He also stuck close to Percival wherever possible, hoping his presence would help his brother to keep his own frustration under the surface.

Whether it worked, and the court's fears were allayed for now, or whether King Matlock just realized he couldn't keep them in Bryford forever, at long last they were released.

Heath couldn't help but feel a bit disgruntled at the timing. If only the king had given them leave to return home one day earlier. The day they spent riding home was Merletta's rest day, so he would have to wait a whole extra week to go to the island. Somehow it didn't even cross his mind to visit Vazula in her absence, as he had once done.

The next six days felt even longer than the six weeks that had come before, but he tried not to show his irritation. He could tell that Percival was growing increasingly suspicious about the nature of his outings with Reka, and watching Heath prowl the manor like a caged bear couldn't be doing much to reduce his curiosity. Heath couldn't think of any convincing reason for why the dragon would be the one who cared what day of the week they went on their expeditions. Days of the week were completely immaterial to an immortal creature.

When the relevant day finally arrived, Heath was on the cliffs outside the manor, with his rucksack packed, by the time the sun rose.

"Reka!" he called. "I'm ready anytime you are." He settled in to wait, watching the sky turn slowly from pink-streaked yellow to the soft blue of a cool spring morning.

"Reka?" he tried again, after an hour. "I'm finally free from Bryford."

He felt foolish. He'd never had to try twice. Reka had always heard him on the first call. And he'd never failed to respond. However superior the dragon might act, Heath knew that as such a young member of the colony, he had no responsibilities to prevent him from leaving Wyvern Islands. And he'd been as eager for their trips to Vazula as Heath had. He was still trying to figure out the story behind the former presence and current absence of Vazula's dragon colony.

Was it possible he'd been going to Vazula without Heath, while Heath was stuck in Bryford, and had solved the mystery? The thought irritated Heath for no sensible reason.

After another half an hour, he was cold, and stiff from sitting so long. He meandered along the cliff face, climbing down once the rocks began to thin into sandy beach. He knew Reka would have no trouble finding him, wherever he ended up. It was too cold to want to dip his feet in the water, but he skimmed rocks across the surface, wondering if Merletta had ever tried that particular skill. It would be hard from halfway in the water, he supposed.

He waited another two hours, his frustration growing until it was even stronger than it had been in Bryford. He was finally home, and yet he was as trapped and powerless as ever.

Eventually, he was forced to admit to himself that there was no point in waiting any longer. The reason, he was unable to guess, but the reality was undeniable.

The dragon wasn't coming.

CHAPTER TWENTY-FIVE

Merletta barely realized when she passed out of Skulssted and into Tilssted, despite the significant difference in the surroundings. She was too lost in thought, thinking about Jacobi's upcoming test, less than two weeks away. She wasn't as nervous as she had been about Sage's test, of course, but she still felt a strong interest in the performance of her fellow first year.

Jacobi was clearly stressed about it. He'd looked so ill when he left the dining hall that morning, she'd almost felt sorry for him. She couldn't blame him for his nerves. They were all on edge after the last test. Well, not Emil, of course. His final test for the program was the day after Jacobi's, but he remained his unflappable self. With good reason—no one doubted the outcome of that test. But the two first years could hardly help being extra anxious.

She shook her head as she swam. It had been a couple of weeks, but she could still hardly believe that Ileana had failed. Speaking of people she never thought she'd feel sorry for...

There was no denying there was a vindictive part of her that had been pleased to hear of the poison-tongued mermaid's failure. But she had the decency to be ashamed of it. Whatever Ileana's intentions toward her, the thought of your life's dreams being so completely shattered was sobering. And even thinking selfishly, she wasn't really glad. Whatever inscrutable reason Ileana had for keeping quiet about the contraband she must surely have seen in Merletta's satchel may no longer apply if she wasn't in the program. Merletta hadn't seen Ileana since she failed her educator test, the other mermaid having disappeared home immediately. But who knew what Ileana would do when next they met?

At least Sage was back from her break now, and into her third year classes. Merletta's nerves had almost been rubbed raw after a month of enduring Ileana's smug glances and sickly sweet greetings without a friendly face to break up the tension.

Merletta made her way quickly through the poorly lit streets of Tilssted, pleased to have her spear with her. She'd snuck out for night time wanderings many times as a child, and had never had the benefit of a proper weapon before. Not that it was night time now. It was barely dinner hour at the Center. But it would be fully dark by the time she returned.

She was glad her outing didn't take her through her old neighborhood. Her mood was low enough already without being reminded of that place. The previous rest day had been the first time she'd seriously considered not even going to Vazula. She could certainly do with the extra study time. But she'd decided that the tension of wondering whether she'd been absent when the Valorian pair had finally decided to reappear would be worse than the disappointment of watching an empty sky all day. And at least when she was floating in the lagoon, she could mull over her various problems without any risk of inter-ruption.

She rounded a corner, her destination in sight at last. Tish's building was quiet, but a couple of the other stone towers occupied by the shellsmiths still rang with the bangs and scrapes of chiseling. They certainly worked them hard. It was a good thing for Merletta to remember any time she felt inclined to complain about the unrelenting schedule of the program.

Merletta slipped into the building as unobtrusively as she could, bracing herself for glares and muttering. The knowledge that visitors—while not forbidden—were generally discouraged, was the main reason she'd come so rarely. She hoped Tish wasn't going to get too much of a hard time after she left.

But to her surprise, no one sent her so much as a nasty look. A mermaid floating through the building's entry glanced at her, taking in the spear in her hand, and the band of a Center trainee on her arm. Strangely, the girl's eyes seemed to light up, and she gave Merletta a tentative smile. Merletta returned it, bemused.

As she made her way up through the floors of the building, the experience was repeated several times. Finally, one floor below Tish's, someone addressed her.

"You're the girl from the charity home who got into that training program at the Center, aren't you?" a mermaid with a particularly loud voice asked. "The first trainee from Tilssted in forever?"

Merletta acknowledged it, a little stunned that they'd heard of her.

"Good on you," the mermaid said stoutly. "You show them what we're made of."

"I'm trying," Merletta said, with a touch of humor.

The other mermaid gave an approving nod before drifting away. Glancing around, Merletta saw that everyone in sight was giving her the same approving look. Rattled by the experience, she hastened up to Tish's floor.

"Tish?" She poked her head into her friend's tiny room, not

surprised to find the pale-haired mermaid bent over a large shell, even though her eyes must be straining in the dim light.

"Merletta!" Tish rose from her seat with delight clear on her face. "It's so good to see you!"

"You too," said Merletta, embracing her friend. "I'm sorry it's been so long since I came last."

"I understand." Tish dismissed the apology with a wave of her hand. "You don't have any more free time than I do. Except for your rest days, of course, and I'm not exactly available to spend those with you." She waved the shell. "Do you mind if I keep working while we talk?"

"Of course not," said Merletta, drifting over to the hammock in one corner, and settling on it to watch her friend. "Still working this late?"

Tish nodded, her head once again bent over the shell which she was working with a sharpened stone. "I haven't quite made my quota for the month."

"Even though—let me guess—you've been working hard from dawn till dusk every day this month, without a rest to speak of?"

Tish just shrugged one shoulder.

"It's servitude, Tish."

"Hush," said Tish anxiously, looking over her shoulder toward the door.

"There's no one around," Merletta reassured her. "I checked. You know I don't want to cause trouble for you."

Tish visibly relaxed. "Of course I do. It's just, you know how it is. The other apprentices are depressingly like the beneficiaries we grew up with. Always someone ready to tattle."

She looked up, meeting Merletta's eye. "I know it's not nearly as grand as working in the Center, but I want to keep this job. It's much better than being on the street. And," she added dryly, "it's not like I can apply at the Center, like you did, if this didn't work out."

"Of course you want to keep it," said Merletta staunchly. "And I'm sure you will." She shuddered internally at the very thought of Tish in the Center. They'd eat her alive. She kept that reflection to herself, leaning forward to get a closer look at her friend's work. "Wow, you're incredibly good at that intricate carving work, Tish!"

"Do you think so?" Tish flushed with pleasure. "The head carver complimented my work the other day. She seems to like me well enough. I'm hoping I might be able to pursue carving, if I can stay on her good side. It's easier work, and better pay, than what I'm doing now."

"It often seems to work that way, doesn't it?" observed Merletta wryly.

"It's just the way of the world," shrugged Tish. "You know, it's really not as bad here as you think. They do work us hard, but we have plenty of food, and somewhere safe to sleep." She lowered her voice. "Some of the other shellsmith towers have terrible reputations, but not here. They only employ women, and they're rigidly strict in the way they run things. Honestly, I've never felt safer."

"Well, that's something," said Merletta. She sighed as she pushed herself off the hammock, floating over to Tish's tiny window and looking out at the grimy street beyond. It occurred to her that Tish was probably safer than she was, given the three times so far she'd been at risk of dying. There was a grim irony to the thought.

"What's up, Merletta?" Tish asked, concern in her voice as she laid her work aside for a moment. "You usually make such a point of being cheerful that it's as clear as day you're not telling me about all the struggles you're facing. I should be glad you're not faking it, I suppose, but all I can do is wonder what's so bad that even the unbreakable Merletta can't put a brave face on it."

Merletta gave a smile that was half grimace. Her friend knew her too well.

"It's nothing so bad, really," she said. "Just lots of little things."

Tish raised an eyebrow, and Merletta laughed. "All right, lots of medium things."

"Why don't you try telling me just one?" Tish suggested. "It might make you feel better."

Merletta drifted back across the room to join her friend. Tish was probably right, as usual. Back when they used to meet weekly on Vazula, she had confided more in Heath than she ever had in any being before, and it did usually make her burdens seem lighter.

Heath's unexplained absence was one of her "medium" problems, of course, but she had no intention of telling Tish about any part of that. It would be dangerous for both of them.

"The Center isn't quite what I hoped," she admitted instead.

"They are unkind to you," Tish said, frowning. "I knew it."

"It's not that," said Merletta, shaking her head. "I mean, some of them are, of course. But not all of them. And that's not what troubles me. I didn't think they'd want me there, exactly, but I did think that once I earned a place there, I would actually be inside."

"What do you mean?" Tish asked.

Merletta hesitated, the desire to share her suspicions warring with her instinct of caution. "Well," she said at last, speaking carefully, "sometimes I think they're not telling me the whole truth. And there's only so much you can learn by reading records without instruction."

"Well, you are only in your first year," said Tish reasonably.

"I'm sure there's a great deal they won't cover until you're further advanced."

"That's precisely the problem," said Merletta, her frustration seeping out of her. "Advancing won't guarantee anything. From all I can gather, the most important training—what they teach the older trainees—is all done orally by the record holders, and can't be found in written records."

"What's wrong with that?" Tish asked.

"What's wrong with that," Merletta said grimly, "is that it means there's no way to keep them accountable about the content of what they're teaching."

Tish had picked her work back up, but she lowered it again, a frown of confusion spreading across her pleasant features. "What do you mean?"

"I mean I can't learn in an environment where I don't know how to trust anything I'm being taught!" Merletta burst out. "What if..." she hesitated, then plunged on, "what if it wasn't just that they weren't telling me everything? What if it was that they're intentionally telling me things that aren't true?"

Tish looked more confused than ever. "Why would you think that?"

Merletta swam over to her friend, taking one of Tish's hands in both of her own. "Tish, do you remember what I told you once, about drying out? Remember how I proved that the head at the home was lying about it?"

"I remember you going without suppers for a week," said Tish dryly. "But they lied to us because we were beneficiaries, with no one to care how anyone treated us. The Center wouldn't do that. They couldn't get away with it."

"Couldn't they?" Merletta challenged. "Who would hold them accountable?"

Tish's frown deepened. "Where is this coming from? Why do you think they're lying to you?"

Merletta released her friend's hand, running one of her own over her face. "There's a lot I haven't told you, Tish."

"I know, Mer, and it's all right. I understand. You're not allowed to talk about what you're learning in your program—"

"I'm not talking about things I've learned in the program," Merletta cut her friend off. "I'm talking about things I've discovered for myself."

"What kind of things?"

Merletta hesitated again. "What if...what if, for example, land wasn't as dangerous as we've been told? What if it could actually help us?"

Tish's eyes flicked past Merletta's shoulder, and Merletta broke off, following her friend's gaze to the window.

"What is it?"

"I don't know," said Tish, sounding nervous. "I thought I saw movement, but no one swims past this high up. It would be incredibly rude."

"I should go," said Merletta, her heart speeding up. She cast her mind back over all she'd said. What would the consequences be for Tish if someone had overheard them? For her?

"It was good to see you," said Tish, touching her arm gently. "And don't let it worry you if you haven't learned everything yet. You haven't even finished your first year." She gave a wry smile. "It's hardly surprising they don't keep written accounts of their most important information. They would hardly want their precious records being read by any old orphan."

She spoke jokingly, but the words sparked something in Merletta's memory. She had forgotten about Jacobi's comments in the records hall, distracted first by the excitement of Sage's news, and then by her alarm over her lost satchel. But they came back to her now.

"Hey, speaking of orphans, have you ever heard anything about something called 'orphan records'?"

Tish shook her head. "I doubt there'd be records about us, Mer. We're not nearly important enough."

"You might be surprised," said Merletta vaguely. "They keep records about all kinds of mundane things in the Center, like harvest reports on the kelp farms, that kind of thing."

Tish shrugged. "Well, I've never heard of something like that, but then I wouldn't have, would I?"

Merletta nodded thoughtfully. "I guess not. Thanks, Tish. Don't work too hard."

Her friend smiled noncommittally. "If you say so."

Despite her curiosity, it was another week before Merletta remembered to actually chase down the so-called orphan records.

But when she found herself studying alone late one night, her attention wandered away from her work for long enough to remember the unexamined corner of the records hall that Jacobi had pointed to. She drifted across the room, sorting methodically through the records until she found what she was looking for.

"Huh," she muttered, running her eyes over the words *Orphan Records*. "He was actually telling the truth."

She leafed through a stack, looking for the familiar name of her own charity home. It had been around longer than she'd realized. The list of names covered many leaves. She sighed as she saw recent scratches on the bottom. New children being abandoned to an experience like hers. It was a depressing thought.

Her eyes caught on a familiar name, and she read Letitia's details with interest. Her mother's name was there, and her date of birth. Merletta remembered Tish telling her that no one had even known who her father was. Not an uncommon story at the home, sadly. There were symbols alongside, and a quick check of the covering leaf for that particular bundle showed that they were used as a code, giving a brief summary of the circumstances surrounding her adoption into the home.

Looking up and down the page, Merletta saw that some names were underlined, and those names usually had few or no symbols next to them. Referring back to the cover leaf, she realized those were the children who'd been abandoned at the doorstep of the home. Also not that uncommon. That was her own story.

She was younger than Tish, and she ran her finger down the leaf, looking for her own entry.

Merletta. There it was, with her date of birth alongside. It was strange to see herself recorded, like her whole existence came down to that one line on a page.

She looked again, her forehead creasing. That couldn't be right. Her name wasn't underlined like it should be. Her eyes widened as they passed along the line. There were no parents named, but the leaf looked damaged. In fact, there was a whole section that was bruised and blotted, as though someone had dropped a chisel on it or something. The part where parents should be listed wasn't legible, on her entry, or several either side. But she could see that something had been there.

Her heart raced, this latest revelation robbing her of breath. Was it possible this was another lie the home had told her? That she hadn't been abandoned after all? But why? The answer to that came easily enough. The head had hated her so much she wouldn't have needed a reason to lie to her about something like this.

Merletta dropped the record like it had stung her. Her thoughts were in such a whirl that she barely saw where she was going as she swam from the records hall. She wouldn't be getting any more study done tonight.

Merletta floated absently toward the round table in the dining hall. It had been days, but her thoughts were still caught up on her discovery in the orphan records.

It took her a moment to notice the tense edge to the buzz of conversation before her. But suddenly she realized the reason. Everyone was always very distracted on a test day, and today had been Jacobi's.

She searched the table for him, feeling a flicker of interest. She'd be sitting the same test soon, after all. But there was no sign of him.

She settled next to Sage, scooping up an octopus tentacle.

"I wonder how Jacobi's test is going. Must be a long one."

Sage stared at her, wide eyed. "You didn't hear?"

Merletta stilled. "Hear what?"

"He failed," Sage whispered. "It's all over the dining hall."

Merletta's mouth dropped open, and she found herself searching the room. Sage was right—the rest of the merpeople were looking frequently at the trainees' table, and muttering amongst themselves.

"Poor Jacobi," said Sage. "I bet his family are furious."

Merletta felt a flicker of sympathy, but it was measured by a selfish relief that she would be rid of another hostile rival. The thought made her feel guilty.

"I wonder if Emil is nervous," she said, glancing at the fourth year. "His test is tomorrow, isn't it?"

"He doesn't look nervous," said Sage dryly.

She was right. The older trainee looked as calm as ever,

eating his meal in his habitual silence with no sign that he was aware of the excited chatter around him.

Merletta let out a long breath. "It makes it feel real," she said, a sick feeling in her stomach as she thought of her upcoming test. "The reminder that some people fail."

Sage gave her arm a reassuring squeeze. "You're not going to fail, Merletta. You've outperformed Jacobi in every practice test."

Merletta gave her friend a tense smile, still feeling slightly nauseated. She could only hope Sage was right.

Emil had no reason to be nervous, of course. To nobody's surprise, he passed his final test the following day, and it filled Merletta with fresh determination. Finishing the program often felt like an impossibly far off dream, but seeing someone else achieve it spurred her on. Not to mention she was now the only one left of the group she'd joined to take her test, and she was determined not to follow in Jacobi's wake.

Merletta looked up at the grim stone wall of the charity home. She was less than eager to be back here, but she had little choice. Her accidental discovery in the records had so thrown her that she'd been unable to focus on her study ever since. And with her test only a week away, she couldn't afford the distraction any longer. Jacobi's failure had rattled her, and she wanted to clear the water before she took the test.

She saw many familiar faces as she swam boldly through the halls of the home, but none she wanted to stop and greet. She gripped her spear tightly, proud of the symbol of her success. Perhaps the weapon was why no one stopped her or asked her why she was there. She passed unhindered to the head's office.

"You." The head looked her over with disfavor, not seeming especially surprised to see her. "Failed, have you? I guess it's been about that long." Her eyes narrowed. "I told you that you couldn't come back here."

"I would live on the street before I came back here," said Merletta coldly. "And I haven't failed anything. I'm yet to sit my test."

"Only a matter of time," the head said dismissively.

"I don't care what you think about my prospects," said Merletta, anger simmering just below the surface of her calm words. "I've come to ask you why you lied to me."

"I don't know what you're talking about," said the head, her voice bored, even as her eyes lingered on Merletta's weapon.

"Was I abandoned?" Merletta asked, not interested in subtlety. "Or were my parents known?"

A wary look came into the head's eyes, and Merletta's heart raced faster.

"I don't even remember," the head said, her attempt at nonchalance not convincing. "So many urchins come through here, there's nothing to make your case special."

"You're lying," said Merletta, her voice shaking. "You do remember. What really happened?"

"I don't have time for your dramatics today, Merletta," said the head imperiously. "Where are you getting these wild ideas from?"

"From a written record," Merletta said, her face unyielding. "In the Center of Culture."

Merletta could have sworn a flash of alarm crossed the head's features, but the mask of boredom descended again so quickly, she couldn't be sure. It was hard to believe there was anything she could say or do that would actually scare the hard-hearted older mermaid.

"I know I wasn't abandoned," she pressed, "so there's no point lying about it. What were my parents' names?"

The head raised an eyebrow, no sign of alarm on her face

now. "I haven't got the faintest clue," she said harshly. "I might have been told at the time, but that was sixteen years ago. Why would I remember something so unimportant? You should be thanking me, not coming in here—"

"Thanking you?" Merletta interrupted furiously. "What would I ever thank you for?"

"For shielding you," the head snapped. "Sometimes we tell children they were abandoned, to save them from knowing the truth about their parents. Half the beneficiaries in here have criminals for parents, or parents who died a shameful death, like yours."

Merletta could feel the blood draining from her face. "What shameful death?"

"I'm surprised you didn't figure it out," the head went on, her expression disdainful. "I can only assume you get it from them. They obviously thought they knew better than everyone else, too. Why do you think I exaggerated my explanation of how drying out can happen?"

"You're saying my parents dried out?" Merletta asked, her voice sounding unrecognizable in her own ears.

"I was just trying to protect you," said the head, with a sniff. "But of course you would see my kindness as an insult."

"Kindness?" Merletta choked out. "You don't know what that is." She turned, her throat constricted, and fled from the home. She could feel herself falling apart, and she couldn't bear for the head to witness it.

She wanted to deny it, but the memory of how she had almost been careless enough to dry out on Vazula kept intruding uncomfortably. She swam blindly through the familiar streets of Tilssted, too distracted to take in her surroundings at all. It was dark now, and she knew she was conspicuous in her haste, but she didn't have the energy even to feel alarmed at the jeers and whistles she received from various late night wanderers.

She had just passed across the city border into Skulssted, some subconscious part of her relaxing as the surroundings became rapidly less seedy. She was therefore totally unprepared for the feeling of hands around her throat, as her weapon was ripped out of her grasp from behind.

Before she could react, she was dragged down a small alley, the grip on her throat so tight that she couldn't have made a sound if she'd tried. She thrashed wildly, her training kicking in as she executed a roll that should have broken the hold of any regular bandit. Her attacker held strong, however, and stars began to burst behind Merletta's eyes at the continued grip around her neck.

She couldn't see a thing, but given that her arms had been grabbed as well, she could only assume there was more than one of them. She summoned her waning strength, and thrashed her powerful tail backward, catching something solid. She'd half expected it to be Ileana again, but the dull oomph that told her she'd connected with a torso definitely came from a merman, and one much older than the trainees.

At the contact, the hold on one of her arms loosened enough for her to rip it free. She didn't waste her opportunity, plunging her hand into the kelp satchel at her side and retrieving Heath's knife. She stabbed backward, and a cry of pain told her that her aim had been true. Her throat was suddenly released, and she jolted forward in the water, drawing in deep, shuddering mouthfuls.

She spun around as soon as she had collected herself, ready for a renewed assault, but her attackers were gone. Her eyes scanned the area wildly, but she couldn't tell which direction they'd taken. Only a lingering trail of blood in the water showed they had been there at all. She heard voices drifting toward her from a nearby street, residents of Skulssted cheerfully discussing the day's activities. Perhaps the potential witnesses had deterred the attackers from a second attempt.

Merletta floated for a moment, touching her throat gingerly as she tried to calm her racing heart. She had almost just died, there was no question. Her eyes caught on her spear, lying on the ocean floor below her fins. She reached down to retrieve it, her eyes widening at the sight of another spear beside it. The knobbly wood was as familiar as the shape of the sharpened stone tip. It was distinctive, and only one group of guards was allowed to carry such weapons. Center guards, or those training for the right to join their ranks.

There was only one conclusion to draw. This was no robbery gone wrong. Someone from the Center had tried to murder her.

CHAPTER TWENTY-SIX

Heath groaned as he reached the top of the rise and caught sight of his home. The carriage entering the gates of Bexley Manor was depressingly familiar. If only he'd extended his morning ramble along the cliffs, maybe he could have avoided Lord Niel's visit. With any luck he could slip through a back entrance unnoticed. Of course, he thought resentfully, if Reka wasn't being so uncooperative, there would be no risk of Lord Niel cornering him at all. He would be long gone—today was one of Merletta's rest days.

He passed through the gateway, trying to be inconspicuous as he strolled across the courtyard. What did the nobleman want now? He hadn't been to their estate in months. He must have left Bryford very early to be here already.

Heath slipped through a side entrance, reaching the sanctuary of the manor's library with a sigh of relief. He was unlikely to be troubled here. No one but him and his father used it much, and it certainly wasn't a place to entertain guests. He was therefore surprised to hear a firm step approaching the door only a few minutes after he'd entered.

"Heath, there you are."

"Father," he said, laying aside the volume he had idly picked up. "Are you looking for me?"

"Lord Niel is here," said his father.

Heath sighed. "Yes, I saw. Do you want me to talk Percival down?"

The smallest of smiles tugged at the duke's lips as he shook his head. "Lord Niel is here to see you, Heath."

"Me?" asked Heath, making no effort to hide his dismay.

The duke nodded. "And he's accompanied by Crown Prince Lachlan."

Heath sat up straight. "The crown prince is here? To see me?" He chewed on his lip anxiously. "The tournament was months ago. Surely I can't still be in hot water over it!"

The duke shook his head. "They're not here to complain, Heath. They have a proposition for you."

Heath frowned. "Why does that make me even more nervous?"

There was a definite twinkle in his father's eye as he gestured for Heath to join him. "Take courage, brave heart. The dragon is waiting."

Heath sighed as he stood up. "If only. Will you think I'm a coward if I admit that dragons don't frighten me half as much as people like Lord Niel?"

"I don't advise you to let him hear you say that," said his father mildly, as they left the room.

The visitors were waiting for Heath, kept company by Percival. Heath's brother was watching Lord Niel with narrowed eyes, as though he thought the nobleman might make off with the good silver if left unsupervised.

The three of them were in the same receiving room where Lord Niel had admonished Heath on his last attendance at the manor. The memory of that encounter made Heath stand a little straighter, his resentment at the nobleman's presumption overcoming his trepidation.

"Your Highness," he said, bowing to Prince Lachlan. "We're honored to receive you here." He turned to the other visitor, inclining his head and speaking with cool politeness. "Lord Niel. I trust I haven't kept you waiting this time."

"Not at all, Lord Heath," said the older man, inclining his head ever so slightly. "And since you have brought up the occasion of my previous visit, let me say that I applaud your wisdom in stepping back from such regular interactions with your dragon acquaintance."

Heath froze, his astonishment quickly fading before his growing anger. Was he being watched, that Lord Niel knew he hadn't seen Reka in months?

It was on the tip of his tongue to give a hot retort, but he glanced at his father, and hesitated. The Duke of Bexley's neutral expression had hardened, so that it looked set on his face. Knowing his father well, Heath could tell that he was surprised by the information as well. And he must surely feel some level of anger. But as his eyes darted to those of his younger son, his expression held no fire, only a warning. Heath drew in a breath, trying to be as detached and prudent as his father. The duke was right, of course. The reminder of the scrutiny they were under should be cause for caution, not angry outbursts. Especially with the prince present.

"I understand you wished to speak with me, Your Highness, Lord Niel," Heath prompted, deciding not to respond at all to the reference to Rekavidur.

"Yes, My Lord," said Prince Lachlan formally. "We wish to offer you a position, on behalf of my father."

"Me?" Heath said, startled from his anger for a moment. "What position would the king want to offer me?"

"That of spokesperson," Lord Niel interjected pompously.

Prince Lachlan shifted ever so slightly, and Lord Niel fell silent, deferring to his young companion with the tiniest hint of disgruntlement.

"Indeed," Prince Lachlan said. "It has not escaped my father's notice that the complexities of regulating the wielding of power might be particularly unsettling for those of our generation."

Heath kept his face straight with an effort. *You mean, the king is particularly unsettled by the power-wielders of our generation.*

"He is of the view," Prince Lachlan continued, "that it might be beneficial to have someone in our generation to act as a representative of the power-wielders, to communicate with the crown on their behalf."

Heath blinked. "And the king wants me to take that role?" Never in his wildest dreams had he imagined receiving such an offer.

"That's right." Prince Lachlan inclined his head.

"But..." Heath was still struggling to gather his thoughts. "Surely there are better choices than me for the role." Involuntarily, his eyes flicked to Percival, then back to the prince. "I mean, I'm barely nineteen."

The prince almost smiled. "As am I. My father is offering the appointment to you. He believes that you are in a unique position to help bridge the gap between those who carry power and those who do not. Are you willing to serve in this way?"

Heath was silent for a moment, shifting uncomfortably from foot to foot. It was clear now why he'd been chosen. It was because he was part of the power-wielding branch of the family, but didn't have any notable magic, and was therefore less likely to be met with hostility from the rest of the court. He didn't look directly at his brother again, but he didn't need to. He could feel Percival's annoyance filling the space between them. But of course he wouldn't be chosen for such a role. Not after the stir he'd made.

"Heath," said his father unexpectedly. "A word, please?" He bowed to the prince. "If you will excuse us, Your Highness."

Prince Lachlan nodded graciously, and Heath followed his father from the room.

"Did you know about this?" he demanded, as soon as the door was closed behind them.

"Not before today," the duke said. His eyes searched Heath's for a long moment.

"Do I have a choice about this?" Heath asked abruptly.

"Of course you do," said the duke calmly. "It's not a command. And I won't push you to do anything. But I do want to advise you—don't turn this position down just because you think Percival wants it."

Heath looked up quickly, surprised by his father's bluntness. "He's welcome to it, as far as I'm concerned. I don't want it."

"He's not welcome to it," the duke corrected mildly. "It's been offered to you, not to him. And you're missing my point. Just because Percival wants it, doesn't mean he's a good choice for the role. And just because you don't want it, doesn't mean you're not a good choice." His eyes scanned Heath's face. "Do you understand what I mean?"

"I think so," said Heath reluctantly.

He looked back at the closed door, Merletta's words about family suddenly jumping to his mind. He had been ashamed of his cowardice in dodging the conflict, and had told himself he would get involved where he could. He would certainly never get a better opportunity than this. But still, as he walked slowly back into the room, he couldn't muster any enthusiasm for the idea.

"What is your answer, Lord Heath?" Prince Lachlan asked without preamble.

Heath locked eyes with the young prince for a moment, surprised by what he saw there. For once, Prince Lachlan's expression wasn't entirely impenetrable. The look lurking in his eyes would, on any lesser person, be called a hint of pleading. The realization that the crown prince actually wanted to find a peaceful resolution to the rising tension, and that he was seeking Heath's help to do it, was what decided him. How could he say no to that, and still live with himself?

"It will be my honor to serve my king."

The walls of Bryford rose up before the carriage, their pennants bright in the noon sun, and Heath held back the sigh wanting to escape. He was here by choice this time, and it would serve no purpose to complain. But there was no denying that an afternoon spent in a carriage with Lord Niel had definitely tested his resolve. He had only vaguely listened to the nobleman explaining importantly that the announcement of Heath's appointment would be made at the Summer Solstice Festival. Heath cared nothing about such details.

But it wasn't like he had anything else of interest to pursue with his time, he thought dully. With Vazula out of his reach, he could do with something to focus on. He had been more or less content with his life in Valoria before he found the island and met Merletta. But somehow since being prohibited from returning there, everything else had seemed pointless.

The carriage rattled over the cobblestones, pulling up before long in the courtyard in front of the castle. Lord Niel climbed out, bustling importantly to the castle entrance to give instructions to the king's steward, who was awaiting them.

Heath hung back respectfully, expecting Prince Lachlan to alight next. But the other young man turned to him instead. The prince had been mostly silent during the hours of their journey, leaving the floor open to Lord Niel, who had been only too happy to drone pompously on about the privilege bestowed upon Heath.

"Thank you," Prince Lachlan said now, surprising Heath with the almost-warmth in his tone. "I'm glad you accepted the role."

Before Heath could reply, a shout sounded from outside the carriage, causing both of them to turn. The prince leaped nimbly from the vehicle. He was immediately surrounded by the contingent of guards who had accompanied him to Bexley Manor, and whose horses had flanked the carriage on the drive back to Bryford.

Heath followed close behind, his alarm growing at the increasing shouts, and even screams, sounding across the court-yard. But the concern turned to surprise as he caught sight of the enormous form descending from the sky immediately above them.

"Reka?" he exclaimed, half to himself. The appearance of a dragon in the city at any time other than the Winter Solstice Festival was extremely rare. It had never happened in Heath's lifetime.

But Reka was undeniably there. The dragon landed in front of him, his talons clicking on the cobblestones a mere few inches from Heath's boots.

"I've come to collect you," the dragon said imperiously.

For a moment, Heath just blinked, the flame Reka himself had lit only months before—on the last occasion he'd seen the dragon—tugging at his vision. Before he could say a word, Lord Niel's outraged voice cut across his bewilderment.

"I should have known the power-wielders wouldn't let you out of their grasp so easily," he hissed. "They clearly won't risk losing your absolute loyalty." He gestured to the prince who, with his guards, was the only one within hearing distance. Everyone else in the courtyard was hanging back nervously. "You see how right I was to warn of the danger, Your Highness. They've sent a dragon to retrieve him rather than let him take a role in your father's court."

Heath turned to the nobleman, his brow darkening. "That's nonsense, My Lord," he snapped. "First of all, I'm not in anyone's grasp. And second, you're beyond foolish if you think the dragons answer to any humans, power-wielding or otherwise."

Lord Niel's eyes narrowed in anger. "You should watch how you speak to me, boy. And you expect me to believe that this beast," he waved a hand at Reka, "has followed you to Bryford by coincidence? I know for a fact he no longer comes at your call."

Those words were a mistake. Rekavidur had so far maintained a disdainful silence, but Heath could sense his anger at the nobleman's characterization of their friendship. He turned his vast head in Lord Niel's direction, a rumble building within his chest. He opened his mouth, and with startling abruptness, the rumble turned into a roar. Lord Niel cowered under the force of the sound, darting back to the edge of the courtyard to join the rest of the onlookers. Prince Lachlan flinched, but would clearly have stood his ground if his guards hadn't physically hustled him away.

"Reka, stop!" Heath called, when a wisp of smoke began to curl from the dragon's mouth.

Rekavidur turned to Heath, the heat of his fire seeming to glow in his eyes even as it died down from his jaws.

"Do you think I am tame?" he demanded dangerously. "Do you think you can train me to respond to you, like you would a dog?"

"What?" Heath demanded, dumbstruck. "Of course not!"

Reka still looked so terrifying that even Heath had to fight the instinct to back away. He stared at Reka, and although nothing he could see with his eyes suggested it, he became suddenly aware of some kind of conflict raging within the dragon. Reka was in distress, although he wasn't showing it, and Heath's heart suddenly went out to his friend.

"Reka, what's wrong?" he asked, alarmed.

For a moment the sternness on the dragon's brow seemed to falter, but it returned almost immediately.

"Nothing," he said curtly. "I've come in response to your call."

"My call?" Heath searched his memory, more bewildered than ever. "The last time I tried calling you was weeks ago."

The dragon nodded. "I have considered the matter, and I have decided to come."

He spoke casually, as though it was normal for him to take weeks to respond, but Heath wasn't fooled. He could still sense the tension just below the surface, as though every part of the dragon was tightly coiled.

"Reka, what's going on?"

"Do you wish to come, or not?" Reka asked abruptly.

Heath glanced behind him. He could see Prince Lachlan, trying to wriggle out from behind his guards for a better look. Many pairs of eyes were on them, but none of the spectators were close enough to hear their conversation.

"It's not the best time, Reka," he said, frustrated. "I want to go back to Vazula, more than anything, but does it have to be right now?"

"I am not your pet, to come when you call me," Reka said, danger lurking behind his stately words. "If you wish to come, I am going now."

Heath hesitated, confused and uneasy. Reka had never spoken this way before, at least not to Heath. Nothing could be a stronger contrast to his unprompted declaration of friendship at the Winter Solstice. What had happened to make him so, well...dragonlike?

But whatever the cause, he could see that Reka meant what he said. If Heath refused to go with him now, he might be giving up his only chance to return with the dragon to Vazula. But if he said yes, they could be there in less than two hours. Merletta might even now be waiting for them in the lagoon...

His father's advice flashed through his mind, and the prince's expression of gratitude. But he pushed them guiltily aside. He hadn't asked for this responsibility, and he didn't want it. If it waited for him, fine. If they decided he was too flighty, and gave the role to someone else, so much the better.

"Yes," he said, a dangerous feeling of abandonment rushing over him. "I want to come."

The words were barely out of his mouth when Reka moved, seizing him in his talons and pushing into the air in one fluid movement. Heath barely heard the shouts of the onlookers as the city turned rapidly from a mighty fortress to a gray dot. He turned his face toward the sea, already visible on the horizon from this height.

He was going back to Vazula at last.

CHAPTER TWENTY-SEVEN

Merletta held her head high as she swam through the entrance to the scribes' hall. She had expected to be nervous about taking her test, but the tension filling her every muscle was something else entirely. Not the best conditions for a such a crucial test, but it couldn't be helped.

After the foiled attack, she had fled to her barracks like a fish trying to outswim a shark, and had huddled in her hammock for the rest of the night, trying to decide what to do. She couldn't sleep—she had no idea if the Center was safe for her, and if she'd had anywhere else to go, she wouldn't have returned there at all. Her first instinct was to wait for the relative safety of the dawn, and make straight for the barrier, leaving the triple kingdoms and whoever was trying to kill her far behind.

But what would she do then? Live alone out in the deep ocean? It might not be as dangerous as she'd been taught, but it was certainly too dangerous for a lone mermaid to survive indefinitely. The shallows around Vazula seemed safe enough, but she would be trapped there, like that turtle in its net, unable to either climb onto the land, or safely return to the sea. That was no way to live.

The attack had frightened her, though, more than she cared to admit. An attack by armed Center guards felt so much more serious even than the deadly pranks of the other trainees. Ileana had hated her from the start, and it was no surprise that she wished Merletta harm. But this...this was different.

She'd known all along that there were those who didn't want her in the program, but that they were actually willing to have her killed to keep her from progressing was terrifying. She supposed she should be encouraged—surely they must be a little afraid she'd pass her test, or they wouldn't feel the need to stop her taking it—but somehow she didn't draw much comfort from the thought.

She had considered reporting the attack, of course. But her memory of her previous attempt to make a complaint to Instructor Wivell made her quickly discard the idea. She had no proof, yet again, and it had already been made clear to her that she was on her own.

She just wished she knew who'd sent the guards after her. Agner was the obvious answer, given that he was in charge of the guards. But it didn't tally with her experience of him. He was the only one who was friendly to her, but also, he could easily have gotten rid of her in training and made it look like an accident. Ibsen would make more sense, perhaps even Wivell, but she had no idea if either of them had the pull with the guards to make such an order.

There was no way to be sure, but long before the gray light of dawn had filtered down to the Center, Merletta had made her decision. She wasn't going to flee like a startled minnow. If someone from the Center wanted to kill her, they could do so whether she was in the program or not. She had no safe corner of the triple kingdoms to swim to.

The thought of her combat instructor bolstered her. The first time he'd met her, he'd told her she was a fighter, and he'd been right. The other trainees hadn't been able to frighten her off, and whoever was behind this attack wouldn't do it either. She had learned more in the last year—both in and out of the program—than in the sixteen years before it, and she had no doubt she would pass that test. It was time to prove that to everyone else, as well.

Still, she couldn't help the way her eyes darted around as she entered the room allocated for the test. What if whoever was behind the attack was determined enough to do whatever it took to stop her from sitting for the examination?

But there was nothing sinister in Instructor Wivell's demeanor as he began the testing, and Merletta soon pushed other thoughts aside, focusing on her answers. She knew this test wouldn't be physically grueling like the second year test. And it wouldn't stretch her too far in remembering what she could and couldn't reveal of her knowledge about the history taught by the Center. The first year test qualified a trainee to become a scribe, and was consequently focused almost entirely on literacy.

It was the easiest aspect of her mental learning to quantify, and Merletta was confident. The test was in multiple parts, even longer than the entry tests, and she went through an astounding number of writing leaves in the process. Every trite saying she'd learned as a technique for remembering information danced across her mind, and more than once she paused to mentally swim through a place far from the small testing room, retrieving information from familiar spots.

But eventually, the morning wore away into afternoon, and she could see from Wivell's tight expression that she was performing well.

When she had answered the final question, Merletta

lowered the coral implement, her hand shaking slightly from the hours of exertion.

Wivell took the writing leaf, clearing his throat half-heartedly.

"I'll need to consider your final answers."

"Yes, Instructor Wivell," said Merletta, a hint of stone beneath her polite words. "I'll wait."

She knew from the other trainees that it was normal to learn the results of your test on the spot, and she had no intention of giving the instructor any opportunity to lose her answers, or change his mind based on input from anyone else. If he was going to falsely fail her, when she knew she'd answered every question, he'd have to look her in the eye right now and do it.

He scanned the answers, clearing his throat again as he looked from her writing leaf to his own. Then, his movements painfully slow, he scratched a mark into the thin slab of stone in front of him, where Merletta could see Jacobi's name as well as hers.

"Well?" she prompted. "Did I pass—sir?" She added the title as an afterthought.

Instructor Wivell cleared his throat one final time. "Yes," he said gruffly. "You have passed your first year testing. Congratulations."

Merletta shot from her seat, giving a cry of delight as she spun joyfully through the water with total disregard for her dignity.

"Thank you, Instructor," she said, inclining her head to him, unable to hold in a smile.

Wivell regarded her. "You closed your eyes more than once during the test," he commented. "Were you accessing your mind palace?"

Merletta hesitated only slightly before answering. "Yes."

Wivell was silent for another moment. "It seems you had success with it at last, then."

Merletta's thoughts soured slightly. Her inability to master the mind palace concept had become something of a snide joke for her detractors in her first few months in the program. Wivell had never shown any sign that he'd realized how much she was struggling. As far as she was concerned, the fact that he had noticed only increased his culpability for never making any attempt to help her improve.

Little did he know, her efforts had improved exponentially without his help. It had been many months ago, when she'd decided to ignore his advice and not base her mind palace on her childhood home. She'd taken a risk, and not based it on any building. It wasn't so much a mind palace now, as a mind journey—specifically, the familiar route from the kelp farms to Vazula. In her mind, she called it her memory journey. She knew every patch of coral, every rocky shelf of those waters, and the journey included the island's beach, as well as the lagoon. Once the exercise had ceased to be connected with the unpleasant memories that dwelt in the charity home, she'd found it enormously helpful.

None of this she intended to share with Instructor Wivell, of course.

"Yes, sir," she said mildly. "Am I dismissed?"

He nodded, and she darted from the room, swimming immediately to find Sage. The other mermaid gave such a squeal of delight at Merletta's news that they earned a reproving look from the senior guard overseeing the third years' training exercise. To all outward appearances, Oliver was ignoring them, his expression as disdainful as ever. But Merletta could see out of the corner of her eye that his head was inclined toward her as she spoke. She hid a grim smile. They could pretend all they wanted, but the other trainees were undoubtedly all as curious about her test as she'd been about theirs. She glanced at the new trainee who had started first year a few weeks before, and saw that even she was watching intently.

Merletta smiled to herself, feeling a surge of affection for her fellow trainees, the unfriendly as well as the friendly. They would be studying together for another year. Much as they had tried to push her out, she was still here. The two most hostile trainees had both failed, and wouldn't be troubling her anymore. Some of the others could be unpleasant, but her life here had already given her so much more fulfillment and freedom than the charity home ever had. And maybe the other trainees would come around to her eventually, as Sage had done.

Her friend soon returned to her training exercise, and with nothing else to do, Merletta floated back to the edge of the training yard to watch. Her eyes passed over the various groups, and she started slightly as she confronted a pair of pale eyes fixed on her with pure malice in their depths.

Merletta turned away, her heart beating more quickly in spite of herself. So much for the failed trainees being out of the picture. Ileana was back from her brief break, now officially a member of the guards. She had still never said a word about the incident with the satchel, and Merletta was nervous about it. She hated the feeling of waiting for the blow to fall, but she couldn't quite bring herself to confront the other mermaid and get it over with. What if, unlikely as it seemed, Ileana really hadn't looked inside?

But Merletta couldn't really believe it. The usual smirk was gone from Ileana's face now, but the look of outright hatred that had replaced it didn't bode well for any future interactions between them. Merletta supposed she would see much less of Ileana now the older mermaid was no longer in the program, but her position as a guard would ensure she remained in the Center. She had considerable further training still ahead of her.

Merletta felt a twinge of dark sympathy for the failed trainee. If only Ileana had stopped a year before, when she passed the formidable second year test, she would be joining the guards by choice, without the humiliation of failing third year. No wonder she was glaring like that. It was clear she'd followed the gist of Merletta's conversation with Sage, and she must know her most hated fellow trainee had passed first year. Merletta was going to have to watch her back more than ever.

"What are you going to do with your break?" Sage asked her cheerfully, as they swam for the dining hall at the end of her training. "I'm guessing you won't go back to the charity home."

Merletta snorted. "Hardly."

She fell silent as she remembered her visit to the home. There was a sort of hollow ache that appeared in her stomach whenever she remembered the head's words. She'd even gone back over the orphan records, willing them to be legible, but it was impossible to make out. She had to accept she'd never know her parents' names. In a tiny, foolish way, it felt like losing them all over again.

It seemed so coincidental that her entry had been in the damaged section of the record. She couldn't help but wonder if someone had bruised the leaf intentionally to stop her from reading it. Such a conclusion seemed to require a drastic overestimation of her importance, though. Of course, it might have been just another heartless prank by Jacobi. It seemed the most likely option, since he'd been the one to mention the records to her. But he was gone, and she couldn't even confront him with it.

She pushed such thoughts aside, trying to speak naturally for her friend's sake. She hadn't told Sage what she'd learned about her parents, and she didn't intend to do so now. This was a night for celebration. She let the memory of her success wash over her. As little as she wanted to be a scribe, at the very least she now had a secure future. She would never have to live on the streets. The thought was hard to take in.

"Will you go back to Tilssted, though?" Sage pressed. "Like you do on rest days?"

Merletta squirmed slightly, guilt niggling at her for the deception. It was true she always went *through* Tilssted, she reasoned with herself.

"I'm not sure," she hedged. "I'll go visit Tish at some stage, tell her I've passed."

"I'm sure she'll be delighted," Sage smiled.

Merletta glanced at the other trainees. "Still no sign of Jacobi coming back," she commented. "Do you think he'll apply directly to the guards, see if he can join Ileana?"

"Oh, of course," Sage exclaimed, "you were already in your test this morning, so you wouldn't have heard. He did apply, and he was rejected."

"Really?" Merletta sat up straighter, her interest caught.

Sage nodded. "Instructor Ibsen told us this morning that Jacobi had received a public reprimand for something, and was barred from holding any office in the Center." She dropped her voice. "The rumor is that his family are just about furious enough to disown him."

Merletta could only stare in astonishment. "What was he reprimanded for?"

Sage shrugged. "I don't know. Ibsen didn't say."

"Not much of a public reprimand, then, is it?" Merletta said dryly.

Sage just smiled. "All I know is that the complaint that led to his reprimand was made by Emil. Instructor Ibsen wouldn't say more."

"Emil?" Merletta repeated, startled. What in the ocean

would Emil have been complaining about Jacobi for? She sat in silence for a couple of minutes, mulling it over.

"Oysters?" Sage's cheerful voice broke her reverie.

She was holding out a turtle-shell bowl, and Merletta reached for it recklessly. Why not? This was the time to celebrate, after all. She'd passed her test, and at least one of her two enemies wasn't going to be around next year. She downed one in a single gulp, her eyes widening. "That's delicious!"

Sage laughed. "Don't tell me this is your first time trying an oyster!"

Merletta nodded, grabbing another one to her friend's continued chuckles. "I suppose I'll have to stay here during my break," she mused, thinking aloud. "But I wonder if it's safe."

"What do you mean?" Sage frowned. "Of course it's safe."

Merletta hesitated, then lowered her voice. "Something happened a few days ago. Something I didn't want to tell you about at the time." With a glance around to make sure no one was in hearing, she quickly described the attack she had sustained when returning from her visit to the home.

Sage's eyes grew wider as she spoke, until they were as round as pearls. "But there must be a mistake," she said at last, her voice a little too loud for Merletta's liking.

Merletta gestured for her to be quieter, and Sage glanced around self-consciously. Following her gaze, Merletta noticed Ileana watching them from across the room. She drew her gaze away, back to Sage.

"There was no mistake."

"But surely no one from the Center would dare to attack a trainee," said Sage, more quietly. "It must have been thieves, who'd stolen the weapon from Center guards."

Merletta gave her friend a look. "You think common thieves overpowered Center guards and took their weapons, and we've heard nothing about it?"

Sage nibbled her lip, her forehead creased. "It does seem unlikely."

"Highly unlikely," Merletta agreed dryly. "I'm almost certain they were Center guards. I know I got one of them, and I've been looking for an injured guard ever since, but whoever it was must be out of sight somewhere."

"But..." Sage hesitated. "Who would want you gone so desperately they were willing to have you killed?"

Before Merletta could respond, her eye was caught by a junior scribe entering the dining hall at that moment. His eyes scanned the crowd, latching on to her. He bustled over importantly.

"Trainee Merletta?" he asked, and she nodded. "I have a message for you from Instructor Ibsen. He wishes to speak with you tomorrow, at noon. Please present yourself to his office."

Without waiting for a reply, the scribe turned, swimming smoothly for the door. Merletta turned to her friend. "Well, that sounds...sinister."

"Probably he just wants to congratulate you on your test result," said Sage, without much conviction.

Merletta raised an eyebrow. "Did he call you to his office to congratulate you on yours?"

Sage shook her head, and Merletta nodded.

"That's what I thought." She frowned, thinking it over. "I guess I have to go. But I'd better take my spear."

"Merletta!" said Sage, shocked. "You can't raise a weapon against Ibsen. Besides, he's an instructor, and you're a trainee. He'd never attack you."

Merletta shrugged. "Can't be too careful."

Sage's frown deepened. "Do you want me to stick around?" she asked. "I was going to go home for the morning, but I can stay if you like."

"No, no," said Merletta, waving a hand. "You enjoy your rest day. I'll be fine."

Sage still looked uncertain, but she let it drop. Merletta turned the topic back to her successful test, hoping to cheer her friend up, and they chatted easily for another half an hour before retiring. Merletta couldn't help glancing back toward Ileana as she left the dining hall.

The other mermaid was still watching her, and something in her expression sent a curl of unease through Merletta's stomach.

Merletta swam into Instructor Ibsen's rooms warily, her spear gripped in her hand.

"Hold on!" A clerk appeared before her, his voice shocked as he stopped her with an outstretched arm. "You can't take that into the office."

"It's all right." Instructor Ibsen's voice wafted out of a large office directly in front of her. "Let her pass."

The clerk still looked offended, but he drew back, allowing Merletta to sweep past him. She was surprised by Ibsen's intervention, but glad. Whatever he had to say, she'd rather hear it with the security of a weapon in her hand.

"Merletta," the instructor said, the moment she entered his office. "Thank you for coming."

She just stared at him, more thrown by his polite tone than she would have been by his familiar hostility.

"You called for me, didn't you?" she asked carefully.

"I did," said Ibsen, folding his hands together on the desk in front of him. "Please, sit."

Merletta did so, sinking warily onto a small bench carved from the bedrock.

"I wanted to congratulate you on passing your test."

"You did?" Merletta asked, before she could stop herself.

A flicker of irritation passed over Ibsen's face, but he smoothed it out quickly. "Of course. It is an admirable feat to pass the first year of the program, and you should be proud of your achievement."

Merletta blinked. "I am," she said at last. "Very proud. Success is even more satisfying when it comes purely from your own hard work, without outside assistance."

Ibsen was slower to stifle the irritation this time, but Merletta kept her face stony. She didn't know why he was pretending to be friendly all of a sudden, but she wasn't about to buddy up to him just because he wasn't currently barking at her like a territorial seal.

"Yes, well." Ibsen contained his annoyance with an effort. "As I said, very admirable. I think you will find the life of a scribe both rewarding and comfortable."

Merletta stared at him for a full ten seconds before realization hit. "Oh, I'm not stopping," she said bluntly. "I fully intend to continue to the program's second year."

Ibsen drew in a breath, the pleasant expression on his face looking so painful that Merletta could only stare in fascination.

"I would strongly advise you to reconsider that. It is most understandable to be swept up in the elation of your pass. But don't let that blind you to your own best interests. It wouldn't be in your interests to continue."

Merletta raised an eyebrow, gripping her spear more tightly. "Is that a threat, Instructor?"

"I beg your pardon?" Ibsen's face and voice were colder than the deepest point of the Center, and Merletta judged it best to subside.

"I am not threatening you," said Ibsen. "I'm attempting to help you. The first year test, while difficult to pass, is not grueling in the way the second year test is. I do not exaggerate when I say that trainees have died during this test in the past. And in my educated opinion as an instructor, there is little hope of you passing it."

"Well then," said Merletta lightly. "It's a good thing I have another year to prepare for it, isn't it?"

Ibsen's temple twitched slightly. "Consider carefully, Merletta. If you stop now by choice, you will have a respected and secure position, and can continue to enjoy all the comforts of the Center. If you continue to second year, and fail, you will have the humiliation of everyone knowing you were not good enough for your chosen course. And you will most likely suffer resentment from your fellow scribes, who will know that you did not consider their role a worthy choice."

"A bit like Ileana's position," Merletta commented.

Ibsen nodded in acknowledgment. "Indeed."

"Well," said Merletta cheerfully. "Thank you for the friendly warning."

"So you'll think it over?" Ibsen asked, watching her closely.

"Oh, there's no need for that," said Merletta brightly. "I've been thinking it over since I was child, and I'm very sure of my course. I'll be continuing to second year." She looked around expectantly. "Do I need to sign something to that effect?"

Ibsen's expression was sour, and the usual venom had returned to his tone. "Notifying me is sufficient," he snapped.

Merletta started to rise, but he stalled her with a hand. "There is one other matter," he said, his voice stiff. Merletta waited in silence, and after a moment, he went on, sounding like the words pained him to say.

"I need to inform you about a reprimand given to your former classmate, Jacobi, this morning."

Merletta sat back in her seat, her surprised gaze fixed on Ibsen's face. She hadn't expected the instructor to fill her in on the announcement she'd missed.

"Oh?" she said cautiously.

"A complaint was received by junior record holder Emil, regarding a comment he overheard Jacobi making."

He fell silent, and Merletta stared at him, still waiting to find out why he was telling her.

"The comment related to you," Instructor Ibsen said, more stiffly than ever.

Merletta started. "Me?"

"Apparently Jacobi indicated that he had been involved in some...ill-advised jokes at your expense, involving pufferfish meat and a venomous jellyfish."

Merletta's eyes were wide, and she could find nothing to say.

"Emil reported the matter," Ibsen went on, not quite able to hide his irritation at that decision. He cleared his throat. "I am aware that you raised these matters with Instructor Wivell, but that there was at that time no evidence to support your theory that these were intentional incidents." He paused. "Emil's testimony has now provided that evidence. Jacobi has been reprimanded, and I have been instructed to inform you that your complaint has been formally recorded."

Which means it wasn't before, Merletta thought. But she didn't say it aloud. Her mind was whirling too much with these revelations. Jacobi had actually been punished for his part in the attacks against her! It was a weak response considering they could have been fatal, but still, it was something. And Emil had used his influence to bring that about! It was the last thing she had expected.

She was glad it was being taken seriously, but she actually felt a flicker of sympathy for Jacobi. She had no doubt he'd been involved, but she also had no doubt who had been the real instigator. She remembered with perfect clarity how nervous, even shocked, he'd seemed in the training yard when Ileana had gone from beating Merletta to attempting to choke her.

Had he taken the fall for Ileana simply because he was the only one who was careless enough to be overheard talking about it? Had he heroically refused to name her? Or perhaps the instructors knew, but were unwilling to reprimand someone currently in training as a Center guard. A failed trainee was an easier target. Either way, Jacobi's future would suffer for it.

And Ibsen said he'd been instructed to tell her all this—by whom? Her thoughts flew to the Record Master, and the brief interest he'd taken in her on Founders' Day. But it seemed unlikely he would involve himself in matters at this level.

"I appreciate the information, sir," Merletta said at last, realizing that some response was expected.

Instructor Ibsen gave a curt nod. "You are dismissed."

"Thank you, sir," said Merletta absently.

Her mind was still churning as she swam from the room. She'd been given a great deal to think about. At least the mystery of Ibsen actually wanting to speak with her was explained. Part of her wanted to be amused by the instructor's blatant attempt to dissuade her from taking her hard-earned place in the program's second year. He should know her better by now.

But it was hard to find the humor when she still didn't know who had tried to kill her through means of the Center guards, and Ibsen was one of the most likely candidates. Was today's conversation his attempt to get rid of her by less gruesome means, since he had failed to do so more permanently? Or was it unrelated, with him totally unaware of the attack on her?

Merletta swam back toward the trainees' barracks, which were mostly deserted, given it was a rest day. The thought startled Merletta. It was a rest day. She had forgotten in the excitement of her test, and the apprehension about Ibsen's summons. It was the first time she had failed to travel to the island in the morning, and the realization that she had forgotten made her sad.

She glanced up toward the distant surface. The light was dim, although it was just past noon, and even from the ocean floor she could see the signs of frenzied movement on the surface of the water. It was clearly stormy up there, one of her favorite times to explore.

She cast her eyes around her, remembering that Sage was with her family in Skulssted. There was no point hanging around here. She turned toward the edge of the Center's boundary. It was a while since she had enjoyed the sight of driving waves lashing the sand of Vazula's beaches. She would keep her one-sided tryst, even if it would be late in the day.

CHAPTER TWENTY-EIGHT

Despite his saturation, Heath's heart lifted as the island came into sight. The feeling of passing through the magic barrier was comforting in its familiarity, although it had been months.

Within half an hour of leaving Valoria, they had entered an enormous rainstorm. The rain still pelted down with exhausting force, and Heath had long since resigned himself to being both wet and cold. The wind lashed at him mercilessly, testing his faith in the dragon's ability to keep his grip on Heath's shoulders. The fat drops of water dinged off Reka's scales, the sound like a fingernail tapping glass.

The journey had been spent in silence, and Heath didn't think the roar of the weather was to blame. It was still abundantly clear to him that something was troubling the dragon. But for the moment, all he could think of was their destination. After all these months, would Merletta be there? Or had she given up on him long ago? He could only hope she'd accept his explanation for so abruptly abandoning their rendezvous.

He looked down at the rapidly approaching island, the

normally bright emerald looking dull through the driving rain, its edges uneven and changing as the waves crashed against every inch of the shoreline.

"What's that?" he shouted, pointing down at the water below them.

Reka glanced, but didn't respond, other than the shrug that passed over his body. Heath squinted down, trying to make sense of what he was seeing. It was hard to make anything out with the conditions what they were, but something was definitely moving in the water. Could it be a shark? The thought made him nervous. He was yet to see one of the dangerous beasts in person, and had hoped they wouldn't come past the reef. Whatever he was seeing now was further out than the reef, but not by much.

As he squinted, he thought he caught a flash of scales through the rain, and his heart did a somersault. Was it Merletta?

"Never mind about going to the lagoon, actually," he called to his friend. "Can you set me down on the beach?" His words were lost in the storm, but he knew that, with the superior hearing of his kind, Reka would have no difficulty catching them.

The dragon changed course, descending rapidly toward the island. Within moments, Heath's feet hit the wet sand. He turned immediately, squinting through the water at whatever it was he had seen. It was even harder to make it out from here.

"Is it her?" he muttered.

"I believe I sensed the signature of Merletta's magic as we passed over," said the dragon, still seeming off. "If that's what you're asking."

Heath's heart lifted. "She must be on her way in. I'll wait here."

"As you wish," Reka said, inclining his head. "I do not wish to speak with the mermaid. I will continue my interrupted search regarding my own kind."

Heath looked at his friend in surprise. He wasn't going to wait to even say hello to Merletta? There was something unnatural about the way he said "the mermaid", as if he'd never met her before. Why was Reka acting so strange? But the dragon was already taking off, flying low over the island.

Heath dismissed the matter for the moment, turning his attention back to the water. He waded out into the shallows, surprised by how warm the water felt. Perhaps it was just that he was already wet all over, so there was no moment of adjustment. After a minute of waiting, he became confused. If that was her, why wasn't she coming in closer?

He waded further, straining his superior eyes to try to make sense of what he was seeing. A tail emerged from the water, and his heart lifted as he recognized the familiar purple and gold of Merletta's scales. But she was still out past the reef. He squinted, excitement and nerves passing through him as he saw another tail, and another. Merletta wasn't alone—was he at last about to meet more merpeople?

But a moment later his anticipation turned to dismay. The rain slackened for the briefest of patches, and an angry shout reached his ears. Then something long and thin broke the surface of the water, falling back with a splash that couldn't be heard above the rain. All at once he understood, his suspicion instantly becoming certainty, although there was little evidence for his eyes.

Merletta hadn't brought other merpeople with her on purpose. She was under attack.

Heath didn't stop to think about the fact that he would not only be outnumbered, but impossibly outmatched in the foreign environment of the water. He knew a moment of regret that he didn't have his bow with him, but the merpeople were too far out for him to see them through the water, anyway. Ripping his boots from his feet, he dove forward, plunging headfirst into the world below the surface.

CHAPTER TWENTY-NINE

Merletta swam through the streets of Tilssted, her mind still on the conversation with Ibsen. She hadn't seriously considered stopping and becoming a scribe, not even for a moment. But she was sobered by the reminder that danger lay ahead on her chosen path. Passing her first year test hadn't removed it—if anything, it may have increased it.

With such thoughts on her mind, she was extra conscious of her surroundings, and the further she swam through Tilssted, the stronger grew the uncomfortable feeling of being followed. She sped up, ducking around a corner and hiding behind a familiar boulder, but no one emerged in her wake. She repeated the exercise multiple times without result, but the sensation lingered.

Uneasy, she tried to convince herself as she passed through the kelp farms that her nerves were just highly strung after all that had passed in the last week. She could hardly blame herself for jumping at currents.

She felt the moment she passed the barrier around the triple kingdoms, and her heart lifted slightly. A stretch of freedom was exactly what she needed to clear her head. She hovered at the edge of the kelp forest to check for patrols, but there was no one to be seen. She moved forward with confident strokes, her focus on the surface some distance above, where the evidence of a serious storm could still be seen.

She had been swimming over a canyon for a couple of minutes when she once again felt that sensation. She whirled around, expecting a shark or some other predator, but the fins she saw disappearing behind a ridge of the canyon definitely belonged to a mermaid. Merletta sucked in a mouthful of water sharply. After all these years, she'd finally been caught out. She'd been lucky to last so long, really.

"Who's there?" she called boldly. If the other merperson was hiding from her, they'd obviously seen her. There was no point playing dumb.

There was a moment's silence, and then a figure emerged, unpleasantly familiar, right down to the smirk.

"Ileana," said Merletta darkly, gripping her spear more tightly. "I should have known." No doubt the other mermaid was incensed by the belated success of Merletta's complaint against Ileana's ally.

"Yes," Ileana sneered. "You should have. I *did* know that you were up to something." She gestured to Merletta's satchel. "Even before I saw the proof."

"There's no need to be sour, Ileana," said Merletta provocatively. "We can't all pass, or the program would lose its reputation for being elite."

Ileana's eyes narrowed furiously. "You overinflated pufferfish," she hissed. "You think you're something special because you passed the first year test? That's child's play. You could never pass third year, Tilssted algae that you are."

"Well, I bow to your superior knowledge of not passing third year," said Merletta, speaking pleasantly, even as her blood pounded in her ears.

Ileana actually growled. "It's irrelevant, since there's no way in the ocean you'll ever make it through second year."

Merletta's false smile faded, as she looked Ileana over thoughtfully. Was it possible she was behind the most recent attack after all? She'd seen how respected the tough trainee was with the junior guards. Had she convinced one or two of them to join her in her vendetta against the unwelcome first year from Tilssted? It would be a relief, in a sense, to think she only had the one enemy after all.

"Was that a threat?" she asked, a dangerous edge to her voice as she shifted her grip on her spear.

Ileana shrugged, lifting her own spear. "If you like."

They began to circle, but before they could engage in the fight both of them were clearly itching for, a voice from the direction of the kelp forest made them freeze. The water was too murky to see far enough to make out their forms, but their conversation quickly identified them.

"A patrol," said Ileana, tilting her head to the side as she listened to the approaching merpeople. "How fortuitous." She gave Merletta a nasty grin. "Seems like you might not get a chance to fail second year, after all. Being caught outside the barrier should be enough to get you kicked out of the program, I would think."

Merletta didn't respond, her heart racing. She wasn't supposed to be out here, and she knew it. The purpose of the patrols supposedly wasn't to stop anyone leaving, and she was fairly sure they weren't empowered to mete out punishment for merpeople found outside. But she also knew there were plenty of merpeople in the Center who were eager for any excuse to get rid of her. She didn't intend to take her chances.

She turned, but before she could make good her escape,

Ileana's hand shot out, gripping Merletta's arm in an unyielding grasp.

"Over here!" the older mermaid shouted. "There's a civ outside the barrier without permission!"

An answering shout told them the patrol had heard, and Merletta squirmed in Ileana's vindictive grip.

"Don't lose heart," Ileana said condescendingly. "I'm sure they can find a place for you on the kelp farms."

It was her sneer that broke Merletta from her panic, hot rage rising up to take its place. This girl had hated her from the moment she laid eyes on her, without any basis beyond Merletta's origins. Hated her enough to try to kill her. She would not let Ileana ruin her future just because she'd failed in her own plans.

Merletta curled her free hand into a fist, picturing Ileana as the predatory shark that she was. Before the other girl even read the defiance on her face, she drew her fist back, bringing it forward in a blow that landed right between Ileana's eyes.

The other mermaid released her with a cry, her hand flying to her head as she reeled unsteadily in the current.

"Hey!"

The shout made Merletta's heart sink, as she realized the patrol had seen her strike Ileana. But they were still too far away for her to make out their faces, which hopefully meant they hadn't gotten a good look at her. She hesitated for one frantic second, trying to decide which way to flee, before plunging forward across the canyon, further from the kelp forests. She surely had a better chance of losing them if she headed away from the triple kingdoms. She would have the advantage—she knew this area well.

She streaked through the water, aware of Ileana's shout behind her, but not daring to look back. She twisted her way through coral and seaweed, darting around a school of mackerel to maintain her rapid pace.

A louder shout behind her made her risk a glance over her shoulder. Her eyes widened in alarm as she saw that it wasn't just Ileana hard on her fins. The newly appointed guard had succeeded in getting the patrol to chase Merletta as well. Merletta flicked her tail, propelling herself through the water with all her might. She had thought she would be able to lose any pursuers in these waters, but they were keeping pace, even gaining on her.

It was only when she caught sight of a familiar reef up ahead that she realized a new danger. If she kept this course, she would reveal Vazula to the whole patrol. She hesitated, costing herself precious seconds. How far into the Center's secrets were regular guards admitted? Did they know anything about land? She was fairly certain that Ileana not only knew about land, but was actually aware of the existence of humans. But this was a patrol of ordinary guards, not Center guards. Would it be a good thing, or a bad thing to expose this layer of the convoluted truth?

All of this flashed through her mind in seconds, but there was no time to make a confident decision. Merletta had slowed as the water became shallower, and the patrol was close enough for her to see the faces of the closest guards. One of them was glancing at the ascending slope of the ocean floor, his face confused and apprehensive as it passed to the choppy surface, now not far above them.

His obvious uncertainty decided Merletta. These guards probably knew nothing of the lies they had all been taught. And quite apart from her desire to reveal the truth, she couldn't help but hope she would be able to slip away in the inevitable confusion that would be caused by their first sight of land.

She swished her tail, pushing herself toward the world

above. But as her head broke the surface, the rain instantly pummeling her face, she realized she had lingered too long in making her decision. A grip on her fins told her just how close her pursuers had come. She dislodged it with a powerful flick, but other hands were on her in a moment.

She thrashed wildly, panic threatening to take hold as half a dozen grim faced merguards advanced on her.

"Don't fight," one said sternly, hanging back as his fellows again attempted to seize her. "You'll only make it worse for yourself. You're in hot water as it is."

"Let go of me," Merletta gasped, incensed by the sight of Ileana floating next to the guard, her expression smug. Merletta brought her tail around to wallop the guard who had just made a grab at her spear. "You have no right to attack me!"

"None of that now," said the same guard, presumably the patrol's leader. "You shouldn't be this far out, and you shouldn't be at the surface. We'll be taking you back with us."

Merletta hesitated, wondering if it really would be best to accompany them without a fuss. But then one of the guards seized her from behind, and she reacted instinctively, bringing the flat of her spear around to strike him in the neck.

He flailed, sinking deeper into the water and dragging her with him, their tails thrashing as they sank.

Another guard cried out in outrage, hefting his spear. Merletta barely dodged it in time, and it sliced through the water, emerging briefly into the air before falling back with a splash.

"Easy now," bellowed the head guard, holding out an arm to the guard who had tried to spear Merletta. "No need to shed blood!"

Worried about me? Merletta wondered dryly. *Or just about attracting sharks?*

"Do you see that?"

The startled cry of one of the guards brought everyone's attention around to her, and several heads broke the surface in order to properly follow the direction of her pointing hand. Merletta joined them, although she didn't need to go above to know what the other mermaid was looking at. Someone had finally spotted the island.

"Is that land?" gasped the guard who still had loose hold of Merletta. He released her, looking rattled.

Everyone's eyes were on the island, even Ileana looking taken aback, but Merletta's gaze dropped to the water in front of her, and her heart seemed to stop beating.

No. No no no. He can't be here, today, after all this time.

But there could be no mistaking Heath's familiar form as he swam across the surface of the water toward the group, his closely cropped dark hair slick against his head from the driving rain.

Merletta cast her mind around frantically, trying desperately to think of some way to prevent the others from seeing him. She hadn't really believed for a moment that he might come today, after months of absence. Such a thought hadn't even been in her mind when she'd made her decision about which way to lead the guards. Exposing Vazula was one thing, but she would never in a thousand tides have chosen to let this group see Heath.

"Merletta!"

His clear voice somehow seemed to cut through the storm, his eyes wide with concern. He must have realized she was in trouble. Her heart beat double time, and only partly because of the danger to him. It had been so long, but nothing had changed. The connection between them was just as strong, and just as indefinable, as ever.

But there was no time to dwell on that. His shout had drawn everyone's attention to him, and one member of the group, at least, hadn't missed its significance.

Ileana turned to Merletta, her shock turning quickly to glee. "I knew you'd seen too much for a slum-dwelling orphan," she breathed. "But I never imagined it had gone this far. They're going to do a lot more than just kick you out of the program. They'll never let you live if you've actually *befriended* one of them."

Her eyes turned back to Heath, who was still swimming swiftly toward them through the choppy water, with touching but misguided confidence.

"Let alone what they'll do to him."

Merletta's blood ran cold, but she wouldn't let the other girl see it. "They can't touch him," she scoffed. "What will they do? Crawl up on the land?"

Ileana narrowed her eyes as her gaze flicked between Merletta and the approaching human. "He's not on the land now, is he?" she taunted, hefting her spear.

"Ileana, no!" Merletta shouted, lunging for her. She seized Ileana's spear, attempting to wrest it from the older girl's grasp. As they struggled, Merletta was dimly aware of the reactions of the other guards to Heath's approach.

"Wait, who is that?"

"You mean *what* is that? Where's his tail?"

"Is that...a human?"

"Impossible," the head guard barked. "Humans are a myth."

Some part of Merletta's brain registered that the guards didn't know what Ileana did. But she had no time to process it. Ileana had always been a stronger, better fighter than Merletta, and Merletta couldn't hold her. The older girl wrenched her weapon free, propelling herself toward the island with deadly purpose.

"It's a land predator!" she called over her shoulder as she swam. "We can't let its kind discover our presence in the ocean. We must destroy it!"

"No!" Merletta cried, but the guards ignored her. They surged forward, clearly spooked by Heath's appearance, and ready to assume that as a Center guard, Ileana knew what she was talking about.

Merletta dove after Ileana, her heart beating frantically as she tried to catch up. The guards swarmed around her, spears raised as they made toward the human.

Heath had obviously seen their approach, and he had stopped swimming, bobbing uncertainly in the turbulent water above the reef. His eyes scanned the group, his features lightening with relief as his gaze latched on to Merletta. She tried to call a warning, but a wave slapped her in the face, sending water down her unsealed throat, making her cough.

Heath was no fool—he must have realized the armed guards swimming toward him weren't friendly. But he made no move to flee, perhaps acknowledging that he couldn't outswim them. He raised his hands in a gesture of peace, and one of the guards just in front of Merletta hesitated.

But Ileana knew no such qualms. She was almost upon Heath now, and she glanced back at Merletta, making sure her rival was watching. Then she ducked below the surface, throwing her spear in the environment most familiar to her.

Merletta's scream was whipped from her mouth by the wind. She dove below the waves, but not quickly enough to miss the shock that transformed Heath's face as the spear buried itself in his side. Another guard had copied Ileana instantly, and the second spear pierced Heath's leg.

Heath sank like a stone, the pain that twisted his face soon replaced by the blind panic of a fish out of water as he tried instinctively to take in air. His form hit the coral below, the waves dragging him mercilessly along the sharp surface.

Merletta reached him in seconds, her stomach churning as she swam through his blood to get to him. The other guards hung back, eyeing the red swirls nervously. It wasn't yet the ideal feeding time for sharks, but you never knew.

"Heath!" Merletta screamed, and his head turned toward her, the movement seeming involuntary. His blue eyes widened slightly as his gaze locked on her, apparently able to see her even through the murky water. He was conscious, then, but clearly incapable of sufficient movement to get himself back to the surface and the precious air he needed to survive. She knew a brief flash of gratitude that humans didn't die when fully submerged, the way mermaids dried out.

She abandoned her spear in the reef, seizing him under his arms and pulling him through the water. When his head broke the surface, he spluttered and drew a rattling breath, but it sounded alarmingly like the gasp of a dying creature, and his eyes were closed now. Panic clouded Merletta's brain as she floated, unsure what to do. The rain pounded against Heath's skin, paler than it should have been, and blood continued to stain the water around them.

"You can't save him, you must know that."

Ileana's taunting words startled Merletta back into action. The young guard, alone of the group, had been bold enough to approach the pair through the dangerous water. Ileana still had her spear in her hand, and it was clear she intended to see it through.

"Stop, please! Do you hate me so much?" The words were wrenched from Merletta, half scream, half sob.

"This isn't just about you," said Ileana grimly, her voice the tiniest bit less vicious as she shook her head. "I know my duty."

Merletta was struggling to stay on the surface, burdened down as she was by Heath's limp form, but with a supreme effort, she brought her tail up to connect with the other mermaid's midriff with a resounding thwack.

Ileana's breath left her in a huff, and Merletta didn't waste the moment of reprieve. She streaked for the shore, pulling Heath in her wake, a trail of red flowing out behind them. The blow had clearly winded Ileana, because she still hadn't caught up by the time the water became too shallow for Merletta to properly swim. She slowed once she was almost sitting on the bottom. She didn't think even Ileana would dare follow her that far in. The ebb and flow of the waves was so dramatic that at some times her whole body was submerged, and at others only half her tail was in the water. Few mermaids would be willing to take such a risk.

Merletta dragged Heath up alongside her, trying to keep his head above the breaking waves. He seemed to be coming in and out of consciousness, and his pallor was alarming. But more concerning was the blood pouring from his wounds. Remembering what she had learned of injury treatment in Agner's training, she cast around for strong enough seaweed to make a tourniquet, but of course there was nothing in the shallows. Her eyes fell on his clothes, and a sudden thought occurred to her. She reached into her ever-present satchel, pulling out his own knife. She used it to rip the shirt from him, slashing it into strips. She could only hope that the principle was the same for humans.

It was difficult to do anything with precision, given the way they were constantly buffeted by the waves. But she bound his leg as best she could. She just managed to tie a wad of material to the wound on his side before a particularly violent wave swept over them, sending Heath tumbling back under the water. Life returned to him for a moment as his head was submerged, but it was the thrashing of blind panic, not any helpful movement.

Merletta's arms shook as she again hoisted him up so his head was above the waterline. She had no idea what to do, and at this rate he would certainly drown even before succumbing to his injuries. She looked back out to sea. There was no sign of any of the other guards, but she could make out Ileana's head, bobbing in the waves, just on the shore side of the reef. The other mermaid was watching to make sure the human didn't survive. No help was coming from that direction.

"Heath!" Merletta cried desperately. "Heath, you have to move! Get out of the water!"

Heath stirred feebly, his eyes opening for a moment and settling on her face as the rain continued to lash them both.

"Merletta," he said, his voice soft. "I'm sorry I was gone so long...I wanted to come..."

"Never mind about that!" Merletta cried, tears mingling with the rain. "I can't save you while we're in the water!"

Heath remained silent, his eyes drifting closed again. She couldn't tell whether he could even hear her.

Merletta swallowed, realizing all at once what she needed to do. If she couldn't save him in the water, she had to do whatever it took to get him out of it. She began to move toward the water's edge, one arm wrapped awkwardly around Heath, and one dragging them across the barely submerged sand. She tried to push him ahead of her, but out of the water, she wasn't strong enough. She had to drag him behind, which was so much riskier for her.

She didn't hesitate. She shuffled ahead of him, pulling him along by the arms, wincing as his poorly wrapped wounds continued to bleed. Sometimes the waves receded so far that only her fins remained wet. She started to feel the dry, prickly sensation she had felt once before, and fear gripped her. But still she continued to inch up onto the land.

"Merletta!" Heath's voice surprised her with its strength. "Stop!"

She turned to face him, and found his gaze locked on her,

his blue eyes blazing with clarity even as his face was still twisted by pain. He had clearly returned to reality for a moment.

"You're too far out of the water," he panted, the words coming out with great effort. "You have to leave me here. Get back to the ocean."

Merletta shook her head in silent refusal, continuing her slow progress. Heath tried to protest again, but his words were interrupted by a particularly violent wave, which crashed over his face and left him spluttering.

"Merletta," he choked, as soon as he could speak again. He reached up as she hauled him further ashore. She thought he would grab her arm, but his hand sought her face instead. She hadn't even noticed that her braid had come loose in the tussle, and she only realized her hair was cascading free when Heath's shaking hand pushed it back from her face. She stilled at his gentle touch on her cheek, and an errant wave crashed unheeded over them.

"Stop, Merletta," he whispered, his voice clear even though weak. "I don't want you to die."

"If I stop," she grunted, her teeth gritted against the pain of the prickling beginning to pass over her whole body, "*you'll* die." She forced herself back into motion, giving an almighty heave to get him out of the path of the waves.

With the movement, his hand slipped limply from her cheek, and fear raced over her. He couldn't be gone. She ripped away what was left of his shirt, feeling for a heartbeat, and was relieved to see that the labored rise and fall of his chest continued.

The water was barely lapping them now, and a dry heat was filling every inch of her body, despite the pounding rain. Some small part of her had hoped that being wet from the rain might be enough to stop her from drying out, but clearly the fresh water didn't count. With one final tug, she pulled Heath's motionless form up onto the sand next to her before collapsing beside him, utterly spent.

Her instincts screamed at her to get back to the water, but the prickling had turned into a fire so intense it paralyzed her. She could no longer feel her arms, or her fins.

She raised her head with one last effort, straining her eyes toward the life-giving water of the ocean. Her gaze locked with Ileana's, and she could see the other mermaid's astonishment that Merletta had been willing to dry herself out to save the human. The former trainee looked from one prone figure to the other, and it was clear from her expression that she was satisfied. She believed they were both finished.

Merletta didn't even consider calling out to Ileana to help her reach the water. Even as Merletta lay dying, there was a hint of malice in the other girl's eyes as she turned her shoulder to the pair, and dove once more below the surface.

Merletta's head fell back against the rain drenched sand. Heath remained unresponsive, and she couldn't help the hot tears that poured from her eyes. Ileana's assessment of their chances was accurate. Merletta had gotten Heath out of the water, but it was all for nothing. She couldn't save him from the injuries the guards had inflicted. Perhaps his own kind could, but she had no way to get him back to his home.

Her eyes shot open. Rekavidur could get him home! She'd seen no sign of the dragon, but if Heath was here, Reka must be nearby.

Hoping dragons' hearing was as good as Heath claimed, she gathered the last shred of energy she possessed, and raised her voice in a desperate cry for help.

"REKAAAA!"

CHAPTER THIRTY

Heath could hear Merletta screaming as if from very far away, and he tried with all his might to open his eyes. But everything was a swirl of pain and darkness and driving rain. His leg throbbed mercilessly, but the real center of the agony was in his side. The pain was so overwhelming, it was all he could do to cling to consciousness.

What was happening? He'd been dreaming about the mermaid, but this time he was in the water with her. He remembered blood in the water, and spears. He gasped as memory returned. And Merletta, drying herself out to save him. He forced his eyes open with the greatest effort of his life, squinting against the heavy raindrops. The familiar shape of Reka was descending from the sky, right on top of him.

Yes, good, he thought, in a detached way. Reka would help Merletta get back to the water, and then she would be fine.

"He's hurt." The faint voice from beside him made Heath turn his head, and his eyes widened at the look on Merletta's face. He had never seen her so afraid.

"I don't know if the humans can save him," she continued, her voice barely more than a whisper. "But please, try..."

"I will carry him to his people," Reka's gravelly voice responded.

"No," Heath tried, but no sound came out. Before he could try again, he felt the dragon's talons closing around him, one set around his shoulders, and the other around his knees. He cried out involuntarily from the pain in his injured leg, and for a moment his senses swam.

He was dimly aware of the familiar sensation of lifting into the air, and by the time his head flopped to the side, Merletta was already shrinking out of sight below him. She was stretched fully on the sand, her shining purple tail curled up around her, and no part of her touching the ocean.

"No!" Heath cried, his protest faint on the wind. "Reka, stop!"

The dragon ignored him, and Heath struggled in his grip.

"Go back! You have to help her get to the water!"

"Stop struggling, Heath," Reka responded, his voice unreadable. "If you fall, you will certainly die."

"But she'll dry out!" Heath cried. "It will only take a moment to help her reach the water!"

Still the dragon didn't turn. He continued to ascend, and when Heath looked down again, Vazula was merely a dot, Merletta no longer visible, even to his eyes.

"It is for the best," Reka said, a hint of sadness in his voice this time.

Heath went still, clinging to consciousness by a thread as he tried to make sense of the dragon's words. Anger rose up within him, but he had no energy left to express it. The pain was overwhelming his awareness. The last thing he knew, Reka was speeding over the water at a pace that put their former journeys to shame, the wind and rain so ferocious against Heath's face that he could no longer open his eyes.

Some part of him remembered that something was desperately wrong, and that it was imperative that Reka turn around. But he couldn't quite grasp the information from the edges of his fading mind, and it was with relief that he abandoned the attempt and sank into blackness.

Heath groaned as awareness returned. The first thing he recognized was the pain in his side, still present, but now a dull throb. The second was his sister's voice.

"He's awake!" There was a pressure on his hand, and the voice spoke again, more quietly. "Heath, you've come back to us."

He opened his eyes slowly, blinking in the dim light of a candle.

"Laura?"

"Yes, I'm here."

Heath looked around, frowning in confusion as he tried to figure out where "here" was. The pieces of his own room came together, and his breathing quickened as the full implications burst in on him. If Reka had carried him all the way home, how long had it been since they'd abandoned Merletta on the beach? Hours?

"How did you get here?" Heath asked stupidly, panic making his brain sluggish. "You weren't here this morning, when I left for Bryford."

Laura hesitated for a long moment before answering. "Edmund and I came as soon as we heard about your...injuries. You didn't leave for Bryford this morning, Heath. It's been three days since Reka carried you in, half dead. You were thrashing around, delirious, I think. The physician gave you something, to help you sleep. But he's been worried. I don't think he expected you to be out so long."

Heath stared at her, frozen. *Three days?*

"No no no no no!" he gasped, attempting to sit upright. "Merletta!"

Pain assailed him at the movement, and Laura put out her hands to stop him, her expression alarmed.

"You can't get up, Heath! Give yourself time."

Heath fell back against the bed, cursing his own powerlessness as the horror of the situation washed over him.

"You...you said that name in your fever dreams," Laura said, hesitantly. "Who is Merletta?"

Heath remained silent, not even looking his sister in the eye. His mind was running back over what had happened, trying to put the fragments together.

"What happened to you, Heath?" Laura tried again, her voice gentle. "We've all been beside ourselves with worry. Your leg, and your side...those injuries look like they were caused by weapons. And your back is covered with these deep scratches... Rekavidur wouldn't tell us anything. He delivered you and left the moment you were taken inside."

Rekavidur.

The name unleashed the dam of anger that had been building inside Heath. His fury bubbled up as he remembered the dragon's refusal to go back and help Merletta. After months of unexplained silence, Reka had turned up just in time to take Heath to watch Merletta die. What had he said as he'd turned his back on the dying mermaid? *It is for the best.*

"REKA!" he shouted, the sudden volume startling Laura so much she jumped in her chair. "Reka, I know you can hear me! I'll never forgive you for this! Never!"

The outburst was met by ringing silence, but Heath knew his friend had heard him. There could be no doubt.

After an awkward moment, Laura cleared her throat. "I was under the impression Rekavidur had saved your life. The physician says that your injuries are severe, that you lost a great deal of blood, and you're extremely lucky to be alive."

Heath turned his face away from her, toward the wall. "You don't understand," he said dully. "Please, I appreciate you coming, but I want to be alone. Just for…just for a little while."

Laura hesitated for a moment, then he heard her rise to her feet. Heath drew a shuddering breath, his throat tight and his eyes stinging as the reality washed over him.

He could still see Merletta's shrinking form in his mind's eye. She'd been so close to the water, and yet it had been clear that, whether from exhaustion or pain, she was incapable of moving a muscle to get herself back to the ocean.

And that had been three days ago. There was no point in hoping. There was only one conclusion to reach. Merletta was dead.

CHAPTER THIRTY-ONE

Merletta squinted into the rain, watching as the dragon and his human burden became smaller and smaller, disappearing altogether in an impossibly short time.

Her senses were awash with the fiery pain of drying out, but her breath caught in her throat as she thought of Heath's injuries. She had no idea if he could survive them, and she couldn't bear to remember the way his face had twisted in pain. Even in his distress, his eyes had been as warm as ever when he had said he didn't want her to die.

Well, she didn't want to die either. But with Reka's arrival, Heath at least had a chance, and that was something. She knew she couldn't have lived with it if she'd been the cause of his violent death. The hope that she hadn't been made it marginally easier to let go, and sink into the darkness crowding her awareness.

The fire had spread to every inch of her now, most strongly in her tail. She could feel its brutal fingers piercing her very scales. She had let go of any thought of getting back to the water. She couldn't move so much as a finger.

She felt a flash of irritation cutting through the pain, both at the thought of all the things she had wanted to do with her life, and at the indignity of her death. Just like her parents, she thought, with a stab of a different kind of agony. She pushed the thought aside, wincing as pain lanced down her fins. She wouldn't have expected drying out to take so long.

A defiant anger passed over her at the realization that she would be robbed of the chance to prove to everyone that she could pass the program, and become a record holder. She had hoped to change things, to do something important.

A final surge of pain, stronger than all the others, shot from her midriff down to the tips of her fins, and her senses swam.

This is it, she thought. *This is death.*

But the pain peaked and faded, and still Merletta was lying on the wet sand. She moved a hand experimentally, and found that full control had returned. She opened her eyes, confused. She felt stiff and uncomfortable, but the pain was entirely gone, as was the sensation of prickling heat. Had she rolled back into the water somehow?

She pushed herself up on her hands, trying to identify what felt so different. She wriggled her fins, and her heart skipped a beat at the terrifying sensation that her tail had been split in two. She looked down at her purple scales, and gave an involuntary shout. The scales stopped much too soon, forming a short covering of sorts. Merletta touched it gingerly, and realized with an eerie thrill that it was no longer attached to her body. She pulled it away to get a better look at what was poking out from underneath it.

The sight that met her eyes caused a dozen emotions to wash over her with such overwhelming force that for a moment she thought she might pass out.

Her tail was gone. Completely gone. No gentle blending of

skin to purple scales, no flashes of pearlescent green, no golden fins. In its place was something else entirely.

She had legs.

The story continues in *A Kingdom Discovered*—Book Two of *The Vazula Chronicles*.

NOTE FROM THE AUTHOR

Thank you for reading *A Kingdom Submerged*. I hope you enjoyed discovering the world of Vazula! I would be so grateful if you would consider leaving a review on Amazon—it would really make a difference!

If you want to find out what adventures await Merletta, Heath, and Reka next, check out *A Kingdom Discovered*, the next installment of the series. More adventure, fantasy, mystery, and romance await.

Join up to my mailing list at deborah-gracewhite.com to be kept up to date on new releases, specials, and giveaways, such as bonus chapters. You'll receive some great freebies, too, including *An Expectation of Magic*, a novella which serves as a prequel to *The Vazula Chronicles*, telling the tale of Heath's parents.

You'll also receive *Dragon's Sight*, an 8,000 word prequel to *The Kyona Chronicles* (a series set before *The Vazula Chronicles*, in the same world), told from the perspective of the dragon Elddreki (Rekavidur's father).

Again, thanks for entering the world of *The Vazula Chronicles*! I hope to see you back again.

ALSO BY DEBORAH GRACE WHITE

The Kyona Chronicles: YA Fantasy

The Kyona Legacy: YA Fantasy

The Vazula Chronicles: YA Fantasy

The Kingdom Tales: Fairy Tale Retellings

The Singer Tales: Fairy Tale Retellings
(releasing throughout 2023)

ACKNOWLEDGMENTS

I don't entirely know where the idea for *The Vazula Chronicles* came from. All I know is that mermaids are awesome, and I wasn't ready for the fantasy adventures in the world of Valoria to end. Merletta's toughness and street smarts impressed me from the moment of our meeting, and I couldn't help but be drawn in by Heath's gentle spirit. So the adventure begins.

I am so incredibly grateful for my team, who didn't hesitate to dive right in (I know, but how could I help myself?) along with me. Always and always, first thanks to Ray, my alpha listener and one-man cheer squad. Thanks for embarking on a new project with me, and for giving such great feedback, that helps make the story so much better.

A massive thank you to my beta readers: Tamara, Andrew, Adrian, Mel W, Melanie, Ali, Steph, Dad, Mum, and Berri.

Special shout out to Melanie, whose beta read was really a full-scale (and extremely helpful!) developmental edit. And extra thanks to Dad for developmental and copy editing.

Karri should get a medal for making this cover happen in spite of my conflicting and constantly changing instructions, and Becca, the map is exquisite!

To you, the reader, thank you for giving me the privilege of being an author.

And most importantly, to God, whose light can be found even at the deepest, darkest point of the ocean.

ABOUT THE AUTHOR

I've been a reader since I can remember, growing up on a wide range of books, from classic literature to light-hearted romps. The love of reading has traveled with me unchanged across multiple  continents, and carried me from my own childhood all the way to having children of my own.

But if reading is like looking through a window into a magical and beautiful world, beginning to write my own stories was like discovering that I could open that window and climb right out into fantasyland.

I cannot believe how privileged I am to actually be living that childhood dream and publishing my own novels. I do so from my hometown of Adelaide, Australia, where I live with my husband and our three little ones.

I've never outgrown my love of young adult stories, so the genre of young adult fantasy was always going to be my niche. Feel free to email me at deborah@deborahgracewhite.com and introduce yourself! Or subscribe to my mailing list at deborah gracewhite.com for free giveaways, sales, and updates.

www.ingramcontent.com/pod-product-compliance
Lightning Source LLC
Chambersburg PA
CBHW060737190726

48285CB00001B/245